HOW TO WEAR A HUMAN FACE

GERDEN IBRAHIM

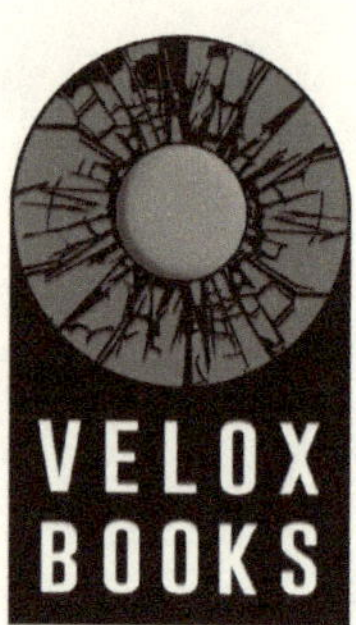

Published by arrangement with the author.

YOU'RE READING ANOTHER TERRIFYING COLLECTION FROM

**FOLLOW VELOX TO KEEP
THE NIGHTMARES COMING:**

CONTENTS

WE NEVER OPEN THE DOOR WHEN THERE'S ONLY ONE KNOCK

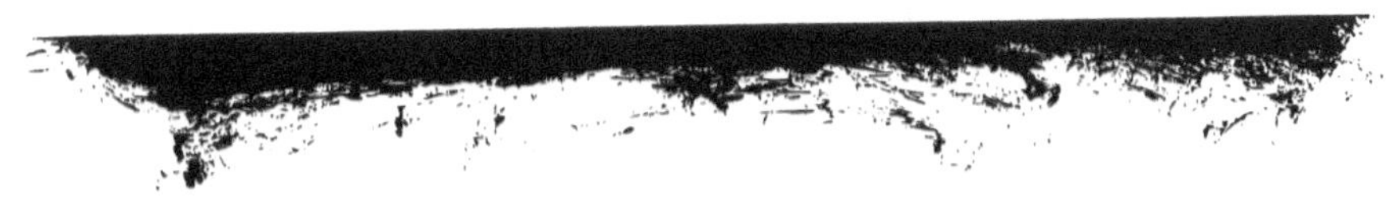

"Please, just let me in. It's getting cold!"

The voice was familiar, only older than I remembered. Very close to detail.

"Lala, please."

Using my old nickname was a nice touch as well.

I sat on the floor next to the door, my arms wrapped around my legs. Of course this had to happen the one week my parents left me alone. They hadn't gone on vacation for years; I practically begged them to get away for a while. For their own good. If I called them, they'd come right back, but I don't think that would have helped me anyway.

Besides, I wasn't an idiot. I heard the knock, and I would not open that door.

When someone comes to your house, they will ring the bell or knock a few times. Most people like to play safe and simply use the bell. And then you open the door as you normally would.

But never, absolutely never, should you open the door when there's only one knock. It was the very first thing we were told when we moved to this neighborhood all those years ago.

There are a bunch of rumors, of people disappearing or suddenly dying after opening their doors, though they all supposedly happened before we even lived here.

I never believed in it, not even when I was little. This town was simply insane; most people here were a little eccentric and unusual. Well, that's what I believed until I heard my lost sister call for me, after the one loud knock on our front door.

"Please, go away," I whispered.

Even after all those years, I recognized her voice. And when I heard it, I jumped right up, ready to open that door wide. But I knew it wasn't her.

I'd looked through the window. There was nobody in front of our door.

I don't know how much time had passed before I finally grabbed my phone and called Max, who's not only our neighbor but one of my closest friends.

"She's here," I said. I knew I wasn't making much sense, but I didn't know how to word my thoughts.

"Who? Where?" he answered.

"Ruby."

Silence.

"Wha—" Max started speaking but stopped.

"She knocked."

That was enough information for him.

"You didn't open, did you?"

I shook my head, which of course he couldn't see.

"I'm coming over now, okay?"

<hr>

I'm not sure how many minutes passed, but Ruby had stopped asking me to open the door.

"Hey, Lainey, I don't think the bell is working," I heard Max. "Maybe they screwed with it."

I swallowed.

"You could knock."

There was silence for a little while, followed by one loud thud.

When I didn't open the door, the sound of Max started shouting loudly.

"Open the fucking door!"

His voice became louder and louder until it hit a frequency that almost made my eardrums explode.

I didn't move, I didn't speak, and finally, the doorbell rang and the voice became silent.

Slowly, I got up from the door to look outside.

This time it was really him.

"The last time I saw her, we had the biggest fight of our lives."

We were sitting in the living room with tea that had already turned cold. I don't open up about Ruby often, but hearing her voice today really messed me up.

"And all because of stupid Jack." I rolled my eyes.

Max smiled.

"A boy?"

I shook my head and laughed.

"Jack was a stuffed toy in the shape of a pumpkin."

I'd never told Max about the fight—in fact, nobody but my parents knew about it.

"I loved that damn thing. Won it at the Halloween carnival. When Ruby saw it, she begged me to give it to her. She cried for hours because she hadn't won it. And even when my parents said they'd buy her another toy, she wouldn't stop. She wanted mine."

"Well, she wanted to be just like you. It's sweet."

I nodded.

Ruby was a year younger than me, but she used to act as if we were twins. She wore my clothes, played the same sports, and always wanted to hang out with me and my friends. When I think about it now, I think it was adorable, but of course back then I found it insufferable.

I sighed.

"For days I took Jack everywhere with me, even to the bathroom. It was probably just out of pettiness, but that toy became everything to me. So when I came home from school one afternoon and saw that Ruby had cut it in half, I screamed at her like never before. She only looked at me with big teary eyes."

Max put his hand on my shoulder.

"Come on, Lainey, siblings fight; it's normal. I saw you with her, though, and you were a damn good big sister."

I nodded. Of course, I knew it was just some stupid fight between kids, but if I could turn back time, I'd give her every shitty toy I owned.

This happened five years ago. Ruby would be sixteen now.

My parents have tried everything for years to find her. I believe the only reason we *still* live here is that they never entirely gave up the hope that she'd come back home one day.

Maybe now she was. Just in a different way.

"Do you think I'm losing my mind, Max?"

He raised an eyebrow.

"I think you lost that a whole while ago," he joked.

"No, I'm serious. I mean, it's not possible that I actually heard her earlier."

He shrugged.

"I mean, you did hear a knock. I don't think it was actually *her*, though."

Max and I used to make fun of the superstition. When we were younger, before Ruby disappeared, we once played ding dong ditch. After a few houses, Max decided to knock once at the door of our neighbor Mrs. Tellski. Someone saw us, though, and Max got the biggest lecture of his life from his grandpa. Like it was a really big deal. My parents weren't happy, either, but Max was grounded for two months, during which his grandpa told him all sorts of horror stories from this town.

"I don't think it was her, either. But I do think it was mimicking her, or trying to," I said.

"For what it's worth, I think it was smart that you didn't open the door. Maybe we're all just a little crazy, but better safe than sorry, right?"

Max offered to stay the night, and I immediately said yes. We got the air mattress and watched movies until I started to hear him snoring.

The good thing about Max was I never felt awkward around him. He regularly stayed over since we were little. Especially often after Ruby was gone. Having him here really helped against the silence.

My mind became easier and my body heavier. Real thoughts started to mix with dreams; I was beginning to fall asleep.

And then there was another knock.

It came from the front door downstairs, but I heard it loud and clearly.

My heart started racing just like it did this afternoon.

"Max, did you hear that?" I whispered, but he didn't answer.

"Lala, it's dark. Please come and get me," Ruby's new voice cried from outside.

"Max, please tell me you hear this."

I looked over at him, but he didn't move. Finally, I collected the courage to get up and turn on the lights.

"Ma—"

My friend's eyes were wide open, but he didn't speak. He didn't move.

"I ran over to him and tried to shake him, but his whole body was stiff. Only his eyes moved."

"LET ME IN!" the voice from downstairs screamed. I didn't know what to do anymore. Max was clearly awake, but it seemed as if something was holding him back. Almost like he was having sleep paralysis but with his eyes open.

"They're pulling me away, Lala. Please help me."

I don't know what happened then, but I immediately jumped up and ran downstairs. Some kind of instinct kicked in. Maybe it was her. Maybe I could pull her back inside. But if this was really Ruby, was she also the one doing this to Max?

My hands touched the cold door handle, moving almost as if I was in a trance.

"I have Jack. They fixed him, Lala. We don't need to fight anymore."

Those words pierced through my body and woke something up inside of me. I stepped away from the door and walked back upstairs, passing my room where Max was still lying still. But I didn't stop. I walked to the next room. Ruby's old bedroom. Everything there looked just the way it did when she was still here. My parents could never change it.

Everything was still the same. And Jack was still placed on her bed where I put it five years ago after I'd sewn it back together.

They almost got me.

MY MOTHER HAS A SPECIAL WEEKLY ROUTINE

My mother had always been just a little peculiar. She liked doing things a specific way and always on one specific day. There was a routine she found herself in since I was just a child, and no matter the situation, the weather, or her mood, the routine would never vary.

On Mondays, she did the planning. She would spend early noon making a list, always on paper, about all the meals we would have that week. Then she would go through the cupboards and the fridge to see what we still had and added everything we needed to the list, in her perfect cursive handwriting.

On Tuesdays, she would go to the fish market just before sunrise, continue to visit the butcher around noon, and finally buy all the other items we needed from the big grocery store just at the outskirts of our suburban neighborhood.

On Wednesdays, she cleaned, or rather we cleaned. While Mum liked things a specific way and would usually go over whatever I did after I was finished, she did always accept my help. I suppose it was more for building my character than for an actual need of help.

On Thursdays, she did laundry. When the sun was shining, she would hang the clothes on a line out in the garden, and if it didn't, she would use the dryer inside. Either way, Thursdays always smelled like lavender softener.

On Fridays, she baked. Muffins and cake and biscuits. With many spices and herbs, she would make her own creations. Those were the only days that smelled even better than Thursdays.

On Saturdays, she would go for a drink. When I was younger, that's when the babysitter would come, but now she could go without having to take care of that. Sometimes she would see her friends and come back in a giggly mood.

Sundays were what we called free days. It was the only day that was not assigned to one specific task.

"We work during the week so that the weekend can be enjoyed."

I heard that sentence more often than I could ever count. As I said, my mother had always been a little peculiar, and as I grew older, I realized she was also a little, if not a lot, compulsive. In all my years in life that I lived in that small suburban house with my mother, I never saw her deviate from that schedule.

Of course, I wasn't always there to observe, but when I came home from school on Tuesdays, the fridge and cupboards would be fully stocked again, Thursdays would smell like lavender, and Fridays we always had fresh baked goods. Even on holiday, she would find ways to squeeze in whatever needed to be done on the specific days of the week.

My mother wasn't always entirely mentally stable, which is something hard to witness as a child and especially to admit. You want your parents to always do well and tell yourself that they are fine even when they're not. However, in most ways, she luckily seemed to be in control of her compulsions.

And most of all, she was always kind and loving. To both of us despite the occasional fight. Especially as I grew older and resented her slightly old-fashioned ways. Still, we were a happy family, and in general, things were all right.

Until last week when my mother, for the first time ever since I can remember, seemed to be out of sync.

It started on Monday when I woke up and found my mother in the living room watching something strange on TV. The sight of that was weird enough already because normally she would never turn on the television by herself before evening, and now she was sitting there, wearing her flowery dress and high heels inside while watching something with complete focus in her eyes.

"Mum?" I muttered.

Her head slowly turned to the left. She looked up, her gaze cutting straight into mine. No words came out of her mouth. When I looked over at the screen to see what she had been so mesmerized by, I noticed the white noise. There was no channel on. I sat down next to her, tried to find the words to ask what was wrong but I couldn't. She was acting as if everything was perfectly normal until Dad came down the stairs with his briefcase in hand.

"Good afternoon, honey. Are you ready for lunch?" she asked him.

My father tilted his head. He could tell that something was wrong, but he didn't mention it either. Instead, he only lifted his briefcase a little and said, "I must go to work."

"But of course." My mother smiled.

I exchanged a concerned look with my father. He definitely knew that something was up, and I wondered whether they had a fight last night. Was that why Mum was acting strange? Before I could talk to him, however, he had disappeared. And Mum jumped up only two seconds later.

"I need to go to the dry cleaners. You can make yourself something to eat, yes?"

<hr>

On Tuesday, I didn't expect to see my mother when I got up. At this time, she normally would be at the fish market to get the freshest catch. Instead, I found her by the kitchen table, nervously writing something down. My dad was sitting opposite her, having scrambled eggs and bacon.

"Are you making a shopping list?" I asked. It was the wrong day, but at least she was acting a little more normal. Even though she was wearing the exact same dress as the day before.

My mother smiled and nodded.

"Yes, is there anything you need?"

"Eggs. And milk. We're out of cornflakes, too."

She nodded.

"Good morning, kiddo," Dad said. They were both sitting together, having breakfast, so I thought that things were back to normal again. He emptied his coffee and got up.

"Time for work!" he called out.

"Oh, honey, could you get some groceries on your way back? Salt, fish, and vinegar, please."

Again my father and I exchanged a look of confusion. Well, the one of mine was the one of confusion, but his look seemed to be of distress. I nodded to silently tell him that I had things in control.

Dad nodded back and then proceeded to head for the door.

"Of course, honey."

On Wednesday, I found her in the garden, digging up dirt. The exact opposite of what we normally would be doing on that day. She was digging a hole, big and wide, and I simply couldn't say what on earth she might need it for. Dad was gone before I had woken up, so I couldn't talk to him, but I promised myself I would do so tonight. Something was wrong with my mother. At first, I was worried, but I started getting scared. Both for her and of her.

"Is something wrong?" my father asked that evening. It was difficult to find a moment alone; Mum always seemed to be somehow around. I hated that I had to get away from her to voice my concerns, but I was worried that she wasn't entirely stable.

"She didn't do anything she normally does. And did you see that hole outside? Dad," I paused for a moment, "I think she might really need help."

Dad tilted his head and looked through the window to the garden. I suppose he hadn't seen the hole out there earlier.

"I will not go to work tomorrow. Stay here with you. Is that all right?"

I sighed in relief. Together we might be able to figure out what was going on, and maybe he could start a conversation with her.

"Yes, thanks, Dad. I think that would be really helpful."

Thursday, I found Mum in the garden again. Normally that wouldn't be so strange as I would usually find her there hanging up the sheets. However, this Thursday it was storming outside. It had been raining all morning, and it didn't appear as if it would end anytime soon.

"What are you doing? It's pouring cats and dogs!" I shouted from the garden door. Dad, who heard me shouting, had appeared behind me and was holding my shoulder.

"Not cats and dogs, fish." Mum turned around and laughed. And that was when we saw what she really was doing out there. She was hanging the chopped-off heads of the fish Dad had bought on the clothesline.

"Mum?" I could only bring out a whisper. "Something is wrong. We need to help her."

Before I could move, Dad was already running outside and guiding my mother back to our living room.

———

Thursday turned into Friday without a moment of sleep. At least for me. I couldn't close my eyes without heads of fish appearing in my mind. And the sight of my mother in that same damn dress and that plastered-on smile.

Tired and exhausted, I stumbled down the stairs to find my parents both sitting in front of the television. I didn't even bother talking to them and went straight to the kitchen.

For the first time in years, there was no sweet smell coming from it. No, instead the stench of vinegar made its way to my nose. We hardly had any food in the house. I supposed Mum had completely forgotten about it and Dad didn't want to leave her in her current stage. He hardly left her side anymore.

Without talking to them, I started with all the chores of the past days, wrote a shopping list, cleaned, and threw some clothes in the washing machine. This might sound as if I only wanted my mother to get back to doing the household, but I swear it had nothing to do with that. I simply was worried because she wasn't herself anymore.

The following morning, all the items that I wrote on the list were sitting in paper bags on the kitchen counter. I assume that Dad had gotten out to buy them.

On Saturday, she did the most terrifying thing so far. A sight I will not be able to delete from my mind anytime soon. It started only in the evening. The entire day both my parents were acting normal. Mum even cooked, and we sat around the table, talking and laughing. She did most of the talking, and I could have sworn she was entirely herself again.

Or she had learned to adapt. At least in some ways. When night came, however, everything turned entirely messed up.

I woke up from the sound of a loud clatter and immediately jumped out of bed. I had been a nervous wreck lately, and it didn't take much to startle me. The sound was coming from downstairs, and my initial thought was that someone had broken in, but then I heard my mother humming something from downstairs.

"Mum?" I called out.

"Go to bed, child!" she shouted back, but I was already making my way to the stairs.

She had painted the walls with strange anagrams using red paint. Still wearing the same dress, she looked up and smiled, but this time it appeared far less sincere. I believe I even saw a twitch in her eye. Dad was sitting on a chair next to her.

"Mum. We need to get you help. I will call the hospital, okay?"

"No, no. I will help," Dad said and took the paint can from her hand.

A tear rolled down her cheek, but the smile never disappeared.

"Why, thank you, honey."

"Families help each other." Dad smiled back.

"Yes, well, I should go and buy more paint. The child will help me," Mum said.

Dad glanced at me.

"What the fuck? It's the middle of the night. Look, Mum, I'm really sorry, but—"

She held my mouth shut with her hand before I could say another word.

"We have to buy paint. Any normal mother and her child do just that. It is of utter importance for a decent home."

Dad looked around at the red paint on the wall and on my mother's face and finally said the last thing I expected.

"That sounds perfectly reasonable. See you soon, honey."

I had no idea what to do. It seemed that both my parents had lost their minds, but I couldn't possibly let my mother leave on her own or let her drive a car in that state. So I went outside with her and sat behind the steering wheel with the intention to drive her to a hospital. However, as soon as I started driving, I couldn't for the life of me remember what direction I had to go.

"Just keep going straight. Follow the street," my mother finally said. Her smile had disappeared, and her leg was shaking.

"Just keep going, honey."

I had no idea what to say, and so I kept going straight until we had left the neighborhood and the surrounding area as well. We found ourselves on the freeway when I couldn't hold it in anymore. I found the nearest exit and stopped.

My mother was trembling, and in the dark light with the splatters of red paint on her face, I finally realized that I might have made a huge mistake.

"Mum?" I hardly brought out the word.

She opened her mouth, but no words came out at first. She swallowed and then finally spoke.

"I am so sorry, my love. I didn't want to believe it. It made no sense."

"What are you talking about?"

She looked at me as if I was the one losing my mind.

"That thing in there. That. That was not your father. Didn't you notice? At first, I thought I would only act slightly different to see if *he* would notice that something was off, but it only copied whatever we were doing or saying." She took a deep breath. "I woke up a few times at night. It never sleeps. It sits in the bed with its eyes open waiting for us to wake up. I—I am so sorry. I just couldn't believe it at first. I thought maybe something was wrong with your father. We should have left or called for help but—" She stayed silent for a moment.

"My memories were blurry, and I had to make sure first. Make sure that it was him and not me."

My palms wouldn't stop sweating, and my head started racing like crazy. This whole week I had been so focused on my mother I didn't notice that Dad only agreed to the things I was saying. He didn't do anything. And suddenly it felt as if something shattered in my mind. My mother had always been a little peculiar. Especially after my father passed away.

"Mum. That wasn't our home, was it?" I gulped. "How did we end up there?"

She looked at me, a reflection of my own fear and confusion.

"I have absolutely no idea. It must have somehow lured us in there and made us forget."

MY FLATMATE IS A FUCKING WITCH

✱ Sorry, typo, I meant bitch. My flatmate is a fucking bitch. And unfortunately moving out isn't really an option for me.

Clara seemed great at first. Of course she did. I mean, I probably wouldn't have moved in if she showed her true face from the start.

No, that's a lie. I was crazy desperate, and all the red flags in the world wouldn't have kept me from moving in. My only other option was becoming homeless, as I was about to be kicked out of my uni flat after graduating. On top of that, the housing market in my town was quite literally hell, so I was happy when I found a place that I could actually afford.

Clara sounded nice on the phone and invited me right over to have a look at the place. Two bedrooms, one living room with an open kitchen, and a decently sized bathroom. She greeted me with a friendly smile and showed me around.

The interior was a bit minimalistic, mostly black-and-white furniture, one or two pieces of art. The kitchen was clean, and she had a shit ton of spices.

"We can share everything in the kitchen. I think it's easiest that way? If you don't want to share groceries, that's fine, of course, but if you wanna use any of my stuff, that's cool," she said during our tour.

"Oh, sharing is fine." I smiled. I wanted her to like me. I needed this room. And I wasn't sure whether me being a guy might be a problem.

I didn't have to be nervous, however; Clara adored me. She called me the very next morning after the tour and offered me the room. And I accepted right away. I felt a great vibe both from her and the place.

And I have to admit when she smiled at me during that first apartment tour with her poison-green eyes, I may have felt a little mesmerized, too.

But not anymore. No, not after going through hell with that bitch.

<hr>

During our tour, she never showed me her own room, which I later learned was the opposite of the sterile and clean apartment. Her room was full of glasses and containers filled with different stuff I didn't recognize. She had all sorts of different candles and a shit-ton of books on the floor, under her bed, and on the shelves. There were around fifteen pillows on her bed and a bunch of lamps everywhere.

Clara never actually showed me her room. I broke in one time when she wasn't home. Yeah, I know that sounds bad, but there was a reason for it, I swear. The consequences of the war that my flatmate herself initiated.

It all started with the passive-aggressive note she left on the fridge door without a reason in the world. It was only one day after I'd moved in, and I swear I hadn't even given this girl one reason to hate me yet.

HOUSE RULES
-No guests after 1 AM
-Any visitor must be announced first
-No pets
-Shared rooms must stay clean at all times
-No going to my room without permission

She came in just as I was reading the rules and smiled like that list was the most normal thing in the world.

"Everything all right? Did you have a good first night?" she asked and smiled at me.

"Yeah, for sure," I answered and then pointed my finger at the piece of paper with a raised eyebrow. "So I just found this."

"Oh yeah, sorry, I always share these when I have a new flatmate. It's important for the place to keep things as they are supposed to be. The other ones really weren't that great, but I have such a good feeling about you." She smiled again, and it felt so genuine that I had to smile back.

"Oh, yeah, me too. If I bring a girl over, I don't have to kick her out at one a.m., though, right?" I joked.

She laughed.

"I am so glad you moved in here, Julius. I don't even think I picked you. The apartment did."

I tried to laugh back politely, but it sounded weird and forced.

To be perfectly honest, I was sure it was all a big joke at first. The stuff she'd randomly say about the apartment and her weird rules but that girl was dead serious, as I'd find out sooner than later.

One time I left a half-empty cereal bowl on the table before going out, and when I came back, Clara had thrown it on my bed. I couldn't get the smell of spoiled milk out of my room for days.

Another time my buddy Matt came over spontaneously, and when Clara saw him she acted super nice and even made him a cup of tea.

As Matt told me later, he spent the entire next day throwing his guts up.

Of course, that could have just been a coincidence, but she acted ice cold to me after that evening. The good vibes were dead. And these were just a couple of examples of our back and forth.

War had begun. And it got worse and worse.

I threw a huge house party, and Clara somehow managed to convince all my friends that I was a vile, disgusting person. She had this effect on people; her charisma was magically persuasive.

When my friends started ghosting me, I decided to buy a pair of birds. I named them Julia and Clarus, which my flatmate didn't find funny at all.

A few days later, I came back to an open birdcage, a living room full of bird feathers, and splatters of blood.

Maybe I should have left then, but I felt the need to confront that psychopath.

I shouted for Clara, but she wasn't home.

I can't even say for sure if I was more angry or scared. Thinking about it now, I should have left right at that moment and never come back. Clara wasn't normal. She looked nice and acted all right in front of strangers, but she was dangerous.

I'm not sure why I didn't leave. Maybe I was too angry to think straight.

So instead of running, I decided to break into her bedroom.

As I mentioned, it was far more whimsical than I'd ever imagined. There was so much stuff and clutter that I wasn't sure what to do next. My initial plan was to trash her room, but instead, I decided to go through her stuff to find something she loved and destroy it. Leave a message to her and then fuck off.

I knew that Clara was weird and clearly had anger issues, but I still didn't expect to find the things that I did.

There was something satanic about this room.

I found books written in Latin or Celtic or whatever. Papers with anagrams, curses, weird lists.

All still somewhat fine, I guess, but then I found the paintings. Paintings of me. Portraits where she burned my eyes off with a lighter and filled the empty holes with red paint. Another one where my eyes were wide open, the flesh of my nose was decaying, and the bones were showing. Another one with dozens of maggots climbing out of my mouth.

It wasn't only the paintings. Her room made me feel sick. I felt nauseated and dizzy, and for a while, I think I even lost track of time.

My blood was freezing. I couldn't move. For a second, my breathing stopped. And that's when I heard the door shut behind me.

***

What happened afterward is a bit blurry in my head. We fought, and Clara shouted things I didn't understand.

I think I pushed her, tried to move her out of the way to get out. She fell, and I grabbed the lamp from the table closest to me and threw it at her. It shattered, and there was blood, but Clara was still moving. I was completely in survival mode, not thinking straight, but so was she.

Finally, I managed to pass through and leave her room. I ran through the living room toward the door, but when I tried to leave the apartment, I couldn't.

I physically couldn't get out. Something was holding me back. Clara had somehow bound me to this place. She cast a spell on me. That was the only explanation that made sense to me.

I kept trying to leave, but it simply wasn't possible.

"This again? Come on, Julius, I thought we were making progress."

I slowly turned around, scared and confused, to see Clara, standing there, looking completely fine. Not a scratch, no blood. She tilted her head and glanced at me with eyes that seemed more tired than angry.

"What's going on?" I whispered. "What did you do to me, you fucking witch?"

She rolled her eyes.

"I'm not a witch, Julius. Come on, we've had this fight at least once a week for months now. Can you make your memory work, please? This is getting exhausting. I can't deal with this rollercoaster—"

Clara was interrupted by the sound of birds tweeting. Loudly, as if they were in this apartment. And I could swear it sounded like Julia, but she and Clarus died months ago.

Months?

Right, months.

I started to remember. Our fight about the birds must have been at least six months ago. Just around the time Matt stopped by for the last time.

Well, the last time he stopped by while I was still alive.

He came once more after he hadn't heard from me in a while. That's when Clara gave him the letter explaining I had left.

"Clara, did you kill me?" I whispered. I really couldn't remember for sure.

"No, well, maybe. I hate this, Julius. Do we really need to do this again?"

I nodded. "Afraid so."

"I killed your birds, which I guess was a little over the top. I didn't mean to. I just wanted to let them free but forgot to turn off the ceiling fan and well—" She took a deep breath. "Anyway, you came to my room, we had a huge fight, and it got out of control. You threw a lamp at me but missed. I threw another one and, well, didn't miss." She mumbled those last words.

The images in my mind were mixing. My memories were not right. Some were of the past when I was alive; some of them were new.

"I forget. All that occult stuff in your room, was that already there?" I carefully asked.

"Some of it. I've always had some interest in it, but it really sparked when I realized that you were still here, even after I got rid of your corpse." She shrugged. "You know this was a lot for me, too."

I sat down on the ground.

This wasn't new. I just had forgotten.

Clara had killed me. But I'd tried to do the same to her. When I finally understood what happened, the first time, not now, we made some type of arrangement.

I was never very close with my family anyway, and I've lost touch with most friends. They believe I'm traveling somewhere, living a new life or whatever.

I'm not sure if other people can see me. I hide the very few times someone rings the bell. This still feels kind of new to me, you know.

Clara stayed because, one, she can't really let anyone else live with me, I guess. And I suppose she really is curious about how any of this is possible at all. And some part of me hopes she'll find some answers for me. My memory is still a bit hazy and time works weirdly.

So I guess we're kind of stuck with each other. Hopefully not forever.

I mean, yeah, my flatmate is a bitch, but who wouldn't be if they had to live with a fucking ghost?

MY DAD IS THE BEST COOK IN THE WORLD

It could be something as simple as a bowl of porridge on a Sunday morning, which technically is just a bowl of slime if you think about it. When my father made it, however, it would be the most delicious breakfast dish in the world.

He used a special kind of oats, or maybe he bought the regular kind and made them special by cutting them even more finely. He would toast them gently to help extract their flavor, as he explained. Then he would boil them on low heat, taking his time as he prepared whatever would accompany the oatmeal or porridge. I'm never sure what the right name is, but I guess Dad's dish would be porridge, simply because it sounds more delicious than oatmeal. My favorite kind of porridge is by far the one he calls birthday cake. He adds in vanilla, colorful sprinkles, and other stuff I forgot, and I kid you not, it's the best breakfast in the world.

I know it doesn't sound as crazily innovative as I make it out to be; I suppose it really isn't. Because I can use the exact same ingredients, trying to mimic his dish, and all I achieve is oat slime with some melted sprinkles. And not because I'm a bad cook. My mum, for example, is a really decent cook as well, but she can never reach the explosion of flavors in a dish quite the same as my dad. Nobody can.

"You are such a liar. He can't be the best in the world. Also, you've never even left town, so how would you know, Chris?"

That's what my disbeliever of a classmate Toby said after I told everyone that I knew for a fact that my dad was the best cook in the world and that one day he would travel to every country in existence to battle the best chefs on earth.

Back then we were around six or seven, and I had realized that my dad being such a genius was definitely something I had to use to impress everyone in elementary school with. And everyone believed me, saying how cool that was, as if my dad was a superhero. Except for that little know-it-all Toby, of course.

"If something is the best you can tell, Toby. It's not that hard. And also everyone who comes to visit us says so, too."

"So what? Anyone that visits is from here, too, so they don't know the world, stupid."

"Shut up, Toby!"

He was right. Nobody who lived here ever left town and came back, so they really wouldn't know. And we never got visitors from outside. I still didn't appreciate him talking back like that though.

Toby was the biggest know-it-all of our class, and I was probably the biggest liar. We would bicker about stuff all the time, for years, which might make it more surprising that we somehow ended up becoming best friends.

But now, ten years later, we are practically inseparable. And thanks to our friendship, Toby even had the luck of trying Dad's food from time to time.

He still thinks saying that he is the best in the world is an exaggeration but simply because he doesn't like to admit that I am right.

If you think that breakfast sounded good, you should see what my father comes up with for dinner. Well, not see, you should taste it, though I'm afraid that's impossible.

Dad only makes dinner for us on very rare occasions. He works a lot, and when he comes home, he is usually too tired to cook. So we only get a home-cooked dinner by my father when we get visitors.

Visitors that are from our town *always*, never from the outside.

A lot of them I know quite well. It's usually the same group, a circle of friends of my parents. They have this dinner party once or twice a year, and it's always at our house because everyone agrees that Dad is the best cook of them all. They spend other events together as well, at other homes or places, but when it comes to dinner, it is always our home. The dinner parties are very similar each time, for me at least. The guests arrive, I say hello, they ask me embarrassingly boring questions about life and school, and then I go back up to my room. I never join them for dinner; instead, Dad brings me up a plate of food that I eat in my room, which I certainly prefer and am thankful for. Often Toby comes over as well, and we hang out in my room, while my parents have their party downstairs.

Dad was hesitant at first when I'd ask if Toby could come as well, but as we got older, he agreed it was fine as long as we didn't disturb the party. It kind of has become our tradition to play video games or listen to music in my room and eat Dad's amazing food while my parents practice their own tradition downstairs.

These nights might sound a little mundane, but I used to love every part of them.

They've been the same for years now. Except for last night.

Last night, things changed.

As before every dinner party, Dad had been in the kitchen all day cooking while Mum decorated the dining room. I helped a little by chopping some vegetables and washing a few dishes in the afternoon. In the evening, before the guests arrived, Toby rang our bell, and the two of us went up to my room to play a new Nintendo game that Toby got as a gift from his uncle. He always gave Toby the best gifts, but he recently moved away from this town.

We got so into the game that I didn't even realize how much time had passed until Dad knocked on the door. As soon as it opened, a sweet smell spread through my room. Hints of cardamom, nutmeg, and most prominently pumpkin.

"Whoa, that smells amazing, Mr. Milner. What did you make?"

"Oh, just some mashed potatoes with pumpkin and greens." We both knew whatever he made was far more special than that. Even when he used the most boring ingredients, he knew how to mix spices so perfectly that they tasted otherworldly. But when Dad said those words, he didn't sound like he was trying to be humble. He seemed exhausted, which was reflected through the empty look in his eyes. I got up to take the tray off his hands that had bowls of soup and two big plates full of the dishes my dad had been cooking all day.

"You all right, Dad?"

"Oh, I am fine. Fine. Just tired. Lots of cooking. Anyway, you know the rules. Enjoy the food but stay in your room, all right?"

We both nodded.

After the door was closed again, I put the tray next to Toby and sat down.

"Your dad seemed weird," he said.

"I don't think he likes dinner parties very much. He has to work, and everyone else just stuffs their faces."

"Or maybe he's not much of a swinger and your mum makes him." Toby grinned.

"For the hundredth time, my parents aren't swingers."

"Right, so why else are we not supposed to see what they are doing down there?"

"Fuck off. Do you *wanna* have dinner with all those old people? They're doing us a favor."

"Right, *dinner*." He grinned again.

———————

There was no part of me that believed that my parents were actually swingers, but Toby dared me to go look, and I wasn't scared to walk around in my own house, so why wouldn't I go check? That's what I said to him. Tried to act cool but some part of me was really afraid of whatever was going on down there. You see, these parties have become such a normal event in our lives that I sometimes forget, or try to suppress, how weird they really are.

First of all, all the guests arrive totally overdressed in cocktail attire and too much makeup. Everyone seems far too excited with big smiles that appear forced. My mother is one of them and enjoys the night to the fullest. My dad is more reserved. One person always brings a big package. I've never seen what's in it, though.

That is usually all I see before going to my room. As I was tiptoeing down the stairs for the first time during a dinner party, my heart started beating so rapidly that I feared it might overshadow the classical music coming from our living room.

"Are you scared?" a voice whispered in my ear as two hands grabbed onto my shoulder. I turned around to see the dark eyes of my friend and a massive grin on his face.

"You were meant to wait upstairs, dickhead," I whispered.

"I didn't want to miss the old guys going crazy."

"Old? Now that is a bit rude, don't you think?"

This time the voice wasn't coming from Toby but Mrs. Callus, a friend of my parents' and dinner guest, who apparently just walked out of the bathroom.

"Oh hi, uhm, sorry, Mrs. Callus. We just came down to—" I started muttering. I don't know why I felt so nervous. This was my home, after all. But something about her big widened eyes and the smeared lipstick around her mouth was extremely unnerving.

"Oh, don't apologize, dear. You two are quite grown up now, after all. I don't understand why your parents hide you in your room all night. I say you join us for dinner starting now! Come on!"

She grabbed first my hand, then Toby's. My friend and I exchanged a look of fear and curiosity.

***

"Look who I just found lurking in the halls." Mrs. Callus laughed loudly as we approached the living room. My mother had really out-done herself with the decorations. Big candles everywhere, black tissues formed into pretty shapes, the chandelier above the table dimmed to a warm yellow. The only thing outshining the decoration was the food on the table.

My eyes met my mother's, who looked less angry than I imagined. Actually, everyone looked at us smiling. They didn't seem that annoyed that we were interrupting.

And luckily, nobody was naked.

"Why don't we make some space for the kids? Let them enjoy the delicious meal with us for once. They look quite grown up to me," Mrs. Callus said, and everyone started mumbling.

"Chris, Toby, do you want to sit with us?" my mother asked in a nervous tone.

I looked over at my father, whose face had turned completely pale. Just as before, he had a strange look in his eyes, but now I realized that it wasn't exhaustion; it was fear.

"No, that's okay, uhm, we still have our food upstairs," I said.

"Nonsense," Mrs. Callus said. "We have two empty seats right here. Tonight you will join us. End of discussion."

It seemed way more normal than I'd have imagined at first until they all started digging into the food as if they were starving animals, ripping off huge bites with their teeth, swallowing whole chunks of meat, and pouring it all down with red wine. No matter how wonderful I normally thought my father's cooking was, at the sight of this I felt a bit appalled. Especially when I saw that my mother ate just as disgustingly. My mother who normally was so incredibly proper and perfect.

Only my dad was not focused on the food; he was staring at me, and his eyes were saying "*Run.*"

Toby looked as if he found the whole event rather amusing and not as creepy or disgusting as it felt to me. I suppose he still thought they would start going wild soon. And in a way, they were, I suppose. Just not the way we imagined.

"You're not eating, sweetie. Why is that? Your father's cooking is simply divine." Mrs. Cullen chuckled with her mouth full. She then proceeded to load a big spoon of Shepherd's pie onto my plate.

I didn't answer but quietly took a small bite out of it. It tasted amazing, of course, like everything Dad makes. But I didn't see this dish on the tray that he brought upstairs for us.

When I looked at all the food in front of us, I noticed something. The food my father had been cooking today, the potatoes and pumpkin mash, the caramelized onions, and the roasted asparagus with sauce hollandaise. He had prepared them perfectly on the plates for Toby and me.

But now I realized that none of the food he had cooked was on this table, and suddenly I completely lost my appetite.

My father was trying to warn us.

The guests we have once or twice a year are friends of my parents. Not by choice, I suppose. Their families have been part of this town for as long as it exists, and so have our ancestors. In a way, I suppose we are part of some kind of elite, although I never really felt like it. Especially because of my dad, who is an incredibly down-to-earth person.

I always thought the only reason he did these parties was for my mother, but as it turns out, there was another reason.

Toby was the first one to leave. He asked to stay over, but I told him I wasn't feeling too well. The other guests stayed until late at night, having the best time you could imagine.

My mother went to bed, exhausted with a full stomach, while Dad sat in the kitchen scrubbing the floor.

The entire house was quiet and dark at this point. He thought I'd gone to bed as well. Monotonously, he scrubbed a stain on the wooden ground.

"Dad?" I asked, my entire body trembling.

He didn't look at me.

"You need to understand, Chris, we have been part of this community for a very long time," he said, his eyes still glued to the floor. "It is not a choice at this point. They tell us the date and we prepare. That's how we stay well and safe."

Finally, he looked at me.

"We are lucky that they enjoy my cooking skills because that way we stay needed. I just wish your mother wouldn't enjoy it so much as well."

Once or twice a year, we have a dinner party at our house. My father spends all day preparing food that only me and sometimes my friend Toby eat.

As the guests arrive, however, they bring one other special ingredient.

Once or twice a year, we have a dinner party at our house. Coincidentally, once or twice a year somebody moves away from this town. And they never come back.

Luckily, I'm a pretty decent liar because I have no clue how I would ever be able to explain to Toby that he devoured his uncle for dinner last night.

I WAS THE STAR OF A CHILDREN'S SHOW THAT DOESN'T EXIST

Part 1

Out of all the fundamental questions we have about life and the progress science has made over the course of time, I find it astonishing how little we know about our own brains. Neurobiology is a fascinating field of research, but even with all the progress we have made, some questions remain unanswered. Why do we dream? Are we ever really conscious? Are we in control over our own minds?

I'm in no way an expert when it comes to these questions, but during my psychology studies, I did try to educate myself more to fulfill this deep need I've always had for exploring the unknown. Something I learned and found particularly interesting is the way in which everything in our brains and bodies is somehow connected. Our senses, our memories, our emotions. They work together in remarkable ways. If you've ever walked down the street and smelled the scent of someone who used to be in your life, you know what I'm talking about. The bittersweet nostalgia. While the olfactory system seems to be especially strong in activating emotion, the other senses are quite powerful as well. It happens to me a lot with music. Turn on a song from 2009 and I'm transported right back to that sweet teenage melancholy.

Except with the sound I heard the other day, the memories weren't sweet. They were buried so deep within me that all they did was leave a feeling of shock and terror that, no matter how hard I tried, I simply couldn't make sense of.

Dun dun du du dun

It was the jingle the show would start with. I was sitting in my car, driving down to my mother's place when I heard it. It belonged to some regional fast food restaurant, nothing too special, but it wasn't the ad that made me worry; it was the jingle they used. This short melody is what woke up the blurry memories somewhere in the back of my mind. As I heard this typical early 2000s tune, I drove down to the next gas station to park. Suddenly I couldn't focus on the street anymore; my breathing became heavy as if there was a big stone in my chest. Something had just been activated inside of my mind. Something I had entirely forgotten about for the past decade.

Dr. Warly's Adventure Club.

Dr. Warly always had a big bright smile on his face. Even when he talked in a more serious tone. His voice was shrill and jolly but deep and rough at the same time. A sound that suddenly made its way back to my ears.

Wonderful afternoon, adventurers and explorers, and welcome, welcome, welcome! Are you as excited we are for another episode of Warly's Adventure Club?...

That's what followed the jingle.

I saw Dr. Warly standing in the middle. He had long, fuzzy hair and would wear peculiar suits in the weirdest color combinations. Next to him were children. I closed my eyes and tried to remember their faces or even their names, but it was too long ago. I laughed out loud, as I started to calm down more. I couldn't believe how I had just blocked this memory out of my mind.

When I was ten or eleven, all I wanted to be was an actor. I was a passionate kid, and when I wanted something, I would do absolutely anything to get it. I'm not sure how exactly it happened. I think I saw an ad somewhere about a new show casting young actors, and while I don't remember the casting process, I knew that I was part of the show. It must have ended when I was thirteen or something, because that's when Mum and I moved away for her new job.

I started my engine again and drove to my mum right away. I suddenly had so many questions.

My mother wasn't home yet, so I decided to do some online research, first but to my surprise, I couldn't find anything about it. Even now. The show wasn't too big and maybe even something more regional if I remember correctly, but I assumed I'd at least find something on YouTube. For a moment, I even doubted if it really happened. As I said, the memories were blurry, and it could have been that I dreamed about it or something. If I'd been the star of a show, I wouldn't have simply forgotten about it, I imagined. I mean, I would have told my friends or something.

This was just so weird, but if it wasn't true, then who the hell was Dr. Warly? And why could I suddenly get that jingle out of my head?

Dun dun du du dun

"Alex?"

I heard my mother say in a panicked tone. I hadn't even heard her come inside. I turned around to see a look of surprise and fear on her face.

"Uhm, hey, Mum, I told you I was coming over yesterday, remember?" I laughed.

"Oh yes. Of course, honey!" She smiled and walked over to give me a hug.

Then her eyes went over to the laptop.

"Warly," she mumbled, and her expression darkened.

"Yes, Mum, I need to ask you a strange question. Was I part of some children's show?" I felt foolish even asking.

My mother walked straight to the kitchen and poured herself a glass of water. She offered me some, but I shook my head.

"I haven't thought about this in years."

She laughed, but I could swear I saw her eyes twitch as she said those words. "You know, honey, I was very busy back then with work, and you were alone a lot. I felt guilty, and you seemed to enjoy acting so much, and those other kids really liked you."

"So it was real?" I interrupted her.

My mum nodded and took a big gulp from her glass.

"You were really young when it started. When your contract expired, you were already becoming a teenager, and I think you started regretting it. Kids change a lot at that age, you know. You thought it was childish and even made me destroy all the tapes."

She walked back to the living room, and I couldn't help but feel like she was hiding something.

"Okay, Mum, sorry, but this is super weird. How the hell did I completely forget about those years?"

My mum looked at me with a concerned look on her face.

"Why was the show cancelled?" I asked.

"You don't remember?"

I shook my head.

"Listen, Alex. You are almost twenty-five now. You've had a nice and normal life, and that is all I ever wanted. Sometimes there's a good reason we don't remember particular times in our lives. Sometimes it's better to keep things buried."

"Mum, you're freaking me out," I exclaimed.

She sighed.

"I wasn't the best mother back then. I spent far too little time with you, and I regret it deeply. But it's also the reason why I didn't see your show much. You'd be picked up by your agent, and I was happy about that. I tried watching the tapes they gave me then, but I couldn't make much sense of it, you know?"

It was true. My mum didn't have much time for me when I was younger. I mainly got raised by babysitters and myself, but that was a long time ago. It couldn't be the only reason my mum was acting so strangely.

"Okay, Mum, I honestly don't care. I don't even remember it. Just why did it get cancelled?" I asked, slightly annoyed.

She made a long pause but finally answered.

"The show was really popular for a while, but then strange things started happening. Children would disappear and leave notes saying they were going on an adventure. You know kids disappear all the time, it's not something we like to talk about, but apparently the notes were all strangely similar. And then there were the suicides."

She had finished her water and went back to the kitchen to refill.

"Suicides? What are you talking about?"

My heart started racing.

"Kids like to copycat. Maybe they heard about other children doing it in the news somehow or I don't know... Look, this was a long time ago. Obviously, it had nothing to do with the show, but people always need to blame someone when things go to shit, right? So it got canceled, and it was honestly for the best anyway. You'd grown too old for that stuff."

"What? How are you taking this so casually?" I started shouting.

My mum shot me an angry look.

"Did you just come to visit me so you can ask questions and shout at me?" she hissed.

I looked at the ground. I guess maybe these memories reminded her of a time where our relationship wasn't the best. But I don't think she understood how stressful it was for me to suddenly remember something so odd about my past. I needed more information, but I knew I wouldn't get it from my mum. I had lost contact with the friends I had as a child, so that wasn't an option, either. I texted some of my middle school and high school friends, but nobody seems to ever have heard of a show with some Dr. Warly.

I hardly slept that night. As I was lying in my old bedroom, having that annoying jingle stuck in my head, more memories started coming back to me. Memories of Dr. Warly's laugh and the stick he always had with him with a purple-and-red swirl. It looked like a big candy cane. The rest of us all wore one specific color each. During every episode, we had the same outfit. There was a boy in green, a girl in yellow, another girl in red, and I was purple. I had the visuals and the sounds but not the content. I have absolutely no idea what those adventures were that we went on, and the weirdest part is that all the memories I did have were about the show. None were about the moments of us filming them. It made sense that I thought I had made it up. I would still be doubting it if my mum hadn't just confessed that it was real.

My eyes shot wide open, and I couldn't help but grin as I got an idea. I got out of bed and slowly opened my door so I wouldn't wake my mum sleeping next door. I tiptoed toward the stairs that went to the attic and climbed up. My mum was the kind of person who never threw anything away, which made it even weirder that she hadn't kept any of the tapes, but

I remember distinctly that she had kept many boxes with old toys and other stuff from when I was a kid. When I moved out for college, we brought some more of my things up here, and I saw many boxes from our old home.

After rummaging through old stuff for what must have been hours, I finally sighed and gave up. I couldn't believe that there was not a single piece of evidence from this strange time of my life. Disappointed, I went back to my room so I could try and get at least a little sleep. I took a look at my phone, and finally, the hope was back.

I had gotten a text from Helen. I had texted her earlier, asking if she remembered the show. She lived next door and went to middle school with me.

This is so strange! I just thought about this the other day... I meant to text you but had been so busy with work. How are you doing Alex?

She had sent this a few minutes ago. Helen works as a nurse now, so I guess she was on her way to work.

Helen! So glad to hear from you. Sorry, I know this is super weird. We definitely need to catch up soon. But can you tell me what you remember about the show? Like any tiny detail would already help!!

She replied a few minutes later.

Uhmm I don't know anything about the show. Your mum would never let us watch it, remember? And it wasn't on tv here. Buuut I remember how we once did a video call with one of your friends from the show. Must have still been msn times lol.

That was all the information Helen had, but it was all the clues I needed. Turns out, I could still access my MSN Messenger contacts. One of the perks of keeping the same Hotmail account for years, I guess. And funny enough, there were a couple of people whose names I didn't remember. I sent each of them an email, trying not to sound too much like I was going crazy. But maybe there was a chance that one of them was actually one of my actor friends.

It took a couple of days, but two people responded.

The first one was someone called Janie, or at least that's what it said in the address, but the email wasn't exactly helpful. All it said was:

Don't ever fucking contact me again.

I kept staring at the screen, wondering whether the real issue with the show wasn't what happened on screen but behind it. It was a scary thought, but maybe there was something that Dr. Warly did. Something that made me want to forget. It would also explain why my mother acted so weird when the topic came up. I wondered whether she made up the thing about children disappearing and the suicides to distract me from something traumatic. My stomach started to turn on the thought of that.

I almost decided to let it go. I started thinking that Mum was right and that sometimes it might be better to not bring up memories we tried to forget.

But then I got another email.

Wow, didn't think I'd ever hear from you again. I have the tape but not online. I can send it to you.

-The boy in green.

The tape? As in one? I hesitated at first. I know sending your address to a stranger isn't very smart, so I gave him the address of a parcel station where I could pick it up as well as my phone number. I asked some more questions, but the only reply I got was this one:

It wasn't our fault, Alex. Don't listen to what I say.

***

Two days later, I finally received the tape.

When Mum was at work, I got the old VHS player from the attic. My hands were shaking as I put the tape in.

Dun dun du du dun

Wonderful afternoon, adventurers and explorers, and welcome, wel-come, welcome! Are you as excited we are for another episode of Warly's Adventure Club?

His voice sounded even more distorted than I remembered.

May I introduce to you our main explorer... Alex!

I saw a ten-year-old version of myself jump onto the screen. I had a big smile on my face and waved furiously. I was small for my age, and my face was plastered with freckles, most of which disappeared over the years.

"And these are my buddies Leigh, Janie, and Millie!" the child version of me said.

The other kids appeared behind me. Leigh was taller than me, and his black hair went in all directions. Millie's hair was red, a few shades lighter than Janie's clothes. Janie had the most serious look on her face. She was wearing big glasses, and her dark hair was pulled into a braid that went around her head.

What's today's adventure? they shouted in unison.

The energy was definitely a little too high, but nothing too strange for some old kids' show. Nothing too worrying, at least. Except after that moment everything we said sounded somehow like gibberish. I wondered if that was part of the concept, but it did feel very weird. I kept listening to the nonsense but at the same time grabbed my phone. I wanted to send Leigh, the boy in green, another email.

"Are you happy?" I heard my own voice say. I looked back at the television and was surprised to see the camera zoomed into my face. Something about it looked somehow off, not just the gigantic smile I had but something about my facial structures was odd. I decided that it was probably just too much stage makeup as the other kids looked a bit weird as well.

All of a sudden, the smile disappeared, and young Alex looked a lot more serious.

"You know she still doesn't love you, right? She never has and never will."

I felt like I had missed some important part, but none of the things said before had made any sense. It didn't even sound like English.

The young version of me started laughing.

The camera zoomed away again, and now the other kids were in the picture once more. Leigh, Millie, and Janie were standing in the back, all laughing. In front of them I saw someone lying on the ground. It looked like another kid but dressed in regular clothes. It was difficult to recognize what gruesome things were going on back there until the camera moved closer. The eyes of the young boy were opened wide, and he wasn't moving. The big candy cane was shoved inside his stomach, staining his clothes red.

I held my breath. This couldn't be real. This was supposed to be a kids' show.

Obviously, there was no way they could ever screen something like this, and at first I wondered if Leigh had sent me this as a prank. Maybe it was some macabre offscreen joke.

The boy—I came closer again and started speaking directly toward the camera.

"Remember how much fun we had, Alex? Let's do it again!"

And that's where the tape ended.

I noticed I was still holding my breath. This had to be a prank; why else would I be talking directly to myself?

Still, for some reason I couldn't bring myself to rewatch the tape.

I don't know how long I was just sitting there, trying to remember anything useful, when my phone started ringing.

It was an unknown number.

"Did you watch it?" I heard a male voice speak.

"Leigh?" I asked.

He was quiet for a while.

"It was a joke, right? I mean, we were young and stuff, but damn, that was fucked up," I added and laughed nervously.

"I hadn't seen the tape for years. I didn't remember any of what was happening in it. But I don't think it was a joke," he finally said.

"What the fuck. It had to be. I even said my name directly to the camera," I responded.

"What are you talking about, Alex? You didn't say anything in that video. It was just me talking. And I told myself to fucking die."

This time I stayed silent. Maybe Leigh was screwing with me, but why would he do that? We hadn't spoken to each other in over ten years.

"I have to go now. Don't show this video to anyone else."

"Wait, Leigh—" I said, but he had already hung up.

Part 2

It probably goes without saying, but I felt fairly agitated after the call with Leigh. Instead of getting answers, I was left with even more questions. It didn't help, either, that my mum acted even stranger around me and seemed to be avoiding me at all costs.

I decided to go for a run so I could try to empty my head a little, but on my way out, I was stopped by Helen. I'd seen her a couple of times when visiting my mum in the past years, but besides the occasional small talk or birthday wishes, we hadn't been in contact much. I guess that's what happens when you grow older. Life happens and you lose touch with your childhood friends. I wonder if that's what happened to me and my actor colleagues as well or whether there was more to it. After seeing that tape last night and talking to Leigh, I wasn't sure of anything anymore.

"Alex!"

Helen walked over and gave me a big hug.

"Can't believe you've been here for days without saying hi!" she said as we sat down at the porch to catch up.

"Sorry! I meant to but—I got a little distracted," I said. It felt strange that only a few days had passed since I sat in the car where that strange jingle activated something buried inside of me. I felt like I had just woken up from a dream just to realize I had entered a nightmare.

"No worries, I'd been pretty busy, too, but as of today I'm officially on summer break!" she exclaimed and raised her arms in the air.

"Summer break? I thought you were working already?" I asked.

"I went back to school to study medicine."

"Oh, wow, we really needed to catch up." I laughed. "That's awesome."

"Yeah, it's exhausting but fun. Anyway, how are you? Did you find out about that show you did as a kid?"

There it was. The knot in my stomach tightened again.

Helen was pretty much my best friend growing up. She even remembered talking to one of my friends from the show when we were younger. I took a deep breath and proceeded to tell her everything that had happened in the last days. All the weird memories that came back to me that I couldn't explain. The weird conversation with my mum, the tape, and the phone call with Leigh. I kept speaking without even taking a break, and she sat and listened to all of it.

"I know how insane this sounds. I still think that the tape was just some weird prank from Leigh."

Helen stayed quiet for a while.

"But that doesn't explain your mum being weird about it," she finally said.

"I mean, maybe she feels guilty or something? I don't know, maybe I'm going crazy, but my gut tells me there's so much more to it. If I could only remember..."

"I did find it a little strange that you forgot about it. It wasn't that long ago, and it's not really something you'd just forget about, you know?"

I nodded.

"But what troubles me the most is that phone call you had with him. You haven't talked to this guy in years and suddenly he tells you that some young version of him told him he should die? Whatever happened or whatever is going on, it sounds like he might need help. Did you try to contact him again?" she asked.

I bit my lip. I hadn't called him again. I basically threw my phone in the corner after the call and tried to forget about it. Of course I couldn't.

I shook my head.

"I should have. It's just... after seeing the tape, I couldn't really think straight."

Helen raised her eyebrows.

"Can I see it?"

I was probably even more nervous showing her that tape than when I was when I watched it myself, but she listened to everything I said and she seemed to be understanding. She didn't make me feel guilty or crazy or anything. I was glad that I opened up to her.

Helen sat down on the sofa as I inserted the tape back in the player. My hands started trembling; I wasn't ready to watch the madness again, so I turned my face toward her instead of the television.

Dun dun du du dun

Wonderful afternoon, adventurers and explorers, and welcome, welcome, welcome! Are you as excited we are for another episode of Warly's Adventure Club?

"Yikes. Dr. Warly looks more like Dr. Molesty," Helen joked.

I stayed silent as I observed her reactions.

"Aww, look at that. What a cutie. You didn't tell me you were the leader of the group! Oh, and that's Leigh, right?"

"The one in green, yeah," I said without turning to the screen.

"Okay, now I don't get it anymore. What age group was this made for?" she asked and raised an eyebrow.

There it was. She must be seeing the messed-up murder scene, I thought. For some reason she stayed weirdly calm.

I finally turned my gaze to the television, but I didn't recognize what was going on. It didn't look like the scene I had seen yesterday. The four of us had a treasure map and were exploring something. The imagery reminded me of Willy Wonka's chocolate factory. There was no blood and no dead child lying on the floor, but it had to be the same tape I saw yesterday as I had gone back to the moment where I started.

"Like, it looks like some scavenger hunt, but what the hell is that language?" Helen asked.

It was the same gibberish I had heard when I watched the tape.

"Wait, hand me the remote." She rewound the tape back to the starting moment. The moment where Dr. Warly introduces us. She got close to the screen and took a photo of my face. Then she went forward to the scavenger hunt and did the same thing again.

"What the hell?" Helen mumbled. "That doesn't look like your face. It doesn't look like a face at all. Did they make you wear masks?"

She handed over the phone and zoomed in. She was right. It was the same thing that I had noticed yesterday. My face looked strange, but this wasn't just makeup. The proportions were slightly off as if someone had plastered a second face on top of mine. But only in the later frames. We checked again, and it was the same for the other faces.

"Maybe," I muttered. "I honestly don't remember anything about the filming part."

"It would be strange to leave the introduction normal but change your looks for the rest. Or maybe the intro was something they always played. Are there any more episodes?"

"I don't know. Leigh only sent me this."

"This is really disturbing," she whispered. "We should try to call him."

It took about six times, but finally Leigh picked up. I wasn't really sure what to say, but Helen took control pretty quickly. After reminiscing about old times for a while, Leigh seemed a lot more relaxed, and I'm not sure how else to describe this, he seemed normal? I was still a bit skeptical, but hearing them talk about regular life helped ease my nerves a little.

Finally, she got to the point.

"So Alex and I watched the tape. Are there different videos? 'Cause he saw something else than I did."

"No. It's one tape. One video. There is just this one episode. I probably shouldn't have sent it, but it's been creeping me the hell out. I constantly have nightmares. And—"

He stayed quiet for a while.

"I haven't talked to anyone about this except my therapist. I wanted to destroy the tape, but then I got that mail from Alex. I'd almost forgotten about you, man."

"Yeah, me too," I said. I hadn't said anything since we started the call even though we had the speaker on.

"You shouldn't have shown it to her, though. I warned you about that."

"It's okay, I didn't find it that scary at all. It was cute," Helen chimed in. "So this might be a little weird, but why don't we meet up? We're old enough now to drive," she then suggested.

Leigh stayed quiet for a while.

"Yeah, fuck it. Why not? But could you come here? I can't really leave. I'm taking care of my grandpa."

<hr>

It all happened really fast, but there we were, driving to the town where I was born. The place I had almost forgotten. There were a lot more trees surrounding the town than I remembered. We passed the sign to Fereway. I remembered how Mum always talked about visiting the town some time, but we never actually did.

"Marden. That's kind of a nasty name," Helen said as we passed another sign to a town.

"It's actually pretty nice. We went there a couple of times to go to the farmer's market. Well, the few times Mum was around."

Helen gave me a sympathetic smile as we drove through more trees. And finally, there it was, the big sign saying "Welcome to Watton." A vivid but gray town somewhere in the middle of nowhere.

I don't know what I was expecting. Some part of me kept thinking this was all some trap and we would be walking right into the arms of Dr. Warly himself. Instead a slightly older version of the green boy from the video opened the door, with a shy smile on his face. Back then he was taller than me, but now we were about the same height. But his eyes were still as green as his costume back then. It was probably why they chose him as the green boy.

"You're not blond anymore," were his first words.

From closer up, I noticed the massive bags under his eyes. His voice had gotten deeper, but I guess so had mine.

"Nope, grown out of that I guess."

I hesitated for a moment before going in for an awkward hug.

"And nice to finally meet you in real life, Helen! Is this your first time in Watton?"

She nodded.

"Yeah. It's... nice," she said with a friendly smile.

"No need to be polite. It's a garbage town. The only reason I still live here is my grandpa." Leigh laughed and welcomed us inside.

"I've been here before," I mumbled as we walked inside the house.

Leigh's parents had passed away when he was very young. His grandparents were the ones who raised him, but apparently his grandmother recently died as well.

"Oh, yeah, you came here sometimes after the show when your mum would work."

"You remember that?" I asked.

He shook his head.

"Not really, but we have some photos. I actually don't remember a lot from back then."

"Yeah, that sounds familiar."

"Have you been in contact with any of the other actors from that show? The girls?" Helen chimed in.

"I chatted with Janie not very long ago, but she didn't want much to do with me."

I got my phone and sent him the response I'd gotten from her the other day.

He nodded knowingly.

"Yeah, that's pretty much what my last interaction with her looked like."

Leigh got us some cups and coffee as we sat around his kitchen table. It didn't take long for us to feel comfortable with each other, and the longer we talked, the more memories of my past came back. But still nothing about filming the show.

"You know, I was actually a little nervous when you sent me that mail. Thought it was some sort of trap. Sounds ridiculous, right?" Leigh said while he poured coffee in our cups.

"Trap?" Helen raised an eyebrow. "From who?"

"Don't know. Dr. Warly?" Leigh laughed nervously. "Or the producers of the show or some crazy fan maybe? Although that's not plausible as the show doesn't even exist."

"What do you mean it doesn't exist? We have the tape right here," Helen responded and pointed toward her backpack.

"Yeah, I mean there is this one video. That's it, though. They aired the same shit every day for like a year. Wait a sec."

He left the room, and we heard him go upstairs.

"Do you think we can trust him?" I whispered toward Helen, to which she only shrugged.

"Okay, this is everything I've collected so far. I know it looks a little obsessive, but well, it's been a rough couple of days."

Leigh was back with a pile of papers, photos, and notes.

"That tape you saw is the only thing we ever filmed. Except I don't think everyone that watches it sees the same thing. And, well, you guys kinda proved that theory. Helen saw some scavenger hunt, yeah? That's what it looked like to my grandpa, too. But this show was super popular with other children. I remember people in school telling me for years how obsessed they were with it."

"Then why did it get canceled?" I asked to see whether Leigh's theory would confirm the things my mother hinted at.

"Because something strange seemed to happen to some kids who watched it. They'd disappear, some apparently started killing their pets and—"

"Some killed themselves," I finished his sentence.

"That's what I heard. I don't know."

"This is so messed up," Helen mumbled.

We went through some of the articles, and it was true. There was a series of seriously messed-up events taking place. For a while, nobody realized that it was connected to *Dr. Warly's Adventure Club*, but then more and more parents found notes from their children saying they were going to explore a new world or similar stuff. The show was canceled shortly after that.

"What is this?" Helen asked as she held up a photo. A photo of the four of us with Dr. Warly taken in the studio. Except Millie's face was blackened out. On top of our heads, someone had written MURDERER in red letters with an arrow pointing toward me and Leigh.

Leigh didn't say anything for a little while. It seemed as if he was carefully collecting his words.

"Janie sent this to me," he finally said.

That photo, it woke something up inside of me. Not a visual memory but a feeling. A terrible feeling. Suddenly the jingle made its way back to my mind, but this time the sound was followed by a cry.

My hands started shaking, and I started sweating nervously.

"Leigh. Is Millie dead?"

He looked me straight in the eyes, with a look that matched mine.

"I don't know," he whispered. "I can't find any information about her."

"Sorry, Leigh, but this is getting really strange."

Helen quickly got up from her seat, her expression a mix of fear and disgust.

"I'm not buying this. You forgot about being part of some murder show and happened to remember it at the same time as Alex?"

I felt terrible seeing Helen so freaked out. And for bringing her here at all. We never even thought about Leigh being dangerous, but what he said next made me understand everything better, even if it didn't necessarily help with the fear.

"I know how eerie this sounds. I'm going fucking insane myself, and if Alex hadn't reached out, I don't know that—After seeing that tape, man, I was so messed up." He took a deep breath. "The memories didn't come out of nowhere. I heard that damn intro song. The weird melody."

"Dun dun du du dun," I mumbled. "Where did you hear it?" I added in a louder voice.

"I heard it on the radio. Well, my grandpa and I did. He's got dementia and doesn't remember much about anything, but when that spot came on, he suddenly whispered, 'Dr. Warly,' and smiled at me. I had forgotten all about it for so many years, but after searching through our basement, I found that tape."

Helen and I shot each other a look.

"The spot? Was it for a burger place?" I asked.

"Not sure if it was burgers, but I think it was called Larry's Wine and Dine or something?"

I got up from my chair, adrenaline rushing through my body.

"I don't think that radio spot was a coincidence, Leigh. Not if I heard it in a whole different state. I think Dr. Warly is trying to reach out to us."

Part 3

Our subconscious is something truly remarkable. Just think about all those skills that we can now perform without being consciously aware. Driving a car, speaking, reading, all without any effort at all. Our autopilot just does it. But at the same time the idea of having all this information inside of us frightens me. Just imagining how much knowledge is hidden somewhere in our minds, all the things we can't control or can't even access. It makes you wonder who is really in charge of yourself.

I'm not sure whether something inside of me was trying to protect me by forgetting the past or better blurring it, or whether there was more to it. I mean, there had to be more to it, considering I wasn't the only person being affected by *Dr. Warly's Adventure Club*.

We had already come too far to just give up. Helen and Leigh agreed. We needed to figure out what had happened all those years ago and whether it was now somehow repeating itself. Because right now, it felt as if Dr. Warly was planning a comeback of some sort.

We had dinner with Mr. Montroe, Leigh's grandpa. He didn't seem to know who I was, but as soon as I saw him, I started remembering the afternoons I would spend here with Leigh and his grandparents. I even believe that Janie and Millie were here from time to time. I didn't ask Mr. Montroe about it, however. Leigh said it's better not to ask him about things from the past as it agitates him sometimes. So we had a nice dinner and played some card games, after which Mr. Montroe went to bed. It was already pretty late at that point, and Leigh invited us to stay. I was reluctant at first, but we had come all the way, and Helen thought it was a great idea. I guess the mistrust she had toward Leigh started vanishing the more tired she got.

Helen was now lying on the sofa, loudly snoring, while Leigh and I quietly went through some more of the clues he had collected.

"You know, it's all right if you go to sleep, too. Looks like you haven't done that in days," I said.

Leigh just shrugged.

"Nah, I'm okay. Every time I try to close my eyes, all I see is that horrible video."

I took a deep breath. I understood what he meant; it was the same for me. The empty eyes of that child being impaled by the candy cane were burned inside my mind.

"What exactly did you see, Leigh?" I asked.

Before answering, Leigh got up and got two Cokes from the kitchen. He offered me one, but I declined. After taking a big sip, he finally answered.

"There was the intro, then some stuff that didn't make much sense. We were speaking and singing in some strange language with voices I didn't recognize at all. It honestly sounded alien."

"Yeah, I saw something like that, and we were dancing in circles or some shit," I added.

"You know what the weirdest part is? Those words don't make sense at first, but I think there's some logic behind it. As in, there's a repetition of things we say and it all sounds kinda similar. Do you think they taught this to us? 'Cause at first I thought it was just random bullshit, but maybe they put those words somewhere in a script."

I hadn't even thought about that. To me, it just sounded like gibberish.

"Anway, after the already weird scenes, it got really messed up." He started whispering. "I think I killed someone. I mean, I don't remember but... there was this scene and Dr. Warly gave me something and—"

"A candy cane?" I interrupted him.

Leigh shook his head. "No, it was a plastic bag. Then he whispered something in your ear. You went to get some kid. A little girl and then I put the bag over her head."

My breathing was getting heavier. We both saw children being murdered, or at least that's how it appeared.

"Was the girl Millie? Is that why Janie sent you that picture?"

"No. I'm not sure what Janie meant by that. I'm thinking maybe she saw something else on the tape; maybe we did hurt Millie. I don't know. I don't know anything."

Leigh was fighting with tears. I understand what this looked like and how he was feeling, but I simply couldn't accept that we supposedly killed any children. I mean, we were children ourselves, for god's sake.

I put a hand on his shoulder and tried to comfort him a little, even if I didn't exactly believe the things I was saying, either.

"It was a show, though, right? I mean maybe we just remember it wrong. Maybe it wasn't made for kids, maybe it was some horror stuff, and we were just too young to understand—"

"No," Leigh interrupted me, "because, after that scene, the camera got really close to my face, the morphed face, and it said that it was my fault that my parents died and that I should follow them." He took another sip from his Coke. "They died in a car crash. What I'm trying to say is that the video was too personal. It wasn't just a scene. It was talking to me."

Thinking about it, the things I said toward the camera were pretty personal as well, even if they weren't as painful as what Leigh had to witness.

"But Helen didn't see that when she watched the tape. And neither did I. That thing is somehow cursed. It's not real," I tried to argue.

"Or maybe it shows us the things that we forgot. Events that really happened. And Helen doesn't see it because she wasn't there," Leigh replied.

"Okay, then how about we watch it now? Together? We'll know whether we are seeing the same things, right?" I suggested. I knew I had to watch this again, and doing it with Leigh, who was an actor in the show like me, made this just a little easier to handle.

We turned on Leigh's TV and turned the volume low enough so we wouldn't wake up Helen but loud enough so that we might be able to hear the made-up language. Leigh suggested we film it with one of our phones so that we could try and unscramble the language somehow.

Dun dun du du dun

The melody was really starting to agitate me.

The next parts were exactly the same stuff Helen saw about the scavenger hunt.

"You know, maybe we did imagine things when we saw it. I don't know how but—"

"STOP!"

Helen shouted from the sofa. She was sitting up straight now, shaking and breathing heavily.

"It wasn't my fault. It wasn't my fault," she muttered.

"Helen, it's fine. You're okay. Try to breathe, slowly." I walked over to the sofa and took her hand. Her heart was beating like crazy.

"It was probably a nightmare. You're safe," Leigh said and came closer as well.

Helen furiously shook her head.

"It wasn't. I saw it. I saw him."

"Who?" both of us asked at the same time.

After a moment, Helen's pulse became slower again, and she gradually calmed down.

"I woke up when I heard the jingle. To be honest, I just wanted to see how you guys were reacting to the thing. 'Cause you saw different stuff when you watched it," she took a deep breath, "but then it changed. It was different."

"You don't have to tell us if you don't want to. We get it," Leigh said.

"It's okay. I was pretty drowsy, so at first I thought I was just imagining things. The children, well you, were talking nonsense again, but then it changed. Dr. Warly invited a child inside."

Leigh and I shot each other a knowing look. We were both afraid of what Helen might say next.

"The boy looked like a patient we had. He was the first person I ever saw die. It broke my heart and my spirit back then. You have no idea how hard that job can be."

"It's not possible, Helen. You were just sleepy. Maybe you imagined something." Leigh tried to comfort her.

"But the worst part was seeing you, Alex. You came really close to the camera, and then you told me it was all my fault."

The next morning we made a plan. We looked up Larry's Wine and Dine and realized that it wasn't that far away from here; it was actually in one of the towns Helen and I passed on our way here: Marden.

"Well, now we know for sure that it's a trap. Why else would they air it where we live? Marden isn't even in the same state," Helen said.

And as if that wasn't strange enough already, Larry's had only opened about two weeks ago.

"Are you guys sure it's a good idea to go there? It's pretty damn obvious it's a trap," Leigh said.

We were already in my car, driving through the alleys surrounded by nothing but trees. I asked Helen if she wanted to go home after last night. I offered to give her my car to leave. I was honestly feeling terribly guilty to have sucked her into this madness, but after the initial shock wore off, she was even more determined to solve this mystery. I think that video made it personal for her.

I had been too afraid to say these words out loud just yet, but there was something else that I started worrying about. Helen didn't just see a man in the video; it was someone who *really* died. Did that mean that the children Leigh and I saw really died as well? Did we just forget?

I was hoping for at least some answers as we drove into the parking spot of Larry's Wine and Dine.

We didn't plan to go inside. It still felt like a trap, but driving there in the middle of the day, just to see the place, seemed safe enough.

We parked far enough away so that whoever was in there wouldn't see us.

"It looks more like a diner, though, doesn't it? The aesthetics don't really match Wine and Dine," Helen said.

"And it's kinda old school. I can't really recognize any people inside, though. It's too far away," I added.

"But check out the walls," Leigh said.

They were purple. A very familiar shade of purple.

"Uhm... guys," Helen whispered. "Do you see that man behind us?"

I turned around and saw a man in his forties sitting on a rusty bike. His face wasn't pointed toward us, but instead it looked as if he was staring inside the diner. He was wearing sunglasses and his hair was shorter, but I would recognize that face anywhere.

It was Dr. Warly.

"Shit, did he see us? What do we do? Should I drive away?" I started panicking, but before I could actually start the engine, Leigh had already opened his door and was rushing out. It all happened pretty fast. Helen and I shot each other a quick look before we followed Leigh, who was now storming toward the man. Before any of us could react, he had punched Dr. Warly right in the face.

Dr. Warly didn't hit back. He just held his bleeding nose and stared at us in shock.

"It's you," he mumbled. He kept switching his gaze between us and the diner, his face a mix of desperation and fear.

"Get out of here. NOW!" he hissed.

The door of the diner opened, and a woman stepped outside. She must have spotted us because she shouted something inside the diner, but I couldn't hear what exactly she said.

Something strange was going on, that much was clear, but I wasn't sure anymore who we needed to be afraid of.

"Guys, I think we should get the hell out of here," Helen said as she rushed toward the driver's seat of the car.

I took another look at the diner where the commotion was getting bigger. I'm not sure if I would end up regretting this, but as I looked at the man with the bleeding nose, I knew that he would have some answers for us.

"Grab his arm, Leigh. Warly is coming with us."

Part 4

His voice was low and rough. It sounded as if this man had spent half his life chain smoking.

"I was young. Not much older than you guys are now. An agent told me they needed an actor for a *revolutionary* kids' show, and while entertaining children in a damned place like Watton felt beneath me, I did need the money. The only reason I could bear it was by being high as a kite on set. That entire year is just a huge blur in my memory. I always thought it was the drugs, but now I'm starting to understand that there is a lot more to it. Whoever these people are, they are dangerous. But I guess you've realized that by now. What brought you to the diner in the first place?"

"How about you answer our questions first, Warly?" Leigh hissed.

We had taken our old acting colleague with us and drove to a coffee shop in the center of Watton. A public place with many people around felt safer for the time being.

"You realize Warly isn't my actual name, right?" He rolled his eyes and sighed. "Anway, for years I had forgotten about the show altogether. I've been living with my sister in Marden, and the other day we got some vouchers for a new diner. I drove down there to get some food, but as soon as I stepped inside, I heard a melody coming from the speakers inside the diner."

"Dun dun du du dun," Leigh and I sang in unison.

"Please don't," Warly said with a disgusted look on his face. "But yeah. That song. I turned right around and left. I wasn't sure why, but at that moment that sound just made me feel sick. Like it triggered some PTSD or whatever. On my way home, the memories came back. I called my agent from back then and asked if she still had any copies of the show. She sent me a tape right away, but I could make absolutely no sense of it. It was even worse than I remembered. So you know, I thought I'd show it to my niece. She's eight, and I figured maybe I don't get it cause I'm too old."

"What did she see?"

Warly's expression darkened. His eyes started watering.

"I have no clue. All I know is that she was basically glued to the screen and even talked to it. I was there the whole time, and I still don't understand what she was seeing. You guys were there, and the two girls, but you spoke in a made-up language."

He sniffed. "That night something happened. My niece disappeared. We don't know how or when, but the next morning she wasn't in her bed, and she didn't come home again. The police couldn't find her. There were no clues left. She even took her shoes. They don't know what happened, but I do. This show does something awful to children."

The three of us stayed silent. To any other people Warly's story would have sounded like madness, but we knew better. We had seen the tape.

"Of course the first one they blame is the ex-junkie uncle, and I get it. But I had nothing to do with it, I swear. The whole mess is repeating itself," Warly finally whispered.

"So the rumors are true?" Helen asked.

"I heard about it back when we were filming. I never believed it if I'm honest, it sounded like bullshit. Stuff like that happens a lot around here, Watton isn't exactly a safe place, but when the little blue girl was taken years later—"

"Wait, what blue girl? Are you talking about Millie?" I almost shouted.

Leigh looked as shocked as I did.

"You don't remember?" Warly asked.

Although as he said those words, something was coming back to me. I remembered meeting them again. But we were older. Fifteen, maybe? Leigh was there, Janie and Millie, too. Was that the last time I talked to her?

"We had a reunion," Leigh whispered as if he had just read my mind.

Warly nodded.

"There was a discussion about bringing the show back. For an older audience. Alex here had moved away, and I was pretty opposed to it, but the network pressured us to talk about it again. A week after that, the girl vanished, and that was the end of the discussion. Apparently she left a goodbye note, but they couldn't make much sense of it."

My hands started trembling. This was getting too real.

"We were children, but you weren't! You were an adult! How could you let any of this happen?" I shouted.

Warly hit his fist on the table, making the cups in front of us spill.

"Do you think I would have let my little niece watch this shit if I knew? I had forgotten, just like you, but I've spent day and night researching, trying to remember."

Leigh put a hand on my shoulder. My heart was still racing.

"Quiet, guys, you're attracting a lot of attention right now," Helen whispered.

We paid the check and got back into the car.

"This doesn't mean that we did it," Leigh whispered in my ear as we made our way to the car. "We don't know what really happened to her."

———

We got back to the car, and I started driving. We headed toward Leigh's home first, where we wanted to drop off Helen. He didn't like his grandpa being alone for too long, and Helen volunteered to take care of him. While we didn't believe that the worn-out actor was exactly dangerous right now, Leigh also didn't want him in his home, which was understandable.

"I tried contacting my old agent again, but she disappeared. I haven't been able to reach her since she sent me that tape. Guys, the show doesn't exist. I'm starting to understand it now. The reason I only remember filming that first scene isn't only because I was high during the other days. It's because we never filmed anything else. The reason they cast us was probably because you kids didn't have any support systems and all of us were troubled in some way," Warly spoke from the backseat.

"My grandparents were just happy I had found a hobby after Mum and Dad died," Leigh mumbled.

"And my mum didn't care much about anything at all," I confessed.

"And I was a wannabe actor who couldn't get his shit together," Warly continued. "I have no idea what happened when we were at that studio, boys, but I've watched the tape often enough now to know that those creatures in the show aren't us. They just used our faces."

"That's what I thought," Helen said. "It just doesn't look real. Maybe they used some computer techniques to make those scenes."

"That must be it. They used us for the normal introduction, maybe as a pilot, and for the rest they plastered our faces on something alien."

"We're at my home," Leigh chimed in.

"All right, I'll see you later, guys, and keep me updated," Helen said and opened the door. "And don't do anything stupid."

She winked and pointed at Leigh's hand, which was still bruised from punching Warly.

"Who is that girl, by the way? Girlfriend of one of you?" Warly asked in a dry tone.

"Helen? No, she's an old friend of mine," I responded.

"And you trust her?" he asked. "You should be careful about that."

Until this point, I hadn't doubted Helen's intentions. I'd known her for years, but it did seem a little strange that she came all the way here with me to investigate a horror show that makes children disappear or even die.

"We trust her more than we trust you, dude. She didn't host a creepy kids' show," Leigh answered instead of me. "And now let's get out of here."

"If that thing about us and the faces is true—I mean, if those things in there aren't really us—does that mean we didn't kill anyone?" I carefully asked as the three of us drove to the closest gas station.

"Is that what you saw?"

Leigh and I both avoided eye contact.

"Right," Warly said. "Honestly, I don't know, boys, but I might have an idea how we can find out more."

"What is it?" I asked.

"Well, obviously we shouldn't go back to that diner, but there is another place we could check. One right in Marden. I remember where the studio is. The one where we filmed the adventure club."

It was an impulsive decision, but it made so much sense. I don't know why we didn't think of it sooner. While the studio might not give us all the answers, at least it could freshen up our memory.

The studio was on a pretty quiet street. There was an old cinema and a small restaurant, but we didn't see many people. The building of the studio itself looked run down as if it hadn't been used in years.

"Are you sure that's a good idea? How will we even get inside?" I asked.

"Yeah, it looks kinda abandoned," Leigh added.

"So what? We'll break in," Warly said as he walked toward the door. He got something out of his pocket and started fidgeting with the lock. After a few minutes, we heard a loud breaking sound.

"Ta-da!" Warly exclaimed and smile. "Easy peasy. It was pretty rusty."

Warly walked inside and gestured us to follow. Leigh shrugged and walked inside. I stayed behind for a moment. It felt like a big deal for me to go back to the place that I had forgotten for such a long time. I needed a moment to collect myself.

"Go ahead, I'm just gonna check on Alex," I heard Leigh's voice say from inside the building. He pushed me outside, closed the door of the building behind him quickly, and whispered, "We need to go," as he grabbed my arm.

We rushed to the car as fast as we could, but Warly was already coming back outside, his eyes glaring at us. He shouted something and ran toward the car. We made it inside just in time to lock the doors. Warly wasn't alone. A woman had followed him outside. Everything was happening too fast for me to understand what was going on.

"GO!" Leigh shouted, and we drove off.

"What the fuck happened in there?" I shouted.

We were both panting.

Leigh held up his phone, which had a text from Helen. I just realized I had left my own phone at his home.

Helen: **GET AWAY FROM WARLY!!!!!**

"I don't know what it's about, but his reaction makes me think we got out of there just in time... Did you see that woman? Dude, I think I remember her. She was my agent," Leigh said in between breaths.

My eyes opened wide. That was the woman who would take me to the studio all the time.

"Call Helen, now," I commanded.

"Guys, where are you? Is Warly with you?" she asked over the speaker.

"No, we got rid of him. What the hell happened?"

"I was watching the tape again. I just had to. And then I realized something. It might be nothing, but it seems weird."

"WHAT?" Leigh and I both shouted at the same time.

"You know how your faces are normal in the intro but then change later? It happens for the four of you but not for Warly. He's in the video later again, and he looks exactly the same. Didn't he say he only filmed the intro? And there was something else, too—"

"We followed him in his trap," Leigh interrupted her. "Helen, you need to get out of there. He knows where I live. Please take my grandpa and get the hell away."

———

Helen dropped off Leigh's grandpa at a nursing home in a different town. A place where he would be safe for now. We didn't want him involved in all of this. The three of us met up again at a motel, hopefully far enough away from Watton. We still had to figure out our next steps, but for now this place seemed safer than Leigh's house.

"What was the other thing you wanted to say about Warly when we talked on the phone, Helen? I got so worried about my grandpa we had no chance to finish talking then," Leigh asked.

"Yes! Shit, I almost forgot to tell you!!" Her eyes opened wide as she quickly got up from the bed. "We were in such a hurry when we left the diner this morning, but I noticed a woman at the door."

"Oh, yeah, I saw her as well," I said.

"Did you see her face?"

"Not really."

"I did, and she looked kinda familiar, but I couldn't place her. Until I watched that tape again. I mean, she's gotten older and everything, but I think it was Millie."

Part 5

Dun dun du du dun

 Wonderful afternoon, adventurers and explorers, and welcome, welcome, welcome! Are you as excited we are for another episode of Warly's Adventure Club?

———

The rest of the night was pretty quiet. After the initial shock wore off, Leigh passed out on the bed. I don't think that guy had properly slept in over a week. Something had changed since the last time the three of us were together, though. The atmosphere had gotten tense. All of us had believed Warly; he seemed so sincere. But then again, he *was* an actor. Still, everything just seemed too coincidental. Leigh and I hearing the same jingle at approximately the same time, remembering everything again now. The fact that Helen had apparently seen Millie and didn't bring it up until we had almost fallen into Warly's trap. Her text came in right at the perfect moment.

Were Leigh and Helen hiding something from me? The paranoia started settling and was rapidly spreading.

As Leigh was sleeping, this felt like a good moment to talk to my childhood friend. She came all the way with me and had been going through some massive stress these last couple of days. I didn't want to mistrust her, but at the same time, I didn't want to be too gullible, either.

"Wanna go outside for a smoke?" I whispered.

Helen hesitated at first, but then she followed me.

———

"Can I ask you something, Alex?"

She started fidgeting with a lighter. For some reason, she seemed more nervous than me.

"Uhm, sure."

"Why did you want to pick up Warly yesterday? I didn't wanna say anything, but it seemed like a dangerous move."

Yesterday. That morning at the diner felt like forever ago.

I raised an eyebrow.

"So we could find out what his deal was. I mean, he was alone and there were three of us."

"Yeah, I know. I just—Never mind."

"Helen, do you not trust me? I told you to go back home. I even offered you my car and—"

"No, of course I do," she interrupted me. "I just think maybe there is a reason you forgot some of the stuff that happened. I'm not blaming you or anything. You know you'd always been like a brother to me."

"Helen, what the hell are you talking about?" I was starting to get impatient.

"You'd left your phone at Leigh's home yesterday, and I know this is a total invasion of privacy, but to be fair, you should have a passcode or something on your cell, Alex."

"I don't care if you used my phone, Helen. Get to the point."

"I looked up Janie's mail address, and then I sent her another mail but from my phone. She wouldn't say much to me, but she told me that it was your fault that Millie disappeared. I tried to explain to her that the tape all showed us different things, that it's not real, but she—Wait."

She got her phone out of her pocket and showed me the last mail from Janie.

I know what I saw and I know that it's true. About nine years ago they wanted to bring the show back. We went to a meeting but nobody really wanted the show to come back except for Alex. He kept pushing, aggressively. I don't remember what happened that day, just that Millie was freaked out after it. I know that it didn't really happen in the show because nobody else I showed it to saw it. But it made me remember. I know for a fact that Alex killed Millie. And Leigh helped him.

Do whatever you want with this information but if I were you I would get far away from those two. And don't contact me again.

I kept staring at the screen, my hands trembling. Finally, I looked Helen in the eyes. I wanted to speak, but I couldn't bring out any words.

"No other mails would go through. I think she deleted the account," Helen said.

"If this is true, why are you still here? Why haven't you called the police or—?"

"Because Millie isn't dead. I saw her."

"You can't even be sure that it was her," I mumbled.

"No, but I know that you're not a murderer, Alex. There is so much crazy stuff happening at the moment that we can't explain. There must be another answer to all this, and I bet it's hidden somewhere in that diner."

"Did you show this to Leigh?"

She shook her head.

"Do you trust him?"

She stayed silent for a moment.

"Yeah," she finally said. "Maybe because I kinda liked him back when we were teens or maybe because I spent some time with his sweet grandpa." Helen laughed. "But my gut tells me he's not dangerous."

"What does your gut say about me?" I asked.

"Alex, I trust you. I wouldn't be here if I didn't. Just try to remember that day. Was there anything that could've given Janie the idea that you had bad intentions?"

I shrugged and stayed silent. After we went back inside, I kept reading that email until I *finally* started remembering the reunion.

The day we came back together and even filmed a new intro. We were too old to be excited to film a children's show, so they tried using the tape against us. To control us. It worked with me and Leigh. We both wanted to come back. I'm not sure what the other two saw, but whatever talked to Millie in the show disturbed her so much that she took her life shortly after.

They had to put a pause on production. I guess they only used the new intro to control the children they had collected all those years ago when *Warly's Adventure Club* aired for the first time.

———

May I introduce to you our main explorer... Alex!

Before I knew what I was doing or could think it through properly, I was already sitting in a cab, going to the diner.

I knew leaving Helen alone with Leigh was a shit move. Or leaving Leigh alone with Helen? I still wasn't sure what to believe.

Could I even trust my own mind?

Right now, I had no other option but to do what I thought was right. It was risky, but the only way for me to finally get some answers was to go to the diner. And, hopefully, end this for good. I had to consciously be there and figure this out on my own terms to really believe my reality.

I was the main explorer, right?

I always had an issue with being too impulsive. When I had a goal in front of me, I would not eat, sleep, or drink until I got what I was looking for. And right now, I had to look for Millie. I had to know if she was alive or if I was responsible for her death.

Before getting out, I looked at my car keys lying on the table but decided to leave them there and take a cab. I also left a note telling Helen to take my car and go back home.

The parking lot was almost empty except for a truck. The warm light inside the diner felt radiating. I peeked inside and saw a man sitting at the counter. There was a waitress talking to him, but I only saw the back of her head. I took a deep breath and opened the door.

I was prepared to be greeted by the strange melody, but instead regular pop music was playing from the speakers. I walked toward the counter. The waitress had disappeared into the back. So far it looked a lot more normal than I would have expected. The man at the counter was drinking coffee and watching something on an old TV.

"Hi, there, take a seat anywhere you like. I'll be right with you."

A young woman in a waitress outfit came out of the kitchen with a plate of food that she brought to the trucker.

I sat down at the nearest table to the door. Just in case I needed to run away quickly.

"Would you like to see the breakfast card?" The girl stood in front of me and smiled.

This was definitely not Millie.

"Breakfast?" I asked. "What time is it?" I mumbled and took a look at my phone.

It was six a.m.

"Uhm, no thanks, just coffee," I answered and tried to reciprocate the smile. "Are you alone here?" I asked without trying to sound too creepy.

"Me and the cook," she responded and started pouring coffee in my cup.

"A friend of mine works here," I lied. "I was just wondering if she was here today. Her name's Millie?"

The girl shrugged first, but then she looked at me again, and her face lit up.

"Oh! Yes, she's in the kitchen. Do you want me to get her?"

My heart started racing.

"No, that's all right, I'll just have my coffee first."

"Okie dokie. You know this is gonna sound weird, but you look really familiar. Have you been here before?" the girl asked.

"Have a great day, see you next time!" We heard the trucker shout as he walked out the door.

"Omg. I do know you! You're Alex!" The girl's eyes opened wide as she walked up to me, and her smile got even brighter. "But you look a little different. And older."

I swallowed.

"Uhm, no, you must be thinking of someone else." I nervously laughed.

"Oh no, it's you. I'm your biggest fan! I came all the way to find you!" she shouted.

I peeked toward the television. *Warly's Adventure Club* was on. Until this moment, this had felt like a regular diner. I guess they were waiting for the other guy to leave.

I had the urge to push her to the side and run away, but I ignored that fearful voice and stayed. I needed to find answers.

"Alex!" a voice shouted from the back. "Our main explorer!"

At first, I thought that it came from the television, but this wasn't Warly's voice, and it wasn't the waitress.

My hand was clutching the door of the diner. A shiver went down my spine, and I felt like I was frozen. I knew that voice.

Slowly, I turned around.

"Millie," I whispered.

Helen had been right; it was her. She looked slightly older than in the tapes but just a little. She didn't look like she was twenty-five, more like sixteen, maybe, but she still had the fiery red hair and the smile with slightly crooked teeth.

"Welcome!" she said.

"Millie, what are you doing here? Are they keeping you here?"

What's today's adventure?

I heard the familiar voices coming from the television, but something was different. We were older. This wasn't the tape I had seen. This was from when we were fifteen or sixteen.

"What's today's adventure, Alex?" Millie started giggling uncontrollably.

"Will you finally film another part? We miss you, Alex," the waitress chimed in.

I looked outside of the big window, and that's when I saw someone was waiting for me outside.

Warly.

And he wasn't alone. The agent was with him, the same woman we saw at the studio, except now I got a better view of her. She appeared slightly older than Warly, around forty maybe, but she didn't look as worn out as him. Her hair was a blinding shade of silver cut into a short bob. She was dressed neatly in a dark violet suit.

That's when I got an idea.

I grabbed my phone and called Helen. Before she even picked up, I muted my phone but kept the speakers on so that she could hear me but I couldn't hear her. Then I let it disappear into my pocket.

I had come here alone to find answers, but that had been stupid. I couldn't do this on my own.

"Oh, Alex, how you've grown!" she said in a melodic voice.

I checked my surroundings. There was nothing around. I could try to run, but where would I go?

"Don't worry, Alex. We're not here to hurt you. Look, no weapons." She held up her hands. "I just have a proposition for you. If you don't like it, you can leave."

Millie and the waitress had followed me outside and were now standing to my left and right.

I was surrounded.

"What did you do to her?" I said and nodded toward Millie.

"We didn't do anything, honey. We would never have hurt any of our actors. The children love all of you. We went looking for her when she disappeared, but when we saw her hanging from the ceiling of the studio, it was already too late. It was tragic, really."

"What are you saying?"

"Millie died, but it wasn't anybody's fault. She chose to do so."

"Bullshit, she's right there!" I shouted.

"That's not her. She's just wearing her face," Warly said in a dry tone.

"That's not possible," I whispered.

"Do you really still believe that any of this is normal, Alex? Because I'm afraid you won't find a logical explanation to it. Believe me, I tried. Accept her proposal, and all of this will be over for us soon," Warly said.

"What happened in the show that you saw, Alex?" the woman asked.

"A child died. And I was talking to myself," I responded.

"But what did *really* happen in the show?"

"I don't know, some weird scavenger hunt."

"Exactly. That's what most people that are alert see. But if you watch with just the right mindset, your imagination will provide something entirely different for you. You will see things that are hidden inside your mind. Your true wishes, fears, and needs. It's not *simple* entertainment. It's revolutionary. Our fans from back then, like little Chrissie over there, don't watch anything except for the adventure club. They are obsessed with it because it provides a form of guidance for them. Something nobody else can. They need the adventure club. But those kids are growing older, and they don't respond to the old shows as well."

"So you want us to film another episode of your brainwash show?" I asked. I had no idea what the hell the things she was saying meant, but all I could do right now was to stall for time.

"We need you, Alex. The children need you. The other actors... they are replaceable. But you are our star! Everyone that watches the show feels like they are talking to you. Come with us and film one more episode. Just so we have a fresh recording of your beautiful face. You can leave after that. We'll provide you with as much money as you wish and you will be left alone."

"That face on the tape isn't mine. Can't you just use your technology to update my face and leave me alone? Take a photo or something."

"I'm afraid it doesn't work that way. We need you to come to the studio. That's the only place where our cameras work," she added.

"What cameras? What are you on about?"

"They make a copy of you. Something that looks like you but isn't. Like that freaky Millie thing over there," Warly said.

"Hush now," the woman hissed at Warly.

"So wait, what if somebody just breaks your equipment?" I asked.

"And why would anyone do that? We are simply a production company. And after filming today, we will move on to somewhere else."

I was praying that Helen was still on the phone and heard all that as I said the next sentence.

"I'm not doing this alone," I said. "I made a mistake to come here on my own. Leigh should be here as well."

"Yes, well, the green boy was very popular with our fans but—"

"But I'm sure I could convince him to come," I said.

The lady lifted an eyebrow.

"What's your plan here, buddy? You think your little friend will come to save you?"

"I don't need saving, do I? We filmed the show before, and I was always fine. I just don't think that I should carry this burden on my own. If you want to influence a new set of viewers, it shouldn't all be on me."

Her mouth turned into a mischievous grin.

"Well, then, give your friend a call. Whatever you think you're doing, better believe that we are always one step ahead. We owe you, Alex."

I looked at the ground.

"I didn't bring my phone," I said.

Her grin grew wider.

"Well, luckily I have his number."

She gestured to Warly to take me into the diner, where they tied me to a chair. The agent then proceeded to call Leigh.

"What if he gets the cops?" Warly nervously asked as the phone rang.

Leigh picked up, and the agent said, "Our lovely Leigh would never call the police. He knows we have connections and that we know where his grandfather is staying."

I heard Leigh cursing and then Helen whispering something inaudible in the background.

"Leigh, I need your help. I'm with the agent. We'll be here at the diner, waiting for you. Please come."

Before he could answer, the lady hung up.

We'd been waiting for at least an hour when she started getting really impatient.

"I want to start shooting now. Screw it. It seems that your friends don't give a shit about you. We don't need—"

Dun du du dun

This time the sound was coming from her phone. This insane woman was using the tune as her ringtone. Her smile came back.

"Don't you love this song?" she said before picking up.

Her smile instantly vanished. Her expression darkened.

"I need to take care of something. Watch him," she said to Warly before taking off.

———

"Were you involved with them this whole time?" I asked Warly after she was gone.

They had tied up my hands and sat me down in a booth.

"Most of the things I told you were true. I really don't remember much of the filming because of drugs. I probably helped them without even knowing. But I didn't trick you because I'm a bad person, Alex. They do have my niece. This was my only way of getting her back," he whispered.

I nodded.

"I guessed so. How about you untie me, we get out of here, and I promise we will help you get your niece back?"

"Sorry, bud, not gonna happen," he responded.

Through the window, I saw a light from afar coming closer and closer. *Finally*.

The light kept getting closer before it stopped right in front of the diner.

Helen and Leigh jumped out of the car and ran inside, both holding up guns.

"Don't fucking move, Warly, or I'll shoot your face off!" Leigh shouted as Helen came toward me to free my hands.

"What do we do with them?" Helen asked and pointed toward Warly and the waitress.

"Wait, where is the Millie copy?" I asked.

She had disappeared.

"Fuck it, we need to get out of here before the woman comes back. We're taking these two with us."

———

We drove Warly and Chrissie to a police station. They were both tied up, and we glued Warly's mouth shut. Chrissie spent most of the ride talking about what a fan she was; she couldn't believe that she was driving around with *the* Alex and Leigh. When we got to the station, we told Chrissie that for today's adventure she had to get to the station and loudly scream for an officer to help her. We untied them, and both got out of the car.

I thought that Warly would run away, but he stood there, frozen. As soon as Chrissie started shouting, we drove off. I felt bad for Warly to a degree, but it was too much of a risk to bring him with us.

"Where the hell did you get those guns from?" I asked after we were finally alone.

"They're toys. We bought them on the way. Figured Warly wouldn't know the difference." Leigh laughed.

I took a deep breath.

"Please tell me you took so long to get here because—"

"We had to go and destroy the studio first?" Helen asked. "Don't you smell the stench of burned ash on us?"

"You *burned* it down?"

They both proudly nodded.

"Well, we didn't stay to watch, but we hope it's all gone."

This entire procedure was risky; we should have talked things through at first. I shouldn't have just left, but I was more than thankful that my friends got the hint during my call. They could have come to the diner instead to help me, but in this twisted game of Warly, you had to be ruthless.

We didn't know if this would end things, but from what it looked like so far, nobody was following us. They had more important things to do right now. Such as trying to get the camera system back.

But it would never stop here. The agent was still alive, after all, but for now we gave them a setback. And at least we managed to save one of the kids.

I wish I could tell you that everything ended on a great note, that we stopped the bad guys and are now living happily ever after, but unfortunately life isn't that easy. Warly is probably in prison for something he didn't do while the real perpetrators still have an army of children and methods that are otherworldly. The children, including Warly's niece, are still somewhere out there. Even if I still don't completely understand so much about this, I do feel responsible for it.

They are being controlled by my face, after all, and I don't even want to imagine what kind of things they hear from me when watching the show. If there is anyone that can get them out of their trance, it's us, which means that we have to try anything to find them.

I don't know how things will look from now on, but at least I have two great friends who I finally trust supporting me.

I can't shake off the feeling that we will be hearing the tune calling us soon. And when that happens, the adventure club will be there to find those bastards.

NEVER LEAVE A CHAIR EMPTY AT NIGHT

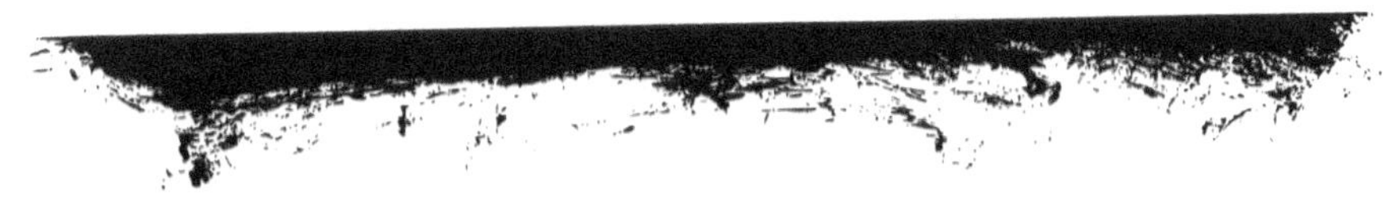

We were pretty superstitious. All of us were. My mum, my dad, grandparents, and teachers. Neighbors, coaches, and bus drivers. We lived our lives by many traditions that might seem naïve and old fashioned at first glance. There is a simple reason for us having them, though. We all lived fine and well obeying the communal gut feeling, and it never disappointed as long as we listened to our sayings. Not all of them sounded as inherently disturbing as the empty chair, of course. Some were just signs we looked out for.

Like, *If there's a butterfly in your house, it means you will get visitors soon.*

Others were little tricks that could ease your life.

If you want visitors to leave your home, a bit of salt poured into their shoes will do the trick.

And some were, well, a bit disturbing, I guess.

If you lean over a railing, the devil will grab you and pull you toward the ground.

That one we can't really fact check, unfortunately.

As I said, there were many of those. Phrases they kept repeating so nobody will ever forget. And the one I've heard the most in my life happens to be the one about the chair.

Never leave a chair in your bedroom empty at night.

Dad repeated it every night like a prayer when I was still little. And Mum would come by later in the evening to make sure I had a backpack, some books, or even just a jacket lying on my desk chair. It was the only one in my room. As I grew older, they didn't need to remind me anymore; the phrase was deeply ingrained into my brain. I still heard Mum's footsteps at night, though. I suppose she wanted to be *really* sure nobody would be taking a seat next to me at night.

When I was younger, I didn't understand why this was so important to everyone I knew. To me, there was one simple solution to the whole hex altogether: simply not having a chair in your room. You don't really need it when you have your bed anyway, except for doing homework maybe. Unfortunately, however, removing the chair is not an option. And there's a reason for that, too, of course. As I said, superstitions are kind of our thing.

As terribly afraid as the people of our community were of forgetting an empty chair, they were even more anxious of what might happen if there was no chair at all. You want to have a space for someone that might visit. You simply don't want them to visit without your approval first. It's a very strange concept, and I can't quite say how it even started. I suppose it's something our village people made up a long time ago. Someone probably once tried to remove their chair and was met with terrible fortune, so they took the risk of having the chair in their rooms with items stacked on top.

———

I never cared for the strange ideas and superstitions of our community much, not until I understood what happens when you don't listen to them.

You can never have every single member of a community obeying the same rules. Some people are inherently against going with the flow. Risk-takers, show-offs, and adrenaline junkies. Then you have the ones who never listened much as kids and grew up not caring for old traditions. Especially when they read and watch all kinds of horror stories and start to realize that something isn't necessarily scary just because someone says so. I suppose many kids now just think that the whole saying is a way for their parents to make sure they keep their rooms clean.

And so of course there were the ones who intentionally kept a chair, or even more, welcomingly empty for whoever might visit at night.

They called themselves brave. We call them cautionary tales.

Because they all would regret it.

When the visitor came.

The story I know the best is the one of Billy Tucker. Billy never cared much for any of the tales the older ones tell. Billy liked to tempt fate more than anything. While he lived with his parents, they made sure he was safe even if he didn't approve, but Billy grew older and bought his own little home on the same street as us. It was the very first night that he would sleep there alone, and I suppose he forgot about the chair. Or possibly he just wanted to see what would happen if he ignored the phrases that had been shoved in his head all his life.

I saw him getting his mail the following day. He looked tired and disturbed. He told me he kept thinking there was someone inside his home, but that wasn't possible. Nobody ever broke into a house around here. He told me he heard someone whisper in his ear to wake him up. When he looked around, he saw nothing but a jacket that wasn't there before, hanging by his closet.

"You know it was probably my ma. That woman is anxiety personified," Billy joked back then.

That was the first day.

After that, Billy hardly left his home anymore. I'd see his parents stop by at times to bring him food, but he never stepped outside. Apparently, he was slowly but surely losing his mind.

It lasted a week until his parents found him hanging from his bedroom closet.

It was a devastating tragedy for sure, but I wasn't completely convinced that it had anything to do with a chair. Billy had been a troubled kid; that was no secret.

However, whether I really believed in it or not didn't matter. My gut feeling had merged with the one of the community. Whether I was afraid of the empty chair or not, as long as I lived in the strange village with all its rules and sayings, I would stick with them. Even if it was just for the sake of my parents' mental health.

And I did. All those years. Until I moved far away from the village.

Living in a big city was far different than anything I'd ever imagined. I suddenly had a sense of freedom I never perceived before. At first, it was overwhelming, all the places I could go to and all the things I could do, but after a while, I realized that this was exactly where I belonged. I found new friends, got a nice studio apartment, and a new sense of my own identity.

But of course the words I heard all my life stuck with me, even far away from our village. I suppose a part of me believed in the superstitions at least to some degree, but I always believed that I left them with me at my old home. I didn't believe they would follow me.

Not until the night.

I came home rather late after drinking at the pub with a few friends. I could hardly keep my eyes open and went to bed pretty swiftly. With the last bit of consciousness, I heard the bag on the chair in my room slip to the ground. My gut kept telling me to go and pick it up, but my drunken and tired mind said that everything would be fine.

I should've listened to the gut.

It was still pitch-dark out when I was woken up by the sounds. It sounded as if someone was moving inside my apartment. At first, I didn't register much. I guess for a moment I forgot that I lived alone. When the realization came to me, my eyes opened wide. My heart started racing, and I had to control my breathing.

I collected all my courage and quietly moved my upper body up so that I could inspect my surroundings. There was nobody there. At least as far as I could tell with the dim light shining through my window.

To calm down my nerves, I got up from the bed and turned on the lights.

The good thing about a studio apartment is there aren't many rooms where someone could hide.

I checked behind my kitchen island; I checked under my bed and in the bathroom. There was no sign of someone being inside.

Until I saw the coat rack.

Most of my jackets are black, so I didn't notice right away, but there was a coat that didn't belong to me as well as a black top hat. My eyes moved to the ground, and when I saw the big leathery shoes with dirt underneath them, my entire body started shaking.

"Hello?" I called out into the empty room.

There was no response.

Of course, I called the police, and they checked every single corner, but there was not a single sign of anyone breaking in. As they arrived, the coat and shoes were gone, but I still saw the dirt stains on the ground. The police were clueless. I'm not sure whether they thought I was insane or on drugs, but finally, they left and I was alone again.

A part of me wondered if I possibly dreamed it all up or if I mixed up the coat with one of my own, but in the end, I knew I was just lying to myself.

Someone had been in here, and it was my own fault for leaving the chair empty.

I figured there was one simple solution to my problem, so the following evening I made sure to stack enough items on top of that chair to make sure nobody would even think about taking a seat in there. It seemed like a decent plan considering the ridiculous superstition I was following. I didn't realize, however, that there wasn't going back after you messed up once. That's what happened to Billy.

On the first night, you question the act. You can't believe that there could be anything true to that old saying, and how could it? You make yourself completely paranoid.

The following night I was still confident. At least to some degree. The fear was still very much present, but I believed to have a solution. I had books and clothes stacked upon my chair, and after a couple of hours of tossing in my bed, I managed to fall asleep.

What you don't realize is the effect the visitor has on you. It starts nibbling on your mind. If you invite it inside once, it learns your scent, and it will continue coming back each night. No matter where you go or if you stay up all night. It won't stop. Until your mind can't take it anymore.

I knew that. I'd heard all the stories; I just never believed how cursed we truly were.

That night, I woke up by the sound of a whisper.

The words made no sense to my mind, but they were near and felt thoroughly unkind. A hand was caressing my face, but when I opened my eyes, there was nobody to see.

The next day, I thought about staying with a friend, but I was afraid I might burden them with the same fate. If *it* followed me. So I got a hotel room instead.

I woke up when I heard a hollow laugh. It didn't stop until the sun came up again. For days, I didn't sleep. Wherever I went, I knew it was there with me, chewing on my mind and swallowing my free will. As the days progressed, the whispers became more clear. It was as if it was pulling me over to a side where we could communicate. A side where I could make sense out of its words.

Come with me.

You won't be missed.

Your choice has already been made.

The voice was omnipresent. It kept whispering and laughing until every moment of my life was drained in the color of nothingness. I didn't eat. I didn't sleep. I didn't feel.

I was just afraid that if it pulled hard enough, I wouldn't be able to come back. Just like Billy.

We were pretty superstitious. All of us were. We all lived fine and well obeying the communal gut feeling, and it never disappointed as long as we listened to our sayings. I thought about that when every other thought in my mind stopped making sense. I thought about the things I was told ever since I was a child. The words that might even be able to help your life.

Like if you want a visitor to leave your home, a bit of salt poured into their shoes will do the trick.

It was a long shot, but the visitor was always polite enough to leave its shoes and coat by the door.

I don't know how permanent the trick is, but last night I finally slept on my own again.

THE PASSENGER I WILL NEVER FORGET

We are all cursed, and we can't even see it. Our eyes won't show us. I was always under the cocky impression that my taxi and I knew the streets of Berlin like no other. You can't begin to imagine the unexpected horrors I've witnessed during my nightshifts. You see, people show far less inhibition when it's dark, and sometimes they even reveal a whole different identity. Still, even my fifteen years of experience couldn't have prepared me for this one night.

Berlin is quite the adjustment if you come from a small Kurdish village like the one I'm from. I've grown to like my work in this city, but it has its goddamn cursed sides, and that's mostly due to the people—peculiar people that might appear friendly and normal during the day but change entirely as soon as the sun goes down. As a driver, I've learned to observe and notice things. Like when I happen to drive a member of some criminal family around. You won't believe how many of those we have in Berlin.

But it's not my place to judge. I'm just a driver.

I have tons of stories, some sweet and some disgusting, but there is only one night of driving in all these years that has left me sick to my stomach—one that left such a bitter aftertaste that nothing I eat brings me joy anymore.

And that's the night I met Julius.

When I don't get a call to go pick someone up, I wait in line with the other taxis at the metro station Neukölln. Sometimes I spend hours there, having coffee and a cigarette with other drivers while waiting for passengers. We tell each other superficial stories about our lives and make bets on who will have the best fare of the night. One time I drove a man to a city two hundred miles away, made the same money I'd usually get for three entire nights.

Julius' fare was in a similar price range, even though we never even left Berlin.

At the end of the night, I didn't ask him for money.

It was a cold and foggy night, typical for the beginning of March. The type of night that you'd rather just spend in bed if you don't have to work like me. I remember thinking that when the passenger door of my taxi suddenly opened from the outside, letting in a cold gust of wind.

The cold swiftly disappeared again as this young man with dark hair and just as dark eyes smiled at me.

"Are you free for a ride?" he asked.

This man could have been twenty or thirty-six, I honestly couldn't say for sure, but I remember vividly how he was radiating something warm and comfortable. He was wearing slacks and a black jacket, a nice white shirt underneath. I don't know much about clothes, but I could tell that someone had perfectly tailored this wardrobe to his body. Maybe that's why I believed him when he said this would be a long ride but that he had enough money to pay for it.

Of course, I said yes and asked if he had any luggage I could help him with.

"Just this." He held up a little wrapped package the size of a book and grinned. "But I'll just put it on my lap."

He sat down in the passenger seat. Some people do that, usually the ones that are alone and feel like talking.

"Where can I take you to? Do you have an address?" I asked.

He fastened his seat belt.

"No, not exactly. I'll just give you the directions as we go, if that's all right."

And that's what he did. It was fine for me as long as the meter was running.

"Dilovan. That's a nice name," he said after looking at the card I have in the front of the car with my name and number on it.

"Thank you," I said while starting the car. "It means heart. It's a—"

I looked behind me to safely leave the line of cars but froze when I noticed that the cars behind me were gone. And not just the other taxis.

Everyone was gone. The entire outside area of the metro station looked deserted.

I looked at Julius, but he didn't even seem to notice anything was wrong; he just smiled. For a split second, I swear I saw something moving in the reflection of the window next to him, but when I blinked, it was gone.

"Heart. That's beautiful," he said casually.

I swallowed and rubbed my eyes. Another look outside proved to me that I'd been imagining things. There were people with bags rushing to their cars, taxi drivers standing around with a cigarette, drunken teenagers loudly chatting. Everything was normal.

It was after three a.m. These things happen during night shifts. Your mind gets foggy. I just couldn't let this man notice; I didn't want to lose a fare that would make such good money.

Luckily, he was oblivious and continued our conversation.

"I go by Julius, but I have no clue what that means."

We both laughed.

"Well, it's nice to meet you, Julius," I said and meant it.

We passed one of my taxi driver buddies as we drove off. He tilted his pale face as he watched us drive off with a distraught look in his eyes. I felt a knot in my stomach as I passed him but didn't yet understand what my gut was trying to say.

When there are passengers in my car, I have the occasional chat with them about the weather or the latest football game, but I'm not a talkative man. Some people pour out their souls, but those are the ones I use the least words with.

Once in a while, however, I'll meet a special person who doesn't simply talk to fill the silence in the car but who is genuinely and truly interested in the lives of others.

Julius was just like that. Special.

"Do you have night shifts often?" he asked as we were driving down a particularly dark road.

"Only on weekends. Money's best Friday and Saturday nights," I said.

"You must sleep away the rest of your weekend, then!" He laughed, and I joined in.

"Well, sleep is a wonderful thing. There's nothing more comfortable than resting your head on a soft pillow after a long night," I said.

"I absolutely agree. If I could sleep forever, I would." He laughed, but it sounded forced. "It's ironic, isn't it? We work so hard to earn a living, but as a result, we wind up losing the time to actually go out and live."

With all his confidence, there was also a melancholic side to him. His charisma reminded me of my older brother. But in some ways, I also saw myself in him.

I sighed.

"If it were up to me, I'd have a simple life. A small house in a village with a garden. Plant my own veggies and maybe have a couple of chickens," I added to his thought.

Julius turned to me with a raised eyebrow. Our eyes met for a second before I had to turn mine back to the street in front of us. His eyes were incredibly dark, as if they only consisted of pupils. I know that sounds creepy, but it wasn't. It felt familiar.

Distracted by our conversation, it took me a while to realize that we were driving down roads I'd never seen before. Driving in between multi-story buildings without any lights on. Well, it was the middle of the night but still. And it felt incredibly strange not to recognize my surroundings. I'm a taxi driver; I always felt like I knew the whole city.

"Well, something must have happened down that road of yours to end up in the biggest city in Germany, then," Julius interrupted my thoughts.

I laughed.

"I'm here because of my family. The village life with chickens isn't for them," I said, surprising myself. I never open up to strangers. No, I never open up to people at all.

"Oh!" Julius called out as he leaned back a little. "You're a family man. Of course you are a family man. And we do everything for our family, right?"

The way he said those words made me feel a little odd for a second, but I shrugged it off.

"Always."

Julius smiled.

We interrupted our conversation as we'd arrived at Julius' first destination, a small kiosk where he needed to drop off his mysterious package.

"I'll be back in a sec. Wait here." He looked at me with a surprisingly intimidating look.

If you don't know what a kiosk looks like, it's basically a tiny corner shop. The windows are filled with beer crates and bottles so you can't see inside too well. I have no idea what happened when Julius was in there, only that after a few minutes all the lights inside the shop suddenly turned off. That little shop that was the only source of light on this dark street anyway now almost disappeared in front of my eyes.

I had weirdly trusted this stranger because everything seemed so fine and I'd felt so comfortable. But after he left the car, I got this odd feeling inside. A new sense of paranoia mixed with a rush of anxiety. Something inside of me was shouting to get the hell away.

I looked for my phone but couldn't find it quickly enough. Impulsively, I set my foot on the gas and got ready to leave, but before I could, the back door of my car opened.

Julius jumped back inside with the same friendly smile through those familiar eyes. Except now he wasn't sitting next to me but behind me.

"Where to now, my friend?" I nervously asked, hoping he didn't realize that I was just about to take off. I don't know why I didn't simply tell him to fuck off. For some reason, I couldn't find any courage.

"I'm glad you called me that. I'd like for us two to be friends, Dil." He took a deep breath. "Just follow the street for now."

I started driving, again following the streets as my passenger instructed me. Finally, I felt like I recognized the area again. We were back in Neukölln.

"Dil, my friend. Let's get back to our family conversation. Do you get along well with your son?"

I stayed silent for a moment.

"We used to be closer. Teenagers aren't always easy to deal with." I laughed.

"Oh yes, teenagers. Things are much better with your daughter, I assume?"

We were driving down a quiet neighborhood again with few lights, and I had to really focus on the street.

"Used to. My daughter, well, she is a wonderful kid but also a little bit off lately. Not quite herself. Teenager, too, I guess—"

I stopped speaking.

We'd been driving around and talking for so long that it really took me a second to realize what had just happened.

I'd never told him that I had a daughter and a son.

"Oh yes, she's more distant—locking herself up in her room, hardly eating any food anymore. That's unfortunate. You still love them, though, am I right?" he said.

I felt incredibly nervous. I'd made some big mistake by trusting this man with my thoughts all night. Something was definitely wrong, but I had to try my best to stay collected. He could have some really bad connections.

"Oh, I have love for my family. But don't we all?" I nervously said.

"No, you don't."

Surprised at his sudden change of tone, I looked into the rearview window to make some eye contact.

Julius, the man I had been driving around with all night, was gone.

I looked into the face of a creature I had never seen before. His dark eyes that felt so kind earlier now looked completely wrong. As if someone had slammed a screwdriver into his eye sockets and filled them with a dark void. There were holes in his face, filled with some kind of fungi.

Repulsed by this entirely wrong face, I forgot to watch the street for a moment and almost crashed into a parked car. I swerved just in time, catching my breath and collecting my courage.

My heart was beating so fast I thought it would jump out of my chest.

It was late at night. I hadn't slept. I hadn't had any water for hours.

I was hallucinating, I told myself. Though at the same time I couldn't bring myself to look in that mirror again.

"Is something wrong, my friend?" He chuckled. I instinctively turned my head around and saw the same Julius with his regular face sitting there, with a smile on his face.

"Yes, sorry," I mumbled. "Long night."

Slowly, I tried to collect myself again.

"What did you do inside that kiosk?" I finally asked, surprised at my own sudden courage. Even if that face was a hallucination, this man still knew things about my children that he shouldn't. He seemed so interested in my life earlier. In reality, he wasn't trying to get any information out of me, though. He already knew everything. What was this man trying to get from me?

I had to get rid of him but be smart about it. So I decided to drive toward my brother's home. My brother, well, he is an intimidating man with a lot of power. A shady man who doesn't shy away from violence. If this Julius meant danger, he'd know what to do.

Julius' eyes were closed, I thought he might even fall asleep, so I quickly changed the direction. I tried to stay confident, but my entire body was shaking at this point. As if he was reading my mind, Julius' eyes opened, and I knew without a shadow of a doubt that this night would ruin the rest of my life.

"Don't try to be smart, Dil," Julius suddenly spoke with a low voice.

I clenched the steering wheel so hard that it looked like the skin on my hands would crack open any second.

"I know where you are going. Don't. I have no interest in meeting your brother. Not tonight," he spoke.

"How do you—" I whispered.

"I know you saw me. In the mirror. You didn't scream. I like that. You know I feel like I can be myself around you." He grinned.

My eyes went to the rearview mirror. None of it was a hallucination.

I don't know how to describe it in better words, but I know for a fact that this thing was not human. It was hiding behind human skin.

"Now I'm gonna be honest because I do truly enjoy your company. This night wasn't about dropping off the package. That's a different business of mine. Tonight was about getting to know you."

A million different thoughts were racing through my mind, but all I asked was, "Why me?"

He chuckled again.

"Oh, please don't be worried, my friend. I can feel this entire car shaking. I'm not here to hurt *you*. This is about your family. It's corrupted. I could smell it on you from miles away."

I swallowed.

"If you're not going to hurt me, what else do you want from me?"

Julius was smiling at me through the mirror, his mouth revealing a set of rotten teeth.

"Being what I am, it's lonely. The fact that your family is corrupted isn't a *bad* thing. You know, maybe you could introduce me to them sometime."

We were on an empty road. There were no people around, nobody that I could ask for help, but I still hit the brakes. I felt sick, but not from whiplash.

"You're wondering whether you should jump out of the car. Wondering if you could outrun me." He sighed. "But you won't."

I took a deep breath.

"No, I won't," I whispered.

"Because you love your family."

I nodded.

"And because you noticed that the eyes of your daughter have recently started to look a little bit like mine." He smiled again, and I stayed frozen.

"Maybe you should check her reflection, my friend. Are your eyes open?"

WHEN THE TOWN SMELLS LIKE CINNAMON, YOU KNOW SOMEONE JUST DIED

Part 1

I've lived in this town named Tattletoe since the moment I was born. When everything smelled like nutmeg. It's quite a beautiful place. Everyone that lives here is being gifted with anything they could ever wish for. Each family has a big house with enough rooms so that generations can live together if they wish to. They receive a car, although that one is quite unnecessary if you ask me. No one ever leaves anyway, and the town is small enough that a bike would be more than enough.

If you want to take a stroll down the town center, you can easily do so on foot. You can watch all the little shops and restaurants. Each and every place is an individual masterpiece run by important members of the community. There is a flower shop growing the most peculiar plants with the brightest colors. There is a store making boots that will make you want to start dancing and never stop. There is a jewelry store with diamonds you have never seen before.

However, the most important place, the one that makes our town what it is, is Mrs. Holly's wonderful bakery. Mrs. Holly is an old woman with rosy cheeks and purple dresses. She likes to sing as she bakes the most delicious pastries, bread, and biscuits. Stepping foot into that wonderful bakery will make you never want to leave again. Unfortunately, we are not allowed to buy any of the things produced, not from the bakery or any of the other *special* shops; the goods are made for export.

There is something particularly interesting taking place in the peculiar place we call Tattletoe. You see, every time a child is brought to life in our little hospital, the town smells of nutmeg, and when someone dies, it smells of cinnamon. That's because as soon as the news reaches the lovely Mrs. Holly, she will start baking a batch of pastry, making sure everyone in town can smell that we gained or lost a member. This is something we have all grown accustomed to, and we wouldn't want it any other way. The smell of a town can tell you a lot about its history, you see. Paris smells like butter, Berlin smells like iron, and Naples smells like basil. Well, I have never been to any of those places myself, so I couldn't tell you for sure, but this is how my grandfather would describe them. He liked explaining the world with his nose. My grandfather was the most remarkable person I knew and one of the very few people who were allowed to leave the town from time to time. He was an exporter.

I still remember the day he was taken away. The cinnamon never smelled sweeter.

Tattletoe is a special place. The people who have the honor of living here are never short of anything they could wish for. But of course, this life of ease and peace comes with a price. If you live here, you need to stick to our rules. They are not many, and it's not that difficult to oblige. You just need to be willing enough.

For example, if you want to live in Tattletoe, you need to work. When a child reaches a certain age, it is assigned to a new job. As I said, we have many special shops. I know, it sounds a little strange. The town committee always says that everything needed is provided for us; if we ever wanted more, it meant we were greedy and not worthy of living in this little paradise.

I never understood much about our ideals. You work all your life but are not allowed to buy anything? It felt strange to me, but my parents taught me from an early age that I needed to follow the rules.

Now that I am old enough to work, I was assigned to my first job. I assumed I would have to work in the toothpaste factory together with Mum and Dad, the toothpaste that makes your teeth go all black and achy, but instead I got a much better job. One that every child in town could only dream of.

I would be working in Mrs. Holly's bakery.

"Deborah, oh please. Come in, come in!" Mrs. Holly greeted me with a warm smile.

It was so early in the morning the sky was still black, but I knew better than to be late on my first day of work.

"Morning, Mrs. Holly, and thank you so much for hiring me. I was a little afraid of what other job I might get."

She gave me a sympathetic smile and waved me inside. She handed me my very own apron as we walked to the back of the bakery.

"I usually work alone, but I heard a rumor that they wanted to assign you to be a shoe tester, and I really wouldn't have wanted your feet to fall off."

I furrowed my brow.

"Why would my feet fall off?"

"Oh, honey, the committee heard about some city somewhere in the states where the people are apparently dancing even when they shouldn't. Now they want to punish them, so production increased. They need testers to see if the new shoes work accordingly."

"Right," I mumbled. All the products were created so someone somewhere could be punished. Don't ask me why; the committee seems to have very clear ideas on how the world should look.

"You know your grandfather was a good friend of mine. I always had a sweet spot for you, my dear. Your parents were smart only to have one child. Some people here—"

She stopped talking and smiled at me as if she had almost said something she shouldn't.

"Anyway, I was just starting to make a batch of snickerdoodles. Why don't you help me with that?"

"Who died?" I blurted out.

"You know the Drottles, right? Well, their oldest son fell in love with Jenny Jenkins. Apparently, he tried getting her a ring. Poor fool. He knew what would happen if they found out."

———

The longer I worked at Mrs. Holly's bakery, the more I started understanding what was actually taking place in our town. The factories and shops were creating something awful. Everyone that was old enough knew about it, but they chose to ignore it. Even if they all had different reasons. Life here was really perfect; you never had to fear for anything as long as you worked and didn't take any of the products from the forbidden shops. There were enough stores giving out legal things for free. The house, the car, the food, the drinks, the entertainment, and everything else you could imagine. Anything that was given to the people for free was a way to make them live happily and not start asking questions.

And there was another rule. Never ask questions.

"What did my grandpa do?"

I know I wasn't allowed to ask. Mrs. Holly could hit me, hurt me, make them burn me, but somehow I couldn't keep myself from blurting out those words. I kept asking myself this question each time I smelled cinnamon. Besides, Mrs. Holly and I had grown closer. I felt like I could trust her.

When I said those words, her eyes opened wide with terror.

"Child, are you insane? Don't you know that—"

"I'm not supposed to ask questions. I know. But you know the other day they took Timmy, my neighbor. He was such a kind and sweet person. They assigned him to the crematory, and he said no. So they threw him in."

I don't know what befell me. Maybe it was the fact that I was getting older or maybe the bakery made me feel dumb and brave. Timmy wasn't the only one they took. Just the one that hurt me the most. He was a kind boy.

Mrs. Holly sighed.

"Your grandfather didn't do his job. He was supposed to travel and sell, but instead, he destroyed the products. He still got the money in different ways, but the committee found out that he was tricking them. This is all I will say and don't ever ask or question anything again."

She got the wooden rolling pin from the desk. I saw the pain in her eyes as she held it up and hit my arm with all her strength. They probably heard what I asked, and they'd know if she didn't do it properly. I knew she didn't want to hurt me, but it was my own fault for asking questions. The broken hand was worth the information she gave me. Besides, my punishment could have been much worse.

I thought I understood Tattletoe, but simple answers can never answer complicated questions. I understand that now. For a long time, I thought it was the smell. The nutmeg would make you happy; the cinnamon would teach you to fear. Except I spent every day in the bakery surrounded by the smells, and only now I'm starting to become skeptical. I'm starting to doubt and to understand. And nutmeg doesn't make anyone happy. Too much of it can even become poisonous.

There was a time where I was afraid of Mrs. Holly and the smell of cinnamon. To me, it meant death. Now I understand that Mrs. Holly isn't trying to scare everyone by alarming them with the smell; she is trying to cover up the smell of burning corpses. I don't even want to imagine how many snickerdoodles she had to bake after they burned all her children and husband when they tried to leave the town.

Part 2

I live in a place named Tattletoe, a place full of mystery. Where death smells like cinnamon and life smells like nutmeg. Everything here is in perfect symmetry. One portion of fear and one portion of happiness fed to the ideal obedient citizen. Perfectly balanced to ensure that the people who live here will do their work for the greater good. What kind of greater good? That's something only the committee members know. It's just all a big hoax, if you ask me, but let's be real here, nobody asks.

It's not simply the fact that they are afraid to die. Of course, nobody believes that they will be the ones being punished. Ignorance can work wonders. And as long as the fear doesn't override the happiness, there is no need to change anything. As I said, life here can be pretty perfect. Although it does ask of some degree of discipline to be surrounded by all these wonderful goods, while not being allowed any.

Honestly, smelling the wonderful creations of Mrs. Holly each day is probably what made me doubt our ways the most. How can they ask me to be surrounded by the most delicious things in the world but forbid me to have a taste? My mouth starts drooling just thinking about it. Sometimes I even dream about her pain au chocolat made with the richest dark chocolate I've ever seen. It straight-out smells like pure luck. I haven't been able to stop thinking about the lemon bars we made the other day. The way Mrs. Holly slowly spread the zest of those bright yellow lemons over the hot and luscious bars. The lemons come from one of the many lemon trees of Tattletoe. Most of the fruits are being exported to some nearby towns, but a few of them are sent to the bakery to be turned into sweet treats. The gardeners here must be very talented; the citrus fruits shine even brighter than the flowers. No wonder Mrs. Holly wore gloves as she prepared them. Oh, and don't even get me started on the cupcakes she made! I would die for trying just one of these marvelous goods.

Well, I would *literally* die if I did.

With a broken hand, I wasn't much use to Mrs. Holly. I would mostly just bring her more flour from the shelf or turn on the ovens. Work had gotten awfully boring, but I kept coming each morning before sunrise. I would put on my apron and sit on the chair waiting for Mrs. Holly to give me a new task. A lot of times we just chatted and drank tea. I couldn't believe my luck. Especially after hearing what kind of jobs some of my neighbor kids were assigned to.

Magnolia Marble started working in the doll store. A place run by an older gentleman who single-handedly creates each and every single doll, which in turn is being exported to children all over the world. I don't like going in there much; the place smells like chlorine, and the dolls are probably the only products that I never wanted to own or even hold in my hands. They are the creepiest things I've ever seen, and I've been around a good portion of bizarre stuff. The resemblance they have with an actual human child is uncanny. You might be wondering what Magnolia has to do in the shop if the dollmaker is the only one in charge of production. Well, she has to go around town and collect items to make the dolls as realistic as possible. One of her jobs is collecting hair or other necessary parts. If she finds some hair in the barber places, she is lucky. She only has to pick them from the ground. Unfortunately, the hairs often belong to adults and are too thick and splintered for a doll. So often she will knock on doors of parents, mainly the ones with many children. As you might imagine, parents are not often happy with that, but if she doesn't find enough hair, the dollmaker gets angry with her. Though if you look at it from the bright side, at least Magnolia never gets tempted to take any of the products she's surrounded by.

The dollmaker uses those hairs, sometimes teeth, even nails, but only the ones that are gentle and nice, and those are made into something I hope you never encounter in your life.

If you've ever come across a doll that just made the hairs on your back turn, a doll that simply seemed to be radiating pure evil, a doll that made you question your own sense of sanity, well, chances are it was produced in Tattletoe's doll store.

"Did you hear the news? Mrs. Musters is gonna have her child soon. It might even be born today!" I said to Mrs. Holly, who was preparing some sort of dough.

The moment those words left my mouth, Mrs. Holly's metal whisk slipped from her hands and loudly hit the ground of the bakery. The batter was splashing everywhere. I quickly got up to pick up the whisk and clean up. Mrs. Holly didn't move; for a good moment or two, she just kept staring into the distance. She looked both scared and angry at the same time. Then I remembered how she had lost all her children and felt awful mentioning somebody else becoming a mother. This must be especially painful for her. And then she has to be the one who spreads the smell of nutmeg for the newborn. I can only imagine what kind of torture that must be. Thinking about it, I wondered how that tradition with nutmeg arose. I know she tries to overshadow the smell of death when she bakes something with cinnamon, but there is no reason for overshadowing the smell of new life, right? It's a celebration.

Maybe it's part of making the people happy. Nutmeg is in a lot of holiday dishes so maybe that's why they like it.

"I'm sorry," I mumbled after cleaning up.

"Oh?" Mrs. Holly shook her head like she was coming back to her senses. "Why are you apologizing, child?" She laughed. "Those are some wonderful news. A child, how lovely." Her words were nice, but the way she spoke made it sound incredibly insincere.

"Hmm, my mum thought it was wonderful as well. She repeatedly said how the Musters' keep getting gifted. Guess because they already have like a dozen kids."

"And they're planning on having even more. Some people just can't seem to get enough, can they?" Mrs. Holly said in a melodic voice.

"Well, I don't. I don't think I want any children at all, if I'm honest."

She smiled at me with that sad expression she had when she broke my hand.

"You know what this means, though, Deborah? We will need to get baking! Will you be a dear and go down to the market to get us nutmeg? As many seeds as you can get your hands on. Stress that they are needed for the bakery! From the looks of Mrs. Musters, she might even be expecting twins. I was thinking of making some gingerbread men—how does that sound?"

"Sounds nice but it isn't Christmas. Where will they be exported to?" I asked.

"We won't export them. They are for the fresh parents," she responded.

I wasn't sure if I could ask, but this did sound very strange. I started furrowing my brow. Mrs. Holly caught my gaze and nervously laughed.

"I know what you're thinking. Our baked goods are not made for the citizens of Tattletoe. There is one small exception, though. New parents always receive many baskets full of gifts, goods nobody else can get, including something made by me."

⁂

I kept my purple apron on as I made my way to the market. Everything on the market was given away for free; those were the goods we were allowed to consume. However, some products were sparer than others, and Mrs. Holly stressed how she needed as much nutmeg as possible. Having the apron would give me some more credibility. Everyone knew and respected Mrs. Holly's bakery, after all.

The market was particularly well visited that day. Townspeople of Tattletoe were walking from stall to stall, enjoying all the new items that were being presented. The market ranged from fine drinks to delicious food, toys for children, clothes, and anything else you might need.

I didn't stop at any of the usual stalls, though. I was here on a mission.

"Nutmeg or cinnamon?" the spice guy asked as I moved up to his stall. I guess he had noticed my apron.

"Nutmeg," I exclaimed.

"Thank god." He took a breath and laughed. "I'm all out of cinnamon. People have been misbehaving a lil lately." He winked at me and handed me a small paper bag with some nutmeg.

"Uhm, I don't think this will be enough," I said.

"This is more than enough, girl! Too much nutmeg can make you all woozy goozy, and if you have too much... well, then Mrs. Holly will need more cinnamon soon," he jokingly said.

I shrugged.

"Mrs. Holly said I should get as much as possible. Apparently they're having twins."

The spice guy shook his head in disbelief as he packed up all the nutmeg he had.

Mrs. Holly was baking all day. She had stopped the production of any other bread, cookies, or cakes. Only gingerbread men were coming out of the oven. The ventilation system was spreading the fragrance all over Tattletoe. The new Musters offspring was born that afternoon.

Mrs. Holly was right. They were twins.

She packed the gingerbread in a big beautiful basket and asked me to bring it to the Musters. On my way up to their house, I met Magnolia, and she asked to come along with me. She needed some hair.

"The Musters usually let me take as much as I want. Makes me feel even worse for those children, but gotta do the job, you know?" Magnolia said with a careless look on her face. Working at the doll store had toughened her up. She used to be my most optimistic friend.

"Why do you feel bad for the kids?" I asked.

"Well, I've been in their home a couple times. Always made me wanna leave right away again. They are some of those folks that collect children for the perks."

"You mean the gifts?"

"Uhu. Though I do get it. The stuff you get is so much better than anything they have at the market. Tattletoe's way of making parents produce new kids." She had gotten a lot more skeptical as well.

"Ssht, Magnolia," I whispered. "Don't get us in trouble."

"Come on, Debbie, this is like common knowledge. Nobody really wants to have children here. The ones that do are just heartless or don't know better."

I got the idea that the Musters belonged to that first group when their father opened the door for us. His eyes went right to the basket, and he pushed his five-year-old son who was reaching for the ginger-bread men away. He laughed it off and opened the door wider so we could walk right inside.

"Just drop it off on that table, love. Magnolia, if you need anything, Joe's losing more teeth lately."

"Just hair today, Mr. Musters. We have more than enough teeth at the moment." She shot me a disgusted look and walked upstairs.

***

It only took a few days. It hit Mr. Musters first. Nobody spoke of his death, but I'm sure it was painful. Mrs. Musters followed him shortly after. I don't think their children were too sad, though. From what I saw in their house that day, those kids hadn't seen happiness in a long time. Not with parents as greedy as theirs. I'm not sure if anyone is suspecting Mrs. Holly and her baked goods. I'm not even sure if the committee knows, or maybe they do but don't care. The Musters had made enough children already who would be having grandchildren, making sure the population was increasing.

It made me see Mrs. Holly in a new light, though. This sweet old lady kept surprising me in new ways all the time, but at the same time she is still the most mysterious woman I know. I wondered whether she did it in spite. You could think that she did it because she lost all her children while those people had so many. But I know Mrs. Holly and that wouldn't be her style. She knows that she is tied to this town, and she is coping with it in her own little way. Or at least that's my interpretation. I wouldn't dare to ask.

They tell us that there are happiness and fear and nothing in between. In Tattletoe, death smells like cinnamon and life smells like nutmeg, but now I know that sometimes the fragrances get mixed.

Part 3

I live in a place named Tattletoe, where death smells like cinnamon and life smells like nutmeg. All because of the wonderful bakery of Mrs. Holly where I work every day surrounded by the most delicious scents in the world. I have to admit that I have grown a little opposed to cinnamon, though, to the point where I feel nauseous just getting a sniff. Unfortunately, the death rates have been skyrocketing lately, and the snickerdoodles, cinnamon buns, and banana bread have been piling up in the bakery, almost leaving no space to work. They haven't been picked up yet by any of the exporters, and I kept wondering what would happen to all these goods. Mrs. Holly didn't say a word about it, though, and I wasn't sure how to ask.

Luckily, we can balance out the smell from time to time with some vanilla, chocolate, or strawberry. Scents only Mrs. Holly and I smell in the kitchen. We wouldn't want to give the town any strange ideas.

"Deborah, get started on the frosting for the cinnamon rolls. Those are his favorite for some unspeakable reason," she mumbled.

"He? As in Mr. V?" I shouted. A feeling of both excitement and fear swept over me. "He wants cinnamon goods?"

Mrs. Holly nodded silently.

Mr. V was the head of our town. The man who doesn't live in Tattletoe but controls it all. I guess you could call him our mayor, except he is more of a businessman who funds more cities, towns, and projects than you could ever imagine. The town had been preparing for his arrival for days now. Thrill and excitement were filling up the air.

The big statue of Mr. V at the marketplace had been cleaned and polished. The painters had been working day and night to give the houses with damage a cordial new look. Every shop owner had been updating their store windows in the most unique ways possible. It was a silent competition in which everyone wanted to be the one to impress Mr. V with the most original idea. The nicest one I'd seen so far was the flower shop whose owner had created a jungle of sorts, with plants growing from all directions. The dollmaker had made a toy-sized Ferris wheel as well as a carousel in which his creepy dolls were taking rounds. The shoemaker had built a theater, including actual spotlights, and his newest collection was the stars. I have to admit, that one seemed a tad ridiculous to me, but the man is absolutely obsessed with his shoes.

Mrs. Holly and I had been baking new creations and were experimenting with different flavors. I figured that she was making new goods because the committee commanded her to. They always want to impress Mr. V. However, hearing that he asked for something cinnamon-flavored was odd, to say the least. I've mentioned it before, but cinnamon only has one specific purpose in Tattletoe, and that is associated with burning corpses. I figured that the goods get shipped to some bakeries or shops around the country afterward. Hearing that Mr. V likes to indulge in them made me think there might be even more to it. If he ate them, they couldn't be so dangerous after all.

The whole time we were baking, she stayed silent. We had grown closer in the time I worked here, and in a way it was like being with my own grandmother. This day was different, though. She was cold and distant, and I was afraid to push her nerves. Asking dumb questions could cost me more than some bruises with the current climate.

Nobody had real answers to the cause of an increase in death lately. Some whisper they were suicides, others say they asked the wrong questions or stopped working. Unfortunately, burnouts are taken far too literally in our town.

There was another thought creeping up in the back of my head, though. Could these new deaths be connected to the upcoming arrival of Mr. V?

"Deborah, you are being given a huge honor tomorrow. Make sure to dress nicely."

Mrs. Holly snapped me out of my thoughts.

"Mr. V asked for our new baker to bring him samples of our goods."

I opened my mouth but couldn't bring out any words. I had never met Mr. V before, and even though he was worshipped here, I was feeling extremely anxious. Besides, he ran the committee, and those bastards commanded the death of my grandfather. Simply because he was trying to help people.

Mrs. Holly smiled at me sympathetically.

"It will be okay," she whispered.

The next day, I got the basket from the bakery and made my way to the office building of Tattletoe. The place where I would be meeting Mr. V.

The overall atmosphere in the town center was incredibly festive. The decorations looked even better than yesterday, and workers were arranging benches and tables for the upcoming beer festival tomorrow. A tradition to lift the spirit of the townspeople and a way to forget about the smell of cinnamon for a while.

I took a deep breath and walked toward the office building where one of Mr. V's employees let me inside. I followed him upstairs as he guided me toward the room where Mr. V was awaiting me.

Inside the room, I saw him. He hadn't changed a bit since his last visit. Dressed casually but still radiating a sense of power. In the back of the room was another person, though. Someone I had never seen before and who didn't match either the Tattletoe aesthetic nor Mr. V's employees. It was a young man, his dark hair looked messy, and he had a bruise on his eye and on his arms. He wore a black shirt with some holes in it, and there were stains on his jeans.

"Oh, don't pay attention to him. That's an old friend of mine who decided to come along for the visit."

Mr. V got up from his chair and gave me a warm smile.

"You must be Deborah Deller!" He got up from his chair and opened his arms so I could hand him the basket with the baked goods.

I nodded.

"Wonderful, just wonderful." He took a deep breath, inhaling all the smells. "Don't you love the smell of cinnamon? It's simply the best."

His green eyes were shifted from the basket to me.

"I prefer chocolate," I said.

Mr. V laughed.

"So did your grandfather. Please, Deborah, have a seat." He pointed me toward his table.

I swallowed. How could he so casually mention Grandpa?

"I know what you're thinking. And I know you're too afraid to ask. But just so you know, I appreciated your grandfather very much. I always liked that he had a mind of his own. There aren't many people like that, you know, the ones who aren't sheep." He sighed. "The committee decided for him to die. I swear those people are useless half the time. But someone gotta do the work, right?"

"I guess."

Mr. V smiled and took another sniff of the basket.

"Now, I understand why Mrs. Holly made such a wide variety, but actually the cinnamon rolls are more than enough. When you get back to her, tell her to make enough for the entire festival tomorrow, will you? You might not believe it, but beer and cinnamon go wonderful together."

Those eyes were basically staring into my soul. I was feeling slightly uneasy but weirdly comfortable at the same time.

"The people here aren't allowed to have any of the baked goods," I responded.

"Sure they can. There's nothing wrong with the cinnamon except that it smells like heaven. Or hell. I guess it depends on your definition," he said as he raised his eyebrows.

I wasn't sure what to say or why I was still here. It didn't look like he was gonna eat any of the goods; he just kept smelling them.

Mr. V smiled again.

"I know you are a smart girl, and I assume working with Mrs. Holly has given you quite some new impressions of this town, so I feel like I can be honest with you. I want to use the cinnamon rolls for a little experiment."

"So you can see if the people will break the rules and burn even more of them?" I blurted out. My heart was racing at this point, but for some reason, I couldn't keep my mouth shut anymore.

Mr. V didn't look angry, though; he just shook his head.

"It shows me their preferences. Cinnamon means death, and I want to see how many of them will happily indulge in the rolls. There's nothing wrong with them, though. You can try one now if you like," he said.

I shook my head.

"Very well," he continued. "Now let us talk about the real reason I invited you here."

I raised an eyebrow, though I had a hunch he didn't just want me to bring the basket. He could have sent for someone to pick it up, after all.

"I have a job offer for you. Well, for now it would be an internship. You can start by taking care of my friend over there."

I looked back at the man in the peculiar clothes. I had almost forgotten about his presence.

"Hello," I said to the man. He waved with a careless expression on his face.

"He's new to town, and I'd love for you to show him around a little. Maybe get him some fresh clothes and a haircut. And bring him to the festival with you tomorrow. He's been staying inside a little too much lately."

Mr. V laughed.

"Do you want me to work as your assistant?" I asked.

"In a wider sense, I guess... Deborah, how would you feel about leaving that old bakery behind you and becoming a member of the town's committee instead?"

I didn't say anything, but we both knew what my answer would be.

It's not like I really have a say in choosing a job here.

Part 4

I live in a place named Tattletoe, where death smells like cinnamon and life smells like nutmeg. Today, however, hop and malt are predominating the town as it is the day of our annual beer festival. And the head of our town had big plans for it.

The crowds had gathered on the streets. The last few preparations were being taken care of. Long tables were reaching all over the marketplace. Children were running around and playing while the adults were working hard to make sure that everything looked perfect. Around the tables, on the corners of the marketplace were beer carts, which were only there for the day. There were seven in total, each one serving a different kind of lager, pilsener, or craft beer. Next to the drink carts were exactly seven food booths ranging from hearty meat and potatoes to sweet candy and salty pretzels. Everything had been imported in advance and naturally not been produced in Tattletoe.

I loved the beer festival. It wasn't the only time we came together to celebrate, but it was one of our most joyous days next to the regular holidays. I would go as far as to say that the beer festival was my second favorite day. This year, however, it felt tainted. I was in no way the naïve girl I used to be last year. I had become an adult working in a place that spreads out the smell of death. And soon I would be joining the town committee. A group of martyrs who burn anyone who doesn't obey the rules of our town.

Of course, first I had to prove worthy by taking care of the outsider who had come to town. This doesn't happen often, so of course many people were watching us with curious looks. Nobody dared to ask out front who he was or where he came from. A couple understood that the head of our town, Mr. V, had brought him along, and that was all they needed to know. Possibly he could be a victim for the town. Maybe a sacrifice, though for who we didn't know.

"You are not even asking why I look the way I do? Is this something you're used to here?"

Of course I had been wondering why he looked the way he did. His clothes ripped and tainted. His face all bloody and bruised.

I shrugged.

"You didn't ask why my arm is broken, either."

"I did assume a few options there. You either had a work accident, although I know you work in a bakery and people don't break their arms often in bakeries. Maybe you fell down during a game or while doing some sort of sport, but I doubt you have a lot of free time for shenanigans like that. So I assume you got it the same way I got mine."

I stopped walking and pulled the man closer to the side of the streets, away from curious ears. Although I knew that whatever we said was by a big chance being recorded.

"So Mr. V didn't do this to you?" I whispered.

He laughed.

"Not directly, but he also didn't care to tell me about the weird rules you have here. I have to admit not asking questions is unbelievably difficult for me. There is nothing more important than questioning everything and everyone. You have to stay critical, but it seems they forbid you to have a mind of your own here."

I didn't understand whether this was some sort of trick to test my loyalty. A way to examine whether I would start talking badly about Tattletoe.

"Will you be leaving with Mr. V tomorrow?"

He laughed again, but this time it sounded much more bitter.

"No. I don't think I will be leaving anytime soon."

I nodded. The tone in his voice told me what I needed to know. He was a prisoner here. I took a deep breath to collect my courage and asked straight out.

"Why did he pick you to come?"

The guy turned toward me; he seemed a lot calmer now.

"You don't have to be afraid to ask questions anymore. At least to some degree. He picked you to be on the committee because he believes you are smarter than the people running it at the moment. They won't harm you. As to me, Mr. V, as you call him, picked me up at a bar and asked me politely to come and join him on this trip."

I raised an eyebrow in disbelief. I didn't care how friendly Mr. V acted; something was awfully wrong with him.

"We go way back, him and I. We hadn't met personally before, but I've been up in his business for a while now. I knew one of his little helpers very well."

"Helper? As what I'm going to be?"

He shrugged.

"As we're both going to be, I guess. By the way," he held out his hand, "you can call me Josh."

"Deborah."

We got Josh some clothes at the marketplace and visited the barber. He was undeniably impressed by everything he saw. It was like watching a child in a candy store. His eyes were big and sparkly like he couldn't believe what kind of little wonderland he had stumbled upon. Or, well, been pushed into.

"Can we go to one of the shops next? I really wanna talk to that doll maker. He seems so wonderfully odd."

"No," I almost shouted. "I guess they didn't tell you about those rules, either. You can't buy any of the products made in the shops. They're only for export. Those dolls have teeth and human hair and strangle you in your sleep if you don't pay enough attention to them."

"Wow," he whispered. "So everything sold here is somehow cursed?"

I shrugged.

"It's punishment. I heard one of the exporters started drinking juice from the lemons he needs to send away. He's become the mere shell of his former self since."

"All right, wait, do you know what I find most astonishing? Sure, yeah, the stuff you make here is demonic in some way, but nobody here uses it. All the things the people that live here consume are ordinary, no magic whatsoever. Why does everyone here obey? Why do the people make things that will kill others if they know something is wrong?"

He was on a real roll, and in my opinion he seemed a little too excited analyzing our lives here, but to be fair, his questions were not uncalled for.

"The people that try to escape die a horrible death. The others like living in their little wonderland," I finally said.

The town had the distinct cinnamon smell again. I felt like throwing up all day, but at least today the smell wasn't due to any deaths, at least as far as I knew. Mr. V had ordered for Mrs. Holly to bake enough cinnamon rolls for the entire town. He called it an experiment, but what he actually wanted to test wasn't clear to me just yet. When I told her the news, Mrs. Holly looked both shocked and disgusted. Never before had she made anything with cinnamon flavor for the townspeople, not even for a festivity. It was plain wrong; we both could tell.

"For a week, we've been making cinnamon for the death. Every single day, there had been a new victim for the crematorium, and now on the day that nobody died, he wants the town to have the smell again?"

Mrs. Holly was fuming. I had never seen her like this before. It was as if she had lost all her calmness at once. Still, she complied and spend the entire night baking. I wasn't there to help as I had to take care of our newcomers, and even though I trusted Mrs. Holly, a part of me was afraid she was filling the cinnamon rolls with an excessive amount of the nutmeg poison.

Or maybe she didn't even have to. We didn't know what eating the cinnamon would do at all. Mr. V could have lied.

The sun was beginning to set when Josh and I made our way to the marketplace. Purple garlands were hanging from the buildings, and fairy lights were spread on the tables, making everyone's faces light up in the dark. There was a small Ferris wheel and even a carousel. They looked just like the miniature ones the doll maker had created in his store. The shops were locked up, but the lights inside were still on, showing off the wonderful storefronts the owners had been creating over the days.

The townspeople had already assembled, and most were sitting at the tables. In front of them, I saw big baskets spread around evenly. They were filled with the cinnamon rolls. So far nobody had dared to touch them. There was one more table in the front on a stage. In the middle of it sat Mr. V, and next to him were two empty seats saved for Josh and me. The rest of the committee, however, was spread around the other tables with notepads and pens.

"The cinnamon rolls will kill them," I whispered.

"No, that would be too easy," Josh responded.

We reluctantly walked up the stage. Mr. V was talking to the people at the moment, and everyone was cheering and clapping. When he announced that everyone was free to eat the cinnamon rolls and that consuming them would not lead to a visit to the crematorium, an eerie silence broke down.

Mr. V laughed out loud.

"Please, friends, don't be afraid to go after your desires. I know many of you are longing for the cinnamon, and tonight I want to fulfill that need for you. Eat, drink, enjoy, for tonight there are no consequences."

It didn't take long for people to start feasting on the cinnamon rolls. Many were stuffing their faces with as much as they could; only a few didn't touch any of it. When I spotted my parents in one of the corners, eating the rolls with enormous smiles on their faces, I jumped up. My heart was racing, and I was about to run down and push them out of their hands. If there was a chance there was poison in there, I couldn't let them do this. However, Mr. V held me back before I could jump down.

"You're killing them," I shouted with tears in my eyes.

He smiled kindly and shook his head.

"You are lucky your parents chose to eat the forbidden fruit. The ones who didn't touch it are the ones we need to have an eye on."

"You're choosing future victims. People who are prone to disobey. That's what those people are writing down," Josh mumbled.

Seeing the happy and healthy faces of my parents and all the others eating the cinnamon rolls gave me a sickening feeling. I fell down back to my seat.

"Our people have been conditioned, my dear Deborah. They understand very well what death smells like, and today they showed us that they enjoy the scent of it."

I WATCHED A TAPE OF MY FOURTH BIRTHDAY

Trauma can be a bitch. That's something I learned quite late as I'd been living a rather sheltered life. My home is a tiny town in the middle of nowhere, which admittedly can sound boring or even suffocating to some. Though to me it was the perfect paradise.

I grew up in a home filled with love and affection on a street with a dozen more similar houses. All beautiful on the outside with bright green lawns and whimsical mailboxes.

I lived alone with my mum and my dad, but that was perfectly fine because our neighbors had children as well. We had everything you could ever wish for. All the best toys that they showed in ads on TV. I was one of the first kids who had a Nintendo and later on a PlayStation. My friends and I had a treehouse where we spent all our free time reading comic books and novels. We were fairly normal in all the typical ways.

Those children had always been my very best friends, and one of them even became my girlfriend and very soon in the future hopefully my wife. Mabel and I moved out of our childhood homes two weeks ago and into our own little dream house not far from our parents. I realize most adults want to leave at a certain point to find their own future, but we'd always known that ours was right here. In Appleton. A place where you know all of your neighbors and never feel out of place. Most people I know never left.

No, that's not perfectly true. Nobody I know has. I never wanted to, either, and I never questioned my life. I never had a reason to. Questions are not necessary when everything is clear. And I swear it was for the longest time.

Until I found the tapes.

And you see, that's the thing with critical thinking. You are fine and well without it, but then you start asking one question, and then there's no going back. If you choose to be skeptical, well, it will make you go crazy. And I had opened the door for it.

I asked enough questions to find out a terrible truth about myself.

Like most children born in the middle of the nineties, I had most of my life recorded on tape after Mum and Dad bought a video recorder when I was three or four years old. My parents filmed school graduations, football matches, picnics, and of course every birthday. I remember we used to watch the tapes quite regularly when I was younger. Sometimes I'm not even sure if the memories I have of my childhood stem from those films or my brain. But then one day our VHS recorder broke down, we hadn't switched from tapes to DVDs, and over the years we kind of forgot those tapes in their dusty boxes in the basement.

When I found the old VHS recorder with Mabel's stuff, I was ecstatic. I hadn't thought about my childhood films in quite a while, but now I could not wait to watch them. I walked the five minutes to my parents' right away. They both weren't home, but I still had my key and went to pick up the boxes from the basement.

I looked through the tapes, which all had different things written on them, and picked the one that said *Jamie 99—X.*

I shoved in the tape, and after rewinding for a little while, I pressed play.

The first video was of my fourth birthday. I saw Mum and Dad dressed in bright sweaters and high-waisted jeans. They were smiling and laughing while Dad was lighting the candles on my cake. My friends and I were sitting around the table impatiently waiting for the cake. There were some other neighbors as well; I guess one of them was filming.

The thing that stood out to me, though, was this one boy. He looked a little older than me, but I'd never seen him before in my life. He had dark hair and very fair skin. His arm was around my shoulder, and he was pointing at the candles on the cake. It seemed normal and fine at first, but then the boy looked into the camera. He started staring and didn't stop. His gaze became uncomfortable and strange until it changed the whole atmosphere of the tape. The camera person started zooming in on my face so he wouldn't be in the picture anymore.

It felt so odd to me because I'd never met a real stranger. Everyone here knows everyone, after all. I recognized the tiny versions of my other friends but not him. So who did this boy grow up to be?

I continued watching my fifth birthday. This time it was a garden party with the same people.

Including the boy.

Again, he was plastered to me. It seemed like we were very close. But while everyone was laughing and being cheerful, his face looked anxious. When the camera came close to him, he'd start staring again. I took a picture of it on my phone so I could zoom in closer, but I simply wasn't able to recognize who he was.

I went on with the following birthdays, and they were the same. Only on the seventh one I finally started noticing a clue as to who this boy might be.

When everyone started singing "Happy Birthday" to me, the strange boy again stared at the camera and mouthed something. I rewind to that exact moment again and again. It felt critical to me to figure out what he was saying. I can't quite explain why, but something about him was pulling me in. I turned up the volume as high as I could.

"Happy Birthday" was blasting through my home. And when everyone was singing, "Happy birthday, dear Jamie," I believe I heard what the strange boy was singing instead.

Luca.

I played the scene a few more times until I was sure. He was singing for Luca.

"What is this noise?" I heard Mabel shout as she shut the door behind her.

I quickly turned down the volume.

"Sorry, love." I laughed. "I found these old tapes and got a little carried away."

Mabel came closer and sat down right next to me. "No way! Look how little you are!" She started laughing.

"Yeah, and there's you! Your hair was still blond then."

As we continued watching the tape, it suddenly went to my eighth birthday.

"He's gone," I whispered.

Mable looked at me with a confused look. I went back to the moments that showed the little boy.

"This boy. He was at all my other birthdays. Do you know who he is?"

Mabel shook her head. "Probably someone's cousin." She smiled. "I'm gonna get some water. Do you want anything?"

I shook my head, unable to take my eyes from the screen. After a while—I don't remember how much time had passed—I heard a familiar voice behind me.

"It's not nice to take something without asking."

I turned around to the strangely uncomfortable face of my mother. My dad was right next to her with frowned brows. "We watched these films when we needed to. You don't need them anymore now, do you?" my father asked.

Mabel was standing behind them with the same smile she had when she left to go to the kitchen earlier. I guess it was an excuse to call my parents, though I didn't understand what suddenly had happened.

"Yeah, sorry, I guess. Just wanted to check out my old—" My eyes went back to the screen. Why did I feel so mesmerized by it?

"Well, then, sweet boy. If you insist on re-watching the past, at least pick a more stimulating film."

"Film?" I asked.

My mother started rummaging through the tapes and finally chose one she felt comfortable with.

Jamie's Happy Times 2004—2008

It was a recording of my parents and me as we went to a park nearby. We were feeding ducks, and later on, other children joined us. All my friends were there, including my girlfriend. In the back of my mind, I was still thinking of Luca, but the nostalgia suddenly took over. It had been a happy time back then. It still was a happy time.

The four of us continued watching the tape, which showed different moments of my life. Most of them together with friends and family. Only Mabel started disappearing in the later parts of the video.

"Weird. I could swear you were there all the time when everyone else was," I whispered to her.

"I have my own life and family, too, you silly goose. I can't be everywhere at once, now can I?" she said without looking away from the screen.

I finally looked away from the tape. Mable was acting particularly odd that day.

"But your parents are right there," I said.

She didn't respond to that.

"Oh well, it has gotten awfully late, hasn't it? You had your fun, Jamie. I believe it is time you get back to reality," my mother instructed as she turned off the tape. My father started collecting all the other ones, and they walked toward the door.

"Can't we keep them here? You don't have a VHS anyway," I said.

Dad looked at me with a strict but friendly face.

"Well, all right, boy. But do not spend all night looking at the past. You need to focus on your future, too."

My mum kissed me on the cheek. She always does that, but I could swear this time her lips stayed on my cheek longer than usual.

When I went back to look through the tapes again, I noticed Dad had left all except for the birthday tape.

The following day the thought of that strange boy and the evening with my parents and Mabel didn't let go of me.

When I woke up, Mabel was in the kitchen making coffee.

"Oh, good morning, sweetheart. Did you have some nice dreams?" She smiled from ear to ear.

"Mabel, who is Luca?" I asked directly.

For a second, her smile disappeared. She let the coffee spoon fall to the ground.

"I never heard that name in my life. Is that a boy or a girl?" she asked as she had collected herself again. However, she didn't even wait for my response.

"The boy in the tape. You said he might be someone's cousin."

Mabel tilted her head like she didn't know what I was talking about.

"I only know Jessica Blitz's cousin. His name is Eli—"

"I fucking know Eli. I'm talking about the boy in that tape," I said in a raised voice, which I regretted shortly after. Mabel looked scared. "I'm sorry. I didn't mean to raise my voice."

"That's fine, love. It's just that I don't know what you're talking about. We didn't watch any birthday tapes."

I sat down at the kitchen table.

"Are you okay?" Mabel asked in a concerned tone.

I didn't respond.

"Do you want me to call your parents and ask if they have any tapes of your birthdays?"

Mabel called my parents and put them on speakerphone. Not only did they agree that we never watched any tapes of my birthdays, but my father also said the only tapes we have of my birthday parties start somewhere around 2005. They lost the other one ages ago.

I almost believed them. I really did.

They spoke in such a kind and loving manner that it wouldn't have occurred to me that they would ever lie. Except I still had a picture of that boy on my phone. A photo of him sitting right next to me with a cake in front of us. A cake with six candles.

I didn't trust either Mabel or my parents with the question, so I started asking other friends. The ones that were at the parties as well.

None of them remembered the boy.

If he was someone's friend or cousin, then someone would have remembered him, right?

I decided to visit my parents and ask them directly about what was going on. This time with the proof of the photo.

I knocked on the door, and Mum opened it. She smiled, but in the corner of her eye, I believed I saw a tear.

"Everything all right, Mum? Can I come in?" I asked.

"But of course you can! You are always welcome here!" she called out enthusiastically but shook her head at the same time.

For a moment, I hesitated. Something seemed wrong, but before I could take a step back, my father appeared behind the door.

"Jamie! Come in, boy. We need to talk to you about something."

I followed my parents to the living room where they were sitting with Mabel and Frank, one of my friends. They were both smiling, but their eyes looked sad.

"What's going on?" I asked.

"Sit down, sweetheart," my mother instructed.

"Look, honey. We haven't been honest with you. Not because we want to hurt you, quite the opposite!" Mabel said.

"I told your parents about the picture... about Luca," Frank chimed in.

My father sat down next to me. "We wanted to keep this from you to spare your poor soul. The boy was a friend of yours. Your best friend even, but—I'm not sure how to say this, so I will just try to be blunt. He died. And the death was partially your fault."

"What?"

My mum sat down as well and started stroking my hair. "You didn't mean to. You went swimming in the lake, and then you pushed him. It was only supposed to be a joke, but he never came back up."

I stayed still. I heard the words, but they made no sense. I didn't have a single memory of that.

"Sometimes your brain makes you forget something that traumatic. Just know that we don't blame you."

"Who are his parents?" I asked.

My parents exchanged a look. Nobody said a word at first. Then, at the same time, Mabel and my father started speaking.

"They moved away—"

"They live down the road—"

"Down the road? Are you stupid?" my father hissed.

"We could've asked someone. You screwed it up!" she shouted back.

I got up from my seat. "What's going on?"

Now they were all looking at me.

"Frank. You can go. Get everyone else. I suppose it's time."

"Time for what?"

My best friend got up and walked outside. Dad grabbed my wrist tightly. "Your mother thought you were doing so perfectly well that we could keep you the way you were, but I told her you were still human! And they always mess it up eventually," my father said. "You see, boy, we came to this place a long time ago, hoping to learn how the world works so we could have our version of it. We built up Appleton ourselves, but we needed something special. Children! We needed to learn how they grow up so we could make our own little versions. You did so well, and many other children did. But we made some mistakes. Some of the children we collected were too old already. They remembered their real parents. At least partially. But we have improved. Just look at you! You were a perfect example. You have ripened just as we needed you to."

He kept speaking, but the words made no sense to me. Until I remembered that the tapes started in 1999. Four years after I was born.

Of course, children that young don't remember anything, but the rest of my childhood was blurry as well.

"Who was the boy?"

Dad shrugged. "We found him on the playground with you."

"Are you even the same girl as the one on those tapes?" I shouted at Mabel. My entire existence was falling apart in front of me.

Mabel shrugged. "Does it matter if I am perfectly correct? I mean, imagine you were a copy. Would it really matter? I don't think it would. I feel fine. No, actually, I feel great."

"Do you want to feel great as well, Jamie?" my mother asked. It was the first thing she said. She didn't wait for my response. Instead, she grabbed my hand.

"Welcome the others. I will prepare him outside."

She continued to pull me toward the garden.

I wondered if I should fight her, but I wasn't even sure where I would go. Dad and Mabel were inside, and Frank was probably on his way with all the neighbors. I was alone in the garden with the woman I thought of like my mother. Though in reality, she was my kidnapper.

"I never killed that boy, did I?" I asked, clenching my fist so I would shake less.

She shook her head. "You shouldn't have started asking questions. They were accepting you." A tear rolled down her face.

She went through her pocket, and I thought she was going to cut me or do hell-knows-what. But instead, she gave me a key as she guided me toward the garage. "Take it and drive. As far as the gas will take you. Never come back."

My hands were trembling. "Mum, what is going on?"

"Marden. That's where we found you, Luca." She looked toward the house with fear in her eyes. "Now, go! They will be here soon, and if they get their hands on you, it won't be pretty."

In the matter of a day, my entire life had fallen apart. Everything I believed in was a lie. The years with my girlfriend. My entire childhood. I had been living in something so right, I should have known it was wrong.

I drove as far as I could. Of course, nobody believed a word of what I was saying at first, but in that town called Marden, I found help. They say I made up this tale as a response to an incredibly traumatic event, but I know that's not true.

I've been looking for Appleton ever since. Those creatures probably never stopped collecting their special children.

There is no map with the small town of Appleton on it, no proof of its existence online. I don't know what to do next. All I have left of that place is the photo I took of the boy who tried to warn me.

And I truly hope he managed to escape back then.

SOMETHING AWFUL HAPPENED TO MY PARENTS

We were on our way home, after watching the new *Hunger Games* movie. My sister Olivia was falling asleep next to me. We were all silent, listening to the radio, when my dad suddenly came to a full stop.

It took me a second to realize what he had seen. A small truck was blocking most of the road in front of us.

"What's going on there?" Olivia asked in a sleepy voice.

That's when a young woman stumbled out of the truck and walked around it to the side that wasn't in view. Her leg seemed to be hurt; she was grabbing the side of the truck to stay in balance.

My parents immediately got into helper mode, seeing a person who didn't look much older than their children. I guess she was around twenty or so.

"Stephen, call 911. I'll go check if she's all right," my father said.

"Maybe we should stay in the car and wait for help, honey. I've seen people tricking people into getting out of their car and—"

"We can't just sit here and wait, Mary. There might be someone even more hurt on the other side."

Before my mother could say anything else, he was already stepping out of the car. My mother opened her door to follow.

"Kids, lock the car and stay inside."

We were stopped on a quiet road, and around us were only trees.

They slowly walked toward the other side of the truck, and my father called out to the stranger.

After that, we didn't hear anything else. I grabbed my phone and called an ambulance.

"Should we check on them?" Olivia asked after a while.

"I don't know. Mum said—"

Before I could finish my sentence, my mother appeared from the back of the truck. Her face had lost all its color; she was walking fast and determined. When she reached the car, Olivia unlocked the doors.

She sat down behind the wheel without a word. Her expression was eerily calm.

"Mum?" I whispered. "What's going on? Is someone hurt?"

My mother didn't respond. And suddenly she opened her mouth as wide as humanly possible and screamed from the top of her lungs.

I unbuckled my seat belt, leaned over, and grabbed her by the shoulder. "Mum?"

"Mum? What happened?" Olivia shouted and grabbed her door handle, but before she could open it, my mother had locked all the doors.

She stopped screaming and took a few breaths before she hit the gas and started driving in reverse.

After we were so far away that we couldn't really see the truck anymore, she turned around and took a different road to our home.

She didn't respond to us; she didn't answer any questions. We kept asking about Dad, but she said nothing.

Next to me, Olivia started crying, and then she took out her phone to call the police again.

When we reached our driveway, my mother finally unlocked the car. Still silent, she walked straight home.

Olivia and I exchanged a look of fear and shock. Then she jumped to the front of the car. "I'm going back. You go inside."

"No, I'm coming with you."

Even from inside the car, we heard the shrill sound of my mother's scream coming from our house. We ignored it and kept driving until we found the road with the trees. I kept trying to call my dad the entire time, but it went straight to voicemail.

There was a police car waiting, but no sign of a truck.

One officer was waiting by the police car, and another one was looking around the side of the road.

We jumped out of the car and asked where our father was.

The officer told us that they arrived a few minutes ago and that there was no sign of anyone. At first, they asked us if we played a prank on them, but when he saw our concerned faces and listened to our story, he said that they would follow us home and talk to our mother.

"Don't worry, we will do anything we can to find your father," he said before we went back into the car.

My entire body was trembling. I had never in my life experienced anything this frightening, and I couldn't stop thinking about my dad. I hated that he didn't listen to my mum's concerns.

When we reached our house, the lights in the kitchen were on.

The officers followed us inside. My mother wasn't screaming anymore, but we heard the kettle in the kitchen.

We followed the sound, expecting to find my mother there. I almost cried in relief when I saw that it was actually my dad.

His hair was greasy, and he had changed into his pajamas.

"Kids, I've been worried sick about you!" he said loudly, and then his gaze shifted to the two police officers.

"Sir, are you all right?"

"Dad, we've been trying to call you! What the hell happened?" Olivia shouted and tried to run to him, but one of the officers held her back.

"I'm absolutely fine. Fantastic even. Except for the fact that I had to take a taxi home. The prices of that—"

"Sir. We need to ask you what happened to the truck and the woman inside."

My dad shook his head. "She was fine. Her car just wouldn't start, so I helped her, and then she drove off. All good."

"Was there anyone else with her?"

My dad shook his head.

"May we talk to your wife?"

"She already went to bed, but I suppose we can wake her up."

One of the officers walked upstairs with my father, while Olivia and I stayed in the kitchen with the other one and explained the situation one more time.

When the other officer returned, he explained to us that my mother told the same story about the broken-down car. Apparently, my mother remembered that the stove was still on, so she quickly drove home with us.

You could hear the skepticism in his voice, but there wasn't much else they could do. They gave us their number and told us to call when anything else came up or parents said anything. After they left, I went to touch the stove, and it was ice cold.

A little after that, my mother started screaming again.

I hardly slept that night. We kept asking my mum what had happened, but she didn't answer our questions. My dad just kept telling us that everything was fine and sent us to bed.

Finally, my mother stopped screaming, and the house turned silent.

The next morning, I walked down and heard the sound of laughter. My parents were standing in the kitchen, making pancakes without a care in the world.

Olivia was already sitting by the table, staring into nothing in front of her, her expression empty. We locked eyes, and I saw that she had slept just as little as I.

"Morning, honey. Did you sleep well?" my mother said in a melodic voice.

"Apparently everything is totally fine," Olivia said in a mocking tone to me.

I sat down next to her, and my mother started stacking pancakes on a plate and walked toward me. She stopped right in front of the table and dropped the plate. The shards flew in all directions. Suddenly her face turned pale again, her eyes opened wide, and then she screamed again, looking at us the entire time.

"Mum?" Olivia jumped up from her seat and grabbed her shoulders.

"Everything is all right, love," my father calmly said.

My mother blinked and looked at the ground. Her face relaxed. "Oh, won't you look at that? What a mess," she said and smiled at us.

We went through the strangest breakfast we ever had. Olivia and I had stopped asking them what was going on; we didn't get answers anyway. Their attempts to distract us were only frustrating and scaring us more.

After breakfast, I followed my sister to her room. Olivia was only a year younger than me, and we'd always been very close. I don't know how I would have dealt with this situation without her. We were both afraid of and for our parents.

"What do we do?" she asked after I sat down on her desk chair.

"I don't know. Should we call someone? Uncle Freddy maybe?"

We didn't have many relatives that lived nearby. Uncle Freddy was the only one, and he was still an hour's drive away.

"Not sure if he can do anything. They are acting like everything is normal."

"Except when Mum screams," Olivia said, and a shiver went down my spine at the thought of it. "Something happened with that truck. I just wish they would tell us," my sister whispered.

"Me too. And Dad is acting even stranger. He doesn't even acknowledge her screams."

We both sat there for a moment, lost in our thoughts, when we heard the door downstairs close shut and a little later the car started running.

Olivia looked out the window. "It's Dad."

"So Mum's alone downstairs?"

We quietly walked down the stairs and made our way to our living room. My mother was sitting on the sofa. In her hand, she held a needle and yarn, but she wasn't moving; she looked completely spaced out. When she noticed us, she slightly moved her face toward us. Her mouth opened, but this time she didn't scream; she just kept it open.

I walked over to her and sat down on the ground in front of her. "Please, Mum. Talk to us. I don't know if you're trying to protect us from something, but this isn't helping. We're old enough, and we are here for you. What happened last night?"

She blinked and then shook her head as if she was just waking up from a daydream. Her mouth closed again.

Her eyes went to me and then to my sister.

"It's hard to remember. Something keeps blocking my memories. I know that something isn't right, but it's almost as if my mind keeps falling asleep. I can't control it."

Olivia came closer and sat down beside me. "Maybe we should take you to a doctor. I mean, the screaming really scares us, Mum."

My mother looked confused. "What screaming?"

I swallowed. "Do you remember anything about that woman?"

We lost her. Her eyes opened wide, and for a moment it looked as if she was smiling, but then her mouth opened so much that her face got all wrinkly.

From the looks of it, it was as if she was screaming but this time no sound came out.

I just grabbed her by the shoulders and shook her. Finally, her expression softened. Her eyes and mouth closed for a moment. She looked at my and my sister's terrified faces. Then she tightly grabbed my arm. "She wasn't a woman. I don't know what she was. It all happened so fast. But kids," a tear rolled down her cheek, "I—I saw your father die. I don't know who that man is that came back to us."

Dread filled my entire body. It felt as if a dark blanket was falling over us. I heard my mother's words, but I just couldn't believe her. I didn't want to.

Suddenly I heard the door slam shut. Olivia got up and pulled out her phone. She was just about to call an ambulance when my father walked into the room.

My mother's face changed again. She was smiling, genuinely smiling.

"M-Mum isn't feeling well. I'm calling a doctor for her," Olivia said with a trembling voice. She looked at me, and I saw how afraid she was of my dad. She was trying to get us out of here.

My father took the phone from her hand and shook his head. "No need. Your mother is fine. Everything is perfectly fine. I was actually thinking we could go to the cinema again tonight."

I forced my body to get up. "That sounds like a fine idea. I haven't seen the new *Hunger Games* movie yet. How about that one?"

He smiled. "That sounds like a terrific idea."

"Yeah, I haven't seen it yet, either," Olivia added. "Can you get our coats from upstairs, Dad?"

He got up without a word and walked up the stairs. Olivia and I each grabbed one of my mother's arms. Together we quickly walked her outside and got her into the car, still wearing our pajamas and no shoes.

"Where are we going?" my mother asked from the backseat.

"We're going to visit Uncle Freddy," Olivia answered in a shaky voice.

"But, honey, we can't just leave your dad here. He'll get lonely."

I JOINED THE ADULTS' TABLE FOR THE FIRST TIME THIS YEAR

"It's not blood that binds us but tradition. Customs that we live by, that we cherish and pass on to our children when they grow old enough. Tradition is everything to this family, and as you are a part of it, you have no choice but to value and live by our rules."

That's literally what I've been told on the car ride to each family function we've ever had. I'm not kidding. Either my father or mother will say those exact same words. One time I jokingly said them myself before either of them could, but then my mum repeated them anyway, acting like she didn't hear me.

They emphasize the importance of tradition so much because they know I can't stand our holiday evening with the extended family. To be honest, I can't stand those people in general. You see, my extended family is incredibly odd. They always have been, forever will be, and every time I see their peculiar faces, I notice even more how strange everything about them is. Especially now that I am growing older.

My grandma was a horrible woman; my uncles are greedy, rude men; my aunts do nothing but pick you apart. And don't even get me started on my cousins. Loud, annoying, and incredibly disgusting little kids that make one evening together feel like being stuck inside a dreadful school cafeteria for an entire month. Luckily, I don't see them often. We only ever get together during the holidays in December. So technically it's not a bad deal, a night spent with the sticky cousins for a year of peace from this family.

My aunt Margaret always hosts. It used to be my grandmother before she passed away a few years ago. As my aunt inherited the house, she also took over the pleasure of being the host for holidays.

"Welcome home, my lovelies!" Aunt Margaret stood on the porch of the familiar old house as we got out of the car. Her red hair was blow-dried, and she was wearing a violet dress that looked like it should have been left in the fifties as well as Grandma's familiar apron with lemons on it.

Mum jumped up the stairs with the kind of energy she never usually has and gave her sister a big hug. Dad followed with the bottle of wine they bought in one hand and a bouquet of flowers in the other.

"Happy holidays, Margie!" he said as he gave her a kiss on the cheek. Everything was exactly the same as always, which meant that I was next.

Margaret waited for me as I made the last step up the stairs to the porch, then she gave me a hug so tight that I felt this morning's breakfast moving up to my throat. Her lavender perfume wasn't exactly helping the sudden nausea I got.

"Oh, Mel, how big you've grown!" she said through those lipstick-stained teeth. "How old are you now? Sixteen?"

I nodded.

"Yeah, my birthday was a month ago."

It's not like any of them sent a card or bothered to call.

"Still a little too young, I suppose," she whispered, and I felt her hot breath against my ear.

As we got into the spacious entry hall, more uncles and aunts appeared to greet us. Kids were running around, playing, and it already felt like being inside a zoo.

I got two wet kisses from Aunt Tully and Trudy, the twins, as well as a handshake from each of their respective spouses. Uncle Ted and Uncle Theo, who both smelled like ashtrays, gave me hugs and made some stupid jokes as the entire company made their way to the winter garden where the rest of the adults were having a drink. That's where we usually sat around to do chit-chat before dinner time.

I could already feel the headache settle in as well as the fear that Margaret might want my help when a hand grabbed me and pulled me back.

"Matteo!" I exclaimed happily. I was already afraid he somehow got out of coming this year. Matteo's the only cousin that I could actually stand. Maybe because he's the only one that was almost my age, less than two years older. Usually, he was the only one that made dinner a little fun for me, but last year my only decent cousin was invited to the adults' table while I had to stay with the kids. The table arrangement is a pretty big deal to this family; we don't even sit in the same rooms.

My cousin looked exactly the same as last year, only an inch or two taller. From our looks, you'd never guess that we're related. Matteo has dark, curly hair; mine is straight and blond. He has blue eyes; mine are brown. He's pale, and I'm tan. The only thing we have in common is the absurd clothes we have to wear because of the dress code. My mother left the purple satin dress with a bow around the waist on my bed this morning, and with it, I had to put on those horrible black patent shoes. Matteo wore a black shirt, and around his neck was the bow tie in the same shade of purple as my dress.

Our family color.

"Come with me," Matteo whispered, and I followed. We walked all the way through the house to the garden, which was on the opposite side of the building to the winter garden, where the rest of the family was.

We sat down on the stairs that led down to the grass, and Matteo pulled out something from his pocket.

He grinned as he showed me the joint he apparently rolled this morning.

"Wanna start our own family tradition?"

I anxiously looked back at the house.

"They won't notice, don't worry," he said and pulled out a lighter.

"So how have you been the past year?" he asked after we sat there for a while.

I shrug. "Pretty much the same as always, how about you?"

"Yeah, same. You know, I wanted to call you the other day. Couldn't find your number anywhere, though. When I asked my dad, he just said no."

Like I said, our families only ever get together during the holidays. We're never in touch except for that.

"He said no?" I laughed, but Matteo stayed serious.

"Weird, right? I also tried to find you online but without luck. Anyway, do you remember the last time we were here?" he said while biting his nail.

"Uhm, yeah. But we didn't really talk then. Remember I had to stay at the kiddies' table?"

Now his eyes opened wide.

"You didn't eat with us?"

"Okay, how much of this did you smoke?" I laughed again.

"It's so weird, Mel, I hardly remember last year, and when we got ready to drive down today, I felt so strange about—"

"There you guys are!" a shrill voice behind us interrupted him.

"Aunt Margie," I said, trying to think of an excuse already, but she didn't seem to care what we were doing.

"The sun's almost down! Come on, come on, it's dinner time!"

We got up, and she put her arms around each of us. "Mel, honey, I know you're still a little young but turns out your uncle Tobias didn't make it, so we have a spare seat at our table! Isn't that marvelous?"

And so I finally was invited to sit with the adults of the family for dinner.

I'd never been inside the dining room before; it was much more spacious than I imagined. The wooden table in the middle of the room could seat at least ten more people; I didn't understand why I was never allowed to sit with them before.

The room was next to the one for the children, though we didn't hear a sound from next door. Around this time, they were probably already being served the food by the kitchen staff. No fancy food. At the kids' table, we always got chicken nuggets, fries, stuff like that. I was curious to see what the adults were eating.

I sat down next to my mother, who smiled with her mouth but not with her eyes. On the opposite side of the table was Matteo, who looked confused, which at that moment I blamed on the weed.

I looked at the table in front of me and was surprised to see that there was no food. No cutlery, either.

We all had one plate with a little black box on it. I reached for it, but before I knew what was happening, Margaret appeared beside me and slapped my hand.

"Not yet."

When I looked up again, I noticed that all the adults were watching me. I swallowed, suddenly wishing I was in the other room with the kids. The atmosphere in the room was so tense, and I didn't understand why.

Until Margaret took a seat at the head of the table.

"Welcome, family. It's not blood that binds us but tradition. Customs that we live by, that we cherish and pass on to our children when they grow old enough. Tradition is everything to this family, and as you are a part of it, you have *no choice* but to value and live by our rules."

I swallowed.

"I realize it hasn't been the same since Mother left," she continued. "She was the heart of our holiday, after all, but with all the obstacles thrown my way, I still try to do my best."

"And you do it so wonderfully!" Trudy shouted out in glee, although something about her speech pattern sounded forced.

"Why thank you, sister. I am glad to see our family grow." She looked at me when she said that, and for some reason, a shiver went down my spine.

"Should we help you serve dinner?" I asked so that the awkward moment would pass by more quickly.

Everyone laughed in response.

Confused, I looked at Matteo, but his expression was empty.

"Now, family. It is time for our tradition. Please open your boxes."

Everyone immediately grabbed the box in front of them, so I did the same.

I lifted the upper part only to realize that it was empty. I looked over at Mom's, and it was empty, too. So were the ones of Dad, Matteo, and pretty much everyone else, it appeared.

Except for Theo's.

He'd dropped the lid and rested his hands on the table. Aunt Margaret got up and walked toward my uncle to take out what was lying inside the box.

A knife.

She smiled at Theo, who turned his hands around so that his palms were facing upward. With the knife, she cut inside his left hand first, then the right hand. Theo moved his hands up above the plate in front of him so that the blood from the fresh wound would be collected inside of it.

I felt incredibly uneasy, close to throwing up. The weirdest part about all of it was the fact that nobody reacted. They stayed still, sitting, watching. And as I looked through the room, I realized that I was doing the same thing.

I opened my mouth to speak, but no words came out. I tried to move, but my body wouldn't listen. We continued watching as Aunt Margaret dipped her index finger into the blood and started drawing a strange symbol on Theo's forehead.

She whispered words I didn't understand, and when she was done, Theo finally got up from his chair, and the two of them started hugging.

"For this year, you will be mine. If you prove worthy, we will all meet again during our holiday in the next year," she finally said.

The rest of the evening felt even stranger. Aunt Margaret led Theo upstairs, where his hands were cleaned and sewn. After they came back, the kitchen staff started serving the food.

There was roast, goose, and duck. Mashed potatoes, gravy, and green beans. Pudding, cakes, and biscuits. Food that you might find if you looked up *festive dinner* online.

The family started laughing and putting food on their plates.

But nobody ate. I'm not even sure if any of the food was edible.

They were merely acting out a dinner party, and even though I knew something was wrong, even though I felt the fear growing and growing inside of me, I couldn't do anything but join. Join the fake dinner and the fake laughter. It was as if something else was controlling me.

This continued until late at night when we finally started saying our goodbyes. We hugged, kissed, shook hands, and then every family got inside their respective cars.

"Mel, you need to listen very carefully. As soon as we are far enough away, we will forget everything that happened tonight." My mother spoke calmly as my father started pulling out of the driveway.

"Mum, what the hell? What was that? Why—" I felt my heart racing inside my chest. All my thoughts felt scrambled.

"Mel, listen!" my father shouted. He was holding the steering wheel so tight that his knuckles got all white. He was trying hard not to shake as he slowly started the gas. Aunt Margaret was standing on the porch watching us.

The other family members were inside their cars, all in front of us. Except for Theo. I saw him through the window. He stood there with an expression of fear and hopelessness in his eyes.

"This is not our family. We are not related to those people. We come here each year. We don't know why. We once got tricked into it, and every year since, we get in the car on that particular day and we arrive at this house," my mother said.

I wanted to say something but decided to stay quiet instead.

"We forget about everything as soon as we leave, and the next year we drive here again. Whatever we do, they manage to pull us back here. We believe the same is happening to those other people who you think are your aunts and uncles, but we don't know for sure," she continued.

"We have no way out of this. And now they have decided that you are an adult," my father said. He was driving so slowly that I could still see Margaret waving through the exterior mirror of the car.

"Dad, why are you going so slow?" I whispered. The sight of her was scaring me even more now. My entire body felt like it was simultaneously frozen and on fire.

"As soon as we leave the street, we will forget. We just wanted you to know, even if you will forget, that we are sorry, and we should have told you sooner. We thought we had another year before they declared you an adult."

"What's going to happen to Theo?" I finally dared to ask.

"We might see him again next year. If things go well for him. If she is happy. She'll let him leave, and he will be replaced by another family member."

All those years I remembered our odd family dinners. Except I was never a part of the real tradition. I was with the kids, which were annoying but not horrifying.

All those thoughts were racing through my mind. Matteo knew that something was wrong, but he couldn't communicate it; he couldn't remember everything. I closed my eyes as we drove down the street and made a turn. I held my breath almost all the way until we were on the freeway.

"Were you ever chosen?" I finally asked. "Did one of you ever stay with her?"

I knew that made little sense because if my parents were gone for a year I'm sure I would have remembered.

"I am so full. What an incredible dinner," my father suddenly said.

"I know, right? How does Margie do it?" My mum rubbed her stomach and giggled.

"Mum, Dad?" I whispered.

"Next year we should contribute. Maybe I could bake something," she continued.

They never spoke about it again. When speaking of family, they would only repeat that bullshit about tradition. Of course, I tried to tell them, but they'd forgotten everything right away and looked at me as if I was losing my mind.

But I remember everything.

I'm not sure why—maybe because I technically joined the adults a year early. I know that my parents must know as well, buried somewhere deep inside of them. I notice the twitch in their eye when I speak about Margaret or any of the other *family* members.

I have tried so much, though, and convincing them seems next to impossible. I finally gave up and decided to start looking for Matteo instead.

So far I've had no luck. No phone number and I haven't found any of his social media, either.

It's gotten so far that I almost started believing my parents. Believing that I was imagining things, that I was losing my mind.

However, almost before I gave up, I did find something else.

I remembered that one person never showed up to dinner.

Uncle Tobias.

So again, after a lot of research, I found something about this man who I don't believe is related to us, either. And I believe that a part of him knew what he might have been facing that day.

He never showed up because he committed suicide on the day of the family dinner.

DEATH OCCURS FAR TOO OFTEN IN MY TOWN, AND THE PEOPLE DON'T CARE

Part 1

Our people are accustomed to death. Well, you have to be if it occurs so unnaturally regularly. Not only to the elderly but simply in general. Mourning is done discreetly and often only by the closest kin.

When you grow up knowing what decomposed flesh smells like, you get used to it, as morbid as it might sound. And I'm not saying someone drops dead every day; our town would have shrunk significantly if that was the case. No, there are rather deadly periods. If you are lucky, you won't be actively involved in one. Usually, if members of your family have been in the past, you won't get the same fate. Although it does mean you were raised by traumatized people, which isn't necessarily better.

Depending on your preferences.

Now of course you could move away. Many have done so in the past, but it doesn't shield you. Death is omnipresent and not bound to borders. At least not when it comes to Drenfield. Here it is bound to your blood and genes.

It's not a curse. Not technically, although it definitely feels like one. It's the consequences of a promise made a long time ago.

A time in which every single child and baby in Drenfield became awfully sick without a warning and without any exceptions. An entire generation would have died in a matter of a week, and there was no doctor that could find a solution to the epidemic they were facing. Until the hunter came.

That's what we call him, even today. Even now that we live in a much more progressed time.

The hunter came and promised to heal all the children if the people of Drenfield made one promise. When the time came, they would join him and hunt. At random, whenever it was necessary, a number of people would become hunters. Usually not more than a handful. And a few more people would be hunted.

And well, considering I introduced all this by telling you how accustomed we are to death, I suppose you can imagine what happens then.

I realize it all sounds like massive bullshit, and it probably is. To a logical, thinking person. To the people of this place, it is the only way they believe to save future generations and live. Together, healthy and happy. As long as it's not hunting season.

Because back then, the hunter didn't only save all those children; he made sure no child of Drenfield blood would ever become sick again. Even adults hardly ever feel unwell. People don't even catch a cold.

And now you might wonder if it's a coincidence, if the hunter really existed or if this is a fairytale the townspeople have grown so used to that it became some sort of self-fulfilling prophecy. Though the custom of hunting and killing to stay healthy would be some hell of a placebo.

Either way, most people are happy with the chances they get; the hunters that are picked are always more than ready. The prey tries to run, but they never get far.

Other than the occasional loss of members, life really isn't too shabby here, though. Small towns tend to be boring, but not Drenfield. There is always something to do here.

There is the cinema, which has a special night of horror once a week. The movies go all the way from your conventional slasher to the more artsy, messed-up tales. My friends and I go at least once a month. Needless to say, we are not exactly sensitive to seeing blood.

Then we have the occasional carnival with adrenaline-inducing rides. A place where we fill our bodies with sugar and grease because nobody's parents tell them to have a healthy diet. We have no rules when it comes to living. Not really.

Of course, there are less gruesome things to do, too. Like going to the three-story-high bookstore, visiting the mall, or trying out different sports in the community club.

The bookstore is where I met Cal about five months ago. Cal was new to town, a son of a former Drenfield family that tried to get away. Cal's mum was chosen as a hunter; she received the letter all the way across the sea. I don't know if she said no or what exactly happened. It is something he doesn't like to talk about. All I know is that both of Cal's parents are dead now.

After the family got blood on their hands despite trying to get away, his grandparents decided to move back with him. After all, at least now the possibility was smaller that Cal would be chosen.

"Wanna watch a movie? Tess and the others are going."

Cal and I would usually hang out alone, just as we did that evening. Just chilling at my home, playing Nintendo.

He rolled his eyes.

"Of course they are. Shouldn't they have seen every fucking movie by now?"

Needless to say, Cal wasn't too fond of my friends.

"Well, not everyone is such a wuss as you. You can't even watch *Coraline*," I joked.

Cal was the only person I'd ever met who was scared of horror movies. It's one of the reasons my friends didn't like him very much when I introduced him for the first time. He was just too different in all the wrong ways, according to them. It was quite the opposite for me. I thought it was fantastic to meet a person that grew up somewhat normal.

"At least I'm not a psychopath," he responded, eyes glued to the screen in front of us. He said it in such a harsh tone it almost made me feel judged, too, but then he turned over slightly and grinned.

I didn't really care that much what my friends thought of him. Honestly, they could be a bit over the top at times anyway. They are the kind of friends you have because you grew up together. Although not all of them were that bad.

Tess was a bit too nosy. She questioned Cal about his parents two minutes after she met him. Hence, he kinda likes her the least. Joe and Mel are the more introverted ones of the group; I probably get along best with Mel. I think she used to have a little crush on me when we were younger. And then there is Marcus, who is Tess' cousin. He is probably the most unpredictable one, ranging from overly friendly to borderline aggressive.

A fun mixture of individuals, I would say. You might think Cal would fit in, too, but there just seems to be a wall between their personalities.

I'm what you'd call someone who always chooses the middle. I usually get along with everyone just fine but never intensely well.

That is until Cal came along, which is probably why I was even more scared for him than I was for myself. On the day that we heard the announcement.

There were letters coming in. A new round of a hunt and it could hit any of us.

***

This would be the third time that I would witness one. I hardly knew any of the hunters or prey of the last ones except for one. Never imagined my elementary school teacher to be a cold-blooded murderer. She was more the kind of woman to encourage you to draw rainbows and who wore those big hippie glasses and colorful skirts. Well, people can surprise you.

The letters would come that evening, and I spent it over at Cal's. I almost felt as nervous as his grandmother, who kept tapping her long nails on the wooden kitchen table.

"Luca, hon, shouldn't you be at home as well? Let's pray they won't, but your family might receive a letter as well."

My great-grandfather on Dad's side had been hunted. My grandma on Mum's side was once a hunter. I had never met either. They passed away before I was born, but it meant that chances were low that a member of my family would be picked. The same family isn't chosen often.

"I'll go in a bit," I lied, knowing I would wait until after eight when the letters are shoved under the doors.

The ticking of the clock in the kitchen was only occasionally interrupted by Cal's grandmother's nails. Other than that, we were all quiet. Cal somehow seemed the calmest.

And then it happened.

The hand of the clock moved to one minute past eight.

There was no letter. I expected to see Cal smile, but his expression didn't change a bit.

"It's not me, but it doesn't mean it's not happening," he said at the door before I left.

The chances of being chosen as a member of society under the age of twenty-five are high. Sometimes older ones get assigned but very seldom. For some unspeakable reason, young people kill and get murdered more often here. Still, I wasn't expecting to be either of those.

It didn't make sense with the probabilities, but I assume I miscalculated. Because when I came home, the letter was waiting for me, and both of my parents were crying.

———

Another month of death was about to be initiated. That is the time the hunters have to murder the prey. Each one receives an individual list of victims. They may decide to kill them all, but they have to choose at least one. They can also decide to let them live for the month and remove them on the last day or start on the first morning of the killing month.

Again, it depends on people's preferences. I don't think either option is that great, though. For some, the first day is used for the prey to start running. To a different city, to a different country. If they choose to run, they will be dead before the last night of the month. No exceptions. If they take their chances and stay, they might not be picked by a hunter. As you might be able to tell, I'm quite interested in probabilities. They are not often in my favor, though, as I started to learn.

I didn't tell any of my friends about my letter. Not even Cal.

I figured they would find out soon enough.

The month begins exactly three days after the letters are handed out, which meant I still had at least three days.

———

Even before the official start, the festivities are initiated. Yeah, you heard right. It is almost like Halloween. People start decorating their homes, many start throwing parties, and people dress up in masks and costumes.

It's all very morbid, but people don't want to appear as if they are against the system. They know there's no way to change it either way, so they might as well go all in.

If an outsider came to town, they'd probably just think we're very whimsical.

"So do I need to clean your blood off the streets anytime soon?" Cal joked as we walked to school next to each other. He still had no idea.

Normally, I would have made some joke, but that morning I didn't really feel like it. I hadn't slept one minute the night before.

I could tell that he knew something was up, but he didn't push it. At the entrance, we split up. He went to chemistry, and I made my way to biology class. People had started drawing slurs on lockers in bloody print.

I'm coming for you first, asshole.

Do you still think I'm that fat? Better watch out.

R U N

Some people fear the day that a letter may come in; some of Drenfield's people, however, wait their whole life to be picked as a hunter.

In class, I sat down next to Mel. She looked almost worse than me. Eyes bloodshot. Leg shaking nervously. At least that's what I thought at first.

"Fuck, did you get a letter, Mel?" I whispered.

She looked at me with an empty expression in her eyes, but then her thin lips grew into a massive grin.

"I sure did." She giggled. Then she proceeded to open her bag to show me what she was hiding inside.

Knives, brass knuckles, and a rope.

"I know I'm supposed to make it look like suicides." She rolled her eyes and laughed again.

I got up from my seat and left class. I didn't look back until I made it to the exit of the school.

She said *suicides*.

She wasn't planning on killing only one. She was going to enjoy being a hunter.

I kept walking all the way home, trying to ignore all the gory decorations on people's homes. Some even put up real animal cadavers, it seemed.

Just in front of our house, I stumbled into our neighbor's daughter. Clara.

She smiled when she saw me. Clara was only eight but incredibly smart and unbelievably sweet.

"Hey, Luca. Are you excited?" she asked.

I shook my head.

"Aw, why not? Uncle Toby is. You know he got chosen even though he is way old!" She giggled.

"Did he now?"

She nodded.

"He is making a special room for them with toys and everything. One that locks from inside."

I swallowed. It seemed that the hunters were overly excited this season.

Cal came over that evening. Unannounced. He wanted to know why I wasn't in school even though we went there together this morning.

I just sat there, in my bed. I had no idea how to tell him. But I didn't need to; he could tell.

"You got a letter."

I couldn't even remember the last time I'd cried, but at that moment I couldn't hold back anymore.

"Fuck."

***

The following days went by like a fever dream. My friends kept calling and texting, asking me to hang out, and I ignored all of them. Especially Mel, even though she was the most persistent. She couldn't wait for a moment together alone, which clearly wasn't happening. Not after I saw the bloodthirst in her eyes.

I already knew Mel was a hunter, and I knew of our neighbor Toby. I also knew who was picked for prey, but I tried to shut it out. There wasn't much time left, though; the hunt would officially begin tonight at twelve.

That evening, Mel stood in front of my house.

"Luca, come out to play! Don't be a bore!"

I stood behind the window, and the second our eyes met, I felt like throwing up.

Finally, though, I opened the door.

"Fuck off, Mel."

She frowned her eyebrows in a playful way.

"I thought we were friends, Luca."

There were only fifteen minutes left.

"All right, come inside. We'll talk."

She ran all the way, probably afraid that I might change my mind. Inside, she slammed the door shut.

"Jeez, Mel, my parents are upstairs," I lied. My parents had left town that morning. They said they couldn't be here to witness it, and I couldn't exactly blame them.

"I know why you're hiding. You're scared," she said in a playful voice. "But you don't have to be. You know Marcus is on the list? He can be such an asshole sometimes."

Her hand was holding a kitchen knife. One of those that could probably cut through glass.

I tried to stay confident, but my palms were sweating like crazy.

"You don't have to do this, Mel. You're not like that. You're—"

"Nice? Sweet? Fuck off, Luca. You never actually cared about me, but now for once, we can mean something."

"Of course I care about you! You're one of my best friends."

She rolled her eyes. "Well, if we're such great buddies, why didn't you tell me about your letter?"

I gulped. "Because I don't want to be a part of this."

She shook her head. "Oh, Luca, you know you have no choice, right?"

And as she said those words, the first announcement started blasting all over town.

Beloved members of Drenfield, there are only five minutes left! Five minutes!

She held up the knife and raised an eyebrow. "It's almost time."

It was getting loud outside. People were on the street, cheering and laughing. It was almost like some festival.

As the noises started getting louder, I finally took my chance and grabbed the knife from her hand.

Her eyes opened wide with excitement, but before she could do anything, Cal surprised her from behind. He had been upstairs in my room this whole time. He slung his arms around her while I got the rope.

Then we locked her in the bathroom.

It wasn't the best plan, but what else were we supposed to do?

***

"Are you ready?" Cal asked, and I nodded.

We grabbed the bags from my room and made our way outside to his car.

At that moment, the public announcement started blasting through town.

Hunting season has now officially begun! We proudly announce our newest hunters... Abigail Morrow, Rania Lizzen, Melanie Smith, Tobias Gorden, and Luca Anderson. Our list of prey is long this year. Please help our hunters the best you can to wipe out Gina Isana, Marcus—

I didn't need to hear the rest. I knew all the names. I had received the names of prey with my invitation to be a hunter.

Something I knew I would never be able to become. No matter the price.

***

Nobody stopped us. Why would they? I was the one that was supposed to be hunting, after all. We left that godforsaken town, but if you paid attention, you know that it won't help me. I'm only stalling for time.

A hunter must hunt or soon they will become prey themselves. I suppose I didn't outrun my fate; it only got delayed.

As I said, death isn't exactly bound to borders.

Part 2

You can't run away from death. If it has you in its grip, holding you tight, you won't get away no matter how hard you try. And if you are from the place where I was born, you can't run away from murdering anyone, either. Because yesterday, the hunting season in Drenfield had begun. And we weren't hunting animals.

"You know we'll have to go back eventually, right?" Cal finally broke the silence.

You might think that my mind was racing, twisting and turning, thinking about what to do and what not to, where to go, and who to leave behind. But no, it wasn't. It was entirely blank. As soon as we drove over the border of the town, my mind was silent. There were so many things I needed to be afraid of. I suppose when you are completely overwhelmed, you just shut down.

Cal hadn't pushed me so far. He kept looking forward, out into the dark road in front of us. I wasn't even sure where he was driving or if he had a destination in mind at all.

"I have a month. Well, minus one day," I responded.

"Well, yeah, to be a hunter. But I meant more because of the psychopath that we locked into your bathroom. If we don't go back, we'll have a murder on both our hands in a while. And it won't even count. How long does it take for someone to die of thirst?"

"Approximately three to five days. But I'm sure someone will find her by then."

"Okay, I didn't expect such a quick answer. Well, if they do, wouldn't that be worse?"

"She might kill Marcus," I whispered.

Now my brain finally began to work again, and the thoughts couldn't be stopped. I had no plan. We had no plan. And that was probably the scariest part of it all. My destiny was determined.

We found a motel somewhere on the side of a road in the middle of nowhere and decided to stay there for the rest of the night.

We were safe. Cal was on no list, and I had a month before I would be punished if I didn't kill anyone. Nobody was after us.

We were safe. I kept telling myself that, hoping that eventually I would believe it. But deep down, I knew that I was lying to myself. Nobody was really safe during this month.

I hadn't slept much the night before, but I didn't feel tired. Cal laid down in bed right away, so I turned off the lights.

"Luca?" I heard him whisper. "Where did your parents go?"

I swallowed.

We were lying in the dark motel room, with only a shimmer of light from a streetlamp shining through the thin shades of the only window the room had.

"I don't know. They didn't tell me; they didn't really say goodbye. Only left a note."

I hadn't told him about that before. Of course, he knew that my parents left so they wouldn't witness what would happen in this month of pain and torture, but I suppose it was still weird. They left their teenage son alone.

I was never the kind of person to open up much. I mostly kept to myself; even my closest friends had no idea who I was on the inside, although to be fair, after seeing Mel getting completely kill-crazy, I guess I wasn't the only one wearing a mask.

"Cal, I wanna ask you something, but you don't have to answer."

He turned over slightly.

"You wanna know if my mum killed anyone?" he blurted out. For a second, I thought he would get mad, but he actually sounded quite okay.

"I kinda guessed she didn't," I said, "but I don't understand what happened to your father. Was he prey?" I regretted those words right after they left my mouth. It was just so disgusting to use that word to describe a person. I've always hated it.

"She did kill someone. Herself."

Now I turned to my left to face him.

"I guess she thought that would end it. She couldn't bear taking some-one's life. Well, that's what my grandmother told me. I was only one when it happened. To be honest, I don't even remember my parents."

"Cal—"

"The following day, my father was murdered. My grandparents were always very open with me when it came to the topic of death. I suppose everyone who grew up in Drenfield is." He breathed out loudly. "They told me about the mark he had on his face. The mark of death left by the hunter who came to get him. Apparently, after what my mother did, he was added to the list of prey."

I wanted to say something, but there were no words that could describe how I was feeling. No words sufficient to demonstrate how sorry I was. But then another thought popped into my head.

"Wait, I thought your parents passed away recently. Isn't that why you moved back to Drenfield?"

"Yeah I kinda made it sound like that, but to be honest, it was only recently that I convinced my grandparents for us to come back."

I wasn't even born when it happened, but now that he told me, a lot more started making sense. An important piece of my family's history, it seemed, was connected to Cal's.

"You knew who I was the first time we met, didn't you?" Now my heart was racing so fast that I thought I might throw up.

Suddenly I knew exactly who had killed Cal's parents.

A cold shiver went down my spine. Had I made a mistake by trusting him? I suppose it didn't matter. I was already a dead man walking.

To my surprise, Cal grabbed my hand and squeezed it so gently and kindly, it didn't feel he had any hate in him.

"Yes. But I figured out very quickly that you weren't like the others here. We are all bound to Drenfield by blood, not by choice."

The following day, my decision was clear. Running away was not an op-tion. Especially not with Cal.

I wasn't entirely sure why he had come with me in the first place, but as much as I tried to tell myself to be wary, I still trusted him.

After a vending machine breakfast, we were sitting in the car again.

"Are you really sure this is what we should do?" Cal asked.

"No. It's what I should do. You shouldn't be involved in any of it."

"Well, buddy," he grinned, "it's too late for that. I'm already on Team Luca."

I don't know why, it was probably completely crazy, but some part of me felt content. We certainly wasted some time and money by leaving for only one night if we were going back already, but somehow, now far away from Drenfield, we were both craving to go back. It was a strange sensation, but being away during the season felt worse than being surrounded by the murderous atmosphere.

Yeah, my initial instinct was to run away. Get as far from that town of horror as I possibly could and take Cal away from what was about to go down there because I had seen enough of it to know that not a single horror movie could compete with the reality of Drenfield, but at least now we had a plan. Even if it wasn't a good one.

"Well, let's go and catch some hunters."

For me, the sight of the town wasn't exactly surprising. Despite being rather young during past hunts, I still remembered them pretty vividly. It looks like an exciting festival as long as you don't know what the true meaning behind all the decorations and events is. For Cal, this was all new. New and frightening.

We passed the invisible border into the outskirts of town. While there were decorations hanging from the few houses and children running on the street with plastic toy weapons, it still appeared somewhat normal. Like a neighborhood celebrating Halloween in summer. But I knew the center would be different. My only hope was that the hunters were taking their time. At least two of the hunters were not going for prey just yet, one by choice and one by being tied down with a rope.

"Why don't we just get the outside world involved? Take pictures? Get help?"

I wondered why he never asked any questions like that before; that's what most logical people would do. Still, I couldn't help but roll my eyes.

"Cal. We live in a town where people like to murder because some hunter healed their children decades ago. A town in which every single person that doesn't obey the rules mysteriously dies. You think if getting someone from the outside to help was an option we would still live like maniacs?"

Cal didn't answer. At first, I thought I pissed him off, but I wasn't the reason for his silence. He was distracted by something else. Something that suddenly made him brake the car out of nowhere, almost giving me whiplash.

We came to a stop on a street close to the center of town. Only five minutes by foot from the marketplace.

"What the fuck?" I shouted. There was nothing in front of us.

Cal didn't look at me. He suddenly seemed frozen.

"Dude, what's wrong? There's nothing on the street."

"Not in front of us," he mumbled, and then he pointed his finger to the roof of the car. "Above."

I opened my door and took a step outside. And then I saw what had shocked Cal so much that apparently, his blood started freezing.

The first corpse.

As we figured out later. This was the first man to die during this year's hunting season.

A young man, wearing a sweater from our high school. A rope had been put right around his neck, and he was hanging down from the traffic light. We couldn't recognize his face because they had put a sack over it with some symbol sprayed on it.

Cal stumbled out of the car and immediately fell to his knees as he started puking his guts out on the side of the road. I wanted to go to him, tell him everything was okay. I had seen scenarios like this since I was a child. I should have been somewhat okay, but as Cal had been frozen from the inside at first, now it was my turn. With my eyes glued to the dead body hanging right above my head, my fists were clenched so tight that my nails started digging into my skin. But I couldn't feel the pain.

The only thing I could think about was whether that dead person was my friend Marcus.

"You fucking assholes!"

"You promised you wouldn't shout, Mel. Do you want me to tape your mouth shut again?"

"You left me here for half a day! You do realize people need to fucking piss, right?"

Mel's entire body was trembling with hate.

"I'm no prey, Luca. You will die. You will die if you keep being such a fucking moron."

"I'm sorry, Mel," I said and really meant it. I didn't want to torture her like this, but I couldn't have her go and murder people.

"—and I will die, too. If you keep me locked up here. I *am* a hunter."

Cal stayed quiet the entire time. I thought that Mel would at least verbally attack him, considering her hands were still tight up, but she didn't even look at him. She was completely focused on me. She wanted to manipulate me.

If we let her go, she wouldn't simply go and kill one person. She would go through that entire list of prey.

That's why we had to stop the hunters. We had to figure out a way to stop this entire mess.

"It's getting dark. Are you gonna be okay with Mel while I check out the hut?" Cal asked.

I nodded.

"But be careful."

***

We need to stop them, at all costs.

That's what I kept telling myself when I stood in front of my neighbor Toby's toy room with matches in one hand and a gallon of gas in the other. It was three a.m., and the street was sleeping. The music had stopped hours ago, and as far we knew there were no other victims just yet.

The toy room was a wooden hut in my neighbors' backyard. Normally, they had some barbecue equipment, toys of Clara's, and other stuff in there. Now it was filled with knives, saws, hammers. All things that would be totally normal inside a shed. Except these were all stained with blood.

That's what Cal told me.

I didn't go into the toy room. I figured I had seen enough gore for one day.

When Cal came back earlier this evening, he told me that Toby wasn't around when he went into the hut. He was inside the house with his family. In all honesty, the plan we had wasn't well thought through, but we didn't have that much time. We decided that I would call Toby and invite him over.

To toast to the month of death with a drink. A drink I had spiked earlier. After he passed out, we tied him up and brought him to a room in the basement. Tomorrow we would figure out what exactly to do with him and Mel and how to keep them under somewhat humane circumstances.

We were creating our own little collection of murderers here.

I repeat, our plan was not very well thought through, but at least now two of the hunters were hidden inside my home. We'd have to think of something to do when people started looking for them, but that was a problem for another day.

We wanted to finish this day on a different note. Namely by sending out a sign into the air by burning down the toy room of that damn Toby Gorden.

So that's what brought me to my neighbors' garden with the gas and the matches to burn down damn Toby Gordon's toy room. Cal asked if I could be the one to actually do it because as a hunter I probably wouldn't get in trouble, which was fine with me. Honestly, it felt pretty freeing to watch the fire and to know that I would be going back inside later to tell Toby that his torture hut was gone.

I was a naïve idiot.

I should have known by the smell. I should have known that Cal wasn't to be trusted.

As the smoke and the foul smell filled our neighborhood, the Gordons stood outside watching their garden hut burn down. Other neighbors were joining them, attracted by the fire. Nobody seemed to mind it; no, quite the opposite—they were cheering and clapping.

Mrs. Gorden was telling everyone how proud she was of her brother. Not only had he found prey so soon into the month and tied them up in his toy room, he now could proudly say that he fulfilled his duty as a hunter.

Except there was one thing that only Cal and Toby knew. And that I was understanding at that moment.

The person, the prey, had been alive in the hut, and it was my first kill, not Toby's.

I WORK IN A LAMP STORE

Part 1

Simply reading the title, you might be wondering right now, *Why the hell would a store selling lamps even be opened at night?* I know because that is exactly what I asked my boss when he offered me the so-called promotion.

"When do you think people need light the most, you silly goose? When it is dark out, of course!"

I'm not gonna lie, I didn't appreciate the way he talked to me, but luckily we were hardly ever inside at the same time. Mainly because it was such a tiny store you could only ever be inside with two or a maximum of three individuals without breaking a light while making a turn. Being cooped up in there with him wouldn't exactly be my fantasy.

To call my boss Mr. Nipps eccentric would be the literal definition of the word understatement. And his personality was reflected in each and every lightbulb and lamp inside this tiny store on Evergreen Avenue. I fell in love with it when I saw the shiny colors in the storefront that very first time I moved to this town. The store was right next door to a pub that we only visited once, and even though I may have been slightly intoxicated, I could have sworn I'd never seen such beautiful art in the form of light. And that was only from the outside.

Hell did I know that I could have simply walked in that night! Seeing that we are apparently open at those times. I did, however, wait until two days later when my hangover had passed but not my curiosity and fortunately miserably drained wallet. Because you see when I came in during the day, the lights were off but the architecture of the lamps stood. It was the very first time I met this peculiar man named Mr. Nipps.

I reached my hand for this gorgeous lamp that was entirely made out of broken mirror pieces when I looked to my right and noticed his pointy nose which was perfectly in line with his only slightly less pointy chin. I looked up and met his eyes, and he smiled, but it was that typical sleazy salesman smile.

He didn't speak but pointed toward a sign

Please do not touch the lamps before purchase.

"Sorry," I mumbled. "It's a really nice lamp. They all are. Do you make these?"

He shook his head.

"No dear, I simply have a good eye for them. And the right nose. It also tells me this lamp might be a little off your budget." He winked.

I would have been offended if he hadn't been entirely correct. This lamp cost more than most of my furniture together, and knowing myself it probably wouldn't have survived more than a few days with me anyway.

I smiled a polite smile and got ready to take off when Mr. Nipps offered to change that problem of mine. In time, of course.

"You seem to have a good eye, too. Not sure about the nose, but I can't be fussy. Would you like to work for me here?"

I certainly wouldn't be working just to afford one lamp. However, I did need work, and this seemed like the perfect place to spend some time while helping the occasional customer that might stumble in.

I accepted there and then. It wasn't much to think through. I needed money and had a lot of free time in between writing. Mr. Nipps gave me the quickest tour, taught me how the register worked, and honestly, that was mostly it. Of course, I was worried, but after working a few shifts alone inside the store full of art in the form of light, I realized something essential.

Nobody ever came in here with the intention to buy. And if they did, they left after seeing the prices.

Of course, the best time to visit us would be late in the afternoon or early in the evening when the combination of deep green, warm red, and bright blue would light up the walls and the ceiling. That's when a few customers would stumble in. They enjoyed the views, had a chat or two, and left again. I did like those times best. During the day, it just felt like a regular boring store, but when it got dark, it became a whole different world. I never worked later than seven, though, so I usually didn't have much time to enjoy it.

I believe that during all those months that I worked for Mr. Nipps, I only ever sold a few lightbulbs and a couple of the discount lamps. I never did ask him how the store was able to run as long as I received my paychecks each month. And with the store being empty most times, I also had lots of time to study.

Now after the initial confusion as to why we would sell lamps at night, I decided not to ask any more questions. Because, for one, Mr. Nipps never ever gave answers to my satisfaction, and second, because the pay would be double what I make now. I couldn't care less why this old gentleman wanted to be open even more to sell even less, but it was none of my business.

So I made my way through the dark to the one shop lighting up the entire street to start my first night shift. I would learn over time that work was surprisingly booming at night.

I assumed that Mr. Nipps would be there when I arrived, but the door was locked. I grabbed my key and opened up.

While I'd never worked at night, I did spend evenings here at times when it was dark out already in autumn and winter. Still, at this particular time, the Evergreen Lamp Store had a mysterious vibe to it. The lights were shining so warm. Some colors were bright, others felt matte, but it only added to the feeling of coziness.

I went behind the counter, logged into the register, and took a seat on the stool. I got the book that I brought from my bag, turned on some music, and got ready for a long night.

Before I knew it, two hours had passed already without a single customer walking inside, which to be fair was not exactly surprising. I got up from my stool and walked up to the door to open it and see if the pub next door was at least open.

I heard some faint music coming from next door, and I believe there were some people walking outside, but I couldn't tell for sure. The entire street was pitch black. Not even a single streetlamp lit up the area. The only light was coming from this peculiar lamp store that I was standing inside.

Which meant that I couldn't point out anyone but they could all see me.

I took a step back and closed the door. This was the first time that I felt a sense of fear. Only then something inside of me seemed to click.

Why exactly had I believed this situation to be acceptable? This was nowhere near regular. This wasn't a diner, a truck stop, or a convenience store but a place that sells lamps, for fuck's sake.

No soul could be thinking, *Well, this is the proper time to go and buy a luxurious, crystal lampstand.*

And I hardly knew anything about Mr. Nipps at all.

"Why are you only now starting to wake up?"

I lifted my head and noticed an older gentleman in the store. His ash-gray hair was half-hidden underneath a purple top hat, he was wearing thick round glasses, and he held a pocket watch in his hand.

"When did you come inside? I didn't even hear you."

He chuckled.

"I noticed. You seemed quite distracted. I do not believe I have seen you in here before. My name is George Golter, and I come here quite regularly."

"I usually only work day shifts. I'm Riley." I tried to smile, but I felt a strange sensation come over me. This whole situation felt so absurd.

"Oh, what a lovely name, Riley. Now I am glad to see some new eyes. The regular fella can be quite rough. Dear Riley, could you help me?"

"Help you with what?" I asked.

He laughed again.

"Well, I would like to purchase a lamp. Isn't that what this store is for?"

He raised an eyebrow.

"Uhm, yes of course. Sorry." I laughed. "I honestly didn't expect any customers around this time, I suppose."

"But you're the only light around! Where else would we go?"

He started walking around the small store, which suddenly seemed far bigger than it ever looked to my eyes before.

"Do you already have something specific in mind?" I asked while trying to act as normal as possible.

"Yes. Glass. Shattered."

"Excuse me?"

He came closer, his eyes piercing right through mine.

"You know which one I'm talking about. Don't act dumb."

I opened my mouth, but no words came out.

I did know which one he was talking about. The lamp made out of broken mirror pieces that I had my eyes on. Without saying anything, I guided him toward the small nightstand lamp.

"Splendid. It is even better than I expected. Bought!"

"Great," I mumbled. Just happy that he would be getting the hell out of here soon.

"So I guess we come to the next point now. There are three prospective receivers currently. A former actor stuck inside a loop he can't seem to get out of. He is sucked into sick games, kidnapping, and drugs, but honestly, he is tough, and I believe he can take more of it. Then we have the lovely lady whose entire life has consisted of being a research rabbit. She has thick skin. She will be fine!"

"You want me to help you pick who gets the lamp? Are those friends of yours?"

He shook his head.

"Oh no. They are interesting individuals who are in need of some future perspective."

I had no idea what he was talking about.

"What about the third?" I asked.

"Oh yes. My personal favorite. She is a trickster. Has cost many humans their life. I believe she sells the organs that they are so fond of?"

"Who are they?"

My breathing was getting heavier. Why did everything he said sound so familiar to me when it was so entirely insane? It was almost as if he was speaking in a language that I knew but forgot.

"Why do we have to pick one?" I asked.

He shrugged.

"Balance of the universe, I guess? Not everyone can have bad luck all the time."

"The lamp gives them bad luck?"

"Seven years to be precise." He grinned.

I grabbed the lamp that was standing right in front of us now. In its light, Golter didn't look like a friendly grandfather anymore. His skin was full of holes, his eyes a poisonous yellow, and the top hat reeked of death.

"No," I whispered.

"Your choice, dumb child," he said in a loud, manic tone.

I held the lamp tight and took a step back.

"Go away!" I cried and closed my eyes. When I opened them again, he was gone, but the lamp was still in my hand, although now it appeared less silver and instead more red.

"What is going on?" I whispered to myself before realizing that the lamp wasn't red. It was my own blood that was tainting the glass. My hands were full of cuts. I dropped the lamp, expecting it to shatter into a million pieces, but it didn't.

It lay there on the floor looking just like before except that my blood kept dripping on top of it.

Drip, drip, drip.

I started seeing stars, and the lights of the store all became one while my body was frozen.

"What is going on?" I repeated again, not expecting that anyone would answer. However, in my blurry mind, I again hadn't noticed that somebody came in. I assumed George Golter had come back.

They grabbed the lamp off the ground.

"Be careful," I whispered even if I couldn't care less if the weird old man hurt himself as well.

"You should be telling that to yourself," I heard the person speak. It was a different voice. A much younger and more pleasant one. I looked up and realized that the eyes in front of me were deep green and friendly. I was greeted by a smile that looked both nice and worried.

"Help me," was all I could say. I felt like I would pass out any second, but he didn't come closer. Instead, he walked toward the door.

"Give it to the third one," I heard from a distance. As he said those words, my vision became clear again. The cuts were gone, and so was the blood.

For a second, I assumed that I had fallen asleep and this was nothing but a bad dream, but the young man with the green eyes was still there. I could see him much clearer now.

"Who are you? What the hell just happened?"

He came closer, but his eyes looked far less friendly now.

"I'm Leon. I usually work nights here. I told that old bastard that he couldn't simply throw you in the cold water, but he's so stubborn.."

"Was I just bleeding?"

"Yeah, and you would have died, too, if I wasn't there. Listen, if somebody wants to buy a lamp, you must help and sell. If you don't, it will hit you instead and much more concentrated, too."

"What do you mean by it?"

"The bad luck, Riley."

"These are just some shitty lamps." I laughed. "This is insane. Tell Nipps I quit."

Leon sighed.

"Look, I can't do all of this again. You choose to not come here anymore. You promise yourself you won't. I do that every day, but when the lights turn dark, I always show up again." He shrugged. "All we can do is pick the right ones to receive bad luck."

I grabbed my keys and headed for the door. Whatever was going on, I needed to be far away from it.

"You can try and leave. Go home where you came from, but be honest, Riley. Do you remember where that is?"

Part 2

When I made my way to work after a day of hardly any sleep, I started seeing this town in a whole different light. This place that I was calling my home now. From my small apartment, it is only a five-minute bicycle ride to Evergreen Avenue where I work, but I decided to walk so I would have a chance to really look around. I never really do that on my bike. I put my earphones in and focus on nothing but the street ahead.

It was getting darker, but where I was walking now, the streetlamps were all shining. I walked through the big marketplace and inspected the little stores. Most were closed; others were getting ready to call it a day. I'd never noticed before, but all those storefronts looked like they would fall over if you only pushed hard enough. Restaurants were still serving the ones sitting and chatting outside on the terrace. The scenery resembled a picture from a magazine. I passed a few people; some greeted me with a smile, but I didn't recognize their faces.

And then there was something else. Something so odd that it surprised me that I never thought about it before.

This town had no church.

It didn't seem right. Even the smallest of towns have at least one church, somewhere in the center. I wasn't particularly religious, maybe that's why I never noticed before, but now that I had made myself conscious of it, I couldn't shake off the feeling that something was off. And now that I let the thoughts of worry inside, there was no way of stopping them.

Until this day I wouldn't have thought of myself as a necessarily suspicious individual, but with only one question, this damn Leon had gotten right to the core of my head.

This town was my home, and it felt like it in every way, but it wasn't where I was born. I lived somewhere else before. I just couldn't quite remember where that was. I wondered why I never went to visit anyone outside of this place, but I never really felt lonely and therefore the need wasn't very present.

If everything felt right, then was it really wrong?

I suppose it was. Or maybe I was craving something that felt wrong because despite what my gut and mind had told me last night, I was back on my way to the lamp store.

After I'd almost died. After I met something that will forever haunt me in my nightmares. And after I played a part in giving someone I didn't even know bad fortune for a very long time.

It all seemed perfectly mad, but then again, Leon was right. I couldn't leave. I'm not sure how or why it never occurred to me before, but I was bound to this place. And while that was the case, I might as well find out as much as I could about this new profession I now had at night. The one involving playing with the fate of strangers.

It's actually rather nice to be making some decisions for once. Even if they are for others.

As I finally got to Evergreen Avenue, the lamp store was prominently lit, guiding my path to work. I was rummaging through my bag looking for my keys when I looked through the glass door and noticed there was someone inside already. Two people, actually.

I wasn't sure whether I was hoping or dreading to meet Mr. Nipps in there, but as I opened the door, I recognized the face of Leon instead. He was talking to some man who turned around the second he heard me walk in.

It wasn't anyone I had met before. This stranger who couldn't be older than thirty-six looked like the kind of person that could actually afford to purchase our extraordinarily expensive lamps. His blond hair was drained of gel, his suit was perfectly fitted, and his bow tie matched his pocket square. His clothes looked new and well-chosen, but you could tell it was only a costume. His face appeared as if it would break any second if he only smiled a little harder. I could swear the light of every single lamp inside this store was reflected in his notoriously bright teeth.

"Good evening."

The man with the perfect smile and waxed mustache spoke. I turned toward Leon, who looked a lot more agitated than yesterday. He stood behind the counter with his fingernails dug into the desk in front of him. His eyes were opened wide, as if he was trying hard not to panic.

"Now thank you for this wonderful offer, you have been more than helpful, but I should get going. It's getting real dark out there." The stranger chuckled.

Leon didn't respond. His eyes seemed empty.

The stranger winked at me and left the store with a big brown shopping bag.

"What the hell was that about?" I asked as the door closed behind him.

"Well, you just missed one of our most horrific customers. He likes to spread torture in bulk. That's why he always gets some artistically crafted fairy lights. Nipps orders a bunch for him alone."

"So he gets to give even more people bad fortune? And you pick them all?" I couldn't believe the bullshit I was saying.

Leon nodded.

"He was here for a whole hour."

I moved closer to the register.

"My shift hasn't even started, and the sun is just setting. Did he come in here when it wasn't dark yet?"

"He came in the in-between period. He's a bit different than the others, so you never really see him in the middle of the night. He comes in before we are even officially opened."

"I don't get any of this."

I thought he was gonna roll his eyes, but he actually looked understanding.

"I thought you weren't gonna come back? I even volunteered in taking your shift," he said.

"Well, it's not really a choice, is it?" I responded.

"Did you think about what I said yesterday?" he whispered.

"About where I'm from?" I asked.

He nodded.

"Yeah, just like you said. I have no idea. I can't say where I was before I came here, but I also don't feel like I'm missing anything," I said.

His gaze shifted toward the door of the store.

"I don't remember, either," he whispered even more quietly, "but I feel like I knew you before."

"Well, I've been working here for a while now. Maybe you noticed me once when I was working days or you saw me in town—"

"No, I only come out here at night. Something is wrong, I can tell."

I sighed.

"More wrong than pushing innocent strangers into their misery?"

Leon got up from behind the counter and started turning on even more lights inside the store like it wasn't shining bright enough already.

"They're not always innocent. You just have to pick the right ones. Usually, that would be whoever the customer is not trying to make you pick."

I nodded.

"I don't know if I can make that distinction. Last night I couldn't choose at all."

"But now you know you will die a horrible death if you don't. And as I'm here now anyway, I don't mind staying a little longer tonight and helping you out a little?" He smiled.

Before I could even answer, we were interrupted by a deafening noise from next door.

"Is the pub open?" I asked.

"Yeah, let me check what's going on. You stay here." He didn't even wait for a response before storming off toward the door. There he stood still for one second as he turned around.

"Whatever you do, don't go out on the street. You're kind of in the spotlight here."

<hr>

I took a seat on the stool, hoping the strange gentleman from before wouldn't come back. He didn't, but it didn't take long before someone else did.

An older lady in a colorful gown. Her red lipstick was cracked and smudged in the corners of her lips. Her black eyeliner was dripping down her face, and her smile showed a set of rotten teeth.

"Hello," I said.

She didn't respond; instead, she started walking through the store smelling the different lamps.

"Can I help you?" I asked.

"It smells rotten in here. Can you breathe?" she asked.

I nodded.

"It's really awfully strong. I just can't identify the source." She shrugged. "Anyway, I would like to purchase a lamp. I saw one in the storefront that seemed perfectly fine."

She pointed her hand toward a crystal lamp.

"If I'm correct, it's made out of diamonds? I am in need of something that might get things bloody."

I swallowed.

"I'm not sure what the lamps do."

"Of course you don't." She chuckled. "But I am sure you will learn. Would you like to hear whose blood will be spilled by a very bad fortune?"

"Do I have a choice?"

"Even better, you have three! Number one would be a young girl whose soul is rather tainted. You could forgive her considering her age, but in time she might put a few more lives at risk. And on top of that, she enjoys it with all her heart."

"How old are we talking?"

The lady only responded with a smile.

"The second prospective recipient is no other than the brother of the girl. In his essence, he has no interest in pain. However, his definition of bad luck would probably be if his little sister was harmed."

I had to pay proper attention. Leon said these customers liked to guide the decision. I just wasn't sure whether that meant that they were lying about the aspects describing the victims. If I had to make a choice, of course I would want the person who does the most harm to receive bad luck, but how could I make that decision with such little information?

"I see your mind working already. It's not always easy to choose the fate of another. Even if it is anonymous."

I nodded.

The lady smiled again, but this time it was more sympathetic.

"Now let us continue with the last one. I have only a little information on this individual. They are living at a place I have little access to. It seems they are already living inside of a curse in a way." She laughed.

"That's not exactly helpful. Maybe we could wait for my colleague to come back and help me decide?"

"Look, girl. Whatever decision you make, it will never be right. You are playing with humans. And yes, many of us do. Well, most of us do. But the decision you ultimately make is based on your sense of right and wrong, so all you can do is try to be informed and hope your gut doesn't lie."

This woman whose appearance scared me at first was starting to make more sense than anyone else I'd talked to in these last days. I figured it might not be a terrible idea to get as much information out of her as I could. Whether those were lies or not would be something I would have to decide afterward.

"How intense are the effects of these lamps? I thought they only brought bad luck, but you were speaking about blood."

She slowly walked through the shop, gently striking different lamps with her fingertip. The lamps had no negative effect on her, which made me wonder why I almost bled out when I grabbed the shattered mirror lamp.

"It can be a bit of bad luck, slipping, waking up late, making awkward conversation in an appropriate setting. Although your very colleague once sold me a lamp that cost a man his life. One man that surely was bad in the past but he was right on his path for the better. It's a tough business."

"Where do the lamps come from?" I asked.

"A place that you won't ever visit, dear. It can't be found, just as this town and this avenue cannot be found. It's for the best, though. That other town is cursed. It reeks of death and poison."

She went back to the front where the diamond lamp stood and turned toward me.

"I'm afraid I will need your answer now."

I swallowed. I had absolutely no idea who to pick. The girl seemed to deserve it the most, but if she received the bad luck, which apparently could even be death, then her brother would be hurt, too.

I suddenly felt an arm over my shoulder.

"I would pick the girl. Most evil, am I right?"

It was Leon.

"When the hell did you come in? And how?" I said as I pulled away from him.

"Back door." He smiled. "Good evening, Ms. Smithel." He winked at the older lady.

He looked fine, a lot more confident than earlier, but something was wrong. Something had happened next door. He had spatters of blood all over his shirt and some on his face.

"What's going on?" I whispered. There was something terrifying about his sudden calmness. Despite the blood.

The lady whose name apparently was Smithel turned her gaze toward me and spoke in a far more monotonous tone.

"Your lovely colleague seems to be an expert in choosing fate."

Her words did not match her expressions. Her eyes were opened wide, and her smile had disappeared. And I could swear that for a second she was shaking her head.

I swallowed. Leon seemed trustworthy so far, but my gut was telling me that this decision was wrong.

"I pick the third one," I blurted out before I knew what I was saying.

I looked at Leon, whose dark eyes were suddenly filled with disgust. A shiver went down my spine. A part of me believed I had made a horrible decision. I'm responsible for this stranger getting hurt.

"Congratulations, you sent some poor soul into its misery. How does it feel?" Leon asked a little too enthusiastically.

I didn't answer. Instead, I got a bag for the lamp that the lady had now officially purchased.

"I better get going now. The sun is about to rise," she said.

I walked toward the door with her, where she took another big sniff of our shop.

"It's even stronger now. You need to do something about this rotten smell."

I had no idea what she was talking about.

"I will be back soon, goodbye!" she called out into the shop, and as I opened the door for her, she turned to me once more and whispered, "Be careful."

I slammed the door shut, filled with both rage and disgust. This night at the lamp store had been even more horrible than the one before because suddenly I had all these intrusive thoughts in my mind. I thought I would throw up any second.

"What was going on next door?"

Leon took a look at his watch and moved his gaze up toward me.

"Oh, just some drunk idiots, nothing to worry about. How are you feeling?"

"Not great."

He smiled.

"It's not an easy job, but you'll get there. Don't worry about that wrong decision today. You'll get the hang of it." He grabbed his jacket and came closer toward the door. "I should get going before Nipps shows up. I'm not supposed to help you."

"Well, my shift is almost over anyway."

I looked outside the glass door. The sun was about to rise. The night hours in here passed surprisingly fast.

"Exactly. And tomorrow you got a night off. Enjoy that." He smiled as he reached around me to get to the door handle.

Before I could ask any more questions, he already walked off into the dark.

I was left feeling even more confused, but at least the sick feeling in my stomach had passed.

I caught myself thinking about the things Leon had told me yesterday and earlier this night. About remembering me. For a moment, I thought I did, too. And I thought maybe he was the one person that I might be able to trust.

But then I realized that he had lied about something earlier.

This store doesn't have a back door.

Part 3

After two disturbing nights filled with confusion, anxiety, and playing with the faith of souls, today I would look at this town in a whole different light.

Daylight.

I hadn't slept much as I left the store quite early in the morning, and while I still felt drained, my mind was restless. Too much had happened. And this new routine of mine was making me forget that there is a whole other world out there. One that I used to live in less than a few days ago.

I passed all the houses and shops again that looked like a copy of reality. That little worm of suspicion was burying itself deeper and deeper inside of my mind. This place was not right, I could tell. But if I knew this was wrong, it could only mean that some part of me knew what was supposed to be right.

I simply wasn't sure where exactly I took that comparison from. My plan was to look through town, maybe talk to some people, but my plans never seemed to work out.

Before I knew what I was doing, my legs had carried me to Evergreen Avenue.

It was just the way it usually looks when I work the regular hours in the lamp store. Or used to. The pub next door was closed, and there were some empty cigarette boxes and trash lying in front showing that there were people in there last night. Well, I already knew about that as Leon had walked in to figure out why they were so loud. Only to come back with splatters of blood and no clear answer.

I had never paid much attention to the other buildings across from our store. Of course, I'd seen them before, but I guess my mind didn't register them consciously. There was a bookstore, a boutique selling clothes that looked rather ugly, and a small kebab shop. All right, the regular stores would be closed at night, but didn't fast food places stay open longer? At least longer than nine p.m., but at night their lights were out just like all the others.

I moved closer to the one place I wasn't planning on visiting, but its magnetism was already pulling me in.

I'd almost forgotten how boring the lamp store looked during the day. All the lights were off and you might guess that the shop isn't open at all. I pushed against the door, and it opened. I took a sniff walking in to see whether I could make out what Ms. Smithel was talking about yesterday, but it smelled just like it always did. A mixture of plastic and metal.

"Riley? You better be looking to buy something because I do not feel like chit-chatting."

It was Mr. Nipps, empty eyes and sparkly grin as always. I have to admit, I felt a little disappointed that it wasn't Leon working. Although I doubt he ever works during the day.

"Well, no. Not now that I know what these lamps do," I promptly responded.

With a scornful snort, he grabbed a pair of scissors.

"Well, while you are here, you might as well help me unpack some of these lamps. We had a dozen delivered this morning!"

"Why so many?" I asked. The store was full to the brink with lamps.

"Another colleague ordered them. Apparently, customers were asking for specific elements."

"Leon?" I asked.

Mr. Nipps rolled his eyes.

"Let me guess? He came to help during your shift even if I told him not to? This boy is the personification of a headache. If I could fire him, he'd be out the door in a second."

I grabbed the scissors and started cutting through the carton. Mr. Nipps seemed awfully chatty considering he had just said he wasn't in the mood.

"This is your store, is it not?" I cheekily asked.

"Well yes, and also no. Even I don't make all decisions on my own," he said with a bitter undertone.

"So did Leon apply or did you ask him, just like you did with me?"

Mr. Nipps shook his head.

"He was suggested, just like you. Around the same time, I believe. I picked him for nights and you for days. Now we're mixing it up a little. The store is awfully vibrant at night, isn't it?"

Mr. Nipps' irritated expression vanished and turned into excitement.

I nodded.

"Well, I hope you enjoy it because soon you might be doing it every night." He grinned.

"Why is that?"

The only response I received was a wink. That was all we talked about. When I realized he was only making me work, I found an excuse and left the store. Again, I hadn't learned much more. Every person I talked to seemed to be speaking in riddles.

When evening came, I wondered what my next step would be. The simplest one would probably be to stay inside my cozy bed and sleep the night away. I could use a few hours of peace, but I knew that this wasn't an option. I'm not the kind of person to sit around and wait; I needed to investigate.

Now the question was, should I stop by the lamp store to try and get some information out of that puzzling Leon, or should I visit the pub?

The answer to this question was rather simple.

I really could use a drink right now.

I waited until it was after twelve before making my way back to Evergreen Avenue. I remember Leon telling me that I shouldn't step outside in the dark, but I'd been out here before. On the specific night that I saw the lamp store for the very first time. When its warm and bright lights attracted my hazy mind. And I'd been inside the pub as well, even if that memory was more of a blur.

Now that I was walking through the pitch-black street, I realized why he had warned me. This darkness of the night was suffocating. All I saw was the lamp store at the end of the street, but what I saw wasn't a problem. It was all that I could hear.

Because while I couldn't make out their shapes, I could tell that I wasn't alone. I listened to the steps surrounding me, heard strange voices giggle and occasionally scream. I tried to hold my breath, hoping they didn't notice me out here while I looked over to the store.

Leon had been right. It really was a spotlight shining on whoever was in there. And I could see that it was him. For a split second, I contemplated walking over. He was alone in there, playing with the lights. He turned them warmer and then colder again. Experimented with different colors and changed the directions of beams. He seemed to be thoroughly enjoying himself.

For a moment, I was so distracted that I'd forgotten the darkness around me. But whoever was out here with me made sure I knew of their presence. I suddenly felt a hot breath against my neck. Instinctively, I turned around, but of course, I couldn't make out who it was. A cold hand touched my arm, but before anything else could happen, I started running.

I ran right toward the door of the pub.

***

The pub smelled of spilled beer on the wooden floor, hints of cigarette smoke and desperation. The lights were dim, but most seats were taken. People were chatting, but I couldn't make out what they were saying through the noise of the music.

I decided to simply walk up to the bartender and ask if they had seen Leon here last night, but on my way there, I caught the last person was expecting to see again today.

Ms. Smithel. The strange older lady that had come to the lamp store last night.

She was sitting inside a booth all alone with her half-empty pint of Guinness.

"May I join you?" I asked.

She looked surprised and yet delighted to see me.

"I don't believe I caught your name last night. You were quite busy asking me questions instead," she said as she gestured me to sit.

I quietly took a seat next to her, unsure how to feel about this situation. Her looks were even more miserable than last night despite the far worse lighting. Most of the other visitors in the pub looked a bit smudged, to be perfectly honest.

"I'm Riley. That's most of what I can tell you, however. You see, I happen to have forgotten a lot about myself," I said.

"Well, we all lose a little of ourselves when we visit this place."

She took a big gulp of her drink.

"Your lamp has been delivered, by the way. The poor fool will be shedding blood soon," Ms. Smithel added without ever looking up from her glass.

I swallowed. I'd tried not to think about what I'd done last night.

"Is it someone I know? Are the victims ever?" I asked.

Ms. Smithel laughed.

"Don't worry, child. You made a good fucking decision." She slowly got up from her seat and finished the last sip of her Guinness. "It might take a day or two until the effects will hit. Until then, you better stay away from that smelling colleague of yours."

With that, she headed toward the door. I jumped up from my seat and followed her. For some reason she was surprisingly fast. All I saw was the door open and her disappearing into darkness before it slammed shut again. When I managed to open the heavy door, I saw nothing outside but a faint light coming from my right side.

Now I had three different choices. Go back inside the pub and talk to the barkeeper, walk into the dark, and hope to find Ms. Smithel, or the dumbest of them all: go next door to the lamp store and talk to Leon.

Of course, I made the worst choice of them all.

As I opened the door, I thought I would turn blind. Leon had turned on every single lamp inside the store, including the new ones, and had turned all of them to maximum brightness.

"What the hell?" I shouted.

As my eyes got used to the sudden burst of light, I finally saw Leon's face among the lamps. His dark eyes were opened wide and his mouth was formed into the biggest smile I'd ever seen. He was dressed just the same as yesterday, including the dried blood on his shirt.

"Riley! Isn't this wonderful? They will all see us now! I've sold five lamps already, and the night isn't even over yet."

Without blinking once he walked closer to me.

"You sold five lamps? So you gave five different people bad fortune?" I asked.

"Do you know what kind of lamps those were, Riley? No regular boring bad luck lamps. The real deal. A murder-suicide, a house fire, a—"

"What the hell is wrong with you? I thought you were stuck here like me. Are you enjoying this?"

"With every fiber of my body." He started maniacally laughing as he walked closer to me. With all this extra light, I could see all the pores in his skin, which appeared like they might burst and explode if he kept moving. Or his whole face might just fall off and shatter on the floor like a fragile lamp. Leon didn't even seem to notice. He never stopped smiling.

Suddenly, I realized what Ms. Smithel was talking about. It *was* smelling rotten in here.

Leon moved his hand toward my face and gently caressed my cheek.

"I thought you'd want this, too. You so quickly made a judgment last night. Don't you understand, Riley? We could take over this whole place."

Leon came even closer. Close enough that his face was right in front of mine. Close enough to realize what I noticed last night but didn't register until now. His eyes were almost as dark as the night out there.

I distinctly remember that the Leon I met here on my first day had green eyes.

Part 4

The days and nights in this town I called home became stranger and stranger. Or at least that's what I thought. In a way, however, I guess they became more normal.

Ever since I'd moved here, the weather had always been absolutely neutral. The sun never shines too bright; it never gets too cold. We'd never seen a heat wave and neither snow. To be perfectly honest, you hardly realize there is *weather* at all. It is just perfectly adjusted to our bodies. Or maybe the other way around. Habituation. If everything's the same all the time, you stop noticing it. That is until there is a sudden change. One that breaks you out of the cycle.

Today exactly that happened.

It started raining.

First, there were only a few drops that I could hear splashing against my bedroom window. I woke up wondering what it was until my tired mind started remembering that sound from a very long time ago.

It used to rain a lot where I was before, and I always found the sound calming.

Not today, however. It simply increased the feeling of wrongness. I stayed in bed for a little while longer watching the drops race down the window. My night, or better day of sleep, was plagued by nightmares. Most of them included Leon and his manic smile. Those eyes that seemed to know nothing but torture. Last night I believed I would be dying inside that store of light. I had gotten away just in time.

Whoever that was that got so close to me, it wasn't the same Leon I had met on my first night shift. Considering I'd only seen him a handful of times, of course I couldn't quite say which one of them was wrong, but I certainly preferred the one with the green eyes. He was a little grumpy but seemed human. This other thing did not.

Tonight I would have to work again. Another night shift on Evergreen Avenue and I most definitely was not ready for it. Especially as I was afraid that the wrong Leon might pay me another visit. If he ever left at all.

None of it mattered, though. Even if I felt nothing but dread and fear, I knew that staying away was not an option. Even if I consciously made the decision of staying home, I always ended up back at the lamp store. It kept attracting me like a moth.

Maybe that was what Leon was, too. He had been poisoned by that place, and soon I would be, too.

———————

At five to nine, I stood in the darkness again. The rain from earlier hadn't stopped; it only got heavier. In front of me, I saw the store. Even if I was getting soaked out here, I waited until it was nine.

As usual, the store was prominently lit and attracted all eyes. Although tonight something was slightly different. The lights weren't as bright as they normally are even though the storefront was filled with even more lamps than on regular days. I couldn't even see the inside of the shop.

Something was wrong. Well, something was always wrong here, but tonight the wrongness was on a new level.

I pushed against the door, hoping it would be locked, but it wasn't, which made me dread that Leon would be welcoming me inside. I was as well prepared as one could be to meet him again. I walked in confidently, planning to tell him to screw off. Tonight was my shift, and it was time I took some responsibility. Leon didn't own this store after all, and I doubt Mr. Nipps would appreciate the way he had been acting.

I admit, snitching to my awful boss wasn't the perfect plan, but it was all I could come up with. I didn't expect to see him so soon, however. In no way could I have predicted what I would be walking into.

I was greeted by Mr. Nipps with his eyes wide. His throat had been cut through. Blood was dripping onto the floor of the store; it sounded just like the rain this morning on my window. His body was hanging from the main chandelier on the ceiling.

I stood there frozen in shock. Mr. Nipps wasn't exactly my favorite person on Earth, but nobody deserved to be brutally murdered like this.

"Riley! Don't worry, love. I'll be out of your hair soon. I know it's your night."

Leon had appeared from the back with a bright grin on his face like nothing had happened. I wanted to run, but something was keeping me from doing so.

"Why did you do this?" I whispered. My hands were shaking, and I couldn't keep my eyes of the empty ones from my eccentric former boss.

Leon chuckled.

"I didn't. You did. I believe you sold a diamond blood lamp?"

I swallowed.

"It's all right, Riley. You can never quite know who it will hit, and to be honest, I think I underestimated you! I would never have made a decision that randomly, but you're bold!"

He walked over, his shoes squeaking as he nonchalantly walked over the puddle of blood underneath the corpse. I turned away, away from Leon and the dead man, and that's when I noticed all the broken lamps on the floor. The shelves were far emptier, too. He must have moved the last decent ones onto the storefront.

"I know I made a mess. Collateral damage, I guess." Leon grinned as he had just been reading my mind.

I tried to peek through the lamps onto the street. It wasn't silent as it is on most nights; the rain had turned into a loud and heavy storm. Even the sky seemed to understand that something was different here.

"Who are you?" I hissed at the imposter. I felt sick to my stomach talking to this thing, but there had to be a reason he was sparing me. He hadn't hurt me last night, and he even seemed happy to see me now.

"Bold asking someone this question if you don't even know who you are yourself." He came closer, and I was sure that I soon would be hanging there next to Mr. Nipps. My breathing got heavier while I contemplated all my options here. There weren't many. "Well, Riley. With that miserable man gone, the store will soon belong to one of us, I assume. I'd like to make sure that person will be me." He grinned.

"I don't give a shit about this store," I responded.

"That's a fucking lie. You keep coming back. You want this," he hissed. His expression was full of hate and anger, and at first, I thought the veins on his forehead would pop any second. Before I realized that those were not veins. They looked more like cracks in his skin.

"What did you do to the real Leon?" I whispered. "Did you kill him like Nipps to take his skin?"

Suddenly, lightning struck, and for a moment all the lamps in our store started flickering before finally losing their light. I stood there in the darkness with a demon who murdered both my colleague and my boss.

The storm outside was the only sound we could hear; the wind became so strong that the front door slammed open.

Nobody would come inside tonight. We had no light.

I heard Leon coming closer, and when lightning struck again, all I saw was his grin in the white light.

This is my moment, I thought. The store was as dark as Evergreen Avenue.

I hoped that there would be another flash, and when it finally came, I ran toward the door and to the one place around here that might have some light and possibly some answers for me.

I fought against the wind and the rain, hoping that the Leon impostor didn't follow me when I grabbed the door handle of the pub.

He hadn't followed me.

I was soaked and afraid, but at least I had achieved getting out of there. The magnetism of the light let go of me thanks to this horrible storm, but I knew the light would come back, and then I would have to go as well. Until then, however, I would try to find the lady that smelled the rotten Leon first.

I walked up to the bar, where I saw the same barkeeper as the other night.

"Hi, sorry, do you know Ms. Smithel?" I asked.

The barkeeper was a man in his early thirties. In a way, he resembled Leon a bit, except he was a bit older and had darker hair.

"You must be Riley," he said in a concerned voice.

I nodded. It didn't even surprise me that he knew me. He started pouring a drink for me and told me to sit down.

"I was hoping you would come here for a drink. I can't really leave myself, you know. At least not as I wish."

I sat down on the barstool.

"Do you know Leon?"

He nodded. "He used to come here at times." His eyes shifted toward the door of the pub. For a second, I was afraid the impostor would come in. "I'm Josh."

"Do you know what happened to him?" I asked.

Josh's eyes went back to the door.

"We don't have much time before you have to leave again, Riley. I was hoping you would come over, however. You see, I'd like to purchase a lamp."

I sighed. "Are you fucking kidding me?"

I thought I had gotten away from that misery for a second, but now I would have to choose another fate. After what I'd done to Mr. Nipps, I certainly wasn't ready for that.

"I already know which one I would like. It's a wooden lamp. A little dark on the outside but bright light. You know which one I mean, right?"

I nodded.

"So who are the victims?" I asked.

"I see, the cynicism has gotten you already. Okay, well, number one is a collector of human components. The second is an artist who enjoys the dance of death. The last one might remind you of Christmas. Unfortunately, that is all I know."

"There is only one right answer, isn't there?" I asked.

"To be perfectly honest, I happen to have my own agenda as well. They are all right for me but only one is for you."

I thought about it for a second. It seemed so absurd, but if I followed my gut, only one felt correct.

"The Christmas one."

I felt a tingle in my hands; it went all the way to my head. Like a migraine moving through my entire body.

"I think I have to go back," I whispered.

Josh nodded.

"Before your shift ends tonight, can you take the wooden lamp and place it next to the door of the pub? Knock three times and leave."

I didn't know why he asked me to do so, but I agreed. With a sick feeling in my stomach, I went back to the lamp store, which from the outside was prominently lit again. The door was wide open, and Mr. Nipps' body was gone with a trail of blood going all the way to the front. Leon must have carried him outside and would probably be back soon.

But at least the storm was calming down.

Part 5

I didn't sleep at all that day. After I finished my shift with no further occurrences, I placed the lamp in front of the bar.

I knocked three times. Not on the door but on the lamp.

Don't ask me why. I believe I lost control over my actions a long time ago. I wasn't a conscious human being anymore but a shell that only came to life in the light of the lamps. The few lamps that weren't shattered, that is. After last night's storm, this paper town was a mess. Trees had fallen to the ground, trash was spread through the streets, but the sun was rising and the wet concrete was starting to dry. It seemed as if we had a warm, sunny day ahead of us. A shimmer of hope.

Of course, these never last long around here.

On my way home, I didn't see a single soul on the streets. It was early, of course, but the quietness made this eerie town feel even more like death. This town, which didn't even have a name. Or a church. Or people who I could trust.

I walked up the stairs to my apartment, more agitated than tired when I found a note stuck to my door.

WELCOME FOR GOOD

I removed the note and checked if there was anything else written on the back. There wasn't.

I took a deep breath. This was my home, the only place where I felt safe so far, but it seemed that was about to change now. With shaky hands, I got my key out of my pocket and tried to open the door, but it wouldn't fit. At first, I thought I was just too tired or shaky due to anxiousness, but no matter how hard I tried, the key did not fit the lock. I sighed, finally ready to give up, though not a clue what that meant. I had no idea where else to go. I wasn't even sure who my landlord was or who I could call.

How had none of these seemingly normal questions ever occurred to me? This wasn't a dream; it felt far too vivid. And I couldn't be dead, either. Even if I didn't know the feeling of death, it couldn't be this. I was placed in the fabrication of a town in a world that was normal. I knew because deep inside I was aware of the real world. You can only tell that something is wrong when you know what right feels like. The only thing that made sense was that a chunk of my memory was missing. Or some part of my brain that would be able to connect reality and fiction.

Though whatever my reality was, I had to cope with it the best way possible. For that, I had to find a way to my home. First, my home here, the apartment. And eventually, maybe, my real home.

I took a look at my left. There was an identical door to mine. Only the number was different. I'd met a few neighbors at times in the hallway. They greeted politely but had no real substance. Just like the people sitting in the fake cafés around town. Still, whoever lived next to me might know who owned this building.

I walked over and knocked.

No answer.

There were no other doors on this floor, and I didn't feel like going further just yet.

So I knocked again. And once more.

Until I finally heard some rattling coming from inside the apartment.

But no, that wasn't right. It didn't come from behind this door but the other one. My door.

There was someone inside *my* apartment.

I heard someone scratching the wall. My breathing became heavier as I contemplated what my next steps would be. It wasn't the middle of the night but early morning. There were other people in this building, even if they didn't know me well. There wasn't any reason to be afraid if it wasn't night, after all. I would just go to a different floor and ask someone for help.

However, as I turned around to move toward the door of the floor, all of a sudden all the lights in this windowless hallway turned dark. I was standing in the darkness, with no sense of orientation. I tried to make out where the door was or at least the light switch, and that's when the door opened.

The door to my home.

"Riley?" I heard a creaky voice.

The blinds inside were shut, and I could hardly make out anything. I didn't know what to do or where to run. Maybe it was due to my new work, but I absolutely hated darkness.

"I was hoping it was you," they whispered. I knew that voice. The hairs on my skin were standing tall when I heard it. My eyes were getting adjusted to the darkness, and the adrenaline was rushing through my body.

It was time to run. Though before I could even try to move, he leaned over and grabbed my arm. His hands were wet.

"Leon, let me go," I said as confidently as I could. He seemed weak. Weaker than before.

To my surprise, he did let go of my arm.

"I remember now, Riley. I remember everything," he said as he started hugging me.

When he let go again, I noticed the blood on his hands, face, and clothes. The same clothes he'd been wearing since the first night I met him.

"Is it really you?" I asked and walked inside the apartment before he could even answer. It had to be the real Leon as the other one wouldn't voluntarily leave the lamp store.

"I thought you were dead. Skinned alive," I said after he didn't answer my first question. He hardly seemed awake, which wasn't surprising if all the blood on him was his own.

Standing in the doorframe of the apartment, I reached my hand for the light switch, but it was no use. Apparently, the electricity in this whole building was cut off. So instead I left Leon leaning on the door and walked toward the window to let in more light.

Finally, I could see fully.

I saw how terrible he looked and how much blood there was on the floor. The floor that didn't belong to my apartment after all. The insides of this place were all different.

"Where am I?" I asked.

"At my home. Didn't you come to see me?" he asked.

I walked back to him.

His eyes looked like they could hardly stay open, but they for sure were green. Of course, this could be another trick, contact lenses, or an even better costume, but this person looked far too broken. He was human.

"Come on," I whispered as I helped him toward the sofa in the corner of the room. This apartment looked exactly like mine, only with different furniture. Leon appeared as if he would pass out any second.

"You need to see a doctor," I said.

He shook his head.

"There are no doctors here. No hospital or schools, either." He sighed. "But don't worry. It looks worse than it is. Mostly surface wounds. I'm just tired. I don't think I've slept at all these past nights."

"Where were you?"

He stayed silent for a moment, simply staring into the distance. Finally, he spoke.

"Outside. In the darkness. But not really. It's hard to explain. I remember leaving the store to go next door. I tried to be quick and get to the pub, but someone grabbed me and pulled me into the night. I was out there with the spirits and demons of this place who kept screaming and threatening me. I tried to come back inside or go anywhere else, but I couldn't, not without a body. At day, I didn't exist. Or I don't remember... I know it sounds absolutely insane."

"Yeah, well, everything here sounds insane. Did you see who pulled you out in the first place?"

He nodded.

"Remember the bastard that comes in to buy fairy lights? He felt like he wasn't spreading enough suffering already. He wanted to be in charge."

Fairy lights. That's what Josh must have meant with the reminder of Christmas.

"Is he gone now?" I asked.

"I'm not sure where he is, but he doesn't have my skin anymore. Tonight at dawn, I heard something. A knock. It somehow led me home. That was you, right?"

"I think it was Josh. He bought a lamp." I smiled, but Leon's expression seemed anxious.

"Josh? Fuck."

"Why? Is that bad? He saved your life!" I exclaimed.

"He's not supposed to. Something is wrong."

———

Leon passed out shortly after. I needed more answers, but I knew I wouldn't get anything coherent out of him in the state he was in. I left his door open so there would be some light and went back to the hallway. I was so sure that this door belonged to my home. Instead, it was Leon's. We'd been living next door to each other without ever meeting. Or maybe we had and forgot.

Earlier, I walked to the wrong door. I was pretty exhausted, after all.

It made sense in a way, but I still didn't understand who was pulling the strings. It couldn't be Nipps, as he was dead. And I doubted it was the man with the fairy lights; I believed that one only looked for chaos.

I guess whoever left the note on Leon's door had something to do with everything.

Could it be Josh?

I walked over to the door next to this one, the one I believed belonged to a neighbor.

As I expected, my key fit. It was my home.

I washed off Leon's blood, put on some new clothes, and got some food for Leon and myself. It was only then when I made my way back to his place that I noticed there was a note on my door as well. Except mine was hanging on the inside.

CHOOSE WISELY.
Someone had been in here.

Leon was sleeping for hours. When he finally woke up, he seemed even more distressed than earlier. We decided that we would go to the store together tonight. To be honest, I couldn't even remember if it was my shift or his.

The streets were layered with a white powder. It was shimmering underneath the twilight.

Snow. That's what it's called. I hadn't seen winter in so long, I almost forgot how the cold smelled. In between the white sheet on the ground were drops of dark red.

"The universe is not in balance anymore. We are corrupted," Leon mumbled.

The sky was turning darker already, but the streetlamps did not shine.

"Don't you think it's strange we've been living next door to each other without ever meeting?" I asked him as we made our way to Evergreen Avenue. He had been rather quiet since he'd woken up again. I didn't want to push him after the trauma he'd gone through, but I needed answers. I was going insane.

"I worked nights. You worked days. We were never home at the same time," he said nonchalantly. It almost seemed like he didn't care anymore.

"Earlier you said you remember something. What did you mean?"

"Huh?" he asked. "Oh, yeah. I just meant what had happened to me. You know, the guy." He kept looking straight ahead as he said that.

"What's going on with you? Ever since you woke up, you've been acting even stranger," I said.

Leon looked at me, and I swore he seemed worried. He took my hand and kept walking through the snow.

"It's almost dark. We need to hurry."

"What is it that you remember, Leon? Please just fucking tell me," I almost shouted.

"I'm sorry, Riley. If I say something, we might end up like Nipps hanging from the ceiling."

I stopped walking.

We were almost at the store, but suddenly I didn't feel so safe with him around anymore. There was nobody there I could really trust. Not even my own mind.

"How do you know about that? You weren't there?"

Leon's eyes shifted toward the lamp store. The lights were on, but it seemed darker than I'd ever seen it before.

"There's someone in there. He'll explain."

Before we continued walking, he grabbed my hand once more.

"It's okay to be selfish sometimes, Riley. Remember that."

When I opened the door to the lamp store, it felt different than usual. There was a cold breeze coming from the inside, one that made you freeze more than the snow outside. It was due to this man. The one that had been waiting for us.

"Hello, Riley. Finally, we meet."

He was of an indefinable age. His skin was picture perfect, as was his whole attire. Only his eyes seemed poisonous.

"Who are you?" I asked.

"I'm the man who owns this wonderful store as well as the town surrounding it and many more. You can call me Mr. V if you like. Though who I am is not as important as what I am about to offer you."

"And what's that?" I asked. Leon stayed quiet during the entire conversation.

"A choice," he replied with a grin on his face and a shimmer in his eyes. "The same one your friend received."

I looked over to Leon, who was avoiding eye contact.

"He promised not to say a thing. You see, it's important you make the decision for yourself. I do believe in free will."

"Is that why you lured me into this hell?" I hissed.

The man who called himself Mr. V shook his head.

"I did no such thing. Both of you came here by mistake, possibly, or maybe because you felt the store calling you. The former man who took care of the lamps is the one who lured you in, I suppose. He was looking for someone to take over. This place leaves a toll on your soul, you see."

I closed my eyes. My head was aching like crazy; the migraine was back even though I was inside. But slowly little drops of memory started trickling in. I saw Leon. Not the broken one, not the impostor. I saw us both in a car, driving and laughing. He was different. He felt warm and kind. I looked at the man I thought was a stranger.

"We came here together?" I whispered to Leon, but he avoided my eyes.

"This town, is it real? Are we still on Earth?" I asked Mr. V.

He laughed. "Of course you are. It's a perfect copy, I suppose. Just like other towns but far more neutral. It needs to be neutral so you have the right surroundings to make decisions that are not corrupted. Well, it used to be."

Mr. V gestured to Leon to go outside. I could see him struggling, but finally he did as told.

"You said you had an offer," I hissed.

"Yes. How did you feel not being able to trust your own mind?"

I didn't respond. It didn't seem like he expected me to.

"And how did you feel making decisions over the fate of others?"

"Awful."

"Ah, yes. Because you believe in good, I suppose? Now, well, at least you were in charge of the decisions. Decisions that will occur no matter what you say. I'm offering you to stay, the two of you, and continue to restore the balance of the lamps. Now, Riley, would you like to be in charge?"

He wanted us to take over the store. He wanted us to stay in the copy of a town that possibly existed in the life we had before. What he didn't say was what the alternative would be.

Would he kill us? Or just me?

I suppose Leon had accepted already. And he told me to be selfish. The store only really needed one person to lead it, but Leon had almost died once. And now that I remembered that he wasn't a stranger, could I let him do all of this on his own?

The last days in this place, I had been frightened like never before. I had felt powerless and used. I was longing for a life I didn't even remember. Maybe Leon was the only thing about that life that I even cared about, and I wouldn't even be able to take him with me. Besides, could I even trust him to make the right choices? There were human lives at stake, after all.

I could think about the different arguments and options forever, but deep inside, I knew what the truth was. Mr. V said he was giving me a choice, but he wasn't really. The decision he offered was merely an illusion. In reality, everything I did and would do was already determined.

I knew I couldn't leave the lamp store. Not after the first night I saw the lights shine.

A SALESPERSON JUST CHANGED MY ENTIRE VIEW ON FREE WILL

I magine you open your door and in front of it stands a person who apparently knows everything about you.

The guy looked just as smug as I imagine a door salesperson to be. Honestly, I didn't know that they even existed anymore. I mean, it does feel slightly intrusive and somewhat old fashioned, especially as this particular guy didn't stop ringing until I finally opened the door.

"Good day, sir. How is your morning going?"

He was remarkably tall but with great posture. He had to look down at me as he was speaking.

"Uhm good, thanks—"

"Well, good to hear that, so you don't have any problems with parasites yet, huh?"

I gave him a confused look.

"Oh, I am sorry. You must not know. Did your parents not tell you? I believed they would have told you before heading off to Spain. Oh, what a luxury to take a vacation in January."

I was standing at the door with one foot outside to make sure he didn't decide to come inside. I had two more meetings and was in no mood to listen to some sales pitch.

"I'm sorry, my parents didn't say anything about... parasites. Did you have an appointment?"

I didn't even question why he immediately assumed that I was their son. But he was spot on; my parents did ask me to watch the house seeing that I work remotely anyway.

The man chuckled.

"Oh, I'm awfully sorry. I have started the conversation in all the weirdest ways. I didn't even introduce myself, how silly! My name is Jonathan Musterman, and I work with ParasiteCorps. Many neighbors have had recent problems in their houses, you see—"

"Oh, you're from pest control?" I raised an eyebrow. He was definitely not dressed like someone who wanted to kill some insects.

He shook his head vigorously.

"No, no. *I* don't want to kill anything in there. I'm simply here to drop off a sample, and if you like it, you can give me a call. Easy peasy. See, if *they* find their way inside. I know you think I'm trying to sell you something you don't need, but you are simply wrong, Owen."

Of course, he already knew my name as well.

I opened my mouth, but he cut me off.

"All right, I don't want to bug you any longer. I imagine you don't want your colleagues to wait too long."

"What—"

He started rummaging through his suitcase and pulled out a black envelope.

"It's pretty much self-explanatory." Jonathan smiled. "Say hello to your parents when you talk to them."

It was a completely odd way to start my morning, but I was just glad that he was gone.

In the afternoon, the door rang again, and I was already dreading who would be behind it. I thought Jonathan was back already to ask what I thought of his sample, which I hadn't even opened.

So I was very positively surprised to open the door to a familiar face instead.

"Mila!"

"Hey, Owen!" She smiled and gave me a big hug. Mila was the daughter of our next door neighbors, and we'd been close friends growing up.

"My mum told me you're here. I meant to come by sooner but had some work to do. Can I come in?"

"Yeah, of course! I was just about to close my laptop for the day."

We walked straight to the living room and sat down on the couch.

"I didn't even know you were in town. How long are you staying?" I asked her. Mila moved away right after high school, so we only see each other occasionally when we're both home during holidays.

She frowned.

"Yeah, but I'm leaving again tonight. Actually, I have to leave really early tomorrow morning, buuut I might be back in a few days. So you won't have to die of boredom."

I have to admit I was a bit disappointed. There weren't many people in town that I was still in contact with.

"Well, I'm not *all* alone. Today I got a really interesting visitor." I grinned. "A guy from ParasiteCorps."

I proceeded to tell her about my weird encounter with Jonathan, and to be honest, I hadn't realized how absurd it truly was until I'd said it all out loud.

"Shit, that guy bugs us all the time, too!" she called out. "He's so creepy, always tries to find a way inside, and I've never seen a truck or any other people from his strange firm. Did he give you anything?"

"Uhm, yeah, some sample, but I don't even know what it is."

"Throw it away!"

Her gaze was all serious now and her voice stern, though I believe I heard some fear in it.

"I can't explain it, but something about him is really wrong. Whatever he gave you, it's probably not good. He'll use it as a reason to come into the house, and you won't be able to get rid of him."

I swallowed. It's not like I'm a little kid anymore, but I suddenly felt very weird about being all alone in this house.

"Yeah, okay, I'll throw it out. To be honest, I wasn't really planning on entertaining him again—but do you think he's dangerous or something?"

She shrugged.

"I don't know. It's more of a feeling, but better safe than sorry, right?"

Mila ordered pizza, and we watched a movie until I almost fell asleep. It was great seeing her again and catching up, especially as my days usually looked the same at the house.

Same breakfast, same workplace, same grocery store, the exact same routine.

So it was quite easy to notice the irregularities.

For starters, I forgot a whole day of work.

I woke up, logged into my laptop, and made breakfast, which I had in front of the television where I stayed until I got hungry again. I randomly found some documentaries on YouTube and somehow kept switching to more and more of them. With my lunch on my lap, I continued the same until it got dark.

I was really lucky that nobody in my team had tried to contact me that day because I wouldn't have been able to explain what had happened. My brain went on autopilot as if it was a lazy Sunday.

And the weirdest part is that I couldn't even say what I'd been watching all day.

When night came, I got so freaked by what had happened that I turned off both my laptop and TV and went for a run to clear my head.

Nothing like this had ever happened to me, and I had a feeling it was connected to Jonathan.

Later that evening, I decided to call my parents and ask them about him.

Neither of them had ever heard of a Jonathan, and they both swore nobody like him ever rang their door.

Forgetting work was unfortunate but not necessarily dangerous yet. But then other things started happening. I woke up in the morning and noticed that the stove had been on and the entire kitchen felt like hell even though I hadn't used the stove in two days.

I noticed in the middle of the night when I went to get a glass of water.

Completely freaked out, I turned it off, happy that I hadn't set anything on fire but still completely out of my mind.

I went to the bathroom to splash some water on my face, and that's when I completely lost control.

I looked into the mirror at my face that somehow didn't feel like it really belonged to me anymore. You know how you don't quite feel like yourself when you stare for long enough?

It was almost like that but a lot worse because before I could move away from the mirror, the left side of my face started twitching.

The corner of my mouth slowly moved up, and it was as if a part of me was trying to smile. I tried to push it back, but then my left index finger pulled the corner of my mouth even higher.

I wish I would have called someone then. Maybe it was all mental; stress and being alone for too long was messing with my mind. Unfortunately, instead of seeking help in those situations, we often hide even more, afraid of the reaction we might get from others.

I can't say if that was really my thought process. All I know is that I finally pulled away from the mirror and went to sleep.

I should have asked for help.

I'm incredibly stubborn, and I truly used to believe that I was in charge of my actions. But slowly the other thing was taking over. The thing that smiled at me in the mirror.

I wanted to believe that it was someone else who was doing this to me, but then I found all the footage. Generally speaking, I'm most suspicious of the way our phones collect data on everything we do, but then I remembered how handy it can be.

Because as it turns out, the other me had been using my phone.

First I checked my YouTube history. Apparently, all the documentaries I watched were on worms, but I don't remember seeing a single one of them.

I knew I needed to go to a therapist or maybe even the hospital. Losing massive chunks of memory like that wasn't normal.

But that was before I checked my gallery.

There were two new videos that I didn't remember recording.

The first one started in the garden. The flash of the phone was shining on the ground with three holes as big as footballs.

"We don't need them now, but we'll hide them here until we get hungry," a voice spoke.

My voice.

Of course, it didn't sound the way I hear it in my head, but I'd heard recordings of me before.

Then my hand came into the frame, and it threw small creatures into each hole.

Squirrels, I believe. And they definitely looked dead.

My stomach started turning at the sight, and my heart started racing. This didn't seem like I was simply sleepwalking. It felt like a different personality took over me.

With my phone still in hand, I ran to the garden where I found three small heaps of earth.

I couldn't bring myself to look into them, but I noticed that there was a fourth hole, slightly bigger, but it almost appeared unfinished. Maybe because of the shovel next to it.

It took me a lot of willpower to check the second video.

This one was only a few seconds short.

I had to rewatch it a few times until I finally understood what I was looking at.

It was a recording of a baby sleeping in a crib. Then the camera turned around, and I saw my own face with eyes wide open and a massive grin.

It was our neighbors' child from across the street. At least that's what I think because I've seen them walk around with a stroller.

"Nothing happened. I would have heard. There would have been police," I whispered to myself, my breath getting faster and faster.

With a shaking hand, I started typing the number of the police. If I really did these things but couldn't remember, I needed to be locked up. Before anything happened to that child.

But while I was ready to call, I simply couldn't. I'm not sure if it was fear of what would happen or if the other part of me was stopping me.

Then my gaze caught something on the ground.

A black envelope.

After Mila had freaked me out about Jonathan, I didn't want it to be inside anymore, even in the trash, so I threw it out in the garden.

I ignored every voice I heard in my head, picked up that envelope, and ripped it open.

A round pill fell outside and a white postcard with this written on it:

Did you have a friendly visitor inside your house lately? Maybe a family member, a handyman, or possibly an old friend? And now think: do you really remember them? If not, give us a call before it's too late. And before they catch on :)

On the other side was a phone number.

My visitor was Jonathan, but as far as I know, he never came inside.

And then it hit me.

I ran inside, through the front door outside, and right to our neighbors.

You might have guessed it by now, but they were really worried about me when I asked about their daughter Mila, who didn't exist.

———

Before they catch on.

I had two options. Fight my thoughts and go to the police, but that would mean that I'd be arrested and probably sent to a mental institution. Or call the number but it was very well possible that Jonathan did all this to me, that he sent *Mila*.

———

"Oh boy, oh boy. They got you so quickly. You should have opened the sample when I gave it to you. You know I can assist, but I can't do *everything* for you."

There he was, the smug salesman back at my door. But this time because I invited him, which I realize sounds incredibly stupid, but I had a feeling that this was what I needed to do. Mainly because my gut was telling me not to and because I don't believe my gut belongs to me at the moment.

"This is insane. What the fuck did you do to me?" I shouted, not caring if any neighbors could hear me.

"Owen, I didn't do anything. I told you there is a parasite infection going around. I'm here to kill them. This really has nothing to do with you. Gosh, you people can be so self-involved."

"Right, asshole, so how do you know everything about me and my parents if you haven't been targeting us?"

I was so furious I wanted to punch this guy in the face, but I knew I'd regret that.

Jonathan smiled.

"I have to know everything so I will notice irregularities. Now you called me for help. Do you want it or do you want to wait until you start getting a craving for human flesh?"

My head started turning.

"Why would I trust you? This didn't happen until you came here."

He shrugged.

"I came because you were new here. Easy target for them. I really am trying my best to be trustworthy. Although if I am honest, I do not care about you. I just want the thing out. But you people always think you're in control. You can't even imagine something else taking over."

"Are you human?"

He burst out into laughter.

"How odd, nobody has asked before. Human, not human, does it matter? Now let's not waste any more time. It will get more power, and then I might become your next meal." He took a deep breath. "Now do you have the pill that was in the envelope?"

Jonathan pushed me aside and came into the house, closing the door behind him.

That's when I knew I'd made a huge mistake. I should have run to the police instead.

He grabbed my arms with incredible strength and pulled me toward the kitchen. He held my right arm with one hand and pulled something out of his pocket with his other.

A small rope.

He used it to tie my arm to a cupboard.

"You're gonna regret this," I shouted. "I will destroy you. I will shred you into pieces!" My voice was deep and full of hate.

"Shhh, quiet now. This will be over soon."

He went through his pocket again, and this time he pulled out a pill.

"You're lucky I always bring extra."

Then he grabbed my face and shoved it down my throat.

I pulled and pushed, feeling rage like I'd never had before. Finally, I freed myself and pushed against Jonathan with all the strength I had. I was ready to kill him for what he had done to me.

But suddenly I felt a sharp pain going through my entire body. It started in my head, a feeling as if it would explode any second, and then it went to my stomach. I fell onto my knees, taking short, quick breaths.

And then I felt it, slowly moving up my throat. I had to stop the urge to swallow because I knew whatever that was, it needed to come out. Except I still can't believe what I saw crawling out of my mouth. A slimy, black worm the size of my thumb.

Jonathan saw it right away, grabbed it, and pulled it out of me.

He poured some liquid over it that smelled like petrol, threw it into the sink, and then set it on fire.

A smell so foul that it shouldn't exist filled the room until the vile creature disappeared and my mind started recovering.

I don't know how long I sat on the ground. When you go through something unbelievable, your head needs time to catch up.

I almost forgot that he was there until the tall man came down to the ground and handed me a glass of water.

"Clear again?"

I couldn't answer.

"You don't need to believe me, but I really didn't do this. I mean, I'm not doing this out of the goodness of my heart, either. I was hired to kill them."

Finally, my voice came back to me.

"By whom?"

"Oh boy, you don't wanna know. This creatures are connected to a lot of other shit going on in the world."

"What?"

He shook his head.

"I'm not supposed to talk about it. Trust me, there are things happening at the moment that you don't even want to think about. You live in one of the *least* messed-up towns. I mean, have you ever heard of Tattletoe, Agsbury, or Marville? Those places are fucked."

IF YOU GET A SONG STUCK IN YOUR HEAD

We fell in love over music.

Cassie always said you could figure out someone's personality solely by listening to their playlists. In a way, I guess she was right. That's how it worked for the two of us. Our best dates were at concerts and festivals. While our tastes weren't always entirely the same, we could discuss our favorite albums, artists, and even music videos for hours.

Maybe her love for music is what inspired the Earworm.

Cassie worked at a tech company. The kind that focuses mainly on finding the newest, biggest, most innovative idea out there. She was a rather big shot in there, which consequently meant that she had to travel a crazy amount of time.

I remember when she told me about Earworm for the first time. Her eyes were shining so bright.

Earworm is basically a little device that you plant inside your ear. You get them in a set of two. One for yourself and one for your significant other. When you get a song stuck in your head, they will hear it, too. Having a song stuck in your head can be pretty annoying, in my opinion, so I wasn't entirely sure why she was so excited about the thing.

"Well, obviously music is only the first step. But don't you think it's absolutely insane that we are able to do this in the first place?" she said as her eyes grew even bigger.

"Can you read thoughts with it as well?" I asked.

"Why? Are you afraid I'll hear all your dirty little secrets?" Cassie laughed. "No, of course not. Although if the technology becomes more advanced, maybe we can in the future." She raised an eyebrow.

I didn't particularly like the work she did or how her ethical boundaries seemed to become more blurry each day. Cassie was in no way evil, but I believe sometimes she got so excited over all the possibilities of innovation that she started ignoring downsides. Not everyone would like what they were coming up with. Although if you think about it, many were—and still are—wary of smartphones when they came out. We've all accepted being tracked; soon enough we probably would be all right with something reading our minds.

Though for now, it was only music. Music that my love and I would share. The annoying earworms as well as the songs that came to our mind when we thought of each other. A way for us to share our biggest interest while we were apart as Cassie had to go abroad for two months to introduce Earworm to their partner company.

"I will be working crazy hours, and I won't have much time for anything else. I just want us to stay connected as well as we can... And you'd help me test the advice as well." She grinned.

"All right. But no musicals!"

***

We got the devices planted inside our ears on the day of her departure. It didn't hurt or anything, but it did feel a little strange. Like it wasn't supposed to be there. At first, there was nothing. Possibly because my mind was pretty blank as I drove my girlfriend to the airport later that day. I guess so was hers.

We stayed quiet for quite some time, but just before we reached the airport, I learned what technological advancement really meant.

Yes, no, maybe, I don't know...

"Can you repeat the questiooon," Cassie suddenly started singing. I hadn't even realized that I was thinking of a song. I was watching *Malcolm in the Middle* that morning. I guess the intro just came to my mind.

"This is insane." I laughed.

"And pretty cool, too, right?" she asked.

"I guess? It's definitely different."

"We'll take them out when I get back. If you want to," she said.

"Depends if you're gonna torture me with your terrible taste over there," I joked as we got her suitcase out of the car.

I hugged her. We kissed goodbye, and that was it. For hours, there was silence. Until she texted me that she had landed.

I read the news today, oh boy

About a lucky man who made the grade

She was listening to music now. I heard it very faintly. Like background music in a movie. I lay in bed just listening to what Cassie heard in her ears all those miles away.

He blew his mind out in a car

He didn't notice that the lights had changed

The following days we hardly called or texted. Our communication went mainly through music, and it was the most exciting interaction we'd ever had.

Sometimes I would be doing something absolutely mundane, like getting groceries, when I suddenly heard a song I loved as a kid but had completely forgotten. I had to keep myself from smiling like a moron in public because Cassie would listen to some trash hits to get my attention and annoy me. We made a game out of it. Who could find the most obscure hits that we would both have stuck in our minds? It was even more interesting when we were listening to music at the same time. Only one of the songs would get stuck in both our minds, or sometimes I'd get hers and she'd get mine.

It was pretty exciting until it wasn't anymore. As with any other type of technology, you get used to it quite quickly. And then you either get addicted to it or you will be bored out of your mind.

As for me, it was just getting really fucking annoying. Cassie had music in her ears most hours of the day, and if she didn't, there would be a tune stuck in her mind. Usually one verse of some annoying song that I would hear over and over again. As we were in different time zones, sometimes I'd hear music until the latest hours. My sleeping schedule was absolutely wrecked.

All I was longing for was a little bit of silence. Just a moment alone with my thoughts and without another sound. I couldn't believe I'd ever reach that point in life, but I was sick of music.

Cassie begged me to keep the Earworm inside just a little longer. She and her team had a big meeting ahead of them, and they needed the data they were collecting through us.

"Can you just try to listen to a little less music? Or maybe shut your mind off a bit?" I asked her over the phone.

Cassie stayed silent for a moment.

"Yeah, I can try. I always wanted to meditate," she joked, "and I won't listen to music when it's night time for you," she promised.

And for days she kept that promise. We still heard each other's earworms at times, but it went back to being nice. On my birthday, she woke me up with my favorite song. She had to get up at three a.m. for that.

To die by your side
Is such a heavenly way to die
To die by your side
Well, the pleasure, the privilege is mine

Despite everything, it felt nice to be connected. Especially through the one thing we loved so much.

There were only a few days left until Cassie would come back, but last night the music was louder than ever before.

I was asleep already when she started playing the song. I knew she had to be listening to it because it was far louder than a song stuck in her head. I'd learned to make the distinction.

This one was blasting through her stereo.

I've been waiting for a guide to come and take me by the hand

Cassie didn't like Joy Division. Maybe she had people over?

I tried to shut off the song in my mind and get back to bed. But it would keep playing on repeat. And it got louder each time.

Lights are flashing, cars are crashing
Getting frequent now

Finally, I had enough and texted her.

Cas, can you turn it down, please? I have work tomorrow.

It still felt strange that I had to tell her to turn down a song in my mind. No idea if that was something I could ever get used to.

She didn't respond to my text. Instead, the song started playing again.

I'm watching you, I'm watching
Oh I'll take no pity from your friends

My ears were almost bleeding, and I was entirely fed up with her. I started thinking that she was pissed at me. Maybe I'd forgotten something important or hell knows what and she wanted to punish me. I felt a migraine settling in. It really drove me nuts. I was so close to just ripping that implant out of my ear. But then all of a sudden I heard something else.

Joy Division was still playing, but it was mixed with a different tune now.

So when you're near me, darling can't you hear me, S.O.S.
And the love you gave me, nothing else can save me, S.O.S.
ABBA, seriously?

I texted her again.

Cas, are you watching *Mamma Mia* **again? You promised no musicals!**

Again, there was no response. It felt strange that she was listening to two songs at the same time, with the ABBA one being so faint in comparison.

I was quite tired then; I'd only woken up, after all. But when I made the connection, I shot right out of bed.

Was she trying to send me a message?

I kept calling her again and again, but she wouldn't pick up. Until all of a sudden, the music was gone.

Though there was certainly no silence instead.

The music was replaced with the most dreadful sound I ever heard in my life. It sounded like pure agony. Voices, that I didn't know, were screaming and crying. It's hard to describe the noises because they were like nothing I'd ever heard before. Something about them just felt wrong, in a way that made the hairs on my skin stand up and my toenails curl.

They were hurting the insides of my soul.

Finally, I couldn't take it anymore. I ripped the device out of my ear, which at this point was already bleeding.

After Cassie still didn't respond to anything I sent her, I called one of her colleagues. A guy that worked in the Earworm team as well. He promised me that he had been testing the device for weeks now with nothing remotely close ever happening to him. But this wasn't only about the device anymore; I could tell that something was awfully wrong.

It took a while, but I convinced him that there might be something happening to Cassie. I was sure that wearing the device was somehow hurting her. Maybe the worm was digging deep into her brain, and she couldn't take it anymore.

He called the rest of the team, but nobody knew what was going on. At that point, it was the middle of the night over there and people were getting worried. When they finally called the police to go and check on her in the Airbnb she was staying at, it was already far too late.

It wasn't the worm that hurt her.

Cassie had been brutally murdered by some monster that the police still haven't found. When the police broke into the apartment, the Joy Division song was still playing on repeat. The song that was supposed to overshadow her screams.

I haven't listened to any music since I lost my sweet Cassie. I don't think I will ever enjoy music again. All I hear now is the sound. The last sound I heard before crushing that implant. It will follow me until the day I die and maybe even beyond.

I believe I heard what death sounds like.

MY GIRLFRIEND STARTED DRAWING AS A FORM OF TRAUMA THERAPY

Part 1

Ever since Evelyn had come back, she had gotten adjusted to very strange ways of doing things. There were a number of particular steps she would go through before conducting the most mundane tasks. The ones we all run with our very own autopilot but hers seemed entirely out of sync.

There were many different things she did with the rules she had come up with herself. To give you only one example, if Evelyn wanted to go to the grocery store, and she went there every day, there were four steps before leaving home. There were more for the way there, but let's start with these first.

"Step one," she would say out loud, to me or maybe to herself, I wasn't sure. "Step one is to get dressed properly. A sundress like the one I am wearing right now is perfectly fine. However, we need to be prepared for whatever the sky might surprise us with. For that reason, we wear a raincoat. A little sweat won't kill us. And we need an umbrella, too, of course."

She put on the yellow raincoat and made sure the umbrella was leaning on the door so she definitely wouldn't forget to grab it.

"Step two: preparation comes in many ways, and we always need to know precisely what we need."

She held up the list of grocery items she had prepared before. It had to be written on a checked paper with a pencil.

"Step three: the grocery bag must always contain one item already, one that is edible and that we bought before."

She shook the tote bag, but there was no sound. So she proceeded to open it slightly so we both saw the lemon that was inside. She nodded at me, and I reciprocated by raising my eyebrows

"Step four—"

"We only pay with coins," I interrupted her and handed over the small wool bag that she had sewed herself. It had become my routine to go to the bank almost every other day to exchange banknotes for coins.

Evelyn smiled. A genuine one, not the one she had been giving me for the last twelve days.

It was twelve days ago that she had appeared back on our doorstep. And it was twenty-four days ago that she had gone to the gym and disappeared without a trace.

Not a letter, not a text or a call. Not to me or anyone else that she knew. She simply vanished. I called the police the very same night, but they couldn't do anything yet. She was an adult, after all.

When there still was no trace of my girlfriend the following days, they started a search troupe. Of course, I had alarmed everyone I knew, posted on all sorts of social media that I otherwise hardly ever used, hung up posters. Some said that she had just left me, but I didn't believe that. People didn't go away without packing a single item. Even her passport was still in the closet.

Others were mumbling that if she hadn't come back by now, chances were high that she certainly must be dead.

They didn't say it to my face, but I knew.

And so after nights and nights of horror and fear and sadness, I nearly had a heart attack when I saw her suddenly standing on our doorstep. Her normally long, curly hair was trimmed to shoulder length. She was wearing the clothes of the day she had gone missing, but they didn't look a bit dirty. And her smile was still exactly the same. That toothpaste smile that I had been thinking about every single day.

One second later, she was jumping into my arms.

I asked her what happened.

The police interrogated her.

Everyone was curious.

She would just shrug and say that she didn't remember but that she was feeling perfectly fine. Nothing bad could have happened because she didn't feel bad.

Of course, that was bullshit. I'm not saying that she was lying. I would never say that even if I almost lost my cool a couple of times. This whole mess was destroying me as well. But I still didn't think she was lying.

No, I believed something so entirely horrific happened to her that her mind chose to forget.

You see, I loved Evelyn, and I didn't mind her newfound routines. When people gave her weird looks for wearing a raincoat on what felt like the hottest day of the year, I went and bought a matching one so that at least they would whisper about both of us. When the cashier rolled their eyes at the sight of all the coins, I'd take the bag with a smile and proceed to carefully choose each one before handing it over. I bought multiple umbrellas, just in case.

I have no idea why, but it somehow seemed to help her. It helped her forget about whatever she went through. After six days, she even started sleeping in bed with me again. Before that, she couldn't stand the thought of not being alone at night and flinched each time I even tried to touch her. After our first hug, physical contact had become close to none.

I was getting used to our new regular quite quickly, but the therapist disagreed when it came to my theory of Evelyn coping by going through steps for everything. That's when he suggested art therapy. A way for her brain to communicate differently.

You see, the left hemisphere of our brain is generally in charge of logical thinking and language production. The right hemisphere is in charge of emotions and creativity. Now the distinction often isn't that important as they are both connected by the corpus callosum—the bridge between both sides, so to say. Without the connection, we wouldn't be able to draw a picture of a word someone gives us. Now, because they are connected, this usually is no problem; however, there is a theory that there seems to be a failure in connection, in communication.

Have you ever felt incredibly sad but simply didn't know the reason why? Possibly the left hemisphere simply couldn't form the words for you to understand.

Now it was very farfetched, but we were desperate to find any solution to Evelyn's case, and that's when the idea of art therapy came up. Maybe Evelyn couldn't find the words for what happened but draw them instead. I went and bought art supplies that same day, and while I thought she might be reluctant at first, she gave me a bright smile when she saw the empty canvases, the brushes, and all the different acrylic colors.

"Are there steps for drawing as well?" I asked.

She tilted her head. "That depends. Do you want to join me?"

"No, let this be your hobby. I might play some music in the meantime?"

She nodded as if I had given precisely the right answer.

"Then we shall keep the steps to ourselves."

<hr>

I was prepared for the worst. The past weeks had been massively nerve-wracking for me as well, though I didn't want to imagine what kind of hell poor Evelyn had gone through that got her this fucked up. There was one thought that kept coming back to me. There was one that seemed rather obvious due to the way she was acting, but I didn't feel proven in my theory until I saw her paintings.

She kept them secret at first.

"I'm not ready for you to see yet."

It took me all the self-control I had not to go inside the small office room she was using as her new atelier, but I stayed patient. I stayed patient, nervously waiting for the horrors I might look at. Well, I tried. I really did.

Everyone loses control sometimes, don't they?

I'm not proud to admit that I didn't stay the patient boyfriend for long. When Evelyn went through the steps of planting a new flower in the garden, I told her I was going to take a nap.

Instead, I walked into the office.

It was strange. I felt like an intruder in my own home, and somehow I was, but I really thought that I needed to help her. That she was overwhelmed by the things she drew and was scared to show me.

Needless to say, I expected anything but the paintings I found.

They were beautiful. Not only the technique she used, Evelyn had always been more of the creative kind, but with the drawings, it wasn't only the style. No, the objects were beautiful as well.

Fields in three shades of green with a baby-blue sky and not a single cloud.

A lake crystal clear that it almost appeared real.

Hills in perfect shape, one only slightly bigger than the next.

I sighed. On one hand, I was relieved not to see blood, dead bodies, maybe the face of a murderer. But at the same time, I felt disappointed. I wished deep inside that this would somehow help us solve the puzzle.

"You've been naughty!"

I jumped at the voice of Evelyn behind me. She spoke in such a shrill voice that I thought she was furious, but when I turned around, she simply looked like an angry child with her arms crossed in front of her chest.

"You made a promise, Nick."

I opened my mouth but didn't know what to say. I should have apologized, but instead, I said, "I thought maybe you drew the place you went to."

"Well, silly. I did. That is the grass I was lying in. I watched the clouds, but they were gone right away. There was no sun but—we didn't mind."

"We?" I asked.

"No, me. You weren't there."

I sighed.

"Ev, you're making no sense. You weren't lying in the grass for three weeks. You were gone. I thought you were dead, kidnapped, or whatever." I couldn't hold it in anymore and hated myself seconds later for raising my voice, but she seemed unbothered. She only shrugged.

"That's where I was. Believe me or not. I told you I was fine."

She turned around, but I grabbed her arm before she could leave.

"Was it a cult? The ones that took you. No. The ones you were with? You can tell me, I won't judge."

She shook her head.

"No."

I didn't get anything else out of her that evening.

Or the next, but I did continue to follow her routines even more. I took part in them as a way to understand her situation better, and somehow it really did seem to help. She trusted me more and more each day, and I could feel that she was starting to open up.

This was why I was completely thrown off by the next drawing she made. This one she didn't hide. No, she hung it right in our living room.

It was the same green field except for this time there was a person in the middle of it. It looked just like me, hyper-realistic. She was talented for sure, but this skill was definitely new.

The person looked exactly like me, but something was different. I had no nose and no mouth. And the eyes, my very own eyes were piercing through me.

That image of me sent the coldest shiver down my spine.

When I asked Evelyn about it, she said that it wasn't me but that I didn't need to worry. He didn't need the nose or the mouth, or ears for that matter. Nobody would hear him scream.

At that moment, I'm not sure if it was progress or a setback but I believed that I was getting just a little closer to figuring out what happened. At least I thought I did. And I needed her to tell or show more, so I made sure Evelyn would be comfortable and keep drawing.

One day she was so sucked into a new painting that she was working at that I suggested getting groceries on my own.

She was reluctant. At first. But then I verbally went through the steps.

"Got my raincoat, umbrella, the bag with an apple inside, coins—"

"And I will write a list. All right, I trust you, honey. Just one moment, yes."

She kept scribbling while looking up after every word she wrote. Then she handed it over.

"Do everything as always, yes?"

I nodded.

"Of course."

I made my way to the store with those damn loud coins and the raincoat that was far too hot, but I had promised it, and I intended to keep it. Until I was finally at the store and got the list out that Evelyn had written.

-200 ml don't listen

-3 pieces to a word I say
-500 grams Do not follow
-1 liter the steps will trap u
-2 jars Don't let Evelyn know
The first two words were all written in cursive. But the others weren't.

Part 2

There is an intruder in my home.

She looks exactly like the woman who lived here. The one that I loved deeply and never wanted to lose. She looks exactly like her, but she's not.

No, this one seems hollow on the inside, which sounds ironic because I believe there are actually two different people in her body. The new Evelyn, the one that laid in the Play-Doh green grass, blissfully watching a sky with no clouds and no sun. The one that goes through a specific number of steps whenever she wants to do something. The one that scares the shit out of me with her paintings of a version of me that can't speak or scream.

And then there is the Evelyn that I love and that loves me. The one who wants to protect me and help me. Unfortunately, the odd one seems to be in charge.

Evelyn was dissociating from herself, which isn't something entirely surprising after a traumatic experience. Her childhood wasn't exactly happy and colorful, either; to be honest, her parents plain sucked. They hardly gave a shit when she went missing, either. With my family living in a different country, we were pretty much each other's family.

And I care.

Yes, that explanation seemed perfectly logical. Maybe her therapist couldn't help her enough; maybe she needed to spend some time in a mental institution. Yes, perfectly logical conclusions to the note she gave me.

Except I wasn't thinking logically. I knew deep inside that something had happened to her the days that she was gone. I was certain that she went to that place that looked so nice and clean but couldn't have been. I knew that a person, with whatever mental challenges they were fighting, could not draw that person I saw on the painting. No, there was something else going on, something unexplainable. but I'd get to the bottom of it.

I would not have them take her away from me again by showing anyone that note. You might wonder if I am completely moronic, losing my mind and risking my life, but I hope that it will all make sense when I tell you how my time with the intruder continued.

I went back home with random groceries I had bought. The note was a little more difficult; I didn't want to throw it away, but I didn't want her to find it again, either, so I hid it in my car and proceeded to go inside, acting as if nothing was different, except that I had left the raincoat in there as well.

The first thing I noticed when walking back inside was the painting. It certainly was a real eye-catcher, but that wasn't the reason for it. Something about it was different.

I walked up close and realized what it was, though I still can't say for sure how I even noticed all the way back from the door. My eyesight isn't exactly perfect, but I knew that something was off, despite all the other things that were already weird about this painting.

Now the creepy Nick suddenly had a nose. Still no mouth. Again this wasn't some cartoonish nose; no, it looked eerily realistic. Something she shouldn't have been able to draw in the thirty minutes that I was gone.

And the paint wasn't wet, either.

I threw the painting in my car where the raincoat and note were, making sure the key was hidden. To my surprise, however, Evelyn didn't mention that it was gone once.

"Would you ever wanna go back to that place?" I asked her during dinner. She hadn't said much since I came back, and I didn't, either, because I wasn't really sure what to say.

"What place?"

"You know. The one where you were before you came back."

She shrugged.

"It is awfully nice there, but it gets a bit boring, doesn't it? Only staring at the sky all day."

I nodded.

"I agree. How come you stayed there for so long, then? Wasn't there a way to get out?"

She looked at me as if she was thinking really carefully about what to say next.

"There was. Otherwise, I wouldn't be here, right?" she hissed back. "It just took some time."

"Right. Sorry," I said, feeling a little guilty for interrogating her. I wasn't a therapist or a detective, but I only had two options—find out for myself what happened or send her away—and the latter just didn't seem right to me. I needed her to be here with me. In no way did I actually believe that Evelyn was dangerous, even if she did scare the shit out of me from time to time since she was back. She wouldn't actually hurt me, though.

"Did you draw some more?" I changed the subject. Now the annoyance vanished from her eyes, and she nodded excitedly.

"Oh, I really do love drawing, Nick. You know it's like being back at home without all the negative aspects."

"Home? This is your home, Ev."

"Yeah, yeah. I mean the other home," she said as if it was the most obvious thing to say

"Fucking hell, you're not making things easy for me."

"Nobody asked you to do anything, Nick. You don't need to be shitty about it. If you don't like the way I am, you can fucking leave."

"Wow," was all I could say. Probably for the first time she was back, Evelyn sounded a little normal.

She took a spoonful of soup and then proceeded. "Having regulated processes for things I'm not used to helps me. Okay? I'm not crazy."

I nodded, feeling somewhat sympathetic but not completely. If it hadn't been for that damn note, I would have been nicer, but I knew that this girl wasn't my girlfriend. At least not all of her.

Hell yeah, you need to get used to things. Because you're probably not human, was what I really wanted to say but didn't.

"I'm gonna draw some more after dinner. Do you want to draw as well? You seem a little anxious, dear."

I stayed quiet for a moment. There were no steps when it came to drawing, but I still wasn't sure if it was a good idea.

"No thanks, you go ahead."

When Evelyn wasn't sure at first if she wanted to sleep in one bed with me, now I was the one who wanted some distance, but at the same time, I didn't want her to know. Some might wonder why I was even staying in a house with someone I found so unpredictable, but at the core of my heart, I knew this one wouldn't hurt me because somewhere inside was my own Evelyn. And my gut was pretty clear on staying here with her. You gotta listen to your gut, right?

Anyway, I told her I was feeling a little unwell and would sleep on the sofa so I wouldn't accidentally infect her. She was fine with that. She actually didn't question it; all she asked was if I needed something.

"Do you want to join me for my bedtime routine, though?" she asked, and I immediately declined.

"Feeling too weak for that."

She understood, but the disappointment was drawn to her face.

"How about I just watch you instead? I think I have enough energy for that."

Look, maybe I was reading too much into what I read on that note. Maybe she did write the things in an unclear state. Like when you are about to fall asleep and mumble nonsense. She was pretty exhausted from all the drawing. Maybe. Or maybe there was an intruder in her mind and the real Evelyn somehow tricked it. Of course, that sounds more than just a little insane, but even if it was all somehow made up by her mind, then one part of her seemed to believe it. And if it did, maybe I could break her out of this state by breaking her cycle. If I was there for the steps, I could manipulate them.

"Alrighty. Nighttime routine. Step one: we light up three candles. Not one, not two, but three."

What she didn't know was that I had thrown away her box of matches earlier.

"Shoot," she mumbled. "Fire, fire, fire, oh!" To my regret, she had extra matches. I should have known that she would be better prepared. Well, I did think about throwing away the candles, but that would have been very obvious, and she probably had spare ones of those hidden away as well.

After lighting up the three candles and placing them precisely one pencil length away from each other, she proceeded to continue with the next one. I moved one of them slightly closer when she was busy getting clothes out of her closet.

"Step two: put on the nightgown. Well this isn't exactly a gown, but it will do," she joked. I smiled.

"Nick."

"Ev, I've seen you naked a billion times."

She furrowed her brows, and I turned around.

"All right," she said after changing. "Step three: remove all of the makeup and brush the teeth. I need to go to the bathroom for that. Are you coming, too?"

"You're not wearing any makeup."

She rolled her eyes.

"But it's a step."

"Can't you just brush your teeth?" I asked.

"Sure," she said and disappeared into the bathroom. When she came back, her face was wet. I should have gone with her, but I couldn't exactly rip the toothbrush out of her hand.

"Step four: now that the teeth are brushed, the hair follows."

I grabbed her hairbrush from the table.

"Can I?" I asked, holding up the hairbrush. Evelyn thought about it for a moment.

"All right. But precisely twenty-one brushes."

"Of course," I lied and made sure to miscount a few times. It all didn't seem enough, though. Little mistakes. There had to be something big.

"Step five: turn off the candles and go to bed," she said as she got ready to blow out the candles.

"Wait!" I interrupted her. "It's so early, and I'm really not tired. Should we watch a movie?"

"I thought you weren't feeling well, dear," she said and raised an eyebrow.

"Yeah, maybe some distraction will help. And I'd be able to sleep better."

She gave me that look. The one that said sorry but not happening.

"Okay."

I moved a step closer. Things had been so weird between us, she needed to know that she could still trust me. I expected her to take a step back, but she didn't. Instead, she came closer, too, and slung her arms around my waist.

Maybe messing with her steps a little did help. She seemed more normal again. So I tried to go just a tiny bit further and moved my neck down a little. She was still not pulling away, so I gently touched the left side of her neck. Instead of moving back, she came closer. And then I missed her.

Again, something we hadn't done in quite a while. She pulled back but smiled, and suddenly I had a new idea.

"How about we draw a little? Together?"

That's when her eyes lit up. The bedtime routine was interrupted.

"I really need to go to bed... but all right. Just for a little bit."

———

For a minute, I really thought things were looking better. Things were feeling normal.

Until I saw it.

I went downstairs to grab some more empty canvases that I had left in the living room. Evelyn had used all the ones upstairs already.

And there it was, hanging back in our living room.

That goddamn painting.

I immediately checked my pocket. The key for the car was still in there. I hadn't taken the pants off, and Evelyn hadn't been close enough to take them until a few minutes ago. Except if she somehow tricked me but even then I don't remember her leaving the house. She went right upstairs to draw and didn't come down the entire time. And I had the key during that time. I checked my pocket several times because I was already feeling paranoid as fuck.

I grabbed the damn thing and ran back upstairs, to the office room where Evelyn was already preparing the paint.

"There is no way in hell that this could have just shown up in here again." I let the painting fall to the ground.

"Did you somehow break into my car?" I shouted, expecting her to show some distressed reaction. I for one was trembling with anger and fear.

She shook her head, completely numb.

"I don't know how that happened. Maybe you brought it here?" she asked.

"I think I would remember if I—Fuck it. Never mind."

I grabbed the biggest brush I could find and slammed it into dark paint. Then I drew over the little figure that now looked exactly like me, except with eyes that would follow you into your nightmares. With hands that showed every vein I had and hair in the exact shade as mine. In a matter of seconds, he was nothing but a black stain, but I didn't stop there; I painted over the entire canvas. When that was done, I grabbed a pair of scissors and slammed them right in the middle of the canvas where I believed the image of me had been before I destroyed it.

Evelyn stood still and watched me the entire time. At first I thought she looked sad or confused maybe, but then I realized the look on her face was one that I had gotten pretty good at myself.

Concern.

My heart was still racing, and I was breathing rapidly. My arms were full of black paint, the scissors still tight in my hand.

"Sweetie. You don't seem very fine," she finally said.

She sounded nice. She sounded like herself.

"No, I'm not fine. You left, Evelyn. You went to some horrible place, and you're trying to tell me it was nice. If it really was so great, then why didn't you call? Why didn't you tell me to come pick you up? Why didn't you ask me to come with you?" I tried to control my voice, but I couldn't; with every word I got louder and louder.

Evelyn avoided my eyes. She looked down, and I realized that she tried to hide her face because of the tears that were now rolling down her cheeks.

This was the first time she'd cried since she was back.

I almost expected her to somehow apologize, to tell me that she left because she wanted to leave me, but then she said the last thing I was expecting.

"Nick, do you want me to show you where I was?"

Part 3

Play-Doh grass, green timbered hills, each one just a little taller than the next, and a lake filled with crystal-clear water. With all my heart I hoped that this place didn't exist. I hoped that Evelyn would take me somewhere so vile and horrible that every fiber of my body would simply scream for us to get away.

I never wanted to imagine this poor girl going through hell. I didn't want to imagine her going through something so traumatic that she changed her entire personality. Of course in my heart, I didn't want that, but my brain needed to understand.

And no part of me could ever understand how she had been at the most beautiful place I had ever seen in my life because it had to mean something far more horrifying than a regular mind could even understand or fight.

We were standing on a road, not far from where we lived, I suppose. We drove for two hours maybe; I can't say for sure. I had lost most sense of time. Well, I drove. She gave directions.

We left at noon. Evelyn had written a list for grocery items, food, and drinks for the road. She was so eager after I accepted visiting the place with her that she wrote it last night. Even after already breaking the steps of her nighttime routine. Highly irregular. In the morning, she offered to go and buy them together, but I insisted that I would be faster on my own. This way we could go to the perfect place even sooner.

I didn't tell her that I took no coat, no umbrella, and certainly didn't use any damn coins. She believed I did exactly as she told me and not only listened to half of her instructions.

The groceries were in my backpack, together with my phone that sent my current location to a handful of friends that I could trust. Although I once believed that the girl I left with was the one I could trust the most. Now she was the one who scared me more than any other person ever before.

And still, I decided to go with her. To the place she was drawing. The place that changed her.

We stood at that empty road looking down at the fields for what felt like an eternity. Not saying one word. Evelyn was smiling, and I felt the knot tighten inside of me.

"Isn't it simply marvelous?" Evelyn finally asked.

I swallowed.

"So where did you stay? Where did you sleep? All I see is emptiness."

"You can look, but I can't show you."

"What do you mean?" I asked.

Evelyn glanced at me, her face a mixture of anticipation and worry.

"I can't go back," she whispered.

"What the fuck? Didn't we come here so you could show me what happened to you? Looking at fucking grass isn't exactly helping our situation, Ev."

"You've gotten meaner in these past days," she mumbled, and I agreed. I'd found it harder to control my emotions.

"So what now?" I asked.

"You can go look. I think if you do, you will understand. It will all make sense again. I promise, Nick."

This beautiful landscape felt suffocating from the outside, but I somehow understood what Evelyn meant. It was pulling me in with its beauty and peaceful nature. It almost seemed as if everything that was on the outside just felt dirty and wrong.

That's what was scaring me.

"If I go there, will I be stuck for weeks, like you were?"

"No, because I will be right here waiting for you. I will make sure we bring you home."

Well, it wasn't an easy choice because, on one hand, this place was not scary. It was the middle of the day, and I saw no other souls out there that would be able to hurt me. If this was just a regular place, then maybe I needed to get used to the idea that it was out of my hands to help Evelyn. Maybe I needed that kind of closure. Maybe we both did. Besides, I had my phone with me and a backpack full of supplies. I would be fine looking at some fields and hills. Maybe I'd stay away from the lake, just to be safe.

It's just that when something seems so easy and fine, then there has to be an issue with it.

"You'll be here when I come back?" I asked.

She nodded.

"One more thing. Nick, this might not come as a surprise to you, but there are steps before going in."

"You're fucking kidding me." I laughed.

"You have to follow them."

I crossed my arms and waited for her to tell me which godforsaken steps she had come up with now.

"All right. Step one: I have to stay here. You have to go alone."

"Yeah, you already told me."

"Yes. Step two: you must go inside one step at a time and leave any extra items on the road," she said as she pointed at the backpack.

"Right."

"Step three: there is no sun inside, but you need to be back before sunset *here*. That one's not easy."

"What if I mess up a rule?"

She didn't answer. Instead, her eyes were piercing through mine. That familiar look. The one that the other version of me had given me on the painting that I destroyed. Not that destroying it helped one bit—it was back in the living room the following morning. Another reason why I had to see this hell for myself. She looked at me with eyes that didn't belong to the woman I loved.

"You're not Evelyn," I finally said. This was the first time I said those words out loud. I expected her to laugh or question me, but she didn't. She kept staring. I got a step closer to the imposter and one more until I was standing right above her, not breaking eye contact. "What did you do to her?" I hissed. My heart was racing, a sudden rush of adrenaline giving me both confidence and anxiety.

Evelyn grinned.

"If you want to see your girlfriend, *follow the rules* I just gave you and walk over." She emphasized the part with the rules.

We were close.

Close to the edge.

Don't ask me why I did the following. Don't ask me what I was expecting, but it certainly wasn't what happened next. I suppose I stopped thinking for a second or maybe I was finally thinking clearly for once, because at that moment it seemed so incredibly logical.

I grabbed Evelyn, or rather her shell inhabited by some sick monster. I grabbed her, and with all my strength, I pushed both of us to the other side, into the grass.

It's hard to describe the feeling of what happened next. A few seconds of the most horrific migraine you could imagine. For a moment, it felt as if glass shattered and splintered inside of my mind and pieces were stuck everywhere. I heard static, loud at first but slowly getting weaker. I had closed my eyes, and when I opened them, the sharpest light was what I saw, radiating from the sky.

It was light as in the middle of the day, but there was no sun. Just like she said.

Evelyn.

I hadn't realized that I wasn't touching her anymore. She had gotten up.

I tried to jump on my feet, at first ignoring my strange surroundings, but I couldn't get up just yet. I thought she would run right over the edge back to the road. I could still see it in front of us, even if it felt as if there was a light filter hanging over the edge to the other side.

She didn't, though. No, she kneeled down, staring at me as if I had just murdered her entire family, then she grabbed my face and pierced her nails inside my flesh. She removed her hand and looked at the blood on it.

She grinned from one ear to the other, but it wasn't a happy or triumphant one. It was a bloodthirsty grin.

"You're gonna regret this, you bastard."

Then she got back up and ran.

At those first moments on that field, I could hardly do anything. My head felt as if a swarm of bees was going to war inside. My cheek was bloody, but I felt no pain there.

At least Evelyn had left the backpack.

As I finally got a little clearer in my head, I grabbed my phone.

No signal.

However, I did have a few messages that were sent before. All saying how the connection broke down. My friends couldn't follow the GPS to where I was. We disappeared from the landscape.

Well, fuck, I thought.

Now there were two pathways in front of me. Well, one of them quite literally. There was a pathway on that field I was standing on, leading god knows where. A pathway I hadn't seen from the outside. And then there was the possibility of leaving if that was possible. I didn't know if that would do any good, but I had a feeling that as soon as I might leave, Evelyn would be stuck here for good, and I wouldn't be able to find her again.

The real Evelyn, that is. So I got on my feet, which were shaky at first but became more steady by the second, and I started hiking up the path.

With everything odd and strange happening, I didn't feel frightened at that moment.

No, as I mentioned. This place was far more peaceful than the outside. It felt welcoming. Familiar because I had looked at it in her drawings for days.

With every step I took, the landscape seemed to change. The vast fields that seemed endless at first were now leading up to something, toward a part of the lake, as it appeared there was more than one. I followed the pathway and was led to a big lake just in front of a hill. There didn't seem anything but nature at first until I got close enough.

Close enough to see the one thing I certainly did not expect at this place.

A house.

It had a small frame and was painted in a lemony yellow. It was fresh; I could smell the paint even from this distance. The door was a rusty red, the windows small, and a bike was leaning on the wall.

This house was an exact replica of the one we lived in. Except it was crooked and unfinished. Like a cardboard version of our home.

I swallowed, standing on this path, unsure whether I should take one more step or run for my life. I certainly should have run, but somehow my feet wouldn't listen, so I approached the wrong, crooked home.

Only as I was standing in front of the house, not able to hide behind anything, I wondered what in the hell I was thinking. There was nothing around me.

This was definitely the place the wrong Evelyn ran toward, and after what she'd done to my face, I didn't wanna know what else she might be capable of. I wondered about the rules she told me about. Was the one about the sunset correct? If so, what time was it now?

The clock on my phone stopped working.

I looked to my left and to my right. There seemed to be more buildings on this road, although much further away. Other homes, all a little crooked, all a little wrong. There was a reason the pathway led me to my own, however, and I needed to find out why.

I collected all my courage and slowly approached the house. On the left side of the door, there was a hedge. I climbed down next to it, took a deep breath, and got ready to have a peek inside.

If she saw me, this could be my end. My heart was racing so fast that all I could hear was the sound of blood rushing through my veins. Completely consumed with fear and anticipation, I was so focused on whatever was inside of this house that I forgot about my surroundings.

That's when I felt the touch of a boiling warm hand wrap around my mouth.

"Nick," a voice whispered.

I grabbed the hand and pulled the person down to the ground with me. Of course, the person was none other than Evelyn. Her eyes were full of panic, and she gestured for me to be quiet. Her hands were shaking, and she looked completely messed up.

Completely different than she had looked before. She was wearing the same clothes, but there was blood on her face, her hair went in all directions, and her clothes were ripped.

"Nick, you have to be quiet. They are in there," she whispered.

Her eyes. Her eyes looked genuinely scared and... real.

"Evelyn, is this you?"

A tear rolled down her cheek, and she gave me that half-smile that I hadn't seen in weeks.

"It was me the whole time, but this thing, it infected my mind. To be able to get out with me. I'll explain, but we need to hide somewhere else."

She grabbed my hand, and I followed. Another possibly stupid mistake but despite all the mindfuckery I still knew that this was her. She had that determined look in her eyes that I knew so well.

———

Evelyn found a safe spot, so she said. It was some tree, one that I didn't remember from her paintings.

"Ev, I don't understand. What the hell is going on?"

She sighed.

"I don't know how to explain. There probably is no normal way to do that. I was here for weeks that felt like years, and I still don't understand it entirely. They somehow infest your mind, and when they dig deep enough, at a place where you can't even feel them anymore, they take over."

"Who are they?"

"The things. I don't know what to call them... When you messed up her routines, you somehow broke her power over me. Little by little. More and more. She wasn't supposed to come back here. It was dangerous. When latched on to a person entirely, they can take their soul with them and slowly replace theirs with their own. I'm pretty sure she only wanted to make sure you got in. When you threw me, us, over the edge, she couldn't latch on for much longer."

"So you're... free?"

She looked at me with fear in her eyes.

"For now. She's in the house. In her own copy of a body. Just like yours. We need to make sure—"

"What do you mean? Just like mine?"

"Nick. It wasn't just me who got infected. When we were here last time."

Now, this was getting ridiculous. I had never come to this weird-ass place in my entire life, and this whole story that Evelyn was telling me now seemed more bonkers than everything she'd done so far.

But then again, I did see that house just now. I just didn't get it.

"But that's impossible. No, you went to the gym, and then you simply didn't come back."

Evelyn shook her head.

"No, we went together. We were there for at least one day. We had a picnic, and it was so nice there that we decided to stay for as long as we could. Of course, that was them manipulating our minds into thinking that. So they had time to melt into one with us... But then you left."

I swallowed. Those words were the hardest to hear.

"I left you?" I whispered.

She took my hand, and I finally remembered how strong Evelyn was. The real one.

"I don't think you did it voluntarily. You weren't entirely in charge of your mind. More so than me, I think, but still not completely. I can't say for sure how that worked because I had her thoughts melted with mine, but I don't know what it looked like for you. I suppose you're memory was more affected, though." She closed her eyes for a moment, and I could feel her pain.

"They took my will. I had no control, and with every step they made me do, they chewed a bigger part of me. When you were gone, I was in that house, which kept growing each day, and with each day that other shell grew, too."

I wanted to ask what she meant by that, but it was incredibly hard to follow already.

"What about the paintings? Do you remember that?"

She nodded.

"Some of it was me. Some of it was the thing. I tried to help you remember. *It* tried to make you go back so that they could switch you out for good. The painting of you in the field. That really was you, the part you left here. I think she tried to lure you in to exchange you with a copy they were creating or make you become one. They are inside here, collecting their strengths now. Growing."

While I didn't want to believe what she was saying, at the same time I didn't have to, if that makes any sense? Remember what I said about Evelyn's autopilot not being entirely in sync? I believe mine did even more without my knowledge. But I still had to be sure. I had to see that we were not both losing our minds simultaneously.

So I walked back to the house.

I walked up the pathway leading me directly toward the door. Alone.

And then I knocked. Three times, as Evelyn told me. I didn't know if I could trust her or if this was even the real one, but that was what I did.

I knocked on the door, which wasn't locked. I don't believe it even had a lock. The door that felt as if it was made out of pasteboard opened wide as my fist hit against it.

I knew that I couldn't exactly expect something nice in front of me, but the look of those creatures brought up the bile inside my stomach.

Evelyn was right. The thing had separated from her, but she had grown while inside of her. Grown to be an almost identical copy.

Almost. It was not fed enough, consisted of more bones than flesh and skin with holes in it. Her hair appeared glued on, the eyes stones instead of irises.

"There you are," she called out in glee with a voice that was eerily similar to the real one.

"There you are," the other one croaked. The one that looked like me with a nose and mouth that were still growing.

I swallowed. I was not ready for this. But I had to be; there was no other option.

I had to make sure that they would stay right where they were. Of course, the copy of me was already trying to get on its feet to move closer to me.

Hurry up, I thought.

"What are you doing?" the fake Evelyn shouted. "What is this smell?"

She looked at me, but I wasn't the one she was talking to. It was my Evelyn who came in from the back while they were distracted to pour out the gasoline before they noticed. She lit up a match and threw it in the liquid.

"Close the door!" she shouted before starting to run.

I slammed the pasteboard door shut and prayed it wouldn't break. One of them was scratching the door from the inside, making noises that no human could ever be capable of.

"Evelyn!" I shouted, praying even more that she had made it out through the door in the back.

The house burned down in a matter of minutes. I suppose that happens when you build a house out of cardboard. It burned down, our parasites with it. And the real Evelyn and I ran outside, back to our world, not looking back once at the wonderful scenery.

You see, I trusted this Evelyn. I knew it was her, the one that wrote that coded grocery list the other day. Because last night she wrote another one when she was in charge of the mind a little more. A list that instructed me to buy gasoline and matches while she told me we needed food and drinks. When she did that, something just clicked. I realized there was still one part inside of her that I could trust, and I could just tell it was this one.

Since we've gotten back, and I still can't believe we did, I have had a hard time adjusting. I don't follow any crazy steps, of course. I just live my regular life as well as I can remember. Evelyn and I even burned the raincoats. The smell of burning plastic really is horrendous but not as bad as our second bodies smelled before they turned to ash.

Evelyn suggested we burn the paintings as well. I thought about it. But I kinda like seeing the painting that once had my imposter on it but now is only a big field.

It even got me in the mood to start drawing. Drawing a place that shouldn't exist with Play-Doh grass, green timbered hills, a crystal-clear lake, and pathways with many different homes that aren't burning yet.

MY NEIGHBORS TAKE THE CURFEW A LITTLE TOO SERIOUSLY

Part 1

I live inside one of those picture-perfect gated neighborhoods. A place where life is always safe and sound because nobody can come in and disturb the peace that is so naturally dear to the residents' hearts. Not with all the security in place. Cameras on each corner watching every step, neighbors that are extra attentive, and then we have this cold and ugly concrete building at the entrance where the security people work. It's probably the only hideous piece of architecture in here and has one of the guards standing right at the gate and greeting everyone who passes by with a friendly wave and smile. That is if they truly belong here, of course.

The loud and busy town isn't far away, but if you stood behind the gate, you wouldn't be able to tell as we are half surrounded by deep forest.

My new neighborhood, named Sanctuary Hills despite not sitting on a hill, is the essence of suburbia. Two-level homes, often in hunter green or eggshell white, embellish the wide streets with long driveways, the homes big enough for generations but usually only inhabited by a married couple with one child and a dog. When a family is very extraordinary, they might have a cat instead, but that's the tip of craziness the people here might express. The people that live here are the kind that cut the grass on their lawns on the same day each week.

Every building here has a spacious pool, many shaped just like kidneys, but most are hardly used. Except for when there is a pool party, of course, and there are many. Usually in combination with a barbecue. In the short time I lived here, I must have been invited to three already, but I didn't make it to one. They usually start very early in the day when I still work.

While I never imagined this to be my cup of tea, I am still astonished by the way I enjoy these surroundings that are so perfect it should be uncanny but somehow it's not. Somehow you do always feel safe. It really is a nice neighborhood, even if I don't entirely fit the demographic. I only came here very recently after my grandmother started getting more unwell. She's been living on her own since Grandpa passed, and as I work remote, it seemed perfectly reasonable for me to come and live with her. She doesn't need anyone to take care of her physically, just company that is around and ready if her head starts to spin. Besides, Grandma is as sweet as grandmothers get. So being here for her is more than simple for me. And I get to live in a beautiful home in a wonderful place.

The only negative side to all this is the lack of people my age. Most residents are either rather old and have been living here for centuries or they're middle-aged with children, seldom plural and in many cases singular. To repeat myself, neither really fits my demographic, but for now, this is totally fine. Especially considering social interactions are currently limited either way.

It's one of the reasons, or possibly the main one, why I didn't mind when I was told about the curfew. I've heard of many places and towns that believe a curfew could be beneficial to our current situation. And, well, here inside Sanctuary Hills, there aren't many places I'd go anyway. Especially not at night.

The curfew begins right after dinner time, which currently is eight p.m., just after sunset. It was one of the first things that Grandma told me when I arrived and something she still repeats regularly.

"Make sure to be back inside before curfew. People really do not appreciate it if you don't. They're a sucker for rules," she said with a smile that didn't match the sentiment in her voice.

"Sure, that's fine. It's not forever, right?" I laughed.

"Of course not, the sun moves with the days. Soon you'll have more time."

"What?"

As I said, physically Grandma was feeling fine; mentally, however, her mind was not as sharp as it used to be.

"Can you go to the store, hun? What time is it now?" she asked now with a much calmer expression.

———

It was only two p.m. when I made my way to the store and less than half an hour later I was standing in the queue waiting for my turn. The store is rather a small shop but has everything we need. If we wanted to splurge, I suppose we could go to the markets in town, but Grandma likes the products here and is very used to them. Grandpa used to enjoy them as well, and honestly, I like them, too. The produce is fresh, and while the brands are unfamiliar, everything tastes nice.

So I was standing in line when I saw the only person so far that truly grabbed my attention in a very different way than the other people here. If I notice the people in Sanctuary Hills, it usually is because they seem so peculiar with their looks and their tastes, with hair too high and makeup too bright, as if they recently escaped out of a book by Dr. Seuss. The person that I saw standing just in front of the grocery store, however, was a young man around my age, dressed in a denim jacket, black pants, and a Kinks shirt. He was holding a cigarette but not even taking a drag; instead, he seemed focused on something in the air or possibly on the lamppost.

I could have just walked out and talked to him, but I used to live in a big city where you usually don't talk to neighbors at all, and somehow I felt too shy. So I found an excuse by buying a pack of cigarettes at the counter, despite not having smoked in years, and asked the stranger for a lighter as I walked outside with my paper bag filled with groceries. I suppose I really was a bit desperate for friends in this lonely place.

"You're new here, aren't you?" he asked after lighting up my cigarette.

I suppressed the urge to cough and answered, "Yeah, I'm staying with my grandma for a while."

He inspected me a second too long and then said, "Abigail Allen?"

"That's her. How do you know?" The neighborhood wasn't big, and if he lived here for a while, it wouldn't surprise me if he knew most people, but guessing simply from my appearance alone was a bit too fast.

He grinned.

"I'm not a stalker, I promise. I know all the people that live here and hear about any newcomers right away."

"Well, that's not strange at all."

He laughed.

"I have a good reason, I swear. I'm in charge of the security systems here and usually install the cameras for the people's homes as well."

He pointed toward the thing he was looking at earlier. It was a security camera hanging on top of the lamppost.

"You know, it's kind of ironic. I usually feel far more unsafe when there is too much security. Like there has to be a reason they're so careful, right?" I said and already started regretting my words, but the guy smiled again.

"To be honest, I don't see the purpose, either, but I get paid so I won't complain."

"So let's hope the people here stay paranoid." I laughed.

We chatted a bit longer, longer than I initially imagined we would, but I assume the stranger—his name was Jack as I found out—didn't have much interaction with peers in Sanctuary Hills, either. He did know people in town, however, and invited me to go for a beer by the river with them. Just after dinner.

"And the curfew?" I raised an eyebrow.

Jack gave me a funny look as if I was a bit clueless.

"How old are you?" Now he was raising an eyebrow.

I rolled my eyes.

"Funny, I'm twenty-five, but you know what curfew I mean. They blast it through the speakers every evening."

Jack chuckled.

"All right, I see. And you live with your grandma, too, who probably doesn't go out at night either way, but trust me, you can. I think it's more so the kids stay inside. Nobody is gonna arrest you for leaving the house after eight, Charlie."

So far I never really had a reason to go outside, but thinking about it, Sanctuary Hills had such a small population, and going to a different place for one evening seemed perfectly reasonable. Depending on how long I would stay here, finding some friends would be nice. Besides, Jack worked for the security system or whatever; if it was that forbidden, he would know.

"All right. I'm in," I decided.

"Cool, so shall we meet at the gate? Just after eight?"

Grandma and I had dinner, but she was rather tired and went to bed early. I hadn't told her about my plans to go out, but I figured I'd leave her a note. And I'd take my phone with me so she could reach me if she needed to.

I noticed that I was a bit late when I suddenly heard the announcements from the street. I'd heard them the past days, too, of course, but somehow they seemed even louder now.

Attention, attention! Residents of Sanctuary Hills. Please be aware that the curfew begins in only five minutes. Find your way home swiftly and have a pleasant Sanctuary evening inside your homes.

The announcement started and ended with a jingle. I must say I felt a bit nervous going outside after hearing the announcement. I'd been a lot more confident when I was talking to Jack. Suddenly I also felt guilty for wanting to leave without Grandma knowing.

I sighed and made the choice not to go out. However, I didn't have Jack's number, and simply not showing up would really be rude. So I decided I would quickly run down to the gate, tell him to leave without me, and come back home.

A few minutes outside past curfew really shouldn't be an issue, after all.

Well, that's the point when I learned oh how seriously the curfew really was taken by the people of Sanctuary Hills. I learned the hard way when I opened the door to my home only a few minutes before eight.

As I opened the wooden door, I was greeted by two bright faces grinning so intensely, it almost appeared as if they were in pain.

A man and a woman that I hadn't seen before. She had red hair with much volume and was wearing round pink glasses. Her lips were bright red, and her flowery dress seemed not casual at all. He completed her look with a button-down shirt, perfectly ironed brown pants, and shiny loafers. They looked strangely old fashioned, even more than the other people here.

"Well, hello there. What a sweet darling you are. Don't you agree, Harold?" the woman said, and the makeup on her face started cracking from her nonstop smile.

"Oh, pleasantly darling, truly my dear."

I laughed politely but mainly nervously.

"Good evening, are you looking for my grandma?" I asked.

"Oh no, dear, we're not. Abigail is a sweetheart and often in bed before the time. She doesn't worry us one bit," the woman spoke.

"Worry? Why would—"

"We hope you did not intend to leave the house. That would be an awful mistake. Haven't you looked at the time? Must have slipped your mind. Well now, now, swiftly go back in and we will forgive and forget." They both laughed, and now all of a sudden they were sounding nervous.

"I'm sorry, have we met?" I asked, and my eyes moved to the clock above our door. I never thought about it before, but it was a strange place to hang a clock.

They didn't answer my question. The man now had his hand in the doorframe, too close for my taste.

"I'm only planning to bring a message to a friend. I'll be right back home," I said, feeling weird that I had to make excuses for doing something so normal.

"No reasonable friend would meet you at a time like that, my dear. Now, will you listen or not?" They were still smiling, but their voices were raised so high I was afraid they would wake Grandma.

"Right. I'm sorry, where do you live?" I asked.

They turned their heads in a half-circle and pointed toward the scarlet red house on the other side of the street. I had been wondering who lived in a house so noticeable.

Their heads moved back so quickly that their necks had no chance to follow. For a second I thought they might break. My feet moved back faster than I could think. My gut started screaming to shut the door; those creatures that called themselves neighbors were far too uncanny. Something was utterly wrong with them, and it made my blood almost freeze.

"How did you—" I muttered and then swallowed. "I promise I won't go outside."

"LIAR," the woman shouted. At that point I was more than worried; these people were scaring me. And the slowly setting sun was only adding to the gloomy atmosphere.

I shut the door without another thought. My hands started shaking, and I didn't understand why. I didn't understand how I was suddenly so scared by such a situation that should be ordinary from an outsider's perspective. I wanted to go and talk to the only person that I'd met and somehow trusted, but I couldn't possibly leave Grandma.

Should I call the police? I wondered. But I changed my mind as those weirdos hadn't actually done anything.

I stood in front of the closed door, but I could still hear them. They didn't leave. I heard them breathing, louder and louder by the second.

I have to go wake Grandma, was my second thought, but it was interrupted.

A shiver went through my body when I felt a sharp pain in my left arm.

"What are you doing?"

I turned my head, and my eyes met the ones of Abigail. My grandmother stared at me with pupils so big I thought her eyes were all black. Her nails were digging into my skin.

When she saw my scared expression, she let go.

"I'm sorry, honey. I told you not to go out after dark. They don't like it. They don't like it one bit."

I thought my grandmother's mind was a bit confused, but after seeing those neighbors, she appeared like the sharp one.

"Come look." She waved me to the window.

My stomach made a turn when I saw Harold and his strange wife standing on our lawn waving. There appeared to be other people behind them, too, but I couldn't look at them for long. Grandmother waved back, and that seemed to make them happy but not happy enough to leave.

No, they stayed. They stayed for hours despite the curfew that they were now breaking themselves. Or maybe it didn't count because they were standing on a lawn?

That's when Grandma pulled me away from the window and closed the blinds. They shielded us from views outside but not from the noise. The noise of ear-splitting screams, painful and sharp. I couldn't exactly tell if they were near or simply so loud that you heard them through the entire neighborhood. My first thought was that it had to be Jack somewhere outside, but I couldn't say for sure. What had I gotten myself into? All I knew was that there was no way I could go outside. I was stuck in here, at least in safety for now.

"You woke them up, and now they'll stay for a bit," Grandma interrupted my thoughts as she gently stroked my hair "but it's all good, love. Just stay inside with me until morning, yes?"

Part 2

Now I know that my reaction might have been just as odd or at least nearly as strange as the neighbors'. I obliged to the curfew and stayed inside despite knowing that something was not right. But then again, what else was I supposed to do? They stood there all night. Even when it started raining and hailing. I couldn't help but wonder if they were somehow helping me, keeping me away from whatever caused the torture outside. However, one look at their stiff faces that had smiles plastered on them assured me that they couldn't possibly have good neighborly duties in mind. And wondering whether it was only them, Harold and her, who had an issue or two proved wrong as well when it slowly became a crowd of people out there on our lawn.

Grandma acted like it was the most normal thing, and I was sure at least one of us was going insane. Or possibly both of us went a bit looney in our own ways. Inside this home and this neighborhood that we weren't leaving. Sanctuary Hills had its hands wrapped around us tightly, and we stayed. Well, Grandma did because she had been living here for ages and saw no reason to leave now. I will elaborate on her far-too-apathetic reaction to the insane neighbors later. I must have been even crazier for not leaving, either, but I believed I had good reasons.

One, I didn't have a car, and my only form of transportation was my feet, and walking or even running from those weirdos did not seem like a great plan. Second, I couldn't possibly leave my grandmother, and as previously mentioned, she certainly was not going.

I did try to call for help as one should in a terrifying situation as such. It seemed logical to me, and under normal circumstances, it sure would have been.

The first one I tried to reach was my mother. My mother, who is the personification of concern and who I normally would choose last to share my fears with simply because she is so terribly anxious. And no, she didn't try to talk sense into me or prove to me that everything was fine and well. No, she acted awfully worse. Our call went just the same way as it did with anyone else I tried to reach.

"Mum, I don't know what to do. I think we might be in danger, Grandma is not—"

"Oh, darling, say hi to your grandmother for me! I haven't called her in ages. I am an awful daughter, aren't I?"

"Mum, no, you need to listen. Something is terribly wrong."

"Are you making sure she is eating well? I know how she adores sweets but—"

"What is going on?" I shrieked. "Mum, I can't get ahold of the police. I don't know what to do."

"Right, oh honey, I almost forgot. Make sure your grandpa takes his medicine!"

After those words, I hung up. My mother couldn't have possibly forgotten that her own father died more than a year ago.

My hands were shaking—no, my entire body was trembling. At first, I believed that only the people in Sanctuary Hills were going insane or had been insane all the time without me consciously noticing, but now it was spreading. Believing that maybe, just maybe, it was only my family, I called others, too. All sorts of numbers I had in my phone. Friends, old colleagues, and even an ex. Every conversation went like me talking about one thing and them responding to questions I never asked.

For the rest of the night, I locked myself and Grandma inside her room. She went to sleep, and I went crazy until morning came.

After numbing down from the shock just enough, my mind started calculating and racing through every logical explanation, as well as illogical ones including their prospective outcomes. Like a machine, my head went through the algorithms. No result was satisfactory, however.

Everything was nice and normal and fine.

That's what Grandma assured me was happening. I still wasn't sure what to do next. Our lawn was empty, but I did see people walking around outside as they did each day. A postman walking around, filling the peculiar mailboxes, gardeners watering plants, and children playing hopscotch. They all appeared so awfully regular that I almost decided to open the door and talk to someone, but somehow I couldn't bring myself to turn the doorknob. I was too anxious.

The curfew wouldn't start for another many hours, but I didn't dare to leave the house. It proved safe last night at least. More hours passed, and I eventually fell asleep from all the exhaustion and from staying up all night. It must have been late in the afternoon when I woke up again.

When there was a knock on the door later in the evening, my heart skipped a beat. I started cold sweating only thinking about those neighbors standing outside again. They had left sometime in the early morning; I saw when I quickly peeked through the curtains.

I tiptoed toward the door and looked through the spy.

It was Jack.

I stood behind the door, suddenly too scared to even move. I wasn't sure if I could trust this stranger. No, I felt like I couldn't trust him one bit because if he was as normal as he appeared yesterday, then he wouldn't be here. Because if he was outside during curfew, then he wasn't safe out there and couldn't stand here normal and fine.

I was genuinely sure that those screams came from him. Now I was wondering if he was the one causing him.

"Mrs. Allen? Charlie? Hello?" I heard him say through the door, and then he knocked three times, but I still didn't move.

I prayed that he would leave so I could just plan my next steps. It felt ludicrous being this anxious when the street seemed normal just as it did the past days that I was here. But it wasn't. After last night, nothing felt normal anymore, even if the appearance tried to make me believe it was.

I slowly took a step back, fearing that he might hear me breathe, but that was a big mistake because before I could help it, Grandma had appeared and opened the door. It all happened so quickly, I didn't even realize she was standing here; I thought she was in bed.

"Good afternoon, dear," she politely said.

"Good afternoon," he responded, and his eyes quickly shifted to me. "Are you okay?" he carefully asked.

I stayed silent.

"I didn't know that you were acquainted. How wonderful that you're making some friends, Charlie. Oh, come on in, dear, let me make some tea." Grandma opened the door wide and then walked toward the kitchen and even had the audacity to wink at me. I couldn't believe her. Did she purposely forget the nightmare we went through?

I was ready to just slam the door shut, but Jack had already made his way inside.

"It's strange how all the houses look exactly the same on the inside." He laughed, and when his eyes met mine again, he suddenly looked a bit more concerned. "Are you ill? I was wondering why you didn't show up. Imagined you changed your mind or something."

I breathed in deeply.

"I couldn't. The curfew," I said, making sure to closely watch how he'd respond.

He raised an eyebrow. "So you decided to be a law-abiding citizen after all?"

I clenched my fist. I surely didn't feel like playing this game after the night I had.

"Why are you here?" I hissed, and he seemed a bit taken back by my sudden anger.

"Uhm, well, I was a bit worried when you didn't show up yesterday but," he paused for a moment, "I didn't want to appear too stalkery, either. We don't really know each other, after all."

"So?"

"So I'm here to check on your grandmother's cameras outside and casually trying to find out if you stood me up on purpose?" He nervously laughed. Somehow, in this moment, he really did seem genuine. I wanted to believe that this was all normal, but how on earth could he be so oblivious to the situation?

"Didn't you hear the screaming last night?" I asked.

He looked confused.

"Screaming?"

"Yeah, and if you were outside, did nobody try to stop you? Because they certainly made sure I would stay inside." I raised my voice again.

"They?"

"The neighbors. The ones from the scarlet red house and all their psychotic friends."

"Oh," he laughed, "I see you met Trudy and Harold. I suppose they are a tad eccentric."

"Eccentric? They didn't leave all night!"

Now he was raising an eyebrow again, and that reaction was really getting on my nerves.

"Charlie, is everything okay?" he said in a worried tone.

"She had a fever last night," my grandmother who appeared behind us with a tray said. "She mumbled all sorts of nonsense all night, nightmares I suppose."

"No, it happened. They were out there, they—"

Now both Grandma and Jack had that worried look on their faces.

"I'm sure something happened, but maybe your mind played some tricks on you?" Jack said.

"Why don't you just show her whatever the camera on my lawn filmed the night before? Possibly that will calm the poor child down."

Cameras. It was the first helpful thing my grandmother said.

Looking at the security cameras must have been the most terrifying experience so far. Not because of what we saw but because of what we didn't.

A couple appeared in the frame. Harold and Trudy. They were dressed just as I remembered from what I could make out on the screen. However, Trudy was holding something in her hand. A basket of some sort. I didn't remember her carrying anything yesterday, but then again, I was slightly distracted by her face, which seemed to be cracking up.

From the view, I could exactly see myself when the door opened. I'm trying to emphasize that it was my face that I saw.

Until that point, it all made sense, and I felt a shiver only thinking about what would happen next.

Except it didn't.

Trudy handed me the basket, I smiled, we chatted some more as it seemed, and then they turned around and left. Soon they were out of the picture and clearly not on our lawn with other neighbors gathering. No, there was nobody, even when we fast forward the tape.

I sat there in shock.

"It's not possible," I whispered.

"Well, darling, you simply cannot and often should not trust your mind. It's trickery!"

Jack laughed at what she said but collected himself quickly.

"I'm sorry, Charlie. I'm sure it felt very vivid. That can happen with fever dreams."

"But it's not possible," I muttered, and then with more confidence, I exclaimed, "The basket! She never gave me a freakin' basket!"

"Oh, honey," Grandma said as she pointed toward the stool next to the bathroom where, of course, sat a wooden basket filled with biscuits and a bottle of wine.

"They really are awfully attentive neighbors, aren't they?"

Jack gave me a sympathetic smile. Until this point, I thought something was wrong with him, but now he must have been sure I was the lunatic.

Grandma had just gone to the kitchen as we all forgot that it was dinner time. I for one had forgotten all other meals as well, and so she jumped up quickly to scramble something up for me that would hopefully unscramble my mind.

"If you like, we can watch some other tapes, too? If that would ease your mind. I mean, I'm technically not allowed to, but you seem really worried," Jack said to me. I really didn't trust what I saw on the tape, basket or not. I was sure that Trudy had doctored it in one way or the other. My mind was hazy and slow at that point; I couldn't think for myself anymore. All I wanted was a bit of truth.

I suppose that's why I didn't consciously notice the announcement. It almost sounded like some sort of background noise that my mind was blocking out.

Attention, attention! Residents of Sanctuary Hills. Please be aware that the curfew begins in only five minutes. Find your way home swiftly and have a pleasant Sanctuary evening inside your homes.

But even tired as I was, it doesn't make sense to me how my legs started moving and following this boy to the threshold of the door. And I swear there was a sparkle in his eye when he took my hand and guided me through it.

Only the sudden movement and the feeling of pain brought me back to the moment.

Grandma had grabbed my arm in a sudden and seldom moment of clarity and pulled me back inside just in time. I didn't believe her weak arms were capable of it, but it was so hard I thought my arm might dislocate.

"You will not have my granddaughter killed just so she stays out there with you, forever and ever. She is here to visit and will leave when the time is right, and she will abide by the rules just as I have for the past years! Do you hear me?" Grandma was shouting louder than ever before.

Jack, seemingly unimpressed, just grinned and turned around.

"We'll see about that, Abigail. We both know she won't be able to cross that threshold."

With that, he slammed the door shut, but he didn't leave. He stayed right outside.

I knew that soon Trudy and Harold and the others would join, but I didn't expect to see their faces glued to our window when I opened the curtain. I jumped back, ignoring the group of neighbors that had gathered. Two groups. The ones that looked old fashioned and were smiling, just like Trudy and Harold, and the ones that appeared bloodthirsty, just like Jack.

"Grandma, what the hell?" I shouted. She looked genuinely shocked by my sudden outburst. She wasn't used to me getting loud with her.

"Charlie," she mumbled.

I clenched my fists. I was so incredibly angry. Although suddenly it made sense that my grandmother never came to visit us. She always had an excuse, like back when Grandpa was alive that he was feeling too sick or that she had too much on her mind to travel. After a while, Sanctuary Hills traps you in.

"Why did you not warn me? Why did you not tell me to stay away?" I collected myself enough to lower my voice, but it surprised me how evil I still sounded.

Grandma looked to the ground. She was mumbling something I couldn't understand.

"I told you at first not to come, but you insisted. And then the thought was nested into my mind, and I couldn't decline."

Strangely, this was the first thing she said that actually made sense to me as I'd been corrupted by their doings as well. They have a way to play with your mind, only a bit, not too much. Not enough to change you entirely, only so much that you won't doubt. You can control it a bit, at least I can. I stop when their manipulative worms dig in too deep. However, Grandma's mind is not as strong anymore.

Not only due to her age. Being here and living here, it gradually changes your interpretation of the surroundings. The longer you stay, the more you interact with the people, the more you become a part of Sanctuary Hills. I've come here before to visit, and I left without a scratch, though I did always leave before dark. Grandfather used to insist that the roads got too dangerous at night. They never let me stay past dinner, and now it made sense why.

I've been corrupted. By Jack and Harold and Trudy and the streets. By the peculiar food we buy and consume, by swimming in the pool. Sanctuary Hills is protecting me but not for my own benefit. It creates its perfect residents. Bit by bit.

If you don't oblige to the rules, it simply will swallow you, as that is the only solution. Jack was helping. Not me but the neighborhood.

"Maybe you can leave, but I never will. You see, my love, I don't even want to. Sanctuary Hills has all I need. I could never go; it would rip my heart out," my grandmother said after a long silence.

I didn't understand what exactly she meant by that, but then I looked outside despite not wanting to see the faces of those neighbors ever again, and I saw someone new waving at me. Someone was standing there waving and smiling, and while I should have been even more terrified by that figure than by anyone else so far, I somehow felt safe. I somehow felt like I belonged just a tiny bit more. He was dressed very well, his hair was combed and thick, and his smile felt truly genuine, maybe because he hadn't been a part of them for long.

And that's when I understood why Grandma felt so safe despite all that was happening here. And why she felt comfortable in Sanctuary Hills.

A tear rolled down my face when I saw the man standing close to the uncanny neighbors because he was not like them, and I whispered, more to myself than to my grandmother, who smiled just as warm as he did.

Part 3

Sanctuary Hills had taken over my mind as it does with anyone that stays too long to only be a guest. We all are swallowed by the need for the neighborhood to be perfect and right. There is not one person, not a community or a committee deciding on the rules. No, they are part of the grounds and the air and the water in this particular place. I haven't quite understood why and when this all started, but I do know that anyone that lives inside the gates does whatever they can to feed it. To make sure that everything here stays the way it has been.

Some do by choice; for others, the choice is made.

I suppose for the people here, Sanctuary Hills is not a place; it's a religion. They all believe in it, but they have different interpretations about how to do right by their belief.

Naturally, they have different approaches to feed the Sanctuary. There are the ones that religiously make sure that the number one rule of the curfew is being obeyed, though that is not the only item they take care of. There are more customs that to this point I hadn't met but soon would.

And then there are the ones that are trapped, that know of the rules, that possibly broke them and now would not be able to go either way, and so they trick anyone new that seems to be an easy target. I don't believe their intentions are inherently evil; no, they are simply bored.

And boredom can, despite its connotation, be a very dangerous emotion.

Harold and Trudy were rule sticklers.

Jack was bored.

Of course, in this scenario, we have the added factor of Sanctuary Hills scrambling minds. Sometimes a little and often a lot and therefore it is difficult to say what and who is right without having a neutral or even believable source.

Although I did find one person who as I'd mentioned before should have been scaring me because they were dead. However, I suppose at this point I had realized that more residents inside these gates were long gone, but their spirits were still going strong.

Which takes me back to when I saw him out there on our lawn. My grandpa, who used to write me letters and put candies inside the envelope and who would encourage me to do what I needed with my life whenever my parents gave me another hard time. And who I felt so incredibly guilty about for not visiting more, especially when I heard the news that he was now gone. Maybe the guilt is the reason that brought me here. Maybe that's why I didn't think during that particular moment, either. Why I didn't use my manipulated mind—I mean my conscious one, of course. Was that my own mind making a blank or was it Sanctuary Hills? I actually believe it was the first.

Well, I did something stupid; I can't deny that. It was just after nine or ten maybe, the exact time doesn't matter, but it definitely was dark out, and that's what should have stopped me. The sun had disappeared just before the creature appeared on our lawn.

And I opened the door.

"Charlie!"

His voice sounded different. Or maybe I didn't remember well because the last time I heard him it was only over the phone.

I thought he looked odd. Well, of course he looked odd. He was dead, after all, but that's not what he looked like. He was different because of his face. The clothes were the same—well, familiar at least. A checkered shirt and brown pants, and colorful dispensers as you don't see them on people often anymore. He waved and another tear rolled down my face. My vision was focused only on him, and I forgot anyone else around. All the terrifying creatures that I couldn't call human anymore were gathered out there while trying to lure me out or force me to stay inside.

Listen to your heart. That's what they say. My heart was telling me to run to my grandpa and ask him to make everything okay.

I took a step. One step and I swear it was tiny, but technically I was outside when I wasn't supposed to. Grandpa smiled, and I saw Jack move closer, and he seemed kind, too. That's what should have stopped me, but they didn't, someone else did.

It was Trudy. She had come far too close again. I hadn't noticed because I was distracted by the look of my deceased grandfather on the lawn. But now she was so close to my face that I could feel a cold breath coming from her mouth or maybe from the air. Her eyes were opened wide, and while she didn't stop smiling, her face appeared furious. Furious enough to crack even more and almost splinter into a thousand pieces.

"You are an awfully lot of trouble, young lady, and you better change that sooner than later," she whispered in a high-pitched voice.

And then she pushed me with unbelievable strength.

The door slammed shut. Trudy was gone, but Harold glued his face back to our window.

When I fell back and the door was closed, I suddenly felt a sharp pain. Not from my elbows, which I fell on, they hurt a bit but not as much as my ankle. When I pulled up my pants just enough to see what was hurting, I saw the bloody imprint of a hand.

I hadn't felt a thing when I was out there.

"Go away!" I cried and shouted toward Harold as I slammed my fist against the window and his distorted face.

I didn't want to see him. I wanted to see my grandfather.

Listen to your heart, they say. However, it doesn't really make sense because your emotions are not in your heart; they're in your brain as well. It's all just a trick.

I suppose in those tiny moments in which I had a clear thought—there weren't many as my surroundings did their best to scramble them—I felt punches in my gut. The ones that told me, "Not now."

I felt Grandma's breath in my neck, and I knew she was thinking of going out there herself. Even after seeing my ankle.

"Maybe," she whispered. "They are all out there, after all. How dangerous can it be?"

I understood her logic. It seemed perfectly understandable because it wasn't intrusive. The intrusive thought was the one telling us to stay inside; we simply weren't quite sure which one to listen to as neither seemed to be our own.

One voice came from the inside. It was the Sanctuary telling us to stick to what we ought to. But then there were the outside voices mocking our fear and telling us to come to play.

"He wouldn't do that to us, though, would he? No, certainly not. He was a kind man with a warm heart that now has turned cold. He would protect us. Cold or not," Grandma said.

I suppose deep inside she knew the truth. She knew, but she didn't mind a little lie as long as she could still see him from time to time. It's what made Sanctuary Hills her place. Even if it was fake.

Even if that man out there wasn't Grandpa, and not his ghost, either. The man out there, in fact, wasn't a man.

Like the basket and the pictures from the cameras, he wasn't right. He wasn't there.

They wanted to lure us out to our demise.

"All right, Grandma. What do we do?"

"Oh, honey, there is only one answer to this question at this particular time of night. We keep our doors shut and go to bed."

Tiny twitches and micro-expressions showed me that she was still inside that shell. The Sanctuary hadn't consumed her entirely.

In the morning, I spent another hour or two making phone calls, but hearing the voices of my loved ones saying only nonsense and wrong things tore me apart even more. The only thing they listened to and responded to normally was the question of whether they should come visit. And I always said no. Not until I knew what fate they might meet inside the gates if the neighbors found out.

I could already picture Jack licking lips on the prospect of fresh blood and corruptible minds.

"All right, hun. I'm off to the market. Do you need anything?"

Grandma called out from the hallway. For a split second, I wondered if everything was normal and I was the weird one. She said it so casually, as if the past nights and days didn't happen. I jumped out of bed and ran toward the door where Grandma was putting on her coat.

"You are what?" I shrieked.

"Sweetie, are you all right? Do you want me to pick up some medicine? Or possibly some fresh ginger and lemon, that always makes me feel just great."

"You're going outside?"

"Why, yes, it's the middle of the day, silly goose. Why wouldn't I? And by the pale look on your skin, I would suggest you get some of those rays of sun on it yourself."

My gaze shifted toward the window, and I saw the lawn, all green and pretty. The sun was shining. It was a beautiful day.

"Perfect weather for the pool." Grandma smiled, and then she left before I could stop her.

Everything was normal. It always was normal when it was day, not entirely normal as it is in other places but normal enough for Sanctuary Hills.

The postman was filling peculiar mailboxes, children were playing hopscotch, and garbage was being collected.

I decided to get dressed and go to the market as well. One, because I didn't like the thought of Grandma alone, and two, because on my way I would also check the gate with the security guard out front. To see what an escape might look like and if I'd even need one in the middle of the day before the curfew begins. Maybe I could somehow go and get help or make a plan to free Grandma before my mind is taken over by the neighborhood.

Grandma was long gone, so I had to get dressed quickly and hurry to meet her there before she went someplace else. She didn't even ask if I wanted to come along.

On my way out the door, I found a card. I'd received a few ones like this before but usually had just pinned them to the fridge to forget about them.

It was another invitation.

Dearest neighbors, Abigail and Charlotte,

What a pleasant weekend for a lovely midday barbecue in our greenest garden.

Yes, you are thinking right: we would like to invite you to another party tomorrow at two p.m. sharp. We know it's very last minute, but we do like to be spontaneous.

Make sure to be on time because as you know time is scarce!

You may bring your swimsuit, but that's up to you.

Besides bringing good fun, a dish of your choice would be swell.

See you tomorrow,

Certainly, not possibly,

Trisha, Tony, and Tina

I stuffed the card in my pocket and made my way to the market. The letter distracted me enough so that I left the doorstep without hesitation. I had been afraid of the thought before, but now I was outside and it seemed all right. I ran all the way to the market, and on my way I could swear I saw Jack sitting on a porch, winking at me and grinning, but I ignored him and ran even faster until I made it to the marketplace.

I'd never seen the market before. It was like a farmer's market with fresh produce being sold as well as little whimsical products. From further away, it looked really nice and inviting, but that was just from the outside. As soon as I stepped inside the marketplace, everything appeared just a little wrong, as it does in Sanctuary Hills.

And the longer I stayed, the more the little wrong turned into horribly frightening.

I recognized a few faces from around the neighborhood but nobody who I'd ever talked to. I've never exactly been the kind of person to talk to neighbors much, and after this experience, I don't think I ever will be. I kept my eyes open for Grandma but couldn't spot her anywhere, so I decided to stroll through the narrow passages.

From far away, it appeared as if there were a dozen stalls, tops. Now that I had actually walked inside the first passage, it changed entirely. Everything did.

There were many people, goods, stalls, and games. Almost like a beautiful Oriental market with lots of colors and products, but it couldn't in any way be possible. I had just entered a labyrinth with fragrances and images too sharp to be real.

In all its wrongness, however, it was perfectly right. A perfect market would suit a perfect neighborhood, and if the space wasn't big enough, then that fact would simply be changed.

Perfectly reasonable for the Sanctuary logic.

I walked toward a stall with the most delicious scent that I had ever smelled in my life. It reminded me of days in the kitchen with my mother when we would bake and cook all days before Christmas. Only as I got closer, I realized what it was that smelled so dangerously delicious.

It was coming from a booth where a man sold jars filled with something I couldn't recognize from far away. I only followed my nose and not my eyes, but I should have focused on the latter. I truly should have, but I didn't because my mind was on the Sanctuary autopilot again.

Standing in front of the booth, I didn't look at the man but only at his products. I had to know what was inside these jars.

"Cinnamon," I whispered. It was the smell of cinnamon except even sweeter and more intense.

"Delicious, isn't it? The sweet smell of death?"

I looked up toward the man who was dressed in a suit that didn't fit the market one bit.

"Excuse me?" I asked.

"The smell. We collect our items from a very special place, you see." He winked.

"A special place? A different place? Have you left Sanctuary Hills, and if you did, can you tell me how?" I spoke without taking a breath.

He didn't answer that question. Instead, he said, "Open a jar and your eyes will see what's inside, doll."

I hesitated for a second but then opened the jar. Even though it was made out of glass, I didn't see what was inside from the outside, but when the lid opened, I dropped the jar right to the floor.

It was filled with eyes.

Human eyes. Stuffed inside to the top.

"You dropped it! How silly of you!"

"I—What—" I muttered.

"It's okay, you can pay me back," he said with his eyes wide open. "Come back tonight and you can pay."

He reached for my arm, but I pulled away just in time and tried running away. I stumbled into too many people; some apologized as if it was their fault, and others whispered as they saw me but I couldn't look at them. I had to get out. I just didn't know which way to go.

I swallowed and kept going until I finally saw her.

"Grandma," I cried and hugged her from behind. She stood in front of a stall selling jewelry.

"Charlie, oh honey, how distressed you look! Are you all right, my sweet child?"

"Oh, she does look awfully distressed but so very pretty. Is she your daughter?" the girl behind the table asked.

She was young, possibly my age, but her clothes looked more like the ones of a housewife from the 1950s. Her caramel hair was curled up perfectly, and her cheeks and lips were rose red.

Grandma giggled.

"Oh, Darla, you make me blush! No, this is my granddaughter. I've wanted to introduce you, either way. She is so lonely here being young and new."

"New?" a new voice said. A male voice.

He had appeared from the side. I hadn't noticed him before. He had the same color hair as Darla, but his clothes were far more normal.

"Grandma, please, let's go home," I whispered.

I wasn't ready for meeting new crazy people.

"Daniel, don't be rude and introduce yourself first, and also I tell you all the time, use entire sentences." Now she was looking at Grandma and shaking her head. "I tell him all the time."

She turned her head toward me and held out her hand.

"I'm Darla, and this is my twin brother Daniel."

I didn't shake her hand.

"Are you gonna ask me to come outside after curfew?" I asked.

"Never!" Darla called out, seemingly shocked.

"Good neighbors obey the curfew," she said in unison with my grandma.

I took a step back.

"I'm sorry, love. I should take Charlie home. She hasn't been feeling too well these past few days, you see."

"Will we see you tomorrow?" Darla asked with big eyes. "I always hope for friends my age at the garden parties, you see." She smiled, and her eye twitched a little.

"Yes. Please come. You *must*," her brother, who had been silent so far, added. He didn't smile, and he didn't twitch but put much emphasis on the last word.

He seemed the most normal, but so had Jack. I didn't trust the neighbors one bit. I couldn't care less about some barbecue. I wanted to take Grandma home and hide inside before the speakers started blasting the curfew call.

***

The whole day had passed. Breakfast, the market, meeting the twins, dinner."

My mission this morning was to get to the gate. To the entrance or preferably the exit.

It was there in the back of my mind the whole time, and still, I didn't move close to the gate even once. As if I had forgotten, but how could I forget the most logical thing to do?

There was no way I would have just forgotten about that. The Sanctuary didn't want me to take action.

It doesn't want me to leave, and so it makes me forget.

With a little help from the neighbors.

EVERYONE IN TOWN LOVES FROCKLE'S FANTASTIC SOUR LIME CARAMELS

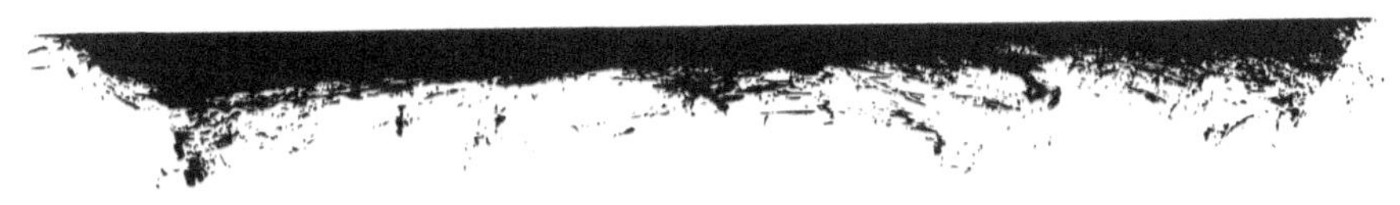

Part 1

I live in a really small town in the middle of nowhere called Hickling. Hickling is so small and boring that everything here comes in ones. We have one cinema, one supermarket, one high school, but most importantly one candy shop. The candy shop is run by an old gentleman named Maximilian Frockle. He is a sweet old man with gray hair, colorful clothes, and a fluffy beard. He looks nothing like his twin brother Maurice. Maurice Frockle is the town's gynecologist. While he always wears the cleanest shoes, the nicest suits, and has his hair perfectly groomed and dyed in the color black, he is just as sweet as his brother.

The Frockle family moved to Hickling before my parents were even born. My grandpa once told me the story of their business. Maurice had just opened his doctor's office and Maximilian bought one of the old buildings in town to start the very first and only candy shop. His high expectations quickly evaporated, and had it not been for his brother, he would have gone bankrupt right away. The candy Maximilian sold was very peculiar. Instead of the typical chocolate, fudge, and gummy bears, his candy had the weirdest shapes and colors. It was too eccentric for the old-fashioned townspeople of Hickling. They were not acquainted with these new tastes, and Maximilian was lucky if one soul per month found its way to his shop.

For almost a year, the shop was closed. Maximilian was experimenting with new combinations and finally presented something he was terrifically proud of. He named it *Frockle's Fantastic Sour Lime Caramels.*

Unfortunately, those were a big bust as well. He tried everything he could, put up signs, was giving out free samples in front of the store, but people seemed weirded out by it. As my grandpa said, they didn't want to take some crazy kind of candy from these people who were strangers to the close-knit community of Hickling.

Luckily, Maurice was a lot more successful with his business. With the nearest hospital being about two hours away, soon every woman in town visited his office. The brothers were smart and came up with a strategy. They would give out free samples of the sour lime caramels to the pregnant women, who were not as opposed to the peculiar flavors of the candy.

There are many studies demonstrating that a child can acquire a certain taste even before birth. When a mother eats a lot of a certain type of flavors during pregnancy, the child gets a similar tendency. It can work for spicy food, sweet treats, or in the case of the Frockles, sour lime caramels.

And boy did it work. Maximilian had to wait a while, but as soon as the first children were born and grew older, they all seemed to crave the sour lime caramels. My grandma had been one of the women going to Maurice, and my mother seemed to be completely obsessed with Frockle's candy and especially the sour lime ones. When she was pregnant with me, she was craving them more than ever; she told me on many occasions how I would always kick in her tummy when she had one of the caramels.

My grandparents passed away when I was only six, but I always loved hearing the story about the Frockles brothers when my grandpa would tell it. He told me it took some time, but soon the town changed into what it is now: a through and through happy place with the best damn candy in the world. Only one thing stayed exactly the same over time: everyone in Hickling loved the Frockles. The brothers became everyone's best friends.

Well, everyone in town is friends with each other anyway. That happens when you live in such a tiny place where everything is connected. All the kids go to the same school; a lot of neighbors work at the same places or go to the same clubs. Hardly anyone ever leaves the town, and if they do, they never stay away longer than a weekend. I once asked my father why we never go on holidays, like the people in TV shows, and he said, "Honey, those people go on vacation to escape from their lives for a little while. Why would we want to escape? We live in the most fantastic place on Earth." He smiled when he said it, but I swore I saw his eye twitch nervously.

He was right, I didn't mind that we never left. I used to love the town when I was younger. My best friends Miles and Kristen lived on the same street, and I spent almost every day with them. We were born in the same year and went to the same kindergarten, elementary, middle, and high school, and we grew up to become inseparable. I loved those two, especially as they were only children just like me. This town had most things a kid could wish for, but I had always wanted a sibling.

A brother to be specific. And when I was nine, I almost got one. I was at the doctor's office with my parents when Maurice Frockle gave my mum the wonderful news that she was pregnant. My mother broke down in tears on the spot.

"There, there. No reason for tears. Those are some wonderful news! A child is always a blessing," Maximilian said while gently squeezing my mother's shoulder.

My mother pushed her teeth together and forced out a smile. "Sweetie, why don't you wait outside and play with the toys?" she told me. Mr. Frockle gave me a piece of sour lime candy and pointed toward the door. I walked out, but as the nosy little kid I was, I made sure to leave the door open just enough that I could hear what they said.

"This can't be possible."

"Oh, but it is! I hear a healthy heartbeat.. And look there, it's a boy!"

I had to really control myself not to jump up and down on the spot. I had always wanted a brother. Maurice started humming while he examined her further. "I'm quite surprised that you didn't notice yet."

"I... I was sure I wasn't able to birth any—"

"Well, then it is a true wonder child. How marvelous."

I didn't hear the rest of the conversation, but I remember the last thing Maurice said to my mother as we were about to leave.

"A boy or a girl, what do you prefer?"

Back then I didn't understand why he would ask that as he had already told her it would be a boy.

My mother didn't stop crying, and when she told my dad the great news, he did something I never saw him repeat again. He punched the wall so hard that his hand started bleeding. And then they both just cried. They sent me to my room, but I heard them whisper all night long. I still don't know exactly what they said, but the next day they packed their bags and left for the weekend. It was the only time my parents ever went on vacation while I stayed at Kristen's home.

When they came back from the weekend, Mum wasn't pregnant anymore.

I wanted to scream and shout. I had never felt this devastated before. Mum didn't even look at me; she went straight to her room, and I heard her cries through the walls. That's when I calmed myself down. I didn't understand everything that was going on back then, but I hated seeing my mother hurt like that. She was usually such a cheerful person. Dad tried to keep up the happy attitude he always had, but I could see that he was struggling. When I asked for an explanation, he told me, "It's something you can't understand yet, but just know that we would do anything to keep you safe. Your mother and I, we love you very much. And isn't that enough? We are just happy to have our one precious child."

Maurice and Maximilian Frockle paid us a visit the following day. Maximilian gave me a big bag of candy, and my parents sent me outside to play with my friends. As I walked out, I heard loud shouting and thumping coming from inside. I was just about to run back inside when the shouting turned to laughter. They sounded cheerful.

When I came back home in the afternoon, my parents acted completely differently. They were happy; my mum was humming and making food, and my dad was playing on the piano. He smiled when he saw me come inside. I wanted to ask them about the bruises they suddenly had on their arms and faces, but they acted so strange that I was afraid to ask. And they seemed genuinely happy.

We never talked about the incident again, and the topic of siblings had become a taboo in our house. None of my friends had brothers or sisters; it didn't matter that I didn't, either.

Only as I grew older I started realizing that it wasn't just my friends and I. Nobody in Hickling had siblings. The only ones that came as two were the Frockles.

When I was about fifteen, Miles, Kristen, and I started resenting the town more. We weren't kids anymore, and we wanted to see the world. Hickling had nothing to offer to us besides Frockle's candy, and we were awfully bored all the time. You can't imagine how excited we were when a new family moved to our street. There were hardly ever any new people in Hickling, and it was even stranger that there was an available house. Nobody ever moved away voluntarily.

We got even more curious when we saw that the new family had children. You read that right, plural.

We were just sitting in front of my home trying out our skateboards when we saw a boy outside of the house. He looked about our age.

"He's cute. Let's go and say hi." Kristen jumped up from the curb.

"Are you sure? We don't know them. My parents didn't say anything about a new family—" I responded.

"Don't be such a wuss, Sammie. Finally something is happening."

So the three of us walked over to see this new boy. He looked about our age, had blond hair, and freckles all over his face.

After chatting with him for a while, we found out that his name was Charlie. He was fourteen and had a two-year-old sister.

"My uncle lived in this house. We came to visit a little while ago, and since then my parents were obsessed with this town. I honestly don't understand why. This place is so fucking weird," he said after we introduced ourselves.

"It is the most boring place on Earth, the only good thing is Fro—"

"Let me guess. Frockle's sour whatever caramel shit? Yeah, my parents talk about it all the time. My uncle did, too," Charlie interrupted Kristen.

"Wait, is your uncle Jeremy Clerkins? I was already wondering why he'd move away. Makes sense that you just moved in with him," I said.

"We're not moving in with him. He died."

The three of us didn't respond. While it wasn't unusual that people of Hickling would pass away out of nowhere, nobody ever talked about it as bluntly as this boy did. I was just about to say something when a woman walked outside with a little girl in her arms. The girl's hair was just as blond as Charlie's, and she held a little pink teddy bear in her hands.

"Oh, look at that! You must be the neighbors! How lovely to meet you! See, Charlie, there are kids just your age here!" His mum seemed just as cheerful as our parents. Charlie rolled his eyes.

"My husband and I were just gonna settle in and then come around and introduce ourselves to everyone here, but first we are awaiting two gentlemen. Charlie, will you go inside and help your dad?" she continued. She gave us a last smile and followed him into the house.

That afternoon, I heard a lot of screaming and shouting coming from the Clerkins' house. My parents acted like they didn't hear any of it, so I did the same. Later that night, someone rang our door. It was the woman, Charlie's mum, and a man who I imagine was his dad.

"Hello, there, we just moved in on the opposite side of the street. I am Peter, and this is my wife Helena. The Frockles paid us a visit already and gave us a big basket of that wonderful candy! We thought we'd share some of it with our lovely neighbors as well."

My mum was just about to say something, but I interrupted her. "Where are your kids?"

"Kids? We only have one child, sweetheart. He is a bit grumpy, hasn't gotten used to the new house yet." She shot my mum a look, who nodded understandingly.

"But what about the little girl?"

"Shush now, Sammie, don't be so nosy," my dad exclaimed.

Mrs. Clerkins' face started twitching. Finally, she said, "Why don't you go over and say hi to Charlie? Maybe you can show him how wonderful life here actually is?" Her husband let out a loud sigh. "We've tried everything, please. Maybe you can convince him?"

I walked over to the yellow house on the opposite side of the street. With a strange feeling in my gut, I rang the bell.

"Hello?" The door was open, but the lights were off. I slowly walked inside the house. I'd never been inside Mr. Clerkins' house, but it looked pretty much like our home. I heard some noises coming from the living room. It sounded like whimpering. As I got closer, I saw someone hunched down on the ground. It was Charlie.

He didn't look at me; he just kept staring at something in his hands. It was a teddy bear. The one that the little girl had in her arms earlier, but it was full of blood.

I walked over and reached inside my pocket to get out one of the little sweets.

"I'm sorry," I whispered. "Try this. It will make things a bit better. I promise."

His tear-filled eyes met mine for a moment before he accepted the Frockle's Fantastic Sour Lime Caramel.

***

Of course, I always knew that Hickling wasn't a normal town. Nobody from the outside ever came to visit. The ones that did would never leave again. Children disappeared all the time. Buildings randomly burned down. I could swear that once an entire street simply disappeared, including everyone that lived there. But nobody here cared about the irregularities. We were happy here.

And life here *can* be good. We have everything we need. We always get the most incredible candy. I don't think I could ever live at a place without Frockle's Fantastic Sour Lime Caramel.

I grew up never leaving town and got married to the best person I could ever imagine. We have our one home, one car, and one life together.

We are happy; we have everything that we need.

Maurice was incredibly kind yesterday when I went to his office—he even gave me a free bag of candy—but for some reason, I can't be happy about the good news. Not since I've found out that I'm expecting twins.

Part 2

I realize that to someone who has never been to Hickling, our way of life can seem strange. When I was younger, there were moments where I wondered if this was really the way to be. Even if I had never spent much time outside of our town, I always knew that the world must have much more to offer. But then again, the world isn't perfect. We have learned about war, crimes, and serial killers in school. The outside world isn't that much better than Hickling.

Hate, anger, sickness. We didn't have any of those things. We had candy, and we were happy. At least that's what I was told every time I showed any signs of concern.

"Everything here is beautiful, Sammie. We can't simply leave that behind," is what my parents told me when I was younger.

"We can live our fantastic life in Hickling or not live at all," is what they said as I grew older.

"There never was an option to leave," is what I've learned now that I'm older. Life isn't as simple as we think when we are young. We all have to do something to get by. I learned to understand that eventually.

And Hickling *is* a special place.

Of course, we had to stick to the rules of our community, but wouldn't you as well, if your payment was a life that was absolutely perfect? Our butcher always has the freshest and juiciest meat even though there are no animal farms close by. Nobody here is ever jealous of anyone. You can go outside on your own in the middle of the night and have nothing to fear. We might only have one out of everything, but the places we have all work extraordinarily well.

As we graduated, I hardly saw my friends Miles and Kristen anymore. They had started dating, and I was quickly out of the picture. Well, that is one reason. The other one is that I kept inviting Charlie to spend time with us, but my friends seemed to feel fed up with him quickly. A lot of townspeople didn't seem to like him. He was too grumpy for their taste.

Of course, these are only assumptions as no one in Hickling would ever directly say anything negatively.

Charlie wasn't a fan of Frockle's wonderful candy store. He must have been the only person in the entire town that had anything bad to say about the sour lime caramels. His parents tried very hard to silence him. They came over all the time to make me convince him.

And I tried. I really did, but he was... different. At times he was happy and jolly just like everyone, and the town could sigh in relief. When he had bad times, his mother wouldn't let him leave the house, but everyone knew what was going on. There was only one possible reason why he was not participating in the town's activities or why he wouldn't come to school for days. And why he looked sick when he did show up.

Everyone knew. Even the brothers.

Charlie didn't eat the candy.

He was the first person I had ever met who had a problem with Frockle's. Even Kristen, who often tried to act badass, was going along just like everyone else. Charlie was different, which is probably the reason I felt so drawn to him. His parents would sometimes lock him up in his room with nothing but candy, hoping the hunger would force him to take some. Sometimes it worked and he would come to school with the biggest smile on his face. When I wouldn't see him for a few days, I would try and climb up to his room to give him some other food.

I knew it wasn't a long-term solution because he would only throw up and look even worse, but when he had those candy-free periods, he would tell me things nobody else did. How our life was far from perfect, how we had to somehow get away but that the chances of that happening were close to zero. Charlie was the only bit of darkness in Hickling, and I loved it.

We just had to make sure to hide it.

Eventually, he had to give in or he would have starved. He became a real part of Hickling. A happy citizen with a belly full of Frockle's Fantastic Sour Lime Caramels. Sometimes I missed his dark side, but at least this meant that we actually had a future together.

When we were twenty-two, we got married and moved to our very own house. We didn't have to take care of anything; the town simply gave it to us after the family that lived there before passed away. Apparently, they decided to go on a vacation. One weekend, not more. But on their way back, it started storming, and their car broke down. They had never spent so much time away from Hickling before, and when they finally did come back, they were so sick that they all died within a day. Not even the candy could help anymore.

They had no family, and people in Hickling don't mourn anyway, so life just continued and we got a perfect new house. It looked the same as the ones we grew up in, but it was closer to the center of town, which was perfect because we could actually see Frockle's from our windows. Charlie got a job as a teacher, and I was hired to take care of Hickling's newspaper. As the news here is basically the same every day, I had a lot of free time on my hands. So I was always the first in the shop in the morning when Maximilian made the fresh batch of caramels.

For a while, our life went on well. Miles and Kristen and their little boy Elliott would come over a lot or we would go to Hickling's hall of movie and entertainment, which had exactly one screen and would show one new movie every month.

Life was great.

More and more people started disappearing, eventually even our parents, but at least we always had enough to eat.

Life was fine.

When Charlie had little moments of darkness, we simply kept to ourselves.

Life was okay.

When Maurice gave me the news of my pregnancy, the illusion that I had built up about my life shattered into little pieces. The only time in my life where I had ever felt remotely close to this sadness was when I got the news that I wouldn't get a brother. Even with the lack of understanding I had, I felt it deep inside of me. I could never choose one of the kids. Just like my mother, I broke down in tears sitting in the office of Maurice Frockle.

He didn't comfort me or tell me about the joy of a child, the way he did with my mother back then. He almost looked sad himself, not that Maurice ever showed any negative emotions. As he reached over to hand me a piece of sour lime caramel, he whispered, "I hope you choose to keep the good one."

"Are you not feeling sick?" I could tell that Charlie tried to smile. This was happy news, after all; we were expecting a kid. But just like me, he was aware that this news was tainted in a dark color. The evil thoughts that we tried so hard to block out, they were making their way back up.

"Of course not. No woman in Hickling feels sick during pregnancy, silly. I feel fantastic."

"GOD, you know how much I hate that fucking word." His pale face was turning red.

"It's been a long time since you've cursed. Bad words aren't very jolly. Have you had any Frockle's Fantas—"

"No. And I won't have any of that poison anymore. And you won't, either. We *need* to get out of here, Sammie. You have changed. We've both changed. We need to go before—" Charlie gagged before he could finish the sentence. He had always been more immune than the other people here, but even Charlie couldn't survive too much time without the candy, and he knew it.

He pulled me closer and held me for a moment that felt like an eternity. Finally, he spoke.

"I will take care of this. For you and for *both* of our future children."

He got the biggest knife out of the drawer in the kitchen, and just like that, he left the house.

He gave no explanation, but I knew what he was intending to do.

He wanted to murder the Frockle brothers.

Charlie had spoken about this many times before. Always in his sleep. Even when he was happy and full of caramels, the hate inside of him always found a way to come out.

I should have been scared. The brothers wouldn't hurt Charlie, but if the townspeople found out that their provider of sour lime caramel was brutally murdered, they would rip my husband to pieces.

I should have been scared, but I knew that it would never come this far.

I knew things would be fine when Charlie came back home. His clothes stained with blood. The knife in his hand.

"The doc is gone," he said.

"And the candy maker?"

"I burned down his shop."

I smiled and gave him a long hug. The blood was rubbing off on my clothes. I smiled because he was alive and because I had to. But I knew that this wasn't the end of it.

Charlie went straight to bed. He was feeling even more ill and kept throwing up all night long, more than should be humanly possible.

The next day, he could hardly get up, but as the sweet smell of caramels filled our street, he pulled himself up, grabbed the knife with stains of dried blood, and left our house.

Again he was tainted red with the blood of the brothers.

"I stabbed both of them." He laughed as he said it.

The next day, he came home saying, "I threw a brick in the face of the candy maker. He collapsed right away."

I nodded and gave him another hug. I knew he needed to do this. Even if I had accepted long ago that it wouldn't change anything. Hickling was a curse and a blessing in one.

"Hello, Maurice." I greeted the Frockle brother dressed in black.

"Hello, love. I'm sad to see that your husband did not take the news of your pregnancy too well."

I didn't dare to look him in the eyes.

"It's just difficult for him. You know he wasn't born here."

"I know, and I know how hard you are trying to keep him happy, but my brother doesn't like it when his candy making is interrupted. Can you at least make sure he only comes for me next time?"

I nodded.

"It's for your own good. The people in town are starting to resent your husband more, and they need their candy to stay peaceful." He winked at me and gave me a bag of caramels. It had Charlie's name on it.

Just like on that first day that we met, I walked to the crying boy that had now become a man and offered him the piece of candy.

"Try this, it will make things a bit better. I promise."

As always, I was the first one in the store. With everything that had happened lately, I needed the candy more than ever. I had no idea that this morning I would be the first one to see Maximilian Frockle's newest invention. I remember feeling extremely euphoric at that moment, thinking how I must be the luckiest person in the world to be the eyewitness of such an enormous change.

I walked inside the bright and colorful store. The most wonderful combination of smells hit my face, and I couldn't help but smile.

"Good morning, Sammie! Isn't it a beautiful day?"

"It truly is, Mr. Frockle. There is only one thing I am missing, and it's those fantastic caramels of yours!"

"Well, then I have to disappoint you, Mrs. Clerkins. I don't have any caramels for you today."

I felt a panic rush over me. This couldn't possibly be true. Never in my entire life had Frockle's been out of caramels. I didn't say a word and already calculated how much candy I had left at home.

Maximilian must have noticed the look of concern on my face because he started laughing.

"The town is shrinking, my love. Don't you know what that means?"

I shook my head.

"Well, it means that our work here is almost done. I cannot sell candy to a nonexistent town. The people of Hickling were too greedy; they expected too much."

"You are talking nonsense, Mr. Frockle. The town is well and fine, and we are still very much in need of you and your fabulous skills."

He smiled even more.

"*Fabulous*. That is exactly the word I had been looking for. I didn't mean to scare you, sweetheart. Of course, I'm not leaving just yet. I have something new to offer, which I hope you will adore even more. I just had to find a way to name it. What do you think of *Frockle's Fabulous Bittersweet Peach Gum?*"

"Bubblegum?" I raised an eyebrow.

"Yes, it lasts longer than the caramels. Would you like to be the first one to try it?"

Part 3

"Not like this, brother. This was not how things were supposed to go."

"It's okay, Mr. Frockle," I chimed in. "I understand this is what I have to do, and I've made my peace with it. I just hope Charlie will understand."

Every morning since we moved to the new house, I would get up, stretch, and open the big window in the bedroom. Usually, I would be alone for this as Charlie went to work pretty early, but this morning he hadn't gotten up from bed yet. He was really awfully sick, and we were out of caramels. All I had were those fabulous bittersweet peach gums. I didn't want to hurt Mr. Frockle's feelings, but there was nothing sweet about that bubblegum. It tasted awful, and I wanted to spit it out right after he gave it to me. That would have been rude, though, so I chewed the gum and told him how delicious it tasted while I listened to the things he told me. Sometimes lying is important. For example, when you don't want to hurt someone's feelings, and I really didn't want to hurt Maximilian Frockle. Not after the agreement we had considering Charlie. The one secret that I'd kept. So that morning instead of having sour lime caramel, I fulfilled my cravings with the disgusting gum.

I felt fine, actually pretty clear, but I hated what this situation was doing to Charlie. After he finally accepted that he couldn't simply murder the brothers, he spent every moment that he wasn't throwing up with planning and scheming. I felt terrible for my poor, sweet Charlie. Yeah, maybe he was a bit different than everyone else here, but that doesn't mean he deserved any of what happened.

I'm getting ahead of myself.

Charlie was still in bed, but he was doing a bit better. I knew how much he resented the caramels, so I offered him some of the fabulous bittersweet peach gum. I figured that he might even like it, with his weird taste buds and all.

"Is that what you're chewing on right now?"

"Yeah," I said and made a big pink bubble that popped a second later. Charlie even laughed at the sight of it. I could tell he was thinking hard again, but then he threw the little pink ball in his mouth and started chewing.

"It's not too bad," he said and shrugged.

I couldn't help but laugh at that.

"It's fucking terrible."

For the first time in a week, Charlie laughed as well. For a moment, we forgot about our troubles.

His smile grew bigger. Bigger than I had seen in a while. He grabbed me by the shoulders and started laughing hysterically.

"Sammie, did you just swear?"

I shrugged. I didn't get what he was hinting at then.

"Sammie. Did you have any of that Frockle's fucking caramel today?"

I hadn't, which was very unnatural for me. This was the first time since... well, since I was born that I didn't start my day off with the candy. And for the first time, I was absolutely fine with it. I didn't crave it at all. I even felt a bit revolved by the thought of it.

"Must be the pregnancy," he concluded.

"Wonderful evening to you, Mrs. Clerkins. Is your husband home by any chance?"

It was our neighbor Mr. Gillster. He had a big smile on his face. This normally wouldn't be too odd; I've never seen him not smiling. This one wasn't quite right, though; he had pinned the edges of his mouth to his cheeks, making his voice sounds slightly distorted.

"I'm afraid not," I responded.

"Well, if that isn't a shame. Would you know where he could be or when he will be back?"

I shook my head.

"I don't mean to make any trouble, love, but could you give me a heads-up when Mr. Clerkins is back? I have a wee question to ask him!"

"Absolutely, Mr. Gillster. I'll make sure to let him know. Bye-bye now!" I slammed the door in his face. He must have been the tenth neighbor ringing our doorbell only in the last twenty minutes. Each time someone rang the bell, their jolly looks were even more static. And they all asked for Charlie. They knew damn well that he was inside and that I was lying. So far they were still trying to be friendly and polite, though.

"How many are they now?" Charlie asked while making sure to stay away from the window.

"Like forty. Looks like their kids are joining as well," I said while staring at the mass of people in front of our home.

"Even more are in front of the candy store."

Maximilian had put up the "CLOSED" sign right after I had left with the bubblegum.

"Fuck, Sammie. They all think it's my fault."

"But it's not. Ma—"

The doorbell rang. It was Kristen. Miles was standing right behind her. He was holding a bat with spikes hammered in.

"Sammie, we know he's in there. I can smell him."

Kristen was pushing her teeth together, forcing the words to come out.

"We don't want to hurt you. All we want is some fantastic sour lime caramel, Sammie. You understand that right? Right?" Miles came closer. "Just let us take him. We've decided. The whole town agrees."

"Listen, Sam, nobody wants to hurt you. We all love you, you know that, right? We just want him. He needs to be punished, and you know it."

I hadn't even noticed that everyone else had come closer. The entire town was standing behind my friends. All staring and smiling while holding a variety of weapons.

"Sammie, go inside," Charlie whispered in my ear. Before I could even react, Miles and Kristen had pulled him outside. I couldn't even say a word or give him a kiss, let alone a hug.

I had to watch how my husband was being ripped into pieces by the horrific people of Hickling. His blood was splashed over the concrete. They took what was left of him and taped it to the storefront of Frockle's candy shop.

If there had been just a bit of doubt left inside of me, it was gone now.

Maximilian and Maurice Frockle were standing inside, looking through the blood-tainted window of the store. In their hands, they were holding big bags filled with something that resembled the fantastic sour lime caramels, but instead of the typical caramel brown and lime green swirl they were black and red. The people didn't care, though; they all started clapping as the smell of caramel filled the streets once again. Nobody but me noticed how terrible the smell really was. It smelled rotten.

The townspeople of Hickling didn't mind, though, and they started cheering and shouting as the Frockle brothers threw the peculiar candy into the crowd. They threw themselves on the ground and filled their mouths like pigs that hadn't been fed in days. It wasn't easy for me to stay calm, but I had to be patient and wait. As Maurice threw out the last pieces of candy, Maximilian cleaned up the bloody remains of my husband and brought what was left of him inside the store.

I took a deep breath and held my stomach, one single tear rolling down my cheek as I saw the entire townsfolk of Hickling slowly falling to the ground like domino pieces. I could hardly get through to the store, fighting my way through the still bodies lying on the ground.

As I reached the candy shop, Maurice greeted me with a sad look on his face. This was the very first time I had ever seen him without a smile.

"Are you sure about this, Sammie?"

"Yes. Fuck Hickling."

We walked inside the store where Maximilian was putting Charlie back together.

"It might take a little, but he will be absolutely fine and healthy again. The bubblegum is even more miraculous than I imagined," Maximilian Frockle said excitedly. He gave me a big smile. "I am so glad you decided to take over the store, Sammie. You were always my favorite person in Hickling. I'm glad your parents chose for you to stay back then."

"It wasn't a very hard decision. I simply picked my family over everyone else." I sighed. "They are not *all* dead, right? I'll need to start somewhere."

"No," Maximilian laughed, "only a few. You'll need some fuel. Let's hope it's the awful ones. Although they are all awful in their own way."

I nodded.

I wasn't lying. It really was an easy decision. After Maximilian Frockle gave me the bittersweet peach gum, I could finally think straight. As he told me the story of Hickling, I was in disbelief, but after seeing what these people did to my poor Charlie, it made a lot more sense. Little did those monsters know that neither of us would be dying anytime soon.

The story my grandpa had told me years ago was only partially true. I don't know if he was too ashamed to admit the rest of it or whether they really all forgot, but there was a lot more to the Frockles.

Maximilian and Maurice Frockle have spent all their life traveling the world to explore the finest locations and build up relationships with communities in need of some sweetness. Maximilian is the most marvelous candy maker in the world, and Maurice loves his brother so much that he has been supporting every aspect of his profession. He knows that it is their destiny to share the candy with the world and ignite Maximilian's spark. They had only good things in mind when they found Hickling all those years ago, but the people here were nasty, cruel beings.

They didn't accept any newcomers, especially not those who were in the slightest different. While they tolerated the inconspicuous and clean-cut Maurice, they absolutely hated Maximilian and his store. They threw bricks into his store, painted degrading slurs on the window, and threw their trash and shit inside just so the wonderful candy store would smell and people would stay out of it. For no other reason than the fact that they couldn't deal with anything new or different or in any way creative.

When one time a little girl found her way to the store, Maximilian was happier than he had been in years and offered her a free sparkling rainbow lollipop. The girl thanked him with a big smile on her face and ran home to show her siblings, who hadn't seen anything like this before.

When the parents found out that Maximilian Frockle had given their daughter free candy, they started some terrible rumors. Rumors about Maximilian doing awful things to the children. Things that make me feel so sick I can't even think about them. Maximilian was heartbroken. Of course, none of it was true, but as the gossip made its way through the town, they all got together to beat him up the way they did with Charlie.

That's when the Frockle brothers realized that Hickling was not a special place. It was hell, and they made it their job to clean it up. You know the rest of the story. Maximilian made his first batch of Frockle's Fantastic Sour Lime Caramels, and the town got addicted to it so much that they lost all control over their free will.

The policy of One was introduced, and the town slowly became the beautiful utopia that it is today. Everything was exactly the same, just as the people wanted. One out of everything, no variety.

With *one* exception, of course, the two single people who were different.

Maximilian noticed that the townspeople weren't as accepting as he thought they were. They didn't tolerate the boy with the blond hair and the freckles that had come into town. They were falling back into old habits. He had to finish things sooner than expected, even if Maurice didn't like it very much. With the gum, he made sure that Charlie and I would be well prepared to take over.

We will make the most wonderful candy and live a happy and long life in the beautiful town that is Hickling. Together with our two little girls.

As for the Frockle brothers? They will move on to the next town that is in need of some of their sweet caramel.

⸻

"So, sweetheart, what will you and Charlie make out of my fantastic store?" Maximilian asked as we got ready to say our goodbyes.

"I actually don't want to change too much. You did a terrific job here; that can't be denied. Well, except for *one* tiny change." I smiled as we took off the Frockle's sign from the storefront.

"How do you feel about *Clerkins' Curious Sour Lime Caramels?*"

I WENT TO VISIT MY DAD AND HIS CONTROLLING NEW GIRLFRIEND

My dad always liked his women clean. He wanted them pretty and kind. He longed for a perfect being without any flaws. Her only thoughts would be love and admiration for him. He has a whole list of qualities that this mythical creature should fulfill, and it might not surprise you that he hasn't had a long-term relationship since my mum left five years ago.

I was sure that he'd never find his perfect match, and even though I love my dad, I didn't think he deserved to find her. However, despite all odds, he did find the *woman* of his dreams, and it's the worst thing that's ever happened to us.

Ever since her presence came into my life, I constantly feel as if something is suffocating me.

Even before my dad officially introduced Jana, I wondered what kind of motives she could have for dating him. He'd started dropping her name during our phone calls a few weeks ago. I don't live at home at the moment because I go to uni in Bavaria, and my dad lives on the outskirts of Berlin in a house that's much too big for him.

I could already tell how excited he was about her, and I was happy for him until I learned more about her.

Jana is closer to my age than his. She is gorgeous, as he always wanted, flawless. Clear skin, shiny golden hair. Her makeup matches her features perfectly, and it's never too much. She dresses modestly but sexy.

Jana cooks five-star meals and makes sure every area of the house is always spotless. She takes care of our overgrown garden and scares away children that try to play pranks.

The question is what does she see in him?

Look, despite his odd views of love, my dad's a nice guy, the quiet type, always in his own head but not really deserving of a live-in maid that fulfills all his dreams. The one thing people might admire about him is his job, but he does some shady stuff with it, too.

He's a surgeon and makes decent money, but some of it comes in pretty shady ways—like when one of his mobster connections, some dead-eyed creep from one of the Kurdish clans in Berlin, drags in yet another cut-up gangster late at night. Honestly, I even wondered if Jana was a *present* from him, but that thought was so nasty that I tried to forget about it right away.

Before I arrived in Berlin, I was skeptical but also curious to meet the woman of his dreams. Now I wish I'd gone to Spain with my friends instead of spending my spring vacation with Dad and his new flame.

"Oh my frickin gosh, what a handsome young man, he looks just like you, Christoph!" the woman with light blond hair shrieked. She was wearing a dress that was certainly too short for Berlin's early spring weather and had her hair put up in a complicated hairstyle that looked painful.

I stood in the driveway in front of my childhood home and tried to keep a smile on my face, but the situation already felt absurd.

"Hi, you must be Jana. I'm Nikolas," I nervously said.

She nodded vigorously but didn't move away from the front door.

Dad took a step forward, grabbed my bag, and waved me inside.

They both looked far too excited to see me, but before I could pass the threshold, Jana's expression fell completely. Her face was serious, her eyes wide open, and she simply stared at me, staying in the doorframe so I couldn't pass by.

She looked angry.

Then Dad appeared behind her and gently put his hands on her shoulders.

"Buddy, Jana really can't stand it when you drag in dirt."

I looked down at my shoes. They were a bit dirty but really not that much. Jana, however, looked at me like I was the antichrist. I cleaned my sneakers and followed the crazy couple inside.

You know how in movies and shows the actors never actually eat any food? For example, they have a lunch scene, and every time they bring a bite to their mouth, the camera shifts somewhere else. Or they play around with their salads without ever taking a bite.

Jana ate like that.

She'd baked a cake. Carrot cake with frosting and small marzipan carrots accompanied with freshly brewed coffee.

We sat in our living room, which had never looked more tidy and clean. Dad shoved one bite after the other in, speaking with his mouth open.

"So, how's school?"

"Got a girlfriend?"

"Boyfriend, maybe?"

Jana sat there the entire time, turning her head to the left to smile at my dad and turning her head to the right to smile at me.

Her perfectly cut piece of cake was sitting on her plate with a neatly folded napkin.

She kept moving her fork near the cake, never really touching it. From time to time she would take the saucer with her cup of coffee. But nothing touched her lips.

Just like in the movies.

"Why are you not eating, sweetheart?" she asked when she noticed I was staring at her. "It's not poisoned, you know. You won't get hurt as long as you don't make anything dirty." She laughed.

"You're not eating, either," I answered in a dry tone.

"Well, you know how women are. Help me finish it?" She tilted her head, and I swear for a few minutes she forgot that people have to blink.

That evening my father needed to go to the hospital for his shift, so I decided I would go to my room to take a nap.

Before Dad left, he came up to my room, which was the only place in the house that still looked messy, and took a seat on my bed. He looked nervous.

"I know it's weird—having a woman in this house again. But I do really like her, Nick." Jana was downstairs cleaning the kitchen.

I nodded.

"Yeah, I get that, but... how do I say this without hurting your feelings... Something is not right about her, Dad," I whispered.

Dad rolled his eyes.

"She simply likes things done a certain way. But don't worry, you'll totally learn. Actually, to make things easier, I wrote a little list." He handed me a piece of paper. "Be a good boy and who knows, we might become a happy little family soon." He grinned and ruffled my hair like I was a little kid.

"You know something's not that right about you either, Dad," I half-joked.

"Ha. See you later, buddy. Don't bug Jana too much."

He went downstairs, and I heard them chatting and giggling in the kitchen. They really were acting like teenagers. Maybe I was exaggerating, I thought, until I took a look at the list Dad had given me.

Jana hates it when you forget to lock the door.

Jana hates television and all form of media. She won't like it if you use your phone around her.

Jana doesn't like it when you use the kitchen.

Jana—

With a loud thud, the front door closed downstairs. Not even a second later, I heard her sprinting upstairs. She stopped right in front of my room, breathing audibly in front of it. I could just imagine her nose pressed against the wood.

For a second, I stood there frozen, too shocked by the situation.

And then she started scratching the door.

"J-Jana?"

"Nikolas," she whispered, "help me with dinner." Her voice sounded raspy.

I swallowed and remembered what Dad wrote on the list.

Jana doesn't like it when you use the kitchen.

"Uhm, sorry, I'm really tired. I want to take a nap."

She kept scratching a little longer, but finally, I heard her leave.

For the next few hours, I stayed in my room.

She was cooking, and I'm not gonna lie it smelled fucking delicious, but I decided I had to get out before she asked me to eat with her.

I grabbed my phone and my wallet and headed downstairs as quickly as I could. Just as I reached the door, I felt her presence behind me.

Ignoring it, I turned the knob, but the door was locked.

"We can't go outside. Dinner is ready."

Jana hates it when you forget to lock the door.

"I'm sorry, Jana. I'm meeting friends in the city." I tried to speak confidently.

"No," she spoke firmly. "Help me set the table."

We had a very awkward dinner where she didn't eat but instead watched me the entire time. She wouldn't even give me a knife and fork to eat with; we were both using spoons for our pasta and for the meat.

I was counting the seconds, and finally, the door unlocked from the outside.

My dad was home again.

"I'm back! What are my two favorite people up to?" we heard him call into the house. Jana's eyes opened wide, and she jumped up to go and greet him with a big hug.

I went back to my room, wondering why the hell I didn't grab my bag and leave for the train station.

It was as if *something* was keeping me here. Not just the locked door.

Nighttime came, and the house turned quiet. I stayed in my room, the only place that felt somewhat normal, until I had to go to the bathroom. I kept it in for longer than I'd like to admit. I'm twenty-two years old, in my own home with my father and some young woman. Why was I feeling so paranoid?

I collected my confidence, went out into the hallway, and remembered why I was feeling so freaked out.

Jana was standing by a window in the hall, her face pressed against the glass. When she heard me, she turned her head and made inaudible noises. The voice hardly escaped her mouth, her lips were pressed tightly together; she pulled them with her fingers, but only muffled sounds came out.

I took a step back, but she grabbed my arm. With her sharp fingernails, she started scratching deep into my flesh. I tried to pull away, but she was holding me tightly.

"What the fuck?" I shrieked. "DAD?"

"Jana, sweetie, don't scare my boy. He'll leave again *soon*," he said in a voice that seemed far too calm.

"Of course not, honey! Do you want a late-night snack? Both of you maybe? You can help me make it, Nikolas." Suddenly her voice was back.

"Uhm, no, thanks," I mumbled.

She smiled at me and turned around to go downstairs.

Unsure what to make out of the situation, I ran to my dad's bedroom, trying my best to convince him that we needed to get the hell away from Jana.

Dad looked at me for a while, but then he smiled.

"She's just some sweet girl. How could she be dangerous?"

I held up my arm, the one she had just turned bloody, and finally I saw some look of fear on my dad's face.

"How did she do that?" he whispered. "I control everything she does."

"What?"

I looked at my arm and noticed that she hadn't simply scratched me. She'd tried to write something.

help

And finally, it clicked.

It was *him*.

The things on the list weren't her rules—they were his. There were no knives because he kept them away from her. She was the one trapped in here.

But why didn't she tell me while my father was at work?

He grinned when he saw my brain working.

"Nikolas, my boy, this is going to be great for us. Jana is only the first step. I can do so much more!"

"H-How?"

"Do you remember Soran? I took care of his people sometimes."

I nodded, a bitter taste filling my mouth. *Soran, the mobster with no remorse.*

"Well, he wanted to say thank you and put this... well, this thing inside of me. At first, I thought it would hurt me, but it doesn't. Instead, it's given me *power*."

His grin got even bigger.

"It's given me the ability to be really convincing. Oh, don't look at me like that. She's happy! I can tell. We get along great, and you know she might be your stepmom soon."

"I don't understand. Dad, that's impossible—"

His expression got more serious, his voice louder.

"How do you think Soran is able to control all of Berlin, huh? He has everything a man could wish for, and now he's shared some of that power with me. I've been stitching up those shitty criminals for decades now! I deserve some reward."

I felt like I was about to throw up; my hands got all sweaty.

He put my face in his big hands.

"Don't look so scared, my sweet boy. You will never be hurt. The three of us will be so happy together. And who knows? Perhaps I'll even be able to let you have a taste of this power soon, too."

WHEN THE CLOCK STRIKES SIX, NOT A SOUL CAN BE FOUND ON OUR STREETS

On the day that we're born and well until we get old, everyone in my town is wired to have but only one desire. To star in a show that displays the reality of the perfection we get to be a part of. The town is called Harmony Hills, and I would imagine you never even heard of it. That's because it can't be found as easily as you might think; only very few find their way here. And to be chosen as a neighbor, you'd have to be darn lucky.

I had the privilege of being born in one of the many vanilla-colored houses with the peppermint roofs. The cozy homes differ only in their sizes and are the perfect place for families of any size to spend their days at ease, supplied with the most brilliant form of entertainment.

The people that live here are so proud of their way to be that they like to reflect that onto their properties. The houses regularly get a new set of fresh paint, the grass gets cut so it won't grow taller than the usual one-and-a-half inches, the rose bushes never grow further than the property goes. The cars are all parked neatly inside the garage, and well, I think you get the gist.

Together with my mum, my dad, and my cat Baby, I live in one of the houses with the bright green lawn in front. We'd never seen life outside of Harmony Hills, and my parents never wanted that to change. After my grandparents left, Mum and Dad put even more of their heart into the community and into our home. They wanted it to appear perfect.

And it's not just the houses. We never wear clothes with any holes in them, and if Mum sees a stain on one of my shirts, she scrubs the dirt right off until her fingers are almost bloody. If my hair grows too long, Dad will stop whatever he is doing to drive me right down to the hair salon.

The town and its people appear perfect because that's what Harmony Hills represents. And now you might believe that the people feel suppressed, but from what I can tell, they all appreciate everything looking so perfectly swell. It gives them a sense of stability. And stability we sure have!

The neighborhood is safe as can be, and the adults like to meet for walks, book clubs, or neighborhood cleanup sessions. The children go to school, have sports clubs, and play games. It's not too different from what you might know. Everyone aspires to be the best version of themselves, and therefore life here is full and happy. Our neighborhood is special. But the most special part of our lives is the one thing we *all* do at six p.m. sharp. That's when you won't meet a single soul out on the street because everyone will be sitting inside their living rooms, no matter how big the family, and everyone will gather around the television and watch our favorite show.

Hidden Hills.

It's a television show produced in Harmony Hills, and from what I can tell, it is unbelievably popular. We have some other shows, like the Harmony Hills news and cartoons for kids, but nothing comes close to *Hidden Hills*. The show has existed for as long as I can tell, and while every season is slightly different, the overall idea is the same. A lucky family gets picked from town. Usually it is the one that values our community the most and reflects it on their exterior. That naturally includes the perfectly groomed house, garden, clothes, and attitude. It's the main reason why everyone in Harmony Hills can be a bit phony. They try far too hard to be interesting in hopes that they will be picked. When a family is chosen for the show, they leave their regular boring home and move into one of the mansions up the hill behind the gates of the restricted area. The only time one of us gets a glimpse of it is when we watch the show.

The individual mansions all have their own movie theater, an indoor as well as an outdoor pool, kitchen with hired chefs who make their dinners, and anything else you could ever wish for. And when their season is finished, they get to stay. Very few will have small parts in other seasons, though for the most part, they just get to enjoy their new luxury lives.

The season that stood out the most to me was the one we watched when I was only ten. It wasn't an entire family that was picked back then but only a married couple. I didn't know either of them, but they were really funny. In the first episode, they went inside the house and turned all the furniture around. Every item, they would lift up and flip all the way. Then they'd look at the camera and laugh uncontrollably. Mum liked that episode the least, but I thought it was hilarious. In the second episode, all the furniture was back to normal, and Mr. and Mrs. Tassy were giving us a walkthrough of their new property. It was breathtaking, and we were even introduced to one of the neighbors, a young gentleman with silver hair and lots of charm. The neighbor would become a regular in the show. In another episode, the Tassys were alone again and were fed all sorts of decadent goods by their personal chef. Without even taking a breath, they were filling their mouths with anything they could. They used that technique where they speed up the film real quick, so it was pretty funny to watch them shovel food in their mouths for what must have been a whole day but we saw it all in thirty minutes. The following episodes were rather boring. The Tassys took walks, went swimming, or played tennis.

And then there was the blood pool. The Tassys had the whole neighborhood visiting them, and they had a big barbecue in their garden. The people who lived in the restricted areas were both families chosen in the past and the rich and beautiful who had always been a part of the town. The ones whose families founded Harmony Hills long before I was even born. The prestige. They were laughing and playing, and I don't remember much more of it except that the entire pool was dyed in red. And they all went swimming in it and smiled at the camera as they did.

Looking back, I know that program sounds absolutely bonkers, but I kid you not, we were all plastered to the screen when it came up. It was the finest television we had. And the families were always all right the next day. No matter how many scratches or bruises they had, no matter how much they were hitting each other or screaming things that sounded other-earthly, the next day they'd go and play golf or show us how to bake a cake in their kitchen, and all was fine and well.

"It's perfectly imperfect, love. A beautiful home, a disgusting inside. *Hidden Hills* portrays what *could* be. None of it is real. It's a show," Mum would always try to shush me when I asked if that scene wasn't painful and how I didn't want to swim in a red pool.

"But, honey, doesn't it look like the most fun? Imagine we would be one of them up there!" Dad would add with a twitch in his eye.

Being accustomed to that sort of violent television, I never saw what could be wrong with it. It was simply what it was. And every day at school, all the other kids would talk about the last brilliant episode, and it would connect us all.

The older I grew, however, the more I started resenting Harmony Hills. I hated keeping everything clean and pretty. I wanted to let loose at times and enjoy the life we had, not the life we could have if we were on television. The only other person I knew who didn't enjoy *Hidden Hills* was our neighbor Mason. He went to my school, and I could actually see his window from my room, but I was never allowed to spend time with him. My parents found that he was a bad influence.

Mason was the complete opposite of the Harmony Hills dream. When he was eight, he stole scissors and cut his hair all crazy. He'd cut holes in the clothes drying in the garden. When he was sixteen, he would regularly screw with both our house and his parents'. He'd draw slurs on the wall with markers, burn little patches of grass, or rip out flowers and secretly leave them for me as a present.

Of course, his parents started hating him soon. Like all others, they wanted to be picked for the show, and their own kin was sabotaging them. They never showed their anger in public; that wouldn't be the Harmony Hills way. Instead, Mason would have another bruise on his face, hidden under layers of makeup. Not that it made him stop, though. He kept ruining anything he could.

No matter how bad his punishment, Mason never stopped, and he never cared. He'd see my mum freak out because her flowers were gone and give a cheeky wink from the opposite side of the street while Mum tried her best not to shout until she was back inside.

Even though we hardly were able to communicate, I felt a connection to Mason. He was the imperfect part of the perfect neighborhood, and I was dying to get closer to him and find out why he was so different from the rest. So on a particularly sunny day when all of Harmony Hills was getting ready to watch a freshly baked episode, I left him a note to come meet me in the park. At 6:05 when all of Harmony Hills would be hidden inside.

It's almost six p.m., guys! Get ready for another juicy look inside **Hidden Hills***! Tonight Deborah is showing her husband how to have a good time... the Hills way! Don't miss out!*

The daily announcement was blasting through the speakers all throughout the town. Just in case somebody forgot what time it was.

I told my parents I would be watching tonight's episode with friends from school and quickly ran out before they could say anything.

It was the very first time I ever missed watching the show.

Mason was already sitting on the swing set in the park. His hair was all messy, and his clothes looked two sizes too big. When he saw me approach he smiled and shouted, "Wouldn't have thought you were a rule breaker, Kelsey!"

I sat beside him but wasn't sure what to say. When you have to be quiet for so long, it feels weird suddenly being free to talk.

"Why do you always screw with our house?" I finally blurted out.

"Isn't that obvious?" He grinned. "'Cause I like you."

"If you liked me, wouldn't you want my family to get called for the show?" I asked with an eyebrow raised.

"Don't you think it's sad? That all anyone here wants out of life is to be a puppet in a show? To entertain the masses so they won't realize that all this life is hideous? That they are living for someone else?"

"It seems to make them happy. I think my mum would die if she never made it to the show." I laughed.

His gaze shifted to the ground, and for a moment, we were both quiet again.

"Kelsey, if I found a way to leave this place, would you come with me?"

I was more than surprised by that proposal. I didn't know anyone besides my grandparents that had ever left. And from what I heard from my dad, they went on to live a dirty and horrible life after they got out.

I shook my head. It surprised me that Mason was actually thinking of disappearing from the picture-perfect neighborhood where everyone aspired to have even more. I knew he liked to sabotage the beauty, but he hadn't always been like that. I remembered he seemed to have a good relationship with his parents when he was little.

"Why do you hate the show so much? I know it's not the finest entertainment but—"

"You know, Kelsey, I'm actually glad you asked me to meet you. I wanted to do the same for a while, but I didn't know if you were ready."

"Ready for what?"

He jumped up from the swing.

"To see the truth behind all that glamour and shine. I wanna show you the restricted area."

———————

The area was surrounded by many trees and a big golden fence. Nobody could simply walk in there, but Mason seemed to have found a way.

"Not exactly inside but it gives you a decent view," he said on our cycle up the hill. We cycled up as far as we could, then left our bikes behind a bush and walked the rest.

"They're probably filming right now. It's not live, though," Mason whispered as we walked in between some trees toward the golden fence.

"Duh, I know it's not live. They record the day before," I responded.

He shook his head. "They film months in advance. And they show the episodes in different orders so people won't realize how bad the things happening in there actually are."

We walked through a dense forest and crawled in between bushes with many stings. They were cutting my skin, but Mason told me to keep following.

Finally, we made it to the golden fence somewhere outside of the area as it seemed. There was just enough space to get a glimpse inside.

"That's the stuff they don't film," Mason whispered.

In front of me, I saw a row of houses. They looked similar to ours, just far bigger with lots of decorations and golden windows. We were on the back of the buildings with a view to the gardens.

And then I saw what Mason was talking about.

There were people hanging from the roofs. They looked empty, as if someone had drained all life of them.

"They cut them open until all blood is out, and they fill the pools with it," Mason said as if he had been reading my mind.

I felt sick to my stomach and just wanted to leave. I wasn't able to say anything for a while, so we just quietly made our way back, but finally I wanted to know what Mason had seen when he came up here first.

"It was a couple years ago. I only came once, and I remembered I loved watching the show back then. I even liked helping my parents keep everything clean 'cause I was so obsessed with moving up here. But when I came, they were filming in one of the homes we saw. They were force-feeding the people until they couldn't take it anymore. They were crying, and one of them seemed to have a stroke. They didn't even care. They're doing whatever they want with them, and for some reason the actors don't say no. It's a sick game I never want to play. For the show, they edit enough so it always looks like fun and games. It's not, though."

"Why didn't you tell anyone?" I asked.

Mason laughed.

"Don't you think I tried? Nobody cares what you say. They just care about what they see on that screen."

Leaving Harmony Hills is difficult because of two reasons. The first one is simple: most people don't want to leave. They either don't know the truth or they know it but want it nonetheless. The second reason is how everyone who lives here wants to keep you inside. They don't like someone getting out and telling the world about their paradise.

When you grow up knowing only one truth, it is hard to break out of it. I thought Mum and Dad would learn, would learn to accept. I knew my grandparents couldn't get them out, as much as they tried. They left before I was even born, knowing that this life was nothing more than misery.

I loved my parents with all my heart. It broke me seeing them cutting the grass with a nail clip so it would be perfectly straight, or how they would climb up the roof to paint it in peppermint colors, how many hours they spent in front of the mirror to look as well as they could. But what broke me the most was seeing them plastered to the screen, watching *Hidden Hills* and wishing with all their heart to be cast as the next dead family. It broke my heart, but I knew I couldn't save them from their wishes.

And no matter how much Mason sabotaged the house, there would be no escape from it. Not until we left Harmony Hills for good.

I knew that for a fact when I got up this morning and saw my mother cry tears of joy. She hadn't even listened to all the things I told her. She just held the paper to her heart and smiled.

"We did it, Kelsey. We finally received our invitation!"

WHEN I WAS A CHILD WE LIVED IN A COPY-PASTE NEIGHBORHOOD

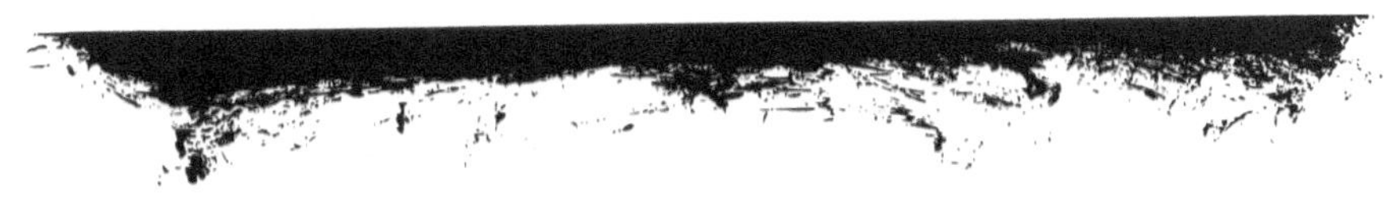

Recently there had been something pulling me back to the street where I lived as a child. A street as unspectacular as it was peculiar. Selen Street had the feel of a different world, and that is because each and every single house in our little neighborhood looked exactly the same way. Not only did we all have the same postbox and the same wooden window frames, but I swear we even had the same type of flowers growing in our gardens.

Those little houses, painted in the same shade of dark ocean blue, have a very particular architecture to them. They are all rather narrow but reach up quite high to ensure that there would always be enough space if more homes needed to be added to the neighborhood.

You would never expect such an awfully individual style being copied, but here they were, twenty identical homes holding very non-identical inhabitants. And you would assume that all the pastel yellow-painted garages hold the same car as well, but as far as I know, my parents were the only ones owning a vehicle. Or at least I'd never seen anyone else in one before.

Luckily, our street wasn't the only place for me to go or maybe I would have turned insane over the years. Our street was rather high up on a small hill overlooking the town where I went to school, where we would buy our food and clothes, and where Dad would go to work. I loved the cycle down to the town, feeling unstoppable with the wind at my back. The way up home was always a drag, however, especially as I had to count not to miss our home when I pulled into our street. It was the fourth house on the left for most of the time. When I was six or seven, I had the brilliant idea to hang up a little sign for me to know where to look or draw a number down on the pavement with chalk, but every time I would come back to look for our home, the signs I made were always gone. I believe Mum removed them as soon as she spotted a change to our copy-paste home. She didn't want our home to stick out next to the neighbors.

When I was younger, I would always wonder how my parents were able to find our home in between all the other ones. Especially if we came home at night from visiting the town. I would sit in the back of the car, my eyes all sleepy, and my thoughts unorganized like I had been just swallowed into a different dimension. Dad would pull into our street, and for a moment I would fear that we would never find our way back. With an eerie feeling in my gut, I would shut my eyes and hope that Dad would carry me inside the right place.

How can it be my home if I can't even recognize it? a voice in my mind would shout. Though deep inside I knew I could trust Dad to bring us to the right place. Mum, on the other hand, seemed to have problems with it at times. Even if she never would confess it to us, I could swear that she accidentally slipped through the yellow door of our neighbor from the opposite side of the street on more than one occasion. I knew she had to be going there by accident as she had lectured me many times that we were never to visit any of the neighbors on Selen Street.

For a child, the world is still quite blank. Your parents tell you what is right and wrong, and you have no other choice than to believe them. My mum never wanted me to bring home any friends. There were no other children on our street except for the baby in house eight on the right side. I'd see mother and child taking a stroll down the street from time to time, and the mum would smile and wave. A few times she even invited me inside and asked if I would like to babysit her little girl, but I always politely declined.

If I wanted to meet friends, I would have to go down to the town. Dad would often drive me; I think he could sense that I was getting a little lonely up there.

"I bet we can convince your mum to let a friend visit sometime," he'd say in a compassionate voice. "She's just a little protective, but I'm sure she won't let us stay all alone up on the hill *forever*." He'd joke, but I knew he didn't like it much, either, that we hardly ever had any visitors.

Things were about to change, though. After an event that I still find hard to make sense of.

I was just finished with school, and normally Dad and I would drive up together, but he was stuck at work longer, so I decided to take a walk up to our neighborhood. The road went quite far up, so I was slightly exhausted when I spotted the sign for Selen Street. I walked down the road and made sure to count to the fourth house.

The door wasn't locked.

"Mum, I'm home!" I shouted.

She didn't respond, and for a moment I was afraid that she had mixed up our house again. That she was inside the home of the smiling woman from the opposite side of the street. But when I spotted the boy standing in the doorframe to the garden that looked exactly the same as ours, I realized that I was the one standing in the wrong house.

"Are you the kid that lives next door?" the pale kid with freckles asked.

I nodded.

"Yeah, I'm Felix. Are you new here?"

"Sure am. Dad and I—"

"Joshua, the boy doesn't really live next door. Their home just makes it appear that way," a man's voice interrupted us. I assume it was the boy Joshua's father.

"You don't?" Joshua said with a disappointed look on his face. "You said I'd make friends here, Dad. That's not fair!"

"Well, maybe you can show Felix your swing set in the garden? And if he likes it he can stay?"

I wasn't sure what to say to that. I knew Mum would certainly not approve of me being here, but then again, these were our neighbors. And Joshua seemed really nice.

The rest of that afternoon is a blur. I know I followed Joshua to their garden. Outside was the same big tree we had in our garden, and I spotted what I assumed was their swing set.

I'm not sure how it happened, but somehow I must have gotten stuck inside the wooden swing's rope. The last thing I remember seeing was

Joshua's smile, but as I woke up, hardly being able to breathe anymore, I heard my parents' screaming and shouting. Dad picked me up, and we drove to the hospital. For days my throat was all red and blue and painful.

———————

When we got back home from the hospital, Dad was angrier than I had ever seen him before. I wanted to explain that it wasn't my fault, that I had counted the wrong number of houses, but my parents wouldn't listen.

Instead, I was sent to my bedroom. Ear pressed against the door, I listened to them fight for hours.

"I built this insane monstrosity of a house for you. I tried. I really did, but I can't do this any longer. This isn't right. This isn't right for me, and it certainly isn't for Felix."

"I love you, George, but I can't leave. You know I can't. I'm sorry," my mother said in a vibrating voice.

"Yes, you can. And you should! You need to let go, Mirren."

I couldn't hear what she said next, but that night Mum came to my room, her eyes all black from the tears. I thought she would ask me to stay or try to explain, but all she did was tell me to go with Dad. That I could come and visit when I was older.

———————

My father was not an emotional man, and we never talked about feelings much. I knew he despised talking about our old home on Selen Street. I knew the pain he felt when thinking about Mum, with whom we had lost touch almost entirely. But I was eighteen by now, old enough to decide for myself if I wanted to forgive my mother for choosing a house over me. I knew it was time to go back, but before I could do so, I had to talk to my father about the night we tried to forget. The night in which I visited the wrong house.

I was older now, and I understood that whatever happened that night wasn't an accident.

Dad and I were having breakfast in the kitchen as I told him about my plans to visit our old hometown and see Mum. While he looked hurt, I could also tell that he understood. He was actually quite compassionate until I brought up the *night*.

"I know we should have talked about this years ago. Sending you to a therapist but not speaking to you about it was cowardly. But you were just so young. I could never have predicted that the loneliness would make you take such measures." Dad suddenly had tears in his eyes.

"What are you talking about, Dad? I had other friends. I wasn't lonely. It was just nice to suddenly have a kid my age live next door. I know I shouldn't have walked inside Joshua's house, but you know it probably wouldn't have happened if we had a freakin' number on ours," I said half-jokingly.

"Joshua? Felix, I thought we made you understand that there was no Joshua."

"Yeah, yeah, I know. I guess they had to leave after what happened." Dad's eyes opened wide.

"Felix, what is going on? You almost sound like your mother. There never was a boy named Joshua who lived next to us. Nobody lived next to us. That was the whole issue. Your mother wanted to have a house on that hill, and the solitude slowly made her go crazy. Apparently it rubbed off on you—"

"What the hell, Dad? What do you mean?" I nervously laughed. "There were, like, twenty houses just like ours. The blue houses with the yellow garages? This really isn't funny, Dad."

Dad put an arm on my shoulder.

"Boy, I can assure you there was no other house like ours. Your mother drew the concept of the building herself. We built it for her because it was her dream home. She was so heartbroken after her mother passed away, I thought nothing could ever make her happy again until we built the house on the hill." For the fraction of a second, he smiled. "I could accept being up there in solitude with all her strange ways, even not getting visitors, but when you tried killing yourself in that backyard and she still didn't want to leave... I just couldn't take it anymore."

I knew Mum was really young when Grandma died. I never even had the chance to meet her. Suddenly it made sense how my father always laughed when I talked to him about all the houses in our street. He thought I was being sarcastic in a time where I didn't even know what that meant.

But Mum spoke to me about the neighbors many times. She saw them, too. And she tried to protect me from them.

Mum didn't draw a house she made up. She drew something that she saw. And that I saw.

My memories of Selen Street were blurry but somehow simultaneously crystal clear. I knew there had to be a reason my mum never wanted to leave that place. And I was about to find out why.

With a knot in my stomach, I drove up the small hill leading to Selen Street. As I pulled into the road, I could already spot the row of blue houses. Just the way I remembered them.

I tried counting the houses on the left side of the street, but I couldn't tell which one was ours. So many years had passed, but they all still looked exactly the same way.

But then I looked to the right side of the street, and there she was, my mother. Her hair had more gray strands now and her face had wrinkles, but her smile was just as warm and her face just as loving. She was sitting on the porch next to the woman she would visit when we were younger. Mum had certainly aged, but the other woman looked just the way she did back then. I'd never noticed before how similar she looked to my mother.

"Felix," Mum whispered. She got up from the porch but looked hesitant. Her hands were shaking. At that moment, I wanted to scream, shout at her for leaving me, but when I saw her tear-filled eyes, I couldn't help but run into her arms the way I always would as a child.

Our house might have been the only real one on the street to the eyes of someone else, but Mum and I knew that this house was the only copy. The imposter house. We weren't supposed to live there. Selen Street was a place for lost souls.

I assume when Mum realized that Grandma was stuck there in one of the blue houses, she thought she could trick the neighborhood if she simply built a house just like theirs. And so we lived in a street that didn't exist. In a neighborhood that only Mum and I could see.

She made a decision all those years ago to stay and protect the soul of her mother. Now I think she deserves to have someone to help her with the job.

Joshua and his father both still live on the other side of the street, the woman and her baby girl still take strolls down the road, and Grandma sits on her porch with a friendly and warm smile.

It gets hard at times not to mix up our home with the other ones. Especially as the neighborhood has been growing over the years.

But I don't mind. I'll just have to be extra careful not to visit any house that isn't our copy-paste one.

WE ARE COLOR-CODED AT BIRTH

They say that everyone in Mallis is born with a distinct color. A color that defines the house they live in, the work they do, and the friends they have. There are exactly three of them. It's not the color of your eyes, your hair, or your skin but a particular spot behind your left hand's thumb. It could be ruby, blue, or green.

The birth of a child is celebrated highly in Mallis. The parents of the new little creature brought to this world are gifted with baskets and presents and many friendly handwritten cards. The mayor himself is present at every birth, dressed up all formally and nice. Of course, the task is quite easy as our town is rather small.

Nobody even cares about the gender of the child. All we worry about is figuring out the color on its thumb. We all act surprised and a little shocked when finding out if the child is a ruby, a blue, or a green. Though in reality, it is all just for show. The child is born to a family of a distinct color, of course, and so their color will usually be the same as the one of their parents and siblings. It is tradition, however, that the mayor himself announces the color of the new child. That's how it's always been, and the people here curiously await his call every time.

Right after birth. Even before the father gets to see his kin.

It is of utter importance to be fast. That's what my mother told me. The color you see doesn't stay forever; a day would be the outer maximum. You need to be sure of the color there and then to ensure that the child fits its environment.

Or else? I wondered back then, but I never quite got the right answer.

Now the color coding is an old tradition, of course, and naturally, we have embedded into current times, though the cultural aspects are still quite present, or at least parts of them. For starters, I am the child of a proud ruby family. The bricks of our house are rusty red, every year for my birthday Mum bakes a delicious red velvet cake, and Dad even says that our blood is ruby while the other blood is tainted. I happen to have red hair as well, although that is just a coincidence even if it's a lucky one. Both my parents are blond. Mum dyed her hair a few times, but it's not quite the same. Not that the color of one's hair should matter.

We live a harmonic life. It's all quite sheltered; we're a close-knit community, and while we are coded in different colors, we still get along nicely with everyone. At my school there are kids of all groups; we do assignments together at times or sit together during lunch. My close friends happen to be ruby as well, but of course, that is not a requirement. I went to preschool in a neighborhood predominated by ruby families, so naturally the first friends I made were ruby just like me. We didn't bond over color but over toys and games and pranks we played. When I got to elementary school, I had a few blue friends, but they usually stayed in their groups as well. Just how it naturally flows. I don't despise anyone. Everyone in town is rather nice anyway.

Well, that is not entirely true. While my parents always taught me to be kind and open-minded, there is one particular family that they warned me about when I was little. Now the paranoia is ingrained into my brain, and unfortunately, it swayed over to other members just a tiny bit. I try not to generalize, but sometimes it's hard. When I first saw the house that my parents warned me about, I was more astonished than scared. It was placed in a green neighborhood, just at the border to a blue one. I only walked past it by accident on my way home from school. Usually, I walked a different route, but I had been lost in my thoughts, and before I knew it, I was looking at a house that wasn't exactly like the others. Now, I'm not entirely sure about the color of the building itself, but it surely looked green with all the ivy covering it from bottom to top. It took me a second look to even recognize the forest green door in between. There was more to it than simply strange looks, too. When I walked by the house, it radiated a smell. One that is not simple to describe but the association in my mind made it feel like *belonging*. It reminded me of the smell of fresh sheets that you get comfortable in with a new set of pajamas after a warm shower. It felt both like nature and home. Despite the cold of November, I stood still on the sidewalk, not able to keep my eyes off it.

I'm not even sure how long I stood there for. A part of me almost walked up the door. It was almost as if something inside of it was calling me, trying to welcome me. That's when I noticed there was someone behind the fogged-up window and heard the noise of something distant but shrill. I saw fingers with sharp nails scratching the window. At first, I thought that this family might have a dog. Curiously, I walked a step closer, only to realize that the eyes of the creature were not friendly. They were red and dark with many bags underneath. As they met mine, the face got even closer to the window, pressing their forehead against it while mouthing something I couldn't understand. When I impulsively took a step back, the whispers became a loud scream.

"What are you doing here, child? Go home!"

At first, I thought it was coming from the house, but when I turned around, I realized that an older gentleman was shouting at me. He was dressed in a blue raincoat, and while his mouth was formed into a smile, his eyes were showing a deep terror.

I started running and didn't stop until I reached my rusty red home. I realized just in time that whatever lived in there wasn't trying to welcome me; it wanted to lure me in.

***

At first, I was unsure whether to tell my parents what I had witnessed. They were quite protective of me. I was their miracle, as Dad liked to say. You see, my parents tried to have children for a very long time before they finally had me. Dad told me how Mum cried the entire first week after I was born because she couldn't believe how lucky she was to finally hold me in her arms. They loved me and proved it each day, which is why I knew they would freak out. Both my parents were more than fond of our beautiful community, and they wouldn't like it if they knew that something here scared me. Little did I know that they would be the ones enhancing my fear.

"Do not ever go near that house again!" my dad said in a stern voice.

"They are not like us. They shouldn't even be here, but we have to accept everyone, you know? It doesn't mean you need to interact with them. They are—not right," my mother added with a little more compassion.

"What do you mean, they are not right?" I asked.

My parents exchanged a glance.

"You know how everyone in Mallis is gifted with a special color? We do that because the old traditions tell us to. With the right color in your mind, you will live a healthy and prosperous life. That's why our crop is always exquisite, why we never get sick but instead grow unusually old. We are lucky because we follow the rituals. Unfortunately, there are some who naturally feel drawn to chaos and pain. And they want to bring it upon all of us."

"What chaos?" I asked.

"They want to spill red. The red that is inside of us," Mother responded.

My heart started beating faster. None of what my parents were telling me matched the image I had of our surroundings. I had never known fear in my life, I was happy, and I had many friends. It got me quite angry hearing that some people wanted to change that for no reason but pettiness.

"Why can't we remove them from town?" I asked.

My parents laughed in response.

"That would be easy, wouldn't it? Though we can't force anyone to leave, they need to do it on their own."

I had to promise my parents to never walk by that street again, but of course, I couldn't keep my promise. I was far too curious. While a part of me was frightened, another told me that it was merely a house. The following day after school, I told my friends I had to run errands for my parents. As they walked back the ruby road, I tried to find my way back to the ivy house.

It wasn't hard to find. Even though it looked a lot different from what I saw the day before.

The house was drenched in blood.

It was coming from the windows and dropping down to the green grass. Big drops of blood.

Of course, it could've been regular paint, but at that moment it didn't even matter. Whatever it was, it appeared to be a sign. I was ready to make my way home, acting like I hadn't seen anything, when I heard a voice. It was quiet, just a whisper, and it sounded like a child.

"Come in."

I looked around, but I was the only other person on the street. I took a small step closer toward the house, and there it was again.

"Come to me."

That's when I stepped back and started running again. My parents were right. There was something awfully wrong with that house and the people living inside. They were trying to create chaos and were succeeding, too.

I didn't think about the house on the green street a lot more after that. I always made sure not to cross it, especially not on my own. As I grew older and got my own driver's license, there was no need to take the shortcut again. Of course, I wasn't as scared as I was back then, but I figured it was better to be safe than sorry.

I did spend more time in the blue neighborhood, however. As I got to high school, I realized that you don't need to be friends with someone simply because you grew up in the same surroundings. My new friends mostly worked helping their parents in the mines or in the factories while I was usually helping out at the ice cream store, but we would meet up after work to do more relaxing stuff. Whenever I invited them to my home, my parents were super friendly. They were smiling and telling them nice things about their parents. They'd usually let us hang out in the living room and bring us snacks. I felt like my parents spent more time with me when friends were around than whenever I was all alone.

I lived quite content with a limited mindset. Until one person came along who would change my view on the color concept of Mallis. Jonas. He came to the ice cream shop every day, ordering a scoop of mint and one scoop of strawberry. A combination that sounded rather disgusting to me but he swore that it fit perfectly. Jonas came back every other day, and shortly he became the one thing I looked forward to the most when going to work. I didn't tell my parents or friends about my new crush. Of course, they all acted very acceptingly and open-minded all the time, but I knew they would be reacting in an old-fashioned manner if they found out that Jonas was born a green baby.

Honestly, after a while, it didn't even matter to me, but the more we hung out, the more he made apparent that we shouldn't tell anyone just now.

"It's our secret for now."

Back then I thought that was romantic. We were from the same small town but still from different worlds.

"What about your family? What are they like?" I once asked him.

"Well, I don't have any siblings, but my parents are very loving. They don't interact much with others here, though."

"Why not?"

He laughed.

"Well, because they're not as appreciated as yours."

Even though he was laughing, I could sense a bitterness in his tone. As a child, I was unaware of it, but by now it was more than apparent to me that the colors in our town meant far more than what kind of neighborhood you lived in. It was a symbol of status. Red families had more money, lived longer on average, and received a better education. Blue families were usually somewhere in the middle, and the green ones were the worst off. They didn't get great jobs, had the worst neighborhoods, and hardly any chance to get out of it. The reds and blues didn't interact with them much, separating the people even more.

Jonas taught me about all that. Sometimes I almost felt like he resented me for the privilege I was born into, though he never showed it. He asked about my day, asked about my parents. He wanted to know how they treated me, what work they did, and everything else. He was way interested in my life but never shared much of his.

I was wearing the biggest rose-colored glasses you could imagine. In my eyes, everything was right about him. I loved his blond hair that would get even brighter in the sun, I loved his kind smile, but mostly I loved the way he smelled.

He smelled just like home.

The glasses only fell off when I came home one afternoon to be greeted by a present in my bed.

It was a flower bouquet. There were roses and tulips but something else. Something that looked very familiar.

Ivy.

That's when it clicked. When I realized that it wasn't a coincidence that Jonas visited me in the ice cream shop. He had been targeting me. It started all the way back then when I walked past that house, but I simply didn't understand why.

Whatever was going on, it was not right. I knew for a fact that my parents didn't let him inside, which meant that he had broken in to leave the flowers on my bed. Until this point, I thought I knew Jonas well, but in that moment it all shattered. I ran down the stairs to grab my phone, but I couldn't find it.

When I heard the noises from the garden and saw my mother's blond hair in between the bushes, I felt intense relief. Mum was out there often. She loved planting flowers. It was her most favorite thing to do. She wouldn't even let me help her.

Quickly, I opened the door and ran outside.

"Mum?"

"Hey, love."

When the figure moved up, I realized that I hadn't seen my mother's hair.

It was Jonas, knees deep inside of Mum's flower bed.

"Did you like your death flowers?" He laughed.

I took a step back and got ready to run, but Jonas had already gotten up from the dirt.

"You can leave in a sec. I just want you to see this first."

There was something strangely calm about his voice. It didn't match the atmosphere at all.

"What are you doing?" I said while trying to sound confident. He had played with my head, and I was fuming.

"I figured it out. I figured it all out."

"What are you talking about? You need to get out of here!"

He just laughed, his eyes radiating malice.

"Don't you understand? You don't belong here. You never have."

"Jona—"

He got up from the dirt. His hands were shaking as he towered over me. But suddenly he didn't look mad anymore; there were tears in his eyes.

"I knew it. They killed them all."

"Who?" I murmured while taking another step back. I had to get away from here quickly.

He waved me over.

"Just have one quick glance, okay?"

He didn't have any weapons. He was digging in the dirt with his hands. I knew Dad would be back home soon. I just needed to stall some time.

I slowly moved toward the destroyed flower bed.

Jonas was pointing at something. Something deep underneath the dirt and flowers that he had spread all over.

They looked like tiny coffins.

"What—What's that?"

Jonas looked at me with a sad smile.

"My dead siblings."

I'm not sure what happened next. Jonas came close, too fast. And before I knew it, everything turned dark.

———

I woke up in a dark room. I was lying in bed, but I wasn't alone. Someone was cradling me. I felt a dry hand move up and down my cheeks. I tried to move, but my body was too stiff. I tried to scream, but before any words came out, the person started whispering.

"Ssht. It's okay. You're home now."

My eyes were heavy, but as they got adjusted, I saw the person. It was an older woman.

Jonas was there as well, holding my hand.

I wanted to crush his hand and his skull next. He had not only betrayed me, he kidnapped me. Took me from my safe home. From my family.

But that was before I realized that I was the one that had taken his life.

Or saved it, depending on how you like to interpret it.

The woman grazed my face and my hair. Her eyes looked just like mine. And in between the gray strands, I could identify a few red ones.

"I'm sorry if my appearance scares you. I haven't been able to leave the house much, you see," she said with a sad smile.

As it turns out, the color behind the thumb of a child doesn't always depend on their family. The privilege we were born into was entirely random. My so-called ruby parents were trying to have a child that would fit their kind but only managed to have babies that were not the right color. Before it was even announced, they made them disappear underneath the dirt. With the prestige my parents had in town, they could do whatever they wanted.

"You and I," Jonas spoke, "we were born on the very same day, in the very same hospital, only minutes apart. You were born red and I was born green to families whose color we didn't match."

Jonas was supposed to die, just like all the other kids my parents had before, but when they saw my ruby-red thumb and the little strands of red hair, they knew they wanted me, and they would do anything to get me. It was perfect. We were born at the same time, and no one would ever know.

My real parents didn't have much of a choice. Nobody in this town would help them. They didn't have the money or power to fight the ruby families. The only thing they could do at this point was to save the life of an innocent boy who otherwise would have been sacrificed.

All their life, they were threatened. My fake family did whatever they could to make sure they stayed far away from me. Sending them blood as a threat, slowly poisoning them and making sure all of the town was against them. For years they were driven by fear.

But not anymore. It was time this concept of color ended.

And we would start by turning their ruby-red house into burning red flames.

EVERYTHING HERE SMELLS ROTTEN IN THE VILLAGE

If you see me staring at you at night, run.

She'd warned me on the very first night, but of course, I didn't listen.

Aunt Sozan's home smells like a delicious blend of spices and herbs, which she uses for cooking, medicine, and making perfumes. Her home is by far the most whimsical place I've ever seen, filled with all sorts of keepsakes, big or small. You can hardly see that the house has any walls because of all the big posters of old cities and movies as well as Arabic wall carpets, from bright purple to deep green. My mother's older sister lives all by herself. She never got married, which is a big deal in our family. But Sozan doesn't mind. She has her own house, her own life, and makes all her own choices.

Her home truly is deserving of the word.

However, as soon as I step out of the comfort of those bright walls, her village seems to suffocate me. I felt the tension of this place the second that I arrived at the train station. Everything was wrapped in a light fog, accompanied by an intense, foul smell that crept all the way down my nostrils.

At first, I was happy to come here for a weekend, to escape the noise of the city and spend some days in a tiny village in western Germany. It was almost May, the sun was back, and I felt almost optimistic. I felt relieved to get away from my parents, my brother, and even from my new boyfriend for a while. The only weird part was that my mum was the one who suggested the trip even though she hates it when I'm in touch with Sozan because "she's a bad influence."

But now I've learned that this place is no home; it's an exile. And there is no sun, or at least you can hardly see it. I have no idea how weather generally works, but I certainly know that it can't be right to sit on a train for six hours and only see one single place that is entirely swallowed by gray.

"Lona!" I heard a familiar voice shout from behind the fog. Aunt Sozan appeared, dressed in a long airy skirt, with at least five necklaces around her neck and six rings on her fingers. Her curly hair that she dyes with henna was going in all directions. When she got close enough, she pulled me into a tight hug and gave me a kiss on each cheek.

She smelled like lavender and roses.

"Let's get you home, sweet girl. You must be starving!"

<hr>

My fun and energetic aunt had made wine leaves filled with rice and herbs, which are my favorite, as well as those amazing semolina dumplings, taboule, and lentil soup. Very typical Kurdish foods. They weren't quite as good as the ones my mum makes, but I didn't tell her that.

After dinner, we sat in the living room, drinking tea and chatting about all sorts of stuff. School, friends, Berlin. After a while, I even told her about Noah, my boyfriend, but only because Sozan is the only person in the family I feel like I can be candid with.

Everything was going close to perfect. Inside her home, I almost forgot how eerie this village was. It was all great until it wasn't anymore. Until our conversation shifted.

Sozan turned her cup of tea around, maybe for a reading of the leaves or maybe it was just out of habit.

"I've wanted to see you for a while now, honey. The last time you were here, you were, what, six or seven? I get that your mother doesn't like visiting but—"

She paused for a moment. *But she's the one who made me leave Berlin,* is probably what she wanted to say. My mum believes that Aunt Sozan casts a bad light on our family.

"She probably just doesn't like the smell. You know how sensitive she is," I tried to joke, but I couldn't even look into her eyes. I hated how my mum abandoned her. I can't stand my brother at most times, and I still wouldn't do this to him.

"Smell?" She raised an eyebrow.

"Yeah, it smells... rotten. Kind of like burned eggs and gasoline. I don't know... Not in here, outside!" I quickly added.

Aunt Sozan turned her cup back around. "Lona, when you were little, did your mum ever warn you about djinns?" she asked, ignoring what I said about the scent.

"Only the one from *Aladdin.*" I laughed, but Aunt Sozan's face didn't move one bit. My mother is quite a religious person; everything evil must stay far away. Ironically.

"They are quite unpredictable. Can change their shape. Not all are evil, actually. Concepts of our morality don't exactly work the same for them... as far as I understand. But some do like to inflict pain on humans and they are rather good at that." She sighed. "Some might find it ridiculous, but I am very aware of them. I don't want to anger any, even if only by accident. And while you're here, I wish you to respect that. Can you do that for me?"

I had no idea where this sudden shift in conversation had come from, but Aunt Sozan was staring at my eyes, not blinking once. There was such an intensity about it.

I nodded. Maybe my aunt had gotten a little crazy living here all by herself. I know I would if I had to live in this industrial little hell hole.

"I'm glad to hear that, sweetie. I've written a few things down. You can memorize them later, yeah?"

The evening had started off so nicely but ended with me alone, locked inside my aunt's guest room, reading a list that made me question her sanity. And my own.

If you smell fire, get away as quickly as possible. They will burn you.

Do not trust animals while you are here.

Iron angers them.

The fog is not there at all times. When it is, don't trust your mind. If it storms, go inside as quickly as possible.

Do not ever stare down the well. They will pull you in.

I don't scare easily, and while odd, I didn't find the list too disturbing. Until I came to the last warning.

If you see me staring at you at night, run.

<hr>

Luckily, I didn't catch a stare on my first night.

When morning came, I almost even forgot about all the weirdness. My aunt had left early for work, and I decided to go grab some croissants at a bakery.

The fog was hardly noticeable that morning, though the foul scent of sulfur was still present. It got even more intense when I stepped inside the bakery, killing my hunger in an instant. But the lady behind the counter was already smiling at me, showing her big teeth. It smelled as if she'd spent the entire morning burning the bread.

"What can I get you, sweetheart?"

I looked down at the goods, but every single pastry was moldy: green and blue with a cotton film.

"Uhm, actually, I'm not hungry. I just wanted to see—"

Her smile disappeared.

"I spend every single day baking. What kind of nasty tone is that? Who the fuck even are you? Who brought you here?"

She talked herself into a rage, spitting with each word. Before I could step back, she grabbed my arm and pulled me closer.

"You don't belong here. You're not rotten yet," she whispered.

With her other hand, she'd grabbed a lighter and held a flame right under my hand.

Finally, I pulled my arm back.

Fight or flight. I heard a voice in my head, but the one whispering *flight* won.

Outside, I checked my hand. There was no burn mark, and I felt no pain. Did I just hallucinate?

My mind was so muddled that I didn't even notice that the fog was back for a good minute or two.

I turned back toward the bakery once more, and when I saw the lady's grin behind the glass, I started running.

Of course, there had to be a correlation between the items on my aunt's list and this lady. My aunt was living in an infected place; it felt clear to me right away. My mother never spoke about demons to me, but I do know that they play an important role in our family.

I used to think they were old village superstitions and never listened much when an uncle or a cousin spoke about rituals or similar, but lately, my mind has grown more interested. Ever since I've started going to a few changes myself.

The thing is it's my father's family who is into this stuff. Not my mum's. So coming to Sozan, I believed I would get a break. But now I knew for a fact that this place was cursed. And I was starting to wonder if I'd fallen into a trap.

<hr>

My nerves were a wreck. I should have run to the train station instead of my aunt's home, but I didn't. Something was keeping me from leaving. This place felt suffocating, but simultaneously it felt as if I belonged here.

Those thoughts ran through my mind when I fell into the comfortable bed of Sozan's guest room. She wasn't home, so I couldn't speak to her yet, and finally, exhaustion took me over and I fell asleep.

When I woke up again, it was already dark.

<hr>

I heard a knock on the door. Then a scratch. Then someone tried to open the door. Sozan would have said something, but whoever it was didn't speak.

"It's fine. It's fine. I locked the door," I kept telling myself, but the rattling only became louder. And finally, I heard the squeaky noise of the door opening.

Sometimes when you're scared, your eyes simply won't open. They try to shield you from what's to come. This time it was different. My eyes opened wide as if I'd just woke from a nightmare. But in reality, I was just falling into one.

My eyes met Sozan's, although hers looked nothing like the warm, almond-shaped ones I remembered.

Instead, they were turned inside out. Like socks that you fold into each other.

"*Chernobog*," an unfamiliar voice whispered from inside her mouth. I have no idea what that word meant, but when I heard it, a shock went through my entire body. It felt as if a million worms inside of my mind were being pulled apart.

The creature that was wearing the skin of my aunt shuffled its feet across the floor, walking closer to my bed.

Again, the voice in my mind whispered *fight or flight*, and this time it wanted to fight. But I remembered the words on the list; I was supposed to run.

So I jumped from the bed before the thing could come any closer, and a shiver went through my body when I passed it. Especially when it tried to reach for me with its fingers. I headed out the door and slammed it shut behind me.

I ran into the darkness of my aunt's house, stumbling into tables and walls but not stopping until I finally stumbled into something soft that smelled like lavender and roses.

"It's okay," the familiar voice of my aunt whispered. "That was not me."

———

"To be perfectly honest, I thought your uncle sent you, but I felt it was too soon to ask. I don't know how much you know about his business."

The drug business or the demons? I wanted to ask. I learned a little while ago that my powerful uncle has access to the underworld in more ways than one. It was one of the reasons I wanted to get away from home.

"Well, this is where used-up hosts come," my aunt continued. "And your uncle sometimes sends the ones he can't control."

We'd turned on all the lights in the house. Sozan made tea, and after a while, I slowly calmed down. The thing is I don't know why I was so afraid. I should've been used to these things by now. I'd learned weeks ago that

I myself was possessed by a creature. Not a djinn but a different type of demon. One that I'd grown accustomed to because it gave me power and confidence. Here somehow it was much weaker, though.

"Used up?" I asked.

She stayed quiet for a moment. "Sometimes humans get sick, old, or they die. But the demon possessing them can stay alive."

"So everyone here is dead or dying? Are you—?"

She shook her head.

"I'm here because your uncle didn't want me near your family. And your mother listens to what he says. But I've started to like it here. I have a purpose. I care for the lost souls." She tried to smile, but her eyes looked sad and tired.

Something inside of me started pulsating, and I wondered if that's why my mum sent me here.

Does my family believe that I'm a lost soul? Are they trying to get rid of me?

MY NEIGHBOR SPENDS EVERY DAY REPAINTING HIS HOUSE

Jeremiah Jones is nothing if not the perfect example of the most stressful neighbor you could imagine. A perfectionist with artistic tendencies, however, I suppose he only ever got them because he is so addicted to the need of having everything right and clean at all times. I don't believe he was always like this. Before his wife passed away, you would hardly see him outside at all. Except for when he came home from the office in his shiny Volkswagen. And now he has all this time. Time that he uses for cleaning and renovation and this almost daily.

He's gotten older and stopped working, though his retirement money should be more than enough after all those years of work. I'm not sure, though. My mother says it is awfully rude to speak about money, especially other people's money, but that's dumb—it's just paper, after all. Maybe being alone and having time is what evoked this hobby or addictive habit of his. Their house was never ugly or dirty when his wife was still there, but she was only out there occasionally. He is far more excessive with his approach.

Anyway, Jeremiah Jones was so addicted to perfection that he wouldn't even take a chance of his home having any sign of dirt on the outside. And I mean that quite literally. It's not as if he watches for a bird or a tree to leave a nasty little mark so he can climb up and paint. No, he is constantly taking precautions matters by painting the roof and the walls every single day.

Excessive, isn't it?

Well, at the beginning, it wasn't that entirely insane just yet. The neighbors even thought that it was a nice habit he had found to distract himself a little. You would see him out there with a big can of blue paint, and he'd be humming while painting the left side of the building. A few days later, the entire house was blue and it looked kinda cool.

An ocean-blue home isn't something you see every day. He smiled and waved when I watched him from our porch. I waved back and even asked if he needed some help, but his smile swiftly disappeared.

"No, you would just do it all wrong!"

When I frowned at his words, he picked his smile up again and added, "I'm just awfully nitpicky, you know."

I nodded and went back inside.

The day after he had finished painting it all blue, he was outside again at five a.m., when the birds weren't even up just yet. I awoke from the sound of something heavy loudly hitting the pavement outside our door. I instinctively jumped out of bed and looked out the window to see what it was, and while my mind wasn't that sharp just yet so early in the morning, I clearly saw blood. It was dripping down Jeremiah Jones's window, and there was a big puddle of it on the ground next to the house.

I screamed and shouted for my parents to call an ambulance. Terrified, they ran to my room, and as the three of us took another look, we realized that what I must have seen was red paint.

Our neighbor was outside again, and the sound I heard must have been a can of red paint falling to the ground and spilling. The kind that he was using to go over the formerly blue walls.

I suppose he had forgotten to paint a white layer first, as the color certainly didn't look as fresh and bright as the blue of yesterday. It looked messy and dirty.

My parents walked outside that morning and talked to him, but I didn't hear what they said. I suppose they told him not to scare me in the morning; Mum was rather furious that he had to start painting so awfully early in the morning. When they came back inside, however, her anger had turned into concern.

"Poor man must be terribly missing Julie," she whispered. That was his wife's name. Julie Jones.

"Is this why he's painting so much?" I asked her.

Mum shrugged.

"She did love that home, and she always wanted things clean. I suppose it's a tribute."

Jeremiah spent the following days going over the walls and the roof until it was bright red and not rusty red, like crusty blood.

In the afternoon, when I had just gone inside, I casually walked by and took a sniff of the wall, simply to prove to myself that it didn't smell of iron.

I know I was tired in the morning, but I could have sworn I saw blood and not paint. However, all that caught my nose were the chemical scents of layers of paint.

The following day, I woke up by sounds from my never-tiring neighbor again. This time nothing was falling, but he was humming a familiar song. I looked outside, and when I saw him with another can on the top of his ladder and a color tassel in his hand, I only rolled my eyes and snuggled back into bed. His humming turned into whistling, and I didn't get another minute of sleep.

In the afternoon, Mum sent me next door with a casserole she had baked earlier that day to make up for her rude attitude toward Jeremiah the day before. She had even talked to other neighbors, and many were worried for the old man. Being so lonely and alone. Many went over to offer their help or have a chat. He often loudly joined in the chats but never accepted any help. It was his work to do.

When I went over with the lasagna that Mum had made, he smiled and climbed down the stairs.

"Tell your mother thank you, but that wasn't necessary. It must be awfully annoying to live next door to a construction site," he joked.

I chuckled. "Oh no, that's fine. I really did like the blue, though." The home was now painted in a rather dark color, a mixture of forest green and brown.

"I thought she would have, too," he said in a sad tone, and I assume he meant that his wife would have liked it.

I wasn't sure what to say at that moment, so I asked, "Was blue her favorite color?"

Mrs. Jones had given me piano lessons when I was younger, and I remembered the wall behind the piano was ocean blue.

"I thought it was," he said with a half-smile. "Though maybe it's not."

He was saying those words as if he had painted the house to please her. Maybe that was what he was trying to do, an act of grief, and maybe if he found the right color he would be able to move on.

I nodded sympathetically and let him continue with his work. I felt bad for being mad at him. He was only trying to find the perfect color, after all.

The next day, it was yellow, and he had started even earlier in the day when it technically was still night. Yellow was the most unfortunate choice because the dark layer the house currently had wasn't accepting of such a light color, though he didn't seem to care and used up at least a dozen cans of yellow paint before noon.

After lunch, I went outside and asked why he didn't put up a layer of ground paint first. I wasn't exactly a professional painter, but it seemed logical to me.

"Because it doesn't matter," he answered in a harsh tone. "It will always shine through."

Then he proceeded to hum loudly, and I quickly went back home.

Sympathy quickly turned into worry when he wouldn't stop for weeks. Every single day he was out there. Especially after it rained.

"What a fortune he must spend on all this paint. He must have sold out every hardware store in town. The layers must be incredibly heavy by now," my father said during breakfast.

And it didn't seem as if Jeremiah was even enjoying his work.

"Dad, how did his wife die?" I asked. I knew she had passed away very suddenly, but I didn't know any specifics.

Das looked uncomfortable.

"Well, uhm, you see. Mrs. Jones had some health issues, but they weren't physical."

He mumbled a few more words, but my father was never good at talking about serious topics. What I could make out of what he said, however, was that she had taken her own life. Inside that house.

If Mr. Jones was the one who found her, I suppose that explained his trauma even more. Especially if he never had much time for her. He even spent nights coming home very late from work. I suppose he was trying to make up for things in hindsight. It made me feel even worse for him.

However, while his coping mechanism seemed to be helpful at the beginning, it clearly didn't seem healthy anymore.

While he used to be happily humming and whistling during his daily activity, it now sounded forced and wrong. He would become louder and more crooked. The song, however, was still the same. And it was loud enough that we could hear it at our kitchen table.

The same melody that sounded awfully familiar but not like something I would usually listen to.

"Even the song," Dad said as if he was reading my mind. "Wasn't that the one Mrs. Jones once taught you on the piano?"

***

Black.

That was the last color he used on the house. The darkest shade of black I'd ever seen before. He must have ordered it online as it was a new and unfamiliar brand. And while he had been cautiously and carefully painting each day before, he now had lost all motivation to do a clean job. He was splashing and pouring the dark color everywhere. Layers on layers of dark paint dripping from the walls.

Neighbors had gathered again. It was evening by then, and Jeremiah Jones was still outside with black splashes all over his clothes and face. Some tried talking to the man, who looked as if he hadn't been sleeping in days, but he ignored them. If he answered, it was only with nonsense.

And that's when I wondered if something else had happened to his wife. Something he had been spared so far because he didn't spend enough time in that cursed home. His wife didn't seem that unwell to me, but I'd only been interacting with her during my piano days, which were a long time ago. However, she was certainly a little nitpicky herself. Possibly the time inside the home alone during those last years had taken a toll on her, and now that he was spending all his time at home, it was getting to her husband.

I tried telling my parents, but they only gave me sympathy smiles for talking about a cursed house. Still, I was convinced there was something going on inside that place, and what I saw the night after the house was painted all black proved my suspicions.

It was late at night. Mr. Jones had gone back inside just an hour back, and the whole street seemed to be sleeping. It was eerily quiet, as it is most nights on Campbell Street. Most people that live here are rather old and boring and go to bed very soon. So I must have been the only one awake, unable to sleep. Maybe it was because I heard our neighbor hum and whistle each day, but I simply couldn't get that melody out of my brain, until I realized it wasn't inside my head.

There was a faint melody playing from outside. In the dim streetlight, the black Jones house was disappearing into the night. There was no light on the inside that I could see, but there was music playing. Very quietly.

I'm not sure how to explain my next set of actions. Maybe I was still half asleep and not thinking well enough, but somehow the music got me so incredibly curious that I put on my sneakers and my jacket and walked out to our lawn.

The melody was slightly more audible outside but still very faint. I doubt it was really coming from the inside of the home. I knew Mrs. Jones had given her piano away many years ago, and the sound was not coming from Mr. Jones. I mean, of course, he could have been listening to it online or on CD, but I could swear that the music was coming from the walls, not from the inside.

I swallowed and took a step closer, now wondering if I was completely out of my mind. I can't quite explain why I felt so drawn to it. Eventually, I had my ear pressed against the outside of the house and immediately moved it away again.

As if doing what I was in that moment wasn't dumb enough already, I had forgotten that the house was freshly painted and therefore wet. I rubbed my face, expecting to see black on my hands, but the gooey substance on my skin was something else.

This time it really did smell like iron.

"The walls are bleeding," I whispered to myself, and that's when the window closest to the wall I was standing by opened up wide. The creaking of the wood sent a shiver down my spine, and I fell back to the ground.

"What are you doing?" Mr. Jones hissed. He was trying to be quiet, I could tell, but his eyes were bloodshot and he looked more terrifying than I'd ever seen him before.

"Do you want to join her? Is that what you'd like?" he added.

I stumbled back, both afraid and ashamed.

I couldn't even explain what I was doing there. I came here almost involuntarily, as if something was calling me.

I opened my mouth to say something, but Jeremiah Jones was already grabbing the frame of the window, ready to climb out. The manic expression on his face was only growing worse.

I tried to scream, but I was entirely in shock. Our neighbor had always been so kind and polite before the recent events. I was afraid the house had turned him insane.

I tried to get up from the dirty ground, but Mr. Jones was almost outside, ready to jump me, and I swear he would have if the commotion hadn't woken someone else up, too. Or maybe it was the fact that I wasn't lying in bed as I should have been, but when I heard the footsteps of my parents running toward the lawn and shouting, I was saved.

Saved from whatever Jeremiah Jones had planned.

More neighbors woke up, and the police were there soon.

At first, Mr. Jones' explanations were sounding crazy, just as crazy as my idea of a cursed house.

"It's bleeding. It's bleeding. It's bleeding and singing. She won't stop bleeding. She should've stopped."

I will never know how any of what happened was possible. I still wonder if I really heard the music and saw the blood because nobody else seemed to have noticed. Nobody but me and our neighbor.

Jeremiah Jones saw the house bleeding each day, which is why he tried to paint over it. Maybe it was a punishment or maybe she tried to warn us and nobody saw.

Because how could anyone have known that she didn't do this to herself but that he was the one who made her bleed?

I GREW A BOYFRIEND IN MY GARDEN

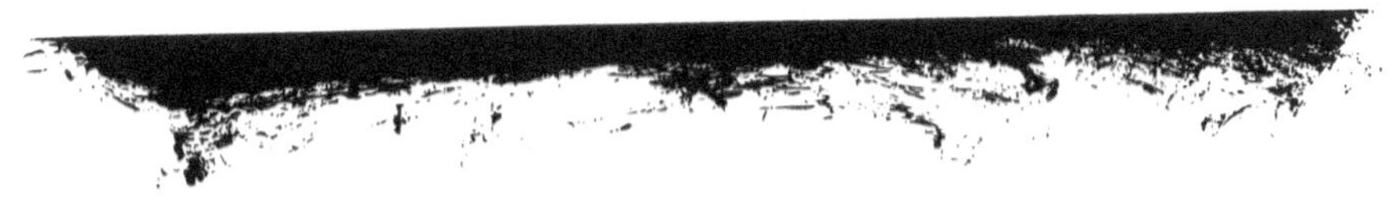

I just grew my very own boyfriend in the corner of my garden where there's always much sun and sometimes a bit of rain. I watched the small bucket filled with fresh potting soil every day to see when the first sprouts make their way out. Turned out it grew much faster than any other plant could.

Now, I didn't intend to grow a boyfriend, of course. Nobody starts a gardening journey having something like that in mind. I'm relatively regular, not entirely odd. It was more of an experiment, the test of a hypothesis. Turns out growing humans is easy! Why do people go through the hassle of childbirth?

I'm exaggerating, of course. I wouldn't be writing to you if everything went fine and well with my lover in soil. Let me tell you where I found the idea and the starting kit.

I moved to this strange town very recently and have therefore been just a bit lonely. It's become hard to meet new people to connect with; it proved even harder in a small town where everyone happens to be rather odd. I spent most of my time getting my small new home in order, decorating, painting, and building, but when the insides were finally ready, I still had all this time, so I proceeded with the garden. Soon I had soil filled with tomatoes, pumpkins, and sunflower seeds. I planted parsley, onions, and basil. Flowers and even a small tree that would provide me with fresh lemons.

When boredom was still far too present, I went to the peculiar market that is only in town on very odd days. The last time it was there was

February the 29th when I had only moved here and had no time. I cannot say for sure why the day I went was odd, but it must have been. I could tell by the weather. The sun was shining as bright as it hadn't been all year, and there were a few clouds on the baby blue sky, but they were fluffy and white like fresh cotton candy. The trail to the market was empty, not a single person was walking on the pebbly road with much green on the left and right, but as soon as I got close to the marketplace, they were all there. Not *all*, but a lot of people.

I strolled through the alleys and saw many interesting booths, but somehow I was attracted to the one at the very end of the second alley. A wooden table, nothing special, but the man behind it smiled and waved as he saw me.

"I know exactly what you need!" he said as I approached.

"And what is that?" I asked.

He pointed at my fingers. "Dirt. Soil. Garden work?"

I nodded.

"Want to grow something extraordinary for once?"

For once? How did he know that not everything I grew was extraordinary?

He played with his waxed mustache and chuckled, and honestly that's when I should have run. But you can't be scared or weirded out on bright, sunny days. The yellow light makes everything seem okay. With his fingertips, he shoved a small brown box over the wooden table until it was right under my nose.

Growing kit for love

"You are a young, pretty girl and pretty girls don't need to be lonely."

While his words were nice and so was his face, I didn't appreciate those words. How did he even know that I was lonely?

The box looked pretty interesting, though. The wood was old and a bit green but not in a disgusting way, and the letters were written with violet paint.

"Do I seem that pathetic?" I nervously chuckled.

"No, you seem like a perfectly great gardener."

I know, I know, both the interaction as well as the situation and the salesman were weird. Did I still buy the kit? Of course I did. What else is there to do in this tiny town that is beautiful but boring?

The box came with one seed, coco peat soil, a small pot, and of course a letter with instructions.

Instructions for growing love

Step 1: Set the dry coco peat soil in a small container and add 27 drops of water. Mix well.

Step 2: Push the seed into the soil and think of your ideal/perfect person.

Step 3: Make sure you start the growing process outdoors and leave the container outside.

Step 4: You will see hints of green growing soon! When your love grows too big, plant them into a bigger container.

Step 5: Bury them.

I followed half the instructions. I did steps one and two, although thinking of a perfect person proved harder than expected. I don't know who would be ideal at all, but I figured maybe my subconscious was thinking of something while my conscious mind was confused. Step three I kinda messed up because I had already started with steps one and two before even reading three. I started the whole process in my kitchen, and then I wanted to place the pot outside, but that night it started raining cats and dogs, so I left him on my kitchen window.

I started calling it *him*.

Please don't think I'm insane. I didn't expect a person to grow out of that soil! I believed it would be just some special plant, but I was excited for it nevertheless.

It took only one night for the first hints of green to sprout. In the morning, the sun and the warmth were back, so I moved the small pot out to the garden.

That afternoon, the plant had grown so big, its small pot was on the brink of breaking, so I planted him into the nicest corner of the garden, the one that is kissed by the sun the most. I would have gone back to the market to ask the mustached man what kind of plant could possibly grow so fast, but as I mentioned before, the market is only there on very odd days.

The following morning he was there. And he was not a plant.

He was a young man with very dark hair and very pale skin that doesn't see the sun often, which makes sense considering he lived underneath the dirt until now.

I am kidding, of course. I have no idea where that guy had come from, but he was suddenly sitting in the garden with a spiky pick in his hand.

"What the hell?" I shouted, and he turned around, seemingly surprised.

"What are you doing in my garden?" I tried to say confidently while searching for my phone with a shaky hand.

"You probably mean *our* garden?" he answered nonchalantly.

Now I should probably mention that I'm not the only person that can reach the garden. The house I live in has the form of a capital square C with other homes on the other sides of the letter. However, the neighbors I have are a mean old lady that never comes outside and a businessman who I only saw once because he is always on the road.

The stranger in my garden smiled and waved as if he hadn't just given me half a heart attack.

"Which home do you live in?"

"This one," he answered without pointing anywhere.

I felt a bit threatened, but then I saw Ms. Morough standing in her window. She often stood there and watched me in the garden, but despite my efforts, she hardly ever engaged in conversation with me. However, now she was smiling at the strange guy in the garden. She even waved. At him, though, not at me. No, I received an eye roll instead.

"Don't worry, she warms up to people eventually."

The stranger jumped up from the ground and reached out his arm. "Aaron Ashton."

I shook his hand. "Fenna Floris."

"That's a very fitting name." He smiled. "Nice to meet you, neighbor. May I ask why on earth you moved to this place?" He laughed.

That was a very legitimate question. Most people move to big cities after graduating to find work. I chose a tiny town surrounded mostly by fields and water. Somehow the quietness was exactly what I was seeking, though.

"I inherited the apartment. And I just couldn't bring myself to sell it."

———

Aaron and I became great friends in no time. He grew up here but had been gone for years because of college. He was the son of the businessman. He showed me gems of the town that I hadn't seen yet, the best bakery and where to get the nicest coffee; he explained to me how this place indeed was a bit odd but could also be very fun.

I was so distracted by this new friendship that I almost forgot about my little project in the garden. I didn't tell Aaron what I had grown there because, well, how do you explain to someone that you tried to grow love? The last time I checked, my plant had been growing toward becoming a tree, but on one Sunday as I went to the garden to have some coffee with Aaron, it was dead.

The plant had fallen to the ground like a lifeless snake. The bright green looked rotten and tainted.

"How do you kill a plant so quickly? It's almost impressive," he said as we were standing above the corpse of my lover.

I shrugged. "I need to bury it now."

Aaron raised an eyebrow.

That was step five of the instructions, but I couldn't tell him that. He didn't question it much longer, though; he simply thought I had much love for plants, which isn't a terrible character trait.

Either way, I didn't really need the plant anymore. I'd found Aaron, after all.

———

We hadn't taken the step from friendship to more yet. I still slept alone in my bed at night. At least that's what I thought.

It was the middle of the night, after four a.m., I believe, when I felt sharp fingernails caress my face. I was still half asleep when it started, but as my mind slowly woke up I felt the anxiety and terror run through my blood. It wasn't enough to mobilize my body yet; however, I was frozen. My heart was beating so fast I thought it would break out of my chest.

There was somebody in my bed with me.

I had absolutely no idea what to do at that moment. Thoughts were flying through my mind, but none landed. I did everything I could to keep my body from shaking. I didn't want this person to know that I was awake.

Finally, they got up. My mattress got lighter as the heavy body stood up. He was standing right above me now, I could feel it, but I kept my eyes closed. The hands touched my face one more time before I heard the heavy steps leaving my bedroom.

It took quite a while until I dared to even move one muscle. I had never lived completely by myself before, and I wasn't so sure anymore whether I liked it. When I collected the courage to get up, the sun was starting to rise, and it wasn't all dark anymore, which helped with the fear.

I tried to listen, but no noises were coming from my home. I wondered whether I had dreamed or imagined what happened that night. My phone was in the kitchen. I had to leave my bedroom to call someone and dreaded who I might meet on my way there.

I was both lucky and unlucky, however. There was nobody in my home, but whatever happened that night was not merely a nightmare.

Dirty footsteps were going all the way from the garden door to my bedroom. In the kitchen, someone had prepared breakfast for me.

A dead bird cut in half neatly decorated on a plate so it almost looked like a heart.

I couldn't control my stomach after that sight and ran outside to the garden, where I immediately threw up. My entire body was shaking. I felt violated and scared.

"Did you do this?" a familiar voice shouted. It was Ms. Morough. She stood in the garden together with Aaron, who looked just as shocked. At first I thought she was screaming at him, but no, it was directed at me. And as I looked around, I understood what she meant.

The entire garden was wrecked. All plants were ripped from the ground, their roots spread everywhere. The tree was broken in two, and dead birds and mice completed the picture.

Aaron quickly walked over, trying to comfort me, I suppose, but I backed away. It was him. It must have been him. He was the newest factor in my life, and in my distressed mindset, I even wondered if he had grown out of that seed.

————

The police came but found no sign of forced entrance. No other apartment had been broken into, either. It was only my home and the garden.

They checked for the footsteps. They weren't mine, nor Ms. Morough's, and they didn't belong to any other close neighbor, either.

And they weren't Aaron's. Somebody else had done this.

My suspicions were wrong.

Aaron was not the boyfriend I grew, though the timing of his arrival could be confusing. I suppose sometimes coincidences exist. It wasn't him. The soil boyfriend arrived at night and acted as if he'd been there all along.

I met him the following evening. After changing the locks and checking every window and gap there might be.

I spent the evening with Aaron, which might have seemed a little naïve considering he could still have been partially guilty. However, I did take some precautions. We stayed outside the whole evening. The weather was nice, and we wanted to clean the mess.

The thing I loved the most about this home, the garden, was now just depressing and sad. We sat there planning which new flowers to plant when *he* surprised us.

"Do not talk to him, Fenna."

He appeared out of nowhere. No, that's a lie. I knew where he grew out. I planted him.

My boyfriend was made out of whatever scraps he could find outside. He had bird feathers glued to his skin with blood. There were holes in his body and his face. He had never seen daylight before; he had only grown out of the ground a day ago and probably was underneath the dirt all day. Surprisingly he could speak, however. I didn't expect that.

"Who is that?" he screamed as he grabbed one of the shovels and went for Aaron, who ducked away just in time.

"What the actual fuck?" Aaron shouted.

"It's okay. It's okay," I said. "He's just a friend. I waited for you."

My boyfriend turned to me and smiled a half-smile that almost broke my heart.

"You did it all wrong," he croaked. "It wasn't supposed to happen this way."

At first, I wasn't sure what he meant, but I suppose it had something to do with how I planted him inside. I messed it all up, but that awful mustached man should have warned me!

"It's okay." With every word, his speech became clearer. "We will kill him and I'll take some of his body."

I nodded. "If that's the only way."

We had to move quickly. I hoped that Aaron realized that, too.

He did. With a swift move, he grabbed the pick that was on the ground and slammed it into the head of my soil boyfriend.

He screamed painfully, and it really did hurt me as well. It was all my fault, after all.

But we had to do it. We had to finish the fifth step.

We buried him deep into the soil. It took us hours; he had grown to be heavy. A tear rolled down my cheek as I poured the last bit of dirt.

Ms. Morough looked out once or twice. She knew what we were doing, but she didn't say a word.

As I mentioned before, the people in this town are all rather odd.

I sighed. This was the hardest thing I ever had to do. Aaron and I were both full of dirt and lots of red and some green blood.

———

"You know, at first I really thought you grew out of that dirt. Lucky for you that I didn't bury you," I tried to joke after we had cleaned up and gone inside. It had been a very stressful day.

Aaron grinned.

"How do you know that seed didn't grow into two plants?"

MORE CHILLS FROM VELOX BOOKS

MORE CHILLS FROM VELOX BOOKS

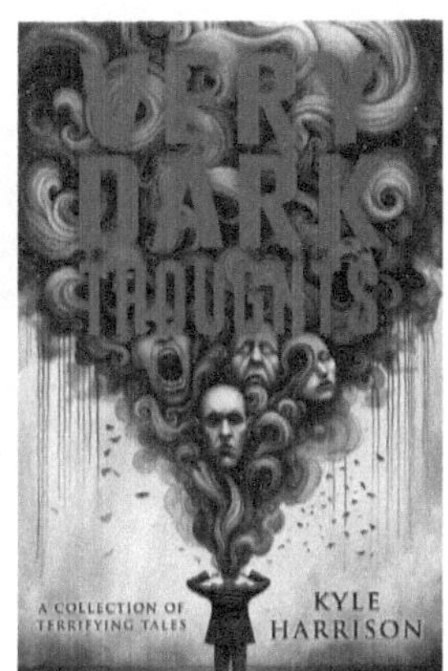